JED HERNE

Across the Broken Stars

Undergrove Press

First published by Undergrove Press 2020

This novel is entirely a work of fiction. The names, characters and incidents portrayed in it are the work of the author's imagination. Any resemblance to actual persons, living or dead, events or localities is entirely coincidental.

Jed Herne asserts the moral right to be identified as the author of this work.

jedherne.com

First edition

ISBN: 978-0-6486819-3-9

Dedication

To Rebekah:

From dinner at the rainforest cafe in London (2017), where I rambled about this story for half an hour,

To helping me edit the final draft in Perth (2019),

Thanks for your friendship, frivolity, and fiendishly fantastic ideas.

Contents

Chapter 1

Leon hated Vahrian airships, but since unloading them put beers on his table, he faked a smile as he picked up the crate.

"Good evening, Captain," he said.

I hope you fall in the sea and drown, he thought.

The captain kept reading his book and reclined further in his chair. Scowling, Leon carried the crate out of the cabin, stumbling down the gangway to reach the old jetty. Wooden planks groaned underfoot and waves slammed against the rocks, spraying him with freezing water. Above Leon, the airship's four-hundred-foot balloon was long and cylindrical, tapering at the ends, with the cabin attached underneath. Straining at the moorings, the ship's anchor ropes twisted and creaked on either side of the jetty as Leon walked along, labouring under the heaviness of the crate.

Towards the end of the jetty, he fumbled the slippery box, but kept hold, staggered off the jetty, then dumped the crate beside the nineteen others he'd unloaded. His back twanged and he groaned. In his Academy days, he could've hauled cargo through a swamp for hours, but now he was forty-three.

Those days were behind him.

He inhaled a lungful of salty air and rested his hands on his hips, puffing. Dozens of vessels crowded the harbour. Airships floated on the end of their anchor ropes, fishing skiffs bobbed in the water, and pegasus-drawn carriages rattled as they entered the harbour from a landing strip that led to the disc's edge. Out of all those vessels, of course the stupid harbourmaster had given Leon the biggest ship to unload.

The captain strode along the jetty and walked past Leon, whistling. Like most Vahrians, he was a head shorter than a Payan, but twice as stocky. Buttons gleamed on his jacket and he bounced as he strolled towards the harbour office – it seemed he still hadn't adjusted to Hargold Disc's gravity, which was half as strong as the Vahrians' planet.

Prick.

Leon watched the captain disappear among the crowds of sailors. It wasn't enough that Vahria had bombed the hell out of Paya's discs in the Invasion War, or that the airship's crates weighed more than an asteroid. No. On top of all that, Leon had to deal with arrogant captains who knew nothing about space travel, yet thought themselves too good to meet a Payan's eyes.

Someone tapped Leon's shoulder. "Leon de Velasco?"

He turned. A young woman stood before him, wrapped in a bulky, dirt-stained cloak. Her tall, slender frame marked her as a fellow Payan. Good. Leon didn't have to hide how annoyed he was at being interrupted.

"What?" he asked.

"My name's Elena. I need your help."

Her voice was a mixture of nervousness and excitement, but she had a confident firmness despite her youth. Leon

2

raised an eyebrow. With dishevelled, shoulder-length hair, a tangled beard, and ratty clothes that reeked of booze, he didn't get many requests for help. Especially from young women.

"Got a ship you need unloaded?" he asked.

"I –"

Two Vahrian soldiers swaggered past and bumped Elena.

"– we'll catch them by tomorrow, chaps," one soldier said.

Leon frowned. Most Payans looked down when soldiers passed, but Elena glared at the Vahrians as they strutted away.

"You were saying?" he said.

"I need to sail to another disc."

What a bloody waste of time.

He turned away. "Can't help. I just unload cargo."

"Wait!" She grabbed him. "I know who you are."

"That ain't so, or you wouldn't have come to me."

He shrugged her off and strode toward the harbourmaster's office, hoping that entering an official building would intimidate Elena and make her go away.

She chased him. "Please. You have to help."

Leon ducked under a pegasus' wing. The four-legged creature neighed and shook its mane, stepping away from Leon as he passed. Elena kept following him.

"Told you, I ain't a sailor," said Leon.

The harbourmaster's office was on the other side of a pack of merchants. Leon would be rid of Elena within seconds.

She shoved something soft into his hand. "I know who you are."

"Karym's horns, girl. I ain't –"

He looked at what she'd handed him.

It was a feather.

3

Panic surged through Leon. The feather was grey, long, and broad, filling the full width of his palm. He hadn't seen anything like it in the twenty years since the War.

If a Vahrian found it, they were both dead.

Leon stuffed the feather in his pocket, dragged Elena down the alley beside the harbourmaster's office, then shoved her against the wall.

"Where'd you get that?" he asked in a low voice.

"You have to –"

"Tell me where you found it!"

"I need your help." Her voice wavered. "I know who you are and you need to know – you're not the last."

Laughter swelled from inside the harbourmaster's office. Elena gasped. She tore herself from Leon's grip with surprising strength.

"Have to go," she said. "Can't let him see me – but I'll find you, okay?"

She sprinted down the alley, vanishing into the shadows. Leon clenched his hand into a white-knuckled fist and strode out of the alley, back into the harbour. This couldn't be real. He'd hidden his secret for two decades, but now ...

She can't know. Can she?

A Vahrian inquisitor limped out of the harbourmaster's office, flanked by soldiers. The inquisitor's left leg scraped along the cobblestones and his foot was twisted at a painful right angle to his body. He leaned on a cane and winced with each dragging step.

Leon's skin crawled. He thought his war wounds were bad, but for this man every stride would be agonising.

The inquisitor saw Leon. "Ah, you're the chap that unloaded my airship, aren't you? What's your name?"

Lean bowed deeply, taking the moment to steady his breath. "Leon, sir."

The inquisitor bowed back. That was nice. Most Vahrians didn't understand Payan etiquette and tried to shake his hand instead of offering the normal greeting.

The inquisitor gave him a handful of coins. "My gratitude for a job well done."

Leon blinked. No Vahrians had directly paid him before. Normally, the harbourmaster paid all the workers at the day's end.

"Thank you, Inquisitor."

The man smiled, but the smile didn't reach his cold eyes. "My dear chap, what's that in your cloak?"

Leon glanced down.

The feather stuck out of his pocket.

Leon's guts twisted. Trying to stop his hand from shaking, he grabbed it and showed the inquisitor.

"Found it in the sea."

The inquisitor hobbled closer, leaning on his cane. Leon's nose twitched. The man reeked of yhona, a foul-smelling painkiller paste.

"Don't be nervous," the inquisitor said. "I'm just looking. It's a rather magnificent feather, dear chap. What creature do you suppose it came from?"

"Don't know," lied Leon. "A pegasus?"

The inquisitor leaned towards the feather. "Ha. Not even close."

Sweat ran down Leon's face.

"Say …" The inquisitor stepped back and Leon breathed out. "May I take that?"

"Yes – of course, sir!"

The inquisitor took the feather. He pulled out a sack that jangled with dorics and gave it to Leon. Leon looked inside. Those coins represented more than he'd earn in a month.

"Thank you, sir."

"You're welcome." The inquisitor examined the feather. "This may be just what I need. Now, Leon, if you find another feather, or anyone who has them, there's more dorics in my pocket for you. Come to the castle and tell them you have a message for Walter Drayton. How's that sound, dear fellow?"

Leon thought of Elena. "Excellent, sir."

Inquisitor Drayton's gaze lingered on Leon. Then he hobbled away. His cane tapped on the cobblestones and his twisted foot scraped along the ground. The soldiers clanked after him.

Another wave smashed against the shore, spraying Leon with water. He clenched his teeth. He'd been safe for twenty years, but now he saw how flimsy that safety had been.

~ ~ ~

Leon staggered to his seat in the corner of the Lowfern Inn, clutching two drinks and trying to ignore the stench of sweat, mud, and stale beer. He glanced around the noisy room. It wasn't like Alvaro to be late. For the last few years, they'd met every Sunday and Wednesday evening to drink and play jonshular. Alvaro never missed an evening without telling Leon, but it was already a half hour past their usual meeting time and there was still no sign of him.

Leon pulled out his hand-carved jonshular board. His thick fingers trembled as he set black and white pieces onto the board's hexagonal spaces.

The woman with the feather – Elena, that was her bloody name – kept appearing in his mind. Her words echoed in his ears: *I know who you are.*

He shook his head and sipped one of the beers, knowing it probably wouldn't help any more than the first three had. He squinted out the dirty window. Glowfung lit the street with purple light and the force field dome encasing Hargold Disc glittered above the rooftops. Stars glowed beyond the field. Leon sighed. That's where he should've been – up there, amongst the stars. Not stuck here, grovelling to Vahrians.

The door opened. Leon looked up, expecting Alvaro, but three Vahrian naval cadets swaggered through instead. Their pale skin and stocky bodies contrasted with the slender, olive coloured Payans crowding the inn. Scowling, Leon finished his drink. The second beer sat in front of him, but he didn't touch it, saving it for Alvaro. If he ever arrived.

"Got any Murmidian Ale?" asked the biggest cadet, a giant man with his hair shaved into a thick strip running down the middle.

"Sorry, sir. We've only got local brewed –"

"Give us whatever's strongest."

Leon stared at the jonshular board and scratched his bushy beard.

Ain't no way Elena knows who I am ... no, she's trying to fool me. For a bet, maybe. Yeah. That's it.

The three Vahrian cadets strode to the cushioned seats by the fire, which held several Payans. The Payans leapt up and scurried away, heads bowed. The cadets sat.

But what about the feather? That was real. Damn it.

Twitching his fingers, he glanced at the door.

He reached under his cloak, pulled out a half-circle pendant, and stroked the marks in the wood. Leon knew the marks by heart, but touching it felt like touching the woman who'd carved it for him, so he cradled it, hoping the pendant would bring him comfort.

He sighed. She would've never been late. Even though he'd made her wait years and given her more hardship than she deserved, Juliana was always there for him. Her, and his best friend Blas ... the three of them inseparable.

The War changed that.

The door opened and Alvaro stumbled inside. Leon jumped out of his chair. Bruises covered his friend's face and a sling wrapped around his arm. He limped over to Leon and they bowed to each other, Alvaro stumbling slightly as he rose upright again.

Leon pulled out Alvaro's chair. "What happened?"

Alvaro slumped onto the seat. "Bloody resistance fighters. Blew up half the Overseer's House as I was delivering flour. Only left the healers' now."

Leon sat. "Blew up?"

"Didn't you hear the great big explosion at noon?"

Leon had been too busy carrying crates to think about the noise and he hadn't talked to his fellow workers all day.

"I thought it was an asteroid hitting the force field," he said.

"Might as well have been. Didn't take out a single blasted Vahrian."

Leon winced and glanced at the Vahrian cadets, who were roaring with laughter. "Careful –"

"For Marym's sake, those dullards can't hear a thing."

Leon nudged the drink he'd saved to Alvaro, hoping it would shut him up. Alvaro grunted thanks and they started a game of jonshular.

"At least the bomb blasted apart the steward's chambers." Alvaro moved a piece. "You should've heard him complain about the dirt on his carpet. Stupid prick."

Leon jumped Alvaro's piece and glanced at the cadets. "Don't speak so loud."

"What are you worried about? We're clean."

"So was Maurice."

"That's different. They were watching him."

"Yeah, because they heard him talking."

Alvaro slammed his piece onto a goal space and flipped it to turn it into a king. "Why so uptight today?"

Leon thought of Elena. "I ain't wanting trouble, okay? I'm close."

"Big payday?"

Leon leaned forward and lowered his voice. "An inquisitor paid a month's earnings for unloading his ship."

"Not bad. So you've only got ... hmm, let's see ..."

"Five months and two weeks. Then the moneylender's off my back and I can start saving for the carriage. We'll leave this disc in no time."

"Leon –"

"You don't want to work in a Vahrian mansion the rest of your life, do you?"

"No. But I've got Teresa to think of, and my stepson."

Leon scowled and nudged his king forward.

Alvaro jumped over Leon's piece, moving his own king back towards the exit spaces. "Come on, man. We've talked about this. A sailor's life ain't for me, and besides, even when you pay off your house, you'll probably waste any extra money in this place."

Leon sipped his beer. "I'm cutting back."

Alvaro raised an eyebrow. "Even so, the pegasus will cost as much as a carriage. Maybe more."

"Yeah, but one step at a time."

"Long as you're walking the right way." Alvaro frowned at the jonshular board. "What did you unload? Must've been important if the inquisitor paid that much."

"You know I don't look."

"I would."

"And that's why you ain't working there."

"Still, must've been special."

"I guess."

Should I tell him about Elena?

If he told Alvaro what happened, that might get her out of his head, but then he'd have to discuss the War, and their one rule was to never talk about that.

Alvaro jumped three of Leon's pieces. Leon cursed. He should've moved his pieces earlier to block that route, but thinking about Elena had distracted him.

Who the hell was she? How did she know his secret? And how had she got that feather? The last time Leon saw one, it was –

No. He wouldn't think about that.

Alvaro's final king jumped two of Leon's pieces and landed on an exit space.

"Another win!" said Alvaro.

"Crap." Leon glared at the board. "Good game."

"You kidding? I wiped you in under ten minutes. Rematch?"

Leon stared at his empty mug. "Sure."

Alvaro frowned. "You alright?"

"Yeah."

A mug shattered by the fireplace.

The biggest Vahrian cadet stood and knocked over his chair. "This crap's piss weak! Barman, you got anything stronger?"

Alvaro's hand clenched into a fist and he whispered, "Sit down, you idiot."

"Shh!" said Leon.

The barman mopped sweat off his forehead. He glanced at the blunted war axe hung on the wall. The weapon was strong and sombre, but against the powerfully built Vahrian cadet it looked like a child's toy.

The barman stared at the dirty floorboards. "I'm sorry, sir. That's the strongest I've got."

"Pah. No wonder all Payans are weak, drinking crap like that."

"Shut the hell up," said Alvaro under his breath.

"Quiet!" hissed Leon.

"Explains why you lost the War," said the cadet. "You're all as weak as that pathetic beer –"

Growling, Alvaro grabbed his mug and cocked back his arm.

Leon grabbed his friend. "No!"

Alvaro threw the mug and it shattered on the wall behind the soldiers. An ominous hush filled the room.

Snarling, the cadet whirled around to face Alvaro. "What the hell?"

Chapter 2

L eon gulped.

A red-faced Alvaro glared at the cadet. "Get out."

The cadet laughed. The other two Vahrians – one male, one female – stood.

Alvaro raised his fists. "Takes three of you, does it?"

He punched and the nearest cadet ducked. The Vahrian slung Alvaro onto the dirty floor, knocking over a table stacked with mugs. Pewter shattered against the floor as the cadets kicked Alvaro. He yelled and curled into a ball, but the blows kept coming.

"Leon!" Alvaro said. "Help!"

The big cadet raised his boot above Alvaro's injured arm. He looked up. Smiled at Leon. Then he stomped and Alvaro screamed. A group of Payans hurried out of the inn and the rest watched with blank faces.

"Want to help your friend?" asked the big cadet.

Leon swallowed. "Please, he don't mean nothing by it. He's drunk –"

"He attacked a Vahrian." The cadet kicked Alvaro's head from behind. "You don't get away with that, Payan scum."

Leon pulled out the bag of coins Inquisitor Drayton gave him, offering a month's worth of earnings to the cadet. "P-

Please, sir. Accept this as an apology."

The biggest cadet – who Leon had decided was the leader – grabbed the bag. "You trying to pay us off?"

"No, sir, no." Leon looked at the floor. "I'm sorry, I ain't meaning to –"

The cadet pocketed the bag and lashed another kick into Alvaro. Leon swallowed. He had a dagger but the Vahrians carried swords. Even if Leon fought, what then? They'd hang him. Or, if he was lucky, ship him to a mining camp in the asteroid belt.

He stayed still and the Vahrians kicked his friend into a whimpering, bloody mess. Leon flushed. He'd always been spineless. No one could say he'd gone against form.

The female cadet grabbed the big Vahrian's arm. "That's enough, Jon."

Jon nodded. He shot another kick into Alvaro's ribs, then he and the other Vahrians picked up the fallen chairs and sat back by the fire.

"Get rid of your friend," Jon said.

Leon grabbed his jonshular set, then dragged Alvaro outside. The night-time street pulsed with purple light, thanks to the glowfung stuck to the walls.

Leon propped his friend up. "You okay?"

"No thanks to you."

Leon's hands trembled. "What the hell were you thinking?"

Alvaro stood, wobbling, and glared with bloodshot eyes. Suddenly he doubled up, coughing blood. Wiping his mouth, he rose again to meet Leon's gaze.

"Someone has to stand up to them, or they'll keep walking over us."

"They walked over you just fine then."

Alvaro spat blood onto the cobblestones. "You're a brave one, aren't you?"

Leon scowled. "I'm realistic."

"You know, cowards like you lost us the War."

Leon's face burned with heat. "Shut up."

"No. You're a bloody coward and you won't even face up to it."

"Shut up!"

Leon stormed away. He stumbled over the cobblestones, hands clenched into fists. His back ached as he staggered around the corner.

What had Alvaro been thinking? You didn't mess with Vahrians. They came from Neebia, a planet with double the gravity of the Payan discs that orbited it, which meant Vahrians were twice as strong as Payans. On top of that, the Vahrian Republic had ruled the Payan discs since the Invasion War twenty years ago. Sure, the Queen still ruled, but everyone knew she was a puppet. The short of it was this: even if you won a fight with a Vahrian, the Inquisition would hunt you and plant your head on a stake. Didn't stop idiotic resistance fighters trying, though.

Leon lurched into a wall. The street wavered and nausea oozed through him. He scowled. This whole thing had given him a splitting headache, but it hadn't wiped Elena from his mind. Maybe a smoke would help.

He stuffed his pipe with kemp and used his shaking fingers to light it with a sulfur match. Leon dropped the match in a puddle, then sucked the pipe, breathing out a thick cloud of smoke that swirled around his face and turned purple in the light of the glowfung fixed to a wall. The smoke softened the rough edges of his headache, but after all that beer he needed to piss.

He staggered into a deserted square. A statue of a Vahrian soldier stood on a plinth that once held a sculpture of a Payan Archangel. Sanded-down carvings decorated the plinth, too faint to see the details.

There'd been a lot of anger when the Vahrians removed the Archangel sculpture. Quiet anger. The anger of people who knew protest was useless. Personally, Leon didn't care then and he didn't care now. Considering what the Vahrians had stolen from him, getting mad over a statue seemed laughable. He'd stayed away from the town's hidden anger and he'd stayed away from just about everything else over these last two decades. But now, with Elena …

Leon puffed on his pipe and sighed. Everything had gone to pieces.

I've got to leave. Catch an airship off the disc, first thing tomorrow.

He swallowed. That flight wouldn't come cheap, but he had to escape before Elena found him again.

He nodded. Wasn't much of a plan, but it would settle his unease. Leon inhaled one last breath of kemp. Then he stuffed the pipe in his pocket, glanced around to check he was alone, and pulled down his breaches to piss on the Vahrian statue, chuckling.

The scent of urine reached him and a memory flashed through his mind. The alley: reeking of piss. The sack: dripping blood. He remembered dumping the sack, whimpering, and running and running and running and he'd never stopped. But now Elena was dragging him back.

He pulled up his breaches. Panting, he hurried out of the square, hands trembling as he stumbled through Hargold's streets. Why did his damn hands always shake? Why couldn't they be still?

He remembered Alvaro's words: *Cowards like you lost us the War.*

Leon slumped. Those words were truer than even Alvaro knew. Leon had been no ordinary soldier and his mistakes had been no ordinary failings.

He reached his house. Like all Payan dwellings, it looked as if a clump of fungus had grown from the ground. The windowless walls were made from fungcrete: a paste daubed over a timber frame, then expanded and hardened to form a solid shell. Leon's house needed re-coating, because the walls looked thin enough to break through. He went to unlock the door, then froze.

The lock was broken. The door was ajar.

Leon swallowed. Who'd broken in? A street gang? Or … no, she couldn't know where he lived.

Right?

He pulled out his dagger. Should he run? Like most fungcrete buildings, his house was windowless, so he couldn't peer inside.

Please, let it be empty.

Holding the dagger, Leon kicked open the door.

Elena stood inside.

Chapter 3

Leon shut the door and pointed the knife at Elena. "Get out."

"Put down the knife, I just want –"

"Get out!"

His hand shook and the bloodstained battleground flickered before him.

"Please," she said, "I can't leave, I need your help –"

Leon snarled and barrelled towards her, his knife outstretched. He wouldn't hurt Elena. He just wanted to scare her and force her out of his life before she dragged him back to the past.

She dodged and tripped him. He crashed onto his bed and his jonshular set dropped out of his pocket. The board smacked into the ground and the hand-carved pieces fell from their drawstring bag. He gaped. That had been a gift from Juliana.

"Please," said Elena. "Don't embarrass yourself. I just want to –"

He roared, rolled over, and swung the knife. She caught his wrist, twisted the blade out of his hand, then flung it away. It landed on the rush-weave matting with a dull thump.

"Could you just –"

Leon punched with his other hand.

She blocked and grabbed his wrist. "– let me –"

Leon tried to pull his hands out of her grip, but she was too strong, so he kicked.

She dodged. "– finish my sentence?"

"Fine." Leon's pulse pounded in his ears. "Let me go and I'll listen."

"Promise not to attack me?"

"If you leave."

"I'll leave, but you've got to hear me out first."

"Whatever."

She let go. He sat up, rubbing his wrists. Slowly, he bent and placed the jonshular pieces into the drawstring bag, hoping to hide his red cheeks. How had a girl half his age bested him, and so easily, too?

Elena sat and leaned on Leon's table. She yawned. There was a haggardness about her, as if she'd spent the last week sleeping in gutters.

"I need your help to find Waverrym," she said.

He stared at her for a few seconds. Then he laughed. Elena's grim expression didn't change. Leon kept laughing until a cough ripped away his breath. He put the jonshular board and the bag of pieces onto the table, then wiped tears from his eyes.

"Waverrym's a myth."

She pulled a leather-bound book out of her cloak. Marks stained the ragged cover, but despite the wear, there was no mistaking the Sarahk.

"It's real." She pointed to the book. "It says so in here."

He snorted. "So you ain't just crazy. You're a fool, too."

"What?"

He nodded at the Sarahk. "It's a book for fools."

Elena gaped. "You don't believe in the Star Spectre, or Her Archangels? Who made these discs, then?"

"I ain't saying they're not real. Karym's horns, there's enough of their relics lying around to prove it, but just because they exist doesn't mean they care about us."

"But you said you don't believe the Sarahk."

"You know what it says? Says you pray to the Archangels and they'll help. Well, I prayed in the War, but it didn't help." He thought of Mangold Pass. "Not one bit. Now stop wasting my time and get the hell out of here."

"You're not supposed to be like this," she said. "You're supposed to be –"

"What? A fool who believes stupid stories?"

"No. You're an angel."

Leon flinched. How the hell did she know?

"When I found out about you, I had hope," said Elena. "I thought you'd be the one to help me find Waverrym. There's an inquisitor hunting me, Leon. A man called Drayton."

Drayton ... that was the inquisitor he'd met at the harbour. The man with the twisted leg.

Elena shivered. "I heard that after the War, Drayton ripped off angels' wings and now he sleeps on a pillow of feathers torn from his victims. He's a monster. If he catches me ... that's why I need your help. In the songs, the angels were always so brave. I thought I'd be safe if I found you."

"Those songs ain't true and I'm no angel."

"You're lying. You are an angel, just like me."

"Eh?"

Elena undid her broach and her cape fell. She turned around, and through her shirt, Leon saw something bunched

19

against her back. With a rustle of fabric, a pair of grey, feathery wings folded out through slits cut in her shirt, and the wings snapped out behind her, wide enough to touch the walls.

Leon cursed and clutched the pendant around his neck. His heartbeat raced.

"I thought I was the last one!" he said.

Elena smiled. "So you admit it. Well, now you know why we have to go to Waverrym."

"I still ain't going."

Her smile faded. "But we're the last ones! The Vahrians have hunted us to extinction. There's none of us left in Paya, but it's different on Waverrym. Angels have lived there for thousands of years, ever since the Great Departure. No one's found it, but if we can, we'll be safe."

"Waverrym doesn't exist, girl. It's a fake disc in a made-up story, and besides, I've been safe for twenty years."

Someone knocked on the door. "Hello!"

Leon's skin went cold and Elena's eyes widened.

"Hide!" he said.

Elena glanced around the windowless house and crawled under the bed, pulling her wings in after her.

The person knocked again. "Hello?"

Leon opened the door. Inquisitor Drayton and a dozen Vahrian soldiers stood outside.

"Good evening, Leon," said Drayton.

Chapter 4

Colour drained from Leon's face as he bowed to Drayton. "Evening, Inquisitor."

He stared at the inquisitor's crippled leg. Bone twisted and bulged under the man's skin, and Leon's stomach churned. Drayton's leg was even worse than Leon remembered. He'd seen bad war wounds, but Drayton's leg looked like it was stuffed with stones.

"Mind if I come in, dear fellow?" asked Drayton.

Leon glanced at the soldiers standing in the street. His heart hammered. Elena was a fugitive and if Drayton found her, Leon was dead.

"Sure."

The inquisitor turned to his soldiers. "Wait here. I'll call if I need you."

Leon held the door open as Drayton limped inside. His twisted foot dragged along the ground and the stench of yhona paste filled the room.

Leon shivered and shut the door. It blocked his view of the soldiers but didn't do much to slow his thundering heartbeat. Drayton studied the brittle fungcrete walls. Despite stooping over his cane, the inquisitor was tall for a Vahrian: only a handspan shorter than Leon.

Must've lived in Paya for a while. Since the War?

Drayton stroked the jonshular board on the table, pried open the drawstring bag beside it, then removed a piece.

Leon tensed. *Get your filthy hands off that.*

"Fine carving, dear chap," said Drayton. "Your work?"

"No. By a friend."

Drayton nodded. He put down the piece and Leon breathed out. The inquisitor examined a chart on the wall, which showed the orbits of the Payan discs.

Then he frowned at the bed in the corner.

Sweat ran down Leon's back. He hoped Elena had enough sense to stay silent. His fingers twitched. He stared at the table, making sure to not look at the bed.

"To what do I owe your visit, Inquisitor?" Leon asked.

Speaking so formally felt damn unsettling. Once, he'd talked like that all the time, but the years working at the harbour had ground away that stupid way of speaking. Just as well. He didn't want to sound like those highborn pricks who'd made the Academy hell.

Drayton lent on his cane and peered at the disc chart. "The discs' movements fascinate you?"

Leon nodded and licked his dry lips. Karym's horns, he was thirsty. He grabbed a water skin, unplugged it, then sculled its contents.

"I respect your intellect." Drayton leaned closer to the disc chart. "You know, there's a Vahrian fellow called Ray Winston, who's created a three-dimensional model of the planet Neebia and the Payan discs that orbit it. His model is perfectly scaled and the discs orbit Neebia with the exactness of a clock. He's in great demand now. I daresay in a few years, one of his models will come to Paya and you may even see it. It's an

22

exciting time to be part of the Vahrian Republic, is it not?"

"It is."

Leon bit his lip. A moving model of Neebia and the Payan discs? Leon didn't need a model to calculate orbits or traverse the discs. He could point to constellations blindfolded. He knew Pomeroy was above them – a disc that appeared every five years. He knew it took six and a half hours to reach Marold, the nearest three-disc system. Four hours if you hitched a ride in the jetstream. Leon knew everything about celestial navigation and this stupid Vahrian scientist thought he was a genius?

"Please." Drayton gestured to the table. "Sit."

Leon sat. He gripped the sides of his chair with white-knuckled hands. He waited for Drayton to sit, but the inquisitor shook his head.

"I'll stand, if you don't mind." The inquisitor gripped his cane harder. "Sitting is … difficult. Ah, but what's this?"

Drayton pointed at the knife Elena had knocked from Leon's hand, which lay on the rush-matting floor beside the bed.

"Yours?" Drayton asked.

"Yes, Inquisitor."

Drayton hobbled over to the bed. Leon gulped. *Don't you dare breathe, girl.*

The inquisitor turned the knife with the tip of his cane. "Most impressive … an angel-issue dagger from the War?"

"Don't know," lied Leon. "Bought it from a smithy a few years back."

"And why does a harbour worker need a military-issue dagger?"

"Cutting ropes."

"I see."

Leon waited for Drayton to say something more, but the inquisitor just stared. A tight silence stretched out between them.

"I'm here to ask for your help," said Drayton.

Leon frowned. "With what?"

Drayton pulled a feather from his cloak. It was the feather Elena handed Leon this morning, which Leon had given to Drayton. Leon tensed.

Drayton put the feather on the table. "I'm not the Vahrian Council's best inquisitor in Paya. However, I'm rather specialised. See, I'm investigating the recent terrorism which has blighted your disc. The bombing of the Overseer's House earlier today is probably the first you've heard of this, but the so-called Resistance has sabotaged Vahrian operations here all week. Now, they could've called any inquisitor to catch these terrorists, but they called me. Why? Well, this case needed a specialist, because the terrorists had a unique aide. An angel."

Leon's heartbeat thumped in his skull as he forced himself to frown. "But they're extinct. They all died in the War."

"Yes, most of the cursed war criminals did, but some survived and kept fighting after the peace treaty. Until I found them. In the War, you see, I was captured by an angel, and there was nothing angelic about how she treated me." Drayton glanced at his crippled leg. "So when it comes to angels, I have history, you might say."

Leon swallowed. *If he finds out who I am, I'm dead.*

"This is why I'm here," said Drayton. "Earlier today, you gave me an angel feather. We must conclude that it came from an angel who was in the harbour this morning. Perhaps they were trying to flee from Hargold. They can't, of course. We've grounded all non-Vahrian airships after the bombing. Nevertheless, I have a request. I want you to help me find this angel. Her name's Elena de Muriel, and she's twenty years old. Now, I will pay for your help."

Drayton placed a large sack of coins on the table. "Twenty dorics."

Leon gasped. That'd take years to earn. Twenty dorics would clear his mortgage, buy a carriage, buy a pegasus, and let him become a sailor. He'd have enough to bring Alvaro with him, too. Sure, he'd still have to deal with Vahrians, but ferrying them between discs would be better than unloading their airships.

And, best of all, he could fly again.

It had been decades since he'd soared through space, floating amongst the stars …

Drayton leaned closer. "I'll give you this, dear chap, if you give me information that helps me arrest her. It doesn't matter how small that information is. If it brings this terrorist to justice, the dorics are yours. What do you say?"

Leon thought of Elena, hiding beneath his bed. He was the only person between her and a hangman's noose, but she was the only thing between him and the freedom of the stars.

"Will you help me?" asked Drayton.

"Yes."

He clenched his hands into fists underneath the table, waiting for her to cry out. She stayed silent.

"Good," said Drayton. "So, can you think of anything that might help me?"

"Hmm. I found the feather in the sea, near jetty two … Didn't spot anyone matching the girl's description. What was her name, again?"

"Ah … I'm disappointed, Leon."

"Sorry. That's all I remember, but I'll try to find her tomorrow."

Drayton pulled another angel feather out of his cloak and said in a quiet voice, "This was on your doorstep."

Leon's chest tightened and his heart raced so fast it felt ready to explode.

Drayton leaned forward and whispered, "She's here, isn't she?"

Chapter 5

L eon's heart thudded. He gaped at the feather in Drayton's hand and glanced at the door. He could sense the soldiers hulking outside. One word from Drayton and they'd burst in, draw their blades, and –

"She's here, isn't she?" whispered Drayton.

A tear rolled down Leon's cheek. "Y-yes."

"Under the bed?" asked the inquisitor, his voice so low Leon almost didn't hear him.

Leon nodded, his lip trembling. Drayton stood. He limped to the bed, pulled out his sword so softly, so gently, that it didn't make a sound. He held it above the mattress. Leon gulped. Looked away and stared at the table.

You ain't changed. You're still a pathetic coward.

He shook his head. "No."

Drayton turned. "What?"

"No," said Leon. "Elena, he's going to stab you!"

Elena pushed up from under the bed, flipping it into the air. The bed knocked Drayton. He stumbled back, crashing through the brittle fungcrete wall to land in the street amongst his soldiers.

"Run!" said Leon.

He charged at the opposite wall and smashed through the

fungcrete. He tripped, falling into the laneway behind his home. Elena leapt through the hole he'd made.

"Get them!" said Drayton.

Elena yanked Leon up. He looked at the jonshular set Juliana had carved, which lay on the table inside.

Soldiers burst through the front door. Leon cursed. No time to grab the set.

He and Elena sprinted through the laneway. The narrow lane was dim, lit by clumps of faded glowfung, and they almost tripped several times. Behind them, armour clanked and soldiers yelled.

"Turn left!" said Leon.

They ripped around the corner, skidding in a trail of mud and crashing through a stack of vases, before bursting into a wide, bright street. Leon's heart raced. They had to use Munrose Bridge to reach Hargold's second disc. In the omnicrop fields, forests, and caves, they'd find places to hide.

He sprinted down the street. "Got a breathfung?"

"Yeah." Elena pelted after him. "So, you'll help me find Waverrym?"

Leon puffed. "What? No!"

"Then why didn't you give me up?" she asked, not sounding the slightest bit short of breath.

"Just keep running."

They tore around the corner. Leon gasped. His lungs burned and his flabby legs ached. Unloading airships had made him strong, but it had been years since he'd run like this.

"There!" yelled a soldier behind them.

Leon and Elena rounded the corner. Ahead of them, Munrose Bridge shimmered behind the domed force field that contained Hargold Disc's air and gravity. Leon swore. Six Vahrian soldiers blocked the bridge. Leon and Elena clattered to a halt a stone's throw away.

"Who goes there?" asked a soldier.

Leon's heart pounded against his ribs. "Back. We've got to –"

Four Vahrian soldiers burst out of an alley behind them. Leon gulped. How would they escape?

Elena grabbed his hand. "Run at the bridge!"

She sprinted forward, dragging Leon along. The soldiers guarding the bridge levelled their spears.

"Elena, we can't–"

"Breathers on, we'll fly over them!"

Elena and Leon pulled breathfung from their cloaks, then attached them to their faces. The fungus wriggled, covering Leon's mouth and sending feelers up his nostrils, which puffed gas into his nose. He felt a familiar rush as the gas readied his body for the shock of space.

They kept running towards the bridge while soldiers chased them from behind.

"I can't fly!" said Leon, voice muffled by the breathfung.

Elena undid her cape as they ran. "But you're an angel!"

Her cape billowed out behind her and her wings unfurled with a snap. The soldiers gasped.

"I can't fly, alright!" said Leon.

"Shit," said Elena.

They charged at the soldiers. Elena flapped, and she grabbed Leon, and his stomach jerked as she lifted him off the ground and they flew over the soldiers and soared through the force field.

Everything went quiet.

29

Gravity vanished.

They glided through space and soared over Munrose Bridge, heading towards Hargold's second disc. Elena's hair fanned around her. Leon's did the same. Despite everything, he closed his eyes. Floating through space always made him calm.

When they flew through the second disc's force field, wind smacked into them and birdsong struck his ears. He grinned. He'd never thought he'd fly again.

But had the ground always moved this fast beneath him, and had he always flown this close to the dirt? Wait – they were too low!

They crashed. The hard-packed dirt smashed into Leon and pain raced through him. He rolled to a stop.

In the distance, soldiers shot through the force field and burst out of Munrose Bridge, clattering onto the disc. Leon stumbled up, groaning. He helped Elena stand and together they staggered toward a field of omnicrop.

"Stop!" said a soldier.

Leon glanced back. Soldiers streamed off the bridge and onto the disc, racing towards them. Leon gritted his teeth. He and Elena had to reach the omnicrop field. The grain's stalks were twice his height and would hide them from the Vahrians.

The soldiers sprinted towards them. One hurled a spear and it stabbed into the ground next to Leon. He and Elena broke into a stiff-legged jog, still bruised from the crash. They staggered into the omnicrop, where the tall brown stalks blocked their view of the soldiers.

"Why can't you fly?" asked Elena as they limped through the field.

He scowled.

"Leon, why –"

"Shut up. They might hear us."

They lurched through the omnicrop field. The towering stalks muffled the soldiers' distant yells. Leon's world shrunk to the space of his next agonising step. He couldn't hear any soldiers' footsteps, but the field must've been teeming with them, all prowling for Leon and Elena.

Wait. Are we walking the right way?

He looked up. Judging by the curve of the domed force field, they were heading towards the disc's centre, which was the right direction.

"Smell that?" Elena asked.

He sniffed. "Smoke."

"Yeah, but why –" Elena gasped. "They've set fire to the field!"

He cursed and stumbled into a jog. Pain spiked up his legs and his lungs strained. Beside him, Elena ran light-footed. Smoke clouded the air. Leon coughed.

He tripped and fell, inhaling a mouthful of stinking manure. He tried to push himself up, but his arms were heavier than stone. Smoke closed around him. He spluttered. All his strength had faded.

Elena heaved him up. She staggered forward, dragging him alongside her. Together, they lurched out of the omnicrop field and into the forest. Leon glanced back. Flames danced in the distance, bathing the forest in flickering light. He swallowed. That field fed half the town.

Ain't nothing I can do.

They stumbled through the forest. The crackle of the fire quietened and the forest grew dark, now lit only by patches of glowfung. After half an hour, the sounds of the soldiers faded. They walked for another few hours to be safe, then pushed through a clump of floatpods and collapsed inside a hollow trunk, exhausted.

Elena rubbed her eyes and yawned. "So how are we going to get off the disc?"

Leon watched sap drip down the bark. Come morning, Inquisitor Drayton would close all the harbours and send every soldier hunting for them. This disc was big, but they couldn't hide here forever.

"Don't know," he said.

He turned to her, wondering if he should say something more, but he needn't have bothered. Elena was asleep. Sighing, Leon laid down, wrapping himself in his cloak. Frayed stitching held the fabric together and it didn't do much to warm him. Still, better than nothing. He shifted position, wincing as pain jolted his stiff muscles, and stared at the trail of sap. In the dim light, it looked like blood.

Chapter 6

Leon woke to the drone of a Vahrian airship. He rolled over, heart beating fast, and peered through a hole in the forest's canopy. The airship floated high above the trees.

"That's the third one I've seen."

He twisted around. Elena sat with her back against the hollow tree trunk they'd slept inside. Leon groaned. For a moment, he'd almost forgotten Elena, the encounter with Inquisitor Drayton, and the fact that he was now a fugitive.

Leon pushed himself into a sitting position, placing his hands with care. This disc was large, but there was no telling how close a Vahrian could be, or how far the sound of a snapping branch would carry.

"If I get you off the disc, will you help me find Waverrym?" Elena asked.

"How are you escaping, girl?"

"Er…"

"You've got no idea, do you?"

She shook her head.

Leon sighed. "Makes two of us."

He pulled his pipe out of his cloak, filled it with kemp, and fumbled in his pocket for matches.

"Why didn't you fly last night?" she asked.

Leon scowled. He stood and stumbled out of the hollow trunk, pushing through a cluster of floatpods. He snagged his foot on the tendril anchoring a floatpod to its host plant and the tendril snapped. The pod floated into the sky, then burst after rising above the canopy, spraying seeds everywhere.

"Did you hear me?" asked Elena.

Leon grunted. He struck the match against a tree and lit his pipe. As he sucked on the pipe, kemp-smoke relaxed his muscles. Elena glared. He smirked and blew a smoke ring, which faded before it reached the canopy. Once he'd finished the kemp, he limped back into the hollow tree trunk, wincing. His legs ached from last night's chase.

"You going to answer me?" she asked.

He packed away his pipe. "Nope."

"Kemp ruins your lungs, you know."

Leon pulled out his hip-flask and swigged lukewarm beer. "This counteracts that."

Elena glowered and opened her mouth to speak, then closed it. The silence suited Leon just fine. He breathed in, inhaling the kemp fumes floating in the air.

"So," she said. "How are we getting off the disc?"

He shrugged.

"Come on, don't you have any ideas?" she asked. "Anyone in town who could help?"

Leon thought of Alvaro and sighed. His friend would've made it home last night, and he'd heal, but Leon still felt guilty over abandoning him.

"You've got wings, girl. Fly."

"My wings aren't developed enough. I struggle to get off the ground. You saw last night. I couldn't glide more than a few hundred feet before we crashed. I can fly through space alright, but not through air, and there's no way we can reach the force field's edge. There'll be Vahrians all around the disc's perimeter."

Another airship droned overhead and despite the soothing kemp, Leon tensed.

"Hang on," said Elena. "Why don't you fly away?"

"Can't fly."

"But you're an angel."

"That a question?"

"I know you're an angel and so does the inquisitor."

Doubt it. If he knew, he'd have arrested me straight away.

"You're lying," he said.

"I can prove it. A few weeks ago, myself and some other Resistance fighters –"

"You work for the Resistance?" Leon thought of the bombing and Alvaro's injured hand. "You bombed the Overseer's House?"

"No, that wasn't –"

"You hurt a lot of Payans, you know."

"We didn't –"

"Save it."

"Leon, we didn't do the bombing. The Resistance doesn't do bombings. It was Drayton."

"What?"

"Drayton blew up the Overseer's House and blamed it on us. That way he'd get the townspeople on his side. It worked. Someone betrayed us. Soldiers raided our hideout a few hours before I found you yesterday. I'm the only one who escaped."

Elena stared at the dirt.

"If you want me to cry, you're out of luck," said Leon. "It's your own bloody fault."

"Shut up, old man." Elena's eyes shone. "Those were my friends."

Juliana's face flashed before Leon's eyes.

"No, you shut up," he said. "I fought in the War, okay? However bad you think you got it? However many friends you lost? It's nothing. Nothing! You and the stupid Resistance – you think it's a game, don't you? You all want to be heroes. Kick the Vahrians off the discs, restore Paya to a new golden age. Too late. Paya lost, Vahria won. Get over it."

Leon crossed his arms and slumped against the trunk. He stared at the forest outside, but he didn't see the trees. He saw the muddy battlefield and the canyon's narrow walls. Crashing metal echoed through the pass and a mass of seething soldiers charged towards him …

Elena watched the floatpods swaying in the breeze. "I know you're an angel, because the Inquisition have files on you."

"Bullshit."

"We broke into the Overseer's House. In the inquisitor's office was a file about you and it said you're the last surviving angel."

"Then why haven't they killed me?"

"They thought other angels would contact you. And they said you weren't a threat."

He glowered. *Got that bloody right.*

"Don't you care?" asked Elena. "They've known about you for years!"

Leon shrugged. "I was fine until you showed up."

"So this is my fault?"

"Damn right."

"You know, the file said you were a miserable, broken-down old man, but I never thought you'd be this pathetic."

None of this is news to me, girl.

Another airship glided above. Was it Leon's imagination, or was this one closer to the treetops? And that distant crunch of leaves … were soldiers prowling nearby, searching for them?

Elena sighed. "Look, forget I said that. Let's just work out how to escape the disc."

Leon glowered. *Forget* … he'd spent two decades trying to forget, but it hadn't happened yet.

"Can't use airships," he said. "They'll be guarded by Drayton's soldiers."

"Okay." Elena pursed her lips. "Are you sure you can't fly?"

"Positive. Even if we get off this disc, where do we go?"

"Waverrym."

He sighed. "Elena –"

She pulled out the Sarahk and flicked to a page. "'For ye that seek safety; for ye that seek freedom; for ye that seek peace; Waverrym is yours. For though ye fathers and mothers and ye ancestors may have sinned, if ye are of noble heart, ye may find the Path to Waverrym.' That's verse one hundred and forty-three from *The Story of Karym's Fall*."

He rolled his eyes. "Waverrym ain't a place. It's a metaphor for becoming good, even if you were raised bad, or some crap like that."

She shook her head. "It's not. I've found the Path."

"Got a map?"

"It's not a map. It's a riddle." She flicked to another page. "Verses eighty-one to eighty-four from *The Prophet Jesphat*."

Leon lent forward. He took out a clump of glowfung and by the fungus' purple light, read:

Find the heart of nobility, and
  find the soul of the realm.
  Find the lungs of Severym, and
  find the path to safety.

Despite himself, Leon frowned. Severym was the Archangel of risers, which were columns of hot air angels used to gain altitude … but what were her lungs?

Leon chuckled. "You think that's a clue? It's a stupid quote that doesn't even make sense."

"It's real, okay? I've talked to a lot of scholars about this, and read a lot of books, and it leads to a real place."

"Whatever. I ain't going to your fake fairy land, so we need to find a place we're both happy with."

"Agreed, but we need to get off here first."

"Damn right."

Leon rubbed his chin. Could they find wild pegasi in the forest? No, that was unlikely. Hargold was the only place they'd find a pegasus or a ship, and they couldn't get there without going past the soldiers.

Leon scowled up at the stars, thinking. Pomeroy – the disc that travelled past Hargold every five years – cast more light over the forest than any other disc, but it wouldn't stay above much longer. Soon, its orbit would carry it away, take it past the Mallean Asteroids, and then it would fly by –

Leon froze. How hadn't he thought of this before?

"Elena," he said. "I've got two answers."

She looked up. "To what?"

"Where we're going and how we're getting there."

Chapter 7

"First, we make a raft," said Leon.

Elena frowned. "You know we're not crossing a lake, right?"

"Course I do, girl. Let me finish. Once we've built it, we gather floatpods and tie 'em to the raft."

He grabbed a nearby floatpod and cut the anchoring tendril with his knife. He let go and the pod glided up into the sky, where it burst into a shower of spores. The wind had faded in the last few minutes, which meant the spores drifted back down towards them.

"Close your eyes," he said as the spores rained down. "It stings if they get into your eyes."

Leon counted to thirty, then opened his eyes. He tapped Elena to let her know it was safe.

"The floatpods take us up, through the force field, and into space," said Leon. "Then you fly us to Pomeroy – it's on an orbit that'll take us through the Mallean Asteroids, and then right past Anshan."

Anshan was the largest Payan system, with a sprawling seven-disc city and a population well over a hundred thousand. Leon hadn't been there for twenty-one years, but if it was like he remembered, it'd be easy to hide in the crowds.

"Anshan sounds good," said Elena. "But what's Pomeroy?"

Leon blinked. "It's a disc. Weird orbit. Appears every five years."

"Yeah, but where is it?"

"You don't know?"

"Course not. There's like eight discs I can see."

"Nine," said Leon without looking. "You seriously don't know –"

"Just tell me which one it is."

He pointed. "See those marks on the disc's underside? And how it's close enough to see detail, but still small?"

"Uh … yes?"

He sighed. "Never mind. Just build this damn raft."

"One question. This is a great plan and all, but don't floatpods pop? To spread their seeds?"

"Yes."

"So … isn't that bad?"

"Karym's horns, girl. Pick the dud floatpods!"

"Oh. How do I tell they're duds?"

"Tap 'em. They'll sound solid, though they'll still float. Most dud ones shouldn't pop. Of course, covering them with tar would be better, because then they'll never pop, but this is the best we can do."

"Er … when you say they *shouldn't* pop –"

"Get extra, just in case."

They set to work building the raft. Leon winced with every snap of wood and every crunch of leaves, but they had no means to silence their work. Hopefully, nearby soldiers would assume the sounds came from animals.

It took an hour to gather enough wood. As they worked, voices echoed in the distance. Once, an airship glided three hundred feet above them and they dove inside the hollow tree to take cover.

They worked faster after that.

Elena used strips torn from their clothes to make ropes, while Leon collected floatpods. He'd just returned to the clearing, holding a clump of floatpods, when Elena tugged one of her knots. It unravelled and she cursed.

He put the floatpods in the hollow tree to stop them flying away. "Can't you tie a knot, girl?"

She stared at the dirt and blushed. "Well ... I've never been out of a town before."

Leon remembered when he'd been a young angel at the Academy. So much he didn't know. So much to prove.

"Here," he said, showing Elena how to make a proper square lashing.

Voices kept echoing through the forest as they worked. Leon gulped.

Are they getting nearer?

"Alright." He stepped back from the raft. "That should do it. Now, let's get these floatpods onto it."

They tied floatpods to the raft. After fifteen minutes' work, the raft rose off the ground. Elena punched the air.

"Don't cheer," he said. "Put rocks on it, girl."

But behind his bushy beard, he smiled. Elena piled rocks onto the raft to stop it floating away.

Leaves crunched as three sword-wielding Vahrian soldiers stepped into the clearing. It was Jon and the other two cadets who'd attacked Alvaro in the tavern last night.

Elena cursed and drew her dagger. Leon's hands fumbled as he pulled out his knife. The cadets outnumbered them, wore full armour, and had swords with better reach than a dagger.

Jon grinned. "Drop the knife, lady."

Leon's legs shook. "We should run."

"I'm done running," said Elena.

The three Vahrians strode towards them. Leon swallowed. He gritted his teeth and turned, ready to sprint away.

Elena grabbed him. "Stand and fight!"

Leon cursed. He struggled out of her grip, but it was too late: the three Vahrians had surrounded them. Leon drew his dagger. He backed up against Elena and they stood on the raft. Floatpods hovered around them.

Jon nodded to the female cadet. She took out a bugle and blew it, sending a low note echoing through the forest. Birds flew out of a nearby tree. A distant bugle blew in response.

Leon's mouth was dry. Everything around him grew sharper. Crisper. He saw the floatpods' veins, heard Elena breathing, and felt every bump in his dagger's worn leather grip.

"Drop your weapons," said Jon. "Last chance."

Leon gulped. "Elena –"

"Not surrendering."

"Didn't mean that." Leon's voice dropped to a whisper. "When I say so, close your eyes."

"What?"

The three Vahrians strode towards Leon and Elena.

"Now!" said Leon.

He slashed at a clump of floatpods, which exploded in a shower of seeds. Leon shut his eyes. Sticky seeds slapped onto his face and the soldiers shrieked.

Leon opened his eyes. The three Vahrians clawed at their seed-splattered faces, cursing. Leon charged at Jon. Elena ran at the other two.

Jon's blade leapt into the air, knocking Leon's dagger out of his hand. The Vahrian snarled, one eye scrunched shut. Sweat streaked down Leon's forehead. Behind him, metal clashed and Elena yelled.

Jon slashed at Leon, who ducked. The blade hissed above him and he dove forward and tackled the soldier and they crashed into the dirt and Jon's armour bruised him as they grappled and Leon twisted the sword out of the Vahrian's hands and Jon drew his dagger and Leon plunged the sword down –

A shock raced up Leon's arm.

Warm blood spurted onto his skin. He stumbled up, chest heaving, and gaped at the sword sticking out of Jon's chest. Blood bubbled from the Vahrian's mouth. He glared at Leon and tried to raise his dagger, but his hand trembled and fell to the ground.

Leon's heart hammered. Blood ran down his forearms and dripped to the soil. He stared. The blood looked like rain falling from a branch. So innocuous. So ordinary. When he'd been a child, he'd always thought blood would look different. Special, somehow. Maybe even sacred.

It wasn't. Blood was a liquid like any other.

Hands grabbed him. "Leon."

He jerked back, twisting out of Elena's grip. On the ground behind her sprawled the other two cadets.

"Can you hear me?" she asked.

He nodded. It was a near thing, though, for she spoke with the muffled softness of a widow whispering through a veil. He realised he was still nodding. He tried to stop, but couldn't.

"Are you okay?" she asked. "Did he get you?"

His hands trembled. "You killed 'em."

"It was us or them."

He stared at Jon's dead body. "I killed him."

"You had no choice." She grabbed a clump of floatpods and tied them to the raft. "Come on. More Vahrians will be here any minute."

Leon stumbled to the raft. He grabbed a floatpod and set about lashing it to the wood, but it slipped out of his shaky grip and shot towards the canopy. A strange look came across Elena's face: a mix of sadness and disappointment, as if she'd expected greatness, only for reality to destroy her dream.

"I can tie these," she said. "You rest, okay?"

"Mmm."

Leon slumped against the tree. He stared at the stars and discs and the great blue orb of Neebia twinkling in the sky. The battlefield flashed before him. He growled and tried to swipe it away, but the blood-stained canyon loomed around him, and the Vahrian army marched forward –

"I just wanted to explore the discs." Leon wiped his eyes. "Didn't want to fight a War."

Elena gave him the smile young people used on doddery grandfathers. "I'm sure no one did."

"No. Some did. Glory seekers. Romantics. Patriots. People like you."

"I'm no glory seeker."

"You're worse." Dry blood caked his hands, but he couldn't muster the energy to clean them. "You're an idealist. You'd die for a cause you believe in."

"It's called bravery, Leon."

"It's called being a fool. Dead heroes and dead cowards both rot in the same grave."

The forest was still sharp and crisp around him. His hands shook. He'd never killed in the War. Maybe he had, but if so it had been his arrows that buried themselves in distant Vahrian chests. He hadn't grappled with the enemy … hadn't smelled their sweat … hadn't punched his sword through their ribcage and had their blood spurt onto him …

"Raft's ready," said Elena.

Leon gritted his teeth. He bundled up all his swirling feelings and stuffed them into the back of his mind.

"Took you long enough." He grabbed the cadets' swords and clipped them onto his belt. "Might as well take these."

Elena's head tilted to the side. "Good thinking."

They climbed onto the raft. Leon stared up at Pomeroy. The disc glided towards them, its silvery underside glowing in the force field's rippling purple light. Horns blew in the distance, getting closer with each blare. Leon fought the urge to release the raft. They had to wait until Pomeroy was above their disc, so that Pomeroy's shadow would hide their raft as they ascended. Another horn blared, scattering birds from nearby trees. Leon clenched his jaw.

Pomeroy slid across the sun's face, plunging their disc into darkness.

"Now," said Leon.

They threw off the rocks and their raft rose and floated through the canopy. The whole of the disc came into view. Leon and Elena rose through a cylinder of shadow cast by Pomeroy above them. Below, the forest was dark, lit by the dim, shimmering purple light of the force field. Further out on the disc, however, sun glowed on the treetops – Pomeroy was only four clicks in diameter, too small to overshadow all of the twenty-click-wide forest disc.

Vahrian airships circled outside the force field. Leon swallowed. If Pomeroy moved too fast, it would take the circle of shadow away and expose them to the airships.

Below, shadow crept across the canopy. Leon cursed. The shadow was moving too fast.

"We're near the force field," Elena said.

He looked up. The translucent field was right above them, casting purple light onto their raft.

"Breathers on," Leon said as they raced toward the field.

Leon slapped his breathfung onto his face and Elena copied him.

"Get ready to jump," he said, his voice muffled by the breathfung. "Floatpods pop when they hit the field."

"What? You didn't say –"

"Jump!"

The raft touched the force field. Floatpods exploded. They leapt through the field as seeds showered the air around them. Gravity vanished. Coldness pierced Leon's chest and his fingers numbed. They floated towards Pomeroy's underside. Elena grabbed his hand, unfurled her wings, and flapped, accelerating them. He swallowed. The disc was moving too fast.

Elena flapped harder, but the disc was too far away. Any moment, it would move aside and the sun would expose them to the Vahrian airships hovering nearby.

Elena's wings beat with silent fury. Cords of muscle strained on her neck. Leon couldn't see her mouth, and he couldn't hear her in the vacuum of space, but he knew she was screaming. He squeezed her hand and she squeezed back. She flapped harder, and faster, her muscles straining and her face turning red. They accelerated. Ahead, the disc loomed.

They were a click from Pomeroy's underside. They were going to make it!

He glanced at Elena, expecting her to slow, but she kept flapping. He cursed.

Stop, girl, or we'll splat into the disc!

He used his free hand to draw a line in the air, then made a chopping motion. Elena frowned, but kept flapping. He scowled. She hadn't trained at the Academy: she wouldn't recognise the sign to slow down.

The disc was half a click away.

He grabbed Elena's nearest wing. The other wing kept flapping, making them spin. He stabbed a finger at the approaching disc. Her eyes widened. He released her wing and she flapped backwards as hard as she could. Leon's mouth was dry.

Ain't going to be enough.

They'd crash into the disc's underside, less than a hundred feet from the edge.

Elena jerked him sideways. Sunlight flashed around them and Leon squinted. They shot past the disc's edge and Elena glided into the force field. Gravity yanked them down. They lost their upward momentum and fell towards the ground. Leon cursed, but Elena stretched her wings and their fall changed into a glide. They skimmed over the flat, desolate disc, and crashed into the loamy dirt.

Chapter 8

Leon peeled off his breathfung, chest heaving. Elena removed hers and puked.

Leon patted her shoulder. "That was some flying, lass."

"Heh." She wiped vomit from her mouth, panting. "Looking forward to being grounded for a while."

He grinned. She beamed. They laughed and tension flowed out of Leon's body and his breathing returned to normal.

We're safe.

He glanced around, still smiling. Pomeroy was flat and he could see from one edge of the disc to the other. Undisturbed soil spread out in all directions, interrupted by small clumps of fungus, tiny ponds, and patches of omnicrop. He stood and drank from a pond, then stumbled to the nearest stalks of omnicrop. The disc was abandoned, which explained why the stalks rose to his hip rather than towering over him – without regular cultivation, the almost-immortal crop hibernated and shrunk to conserve energy.

"You planning on milling that thing?" asked Elena.

"No need." He ripped a handful of omnicrop from the ground. "Roots are edible."

"Urgh. They look gross."

He sat next to her, handed her a root, and gnawed on the roots of his own stalk.

"Taste great," he said, somehow keeping a straight face.

Elena chewed a root.

She screwed up her face. "Liar."

He chuckled. "Best source of nutrients to grow your wings, you know. Back at the Academy, they fed us these four times a day."

"The Academy?"

"Her Majesty's Royal Naval Academy. It's where all angels got trained, back before angels were ..."

His voice faded and so did his smile.

Before angels were dead? Was I going to say that? Go on, don't stop. Spit it out!

Elena munched on her root, grimacing. "Did they force feed you these so if you got tortured, you were prepared for the worst?"

He laughed and the voice in his head vanished. "You know, they're good for you and they'll even cure poisons. Lots of paranoid highborns keep them around for that reason."

"Still gross."

He smiled. He remembered camping with Juliana when he was eighteen. She'd hated omnicrop roots, too. Leon had worried about telling her that he knew the roots were edible because they were one of the main things his mother fed him. But when he told her, she didn't laugh. She was no snob, not like the other angels at the Academy.

He turned away and stared out into space. The two discs composing the Hargold system were the size of his hand and shrunk with every second. Inky blackness surrounded the discs, broken by purple spots that signified the glowing force fields of faraway towns.

"You okay?" Elena asked.

"Just tired."

He lay down and wrapped himself in his cloak. Elena did the same. After a while, her breathing lightened. Leon screwed his eyes shut, but sleep eluded him, so he passed the restless hours by watching the stars.

~ ~ ~

Leon woke to find Elena kneeling in the dirt and muttering, her head bowed and her palms pressed against the ground. The Sarahk lay open in front of her.

He sighed. "Don't tell me you're praying."

She kept mumbling psalms.

"No one's listening," he said.

She closed her eyes and kept whispering. After a few minutes, she clasped her hands together and touched her interlocked fingers to her chest, right above her heart.

"You can join me," she said.

"Ain't wasting my time, thanks."

"Why don't you believe, Leon?"

"I used to. Back when I didn't know better."

"Why'd you stop?"

"The War," he said. "Prayers didn't make the Star Spectre and Her Archangels fix things. Lots of other people thought they would, though. Didn't help 'em survive."

Elena tilted her head to the side. "How did *you* survive?"

He scowled. "Luck."

"No," she said. "That's not it. The War wiped out almost every angel. The battles were ruthless."

"Let's not talk about this."

"The only angels that survived …" Elena's eyes widened. "Were ones that fled from battle."

He stood and stomped away, hands shaking.

She raced after him. "You're a deserter, aren't you?"

That's putting it kind. I'm scum. I'm a coward. All those people who called me a bastard, a half-breed flyer, a fake angel … they were right. They were more right than they could've imagined.

"Not a deserter," he said.

Elena kept pace with him as he strode. "It's okay. What you said before – you were right. I can't imagine what the War was like. It would've been horrible and I get why you –"

"I didn't desert."

"It's fine. Believe me, I'm glad you lived, or I wouldn't have help to find Waverrym."

He rolled his eyes. "Not this again."

"I've got the clue here, see: 'Find the heart of nobility, and find the soul of the realm. Find the lungs of Severym, and find–'"

"'The path to safety,'" said Leon. "Verses eighty-one to eighty-four from *The Prophet Jesphat.*"

Elena narrowed her eyes. "You said you don't believe the Sarahk."

"I don't."

"Oh. What do you think it all means, then?"

"Shit all."

He changed direction, but Elena stuck by his side.

"The Path leads to the Disc of Waverrym," she said. "He was the Archangel of Peace. In some Sarahk translations his name means place-of-refuge, which is a reference to how he became a disc after Karym murdered him, of course."

51

Back at the Academy, all those years ago, Professor Nane told Leon something along those lines. But Elena was stupid. There was no Path.

"Leon, we made such a good team yesterday –"

"I ain't helping you."

"But –"

"Once we get to Anshan, I'm gone. Do whatever the hell you want, but I ain't coming with you."

Elena was silent for a while. Leon could tell she was trying to find an argument to convince him.

Save your energy, girl. I ain't changing my mind.

"This is your chance to redeem yourself," she said.

He scowled. "For what?"

"Whatever you did in the War."

Leon's hands clenched into fists.

"I'm not saying you're a deserter," she said. "But you've been carrying something around since the War. Some kind of hurt. Finding Waverrym is your chance to let it go."

"Piss off."

"There'll be other angels in Waverrym. And an Archangel, too! The Sarahk says so: 'and as penance, Marym stayed behind on the Disc of Waverrym after the Great Departure. She watched over the angels that lived there peacefully, under a pledge to honour Waverrym forever.' That's from –"

"*Karym's Treachery*. I ain't an idiot. I know the story. Thing is, it's just that: a *story*."

"Gah! Why are you like this? We're the last angels in the realm. We're meant to find Waverrym. I know it!"

"Told you: I ain't helping. So shut up."

"Okay. What if I say this, then?" She cleared her throat. "'I am sworn to valour. My heart knows only virtue. My words uphold the peace. My blade defends the helpless. I care for the greater good, and I care naught for myself. My soul belongs to the realm, and, if need be, I pledge to lay down my life for the good of the realm. This I swear in the name of the Archangels.' Know what that's from?"

Leon thought of what Professor Nane had told him at the Academy, all those decades ago. *An angel cares for the greater good. An angel cares naught for himself.* She'd been a wonderful teacher, but the only reward for her bravery was a shallow grave.

"That's the Angel's Oath," Elena said. "An angel swears it every day, right?"

Only if they're a fool.

"How long since you said it?" asked Elena.

He scowled. *Not since my friends died.*

"Please." Her voice softened. "There's angels on Waverrym. They deserve to know what's happened in Paya."

"Waverrym ain't real!"

Leon's hands shook. What the hell was Elena thinking? She couldn't talk about the deaths of his friends – no, his *family*. She couldn't understand what it meant to lose everyone. She didn't know about the pain he lived with.

"Leon –"

He bellowed and swung a blow at Elena, who ducked.

His nostrils flared. "I was safe until you arrived. You've ruined everything and you ain't dragging me on a stupid quest for a place that doesn't exist!"

Her lip curled. "I don't know why you can't fly, but even if you could, you wouldn't be a true angel. You disgust me."

She stopped. Leon kept walking and he glowered.

What does she matter? We'll reach Anshan tomorrow and then

53

I'll never talk to her again.

Chapter 9

Leon stalked around Pomeroy, wishing the disc was bigger. No matter where he went, he could always see Elena in the distance, reading the Sarahk. He glowered. It was disturbing to see her put so much faith in that stupid book. Part of him wanted to rip it from her hands and toss it through the force field, but after all those years at the Academy, all those years of treating that book as the most sacred object he owned ... he couldn't do it.

Leon finished his hip flask by midday and almost exhausted his kemp supply by mid-afternoon. He stuffed the pipe into his deepest pocket and tried to distract himself by searching for a new clump of breathfung. His current clump looked brownish-green, which meant it was almost dead. The force field had grown dark and was dimming the sun by the time he found a fresh breathfung, hidden in a patch of omnicrop. He squished the new breathfung into his old one. The fungi wriggled in his hands as they merged.

His stomach rumbled. Leon gathered an armful of omnicrop roots. When he took a bite, Juliana's smiling face appeared, along with their campsite from all those years ago. Leon grimaced. He dropped the roots and stomped off to find a place to sleep.

~ ~ ~

Leon rolled over into a patch of mud and coldness seeped through his cloak. He opened his eyes, groaning. His knees ached, his back hurt, and dryness filled his mouth.

He struggled up into a sitting position and lit his pipe. The kemp-smoke calmed him a little. Then something flashed overhead and he cursed and dropped the pipe. He glared up at Elena, who soared through the air.

Leon retrieved his pipe and watched her fly. She lost too much speed in her turns and struggled to keep a consistent altitude, but aside from that, she flew well for someone without formal training.

She landed with a stagger and fell. Dusting dirt from her wings, she stood and gazed at the stars beyond the force field. Her eyes held the kind of longing only the young could possess. Leon's eyes had shone like that, once, but it hadn't taken long for life to crush the joy out of him.

He put away his pipe and strode over to her. "Nice flying."

"Thanks."

Leon stroked his beard. He didn't have to say anything else. He owed her nothing and in a few hours they'd land on Anshan and part ways. Besides, saying something might spark another argument.

But despite all this, he said, "You flap too much."

"Sorry?"

Leon sighed. *Why do I do this to myself?*

"When you're flying, you rely too much on strength," he said. "You're fighting the air."

"How else am I supposed to fly?"

"By gliding. Think of it like swimming."

56

She looked down. "I can't swim."

"Oh. Well, when you swim, it ain't about strength. It's about gliding through the water. Same story here. Your mindset, your technique, and then your strength – that's the order of importance. Here, I'll show you."

He made Elena lie face-down on a rock and flap her wings.

Leon shook his head. "Your action's wrong. It needs to be like this."

He held her wings with his calloused hands and guided her through the correct motion. "That's how it should be. You try."

She flapped. This time, her wings moved closer to the right path.

"That's it," he said. "How you flapped before burns too much energy. Now that you've got the right action, flying will be easier. Okay. Onto gliding."

"Can't you show me how to do it with your wings?"

Leon stiffened. "Told you. I can't fly."

"But you can show me without flying. Lie on the rock like I did."

"No."

Elena opened her mouth, but it seemed she also didn't want to start an argument because she kept quiet.

"Now, onto gliding," said Leon. "Those feathers on your wing-tips – yes, those – ain't for decoration. Use 'em to control speed, steer, and keep stable."

"How?"

"Start by not twitching 'em around all the time. That'll ruin your stability. "

"I did that?"

"Sure did."

57

"Oh." She looked at the dirt. "How do I fix it?"

He frowned, trying to remember his lessons at the Academy. "Keep your wing-tips straight. Over time, you'll subconsciously use 'em to change direction. Oh, yeah. That's the other thing: move this wing-tip." He tapped her feathers. "Just this one."

She tried, but also moved a half-dozen other feathers.

"Work on that," Leon said. "Once you can move each wing-tip individually, gliding will be easier. Now, let's get you up in the sky."

Elena stood, brushing dirt off her chest. She ran, her wings pumping in sync with her arms, and after a few seconds of sprinting, she took to the skies.

"Wrong!" said Leon. "Back down here."

She landed and walked to him, shoulders hunched. "What'd I do?"

"You can't have a fifty-foot run-up for your take-off. You need to fly from a standing start, or at most a twenty-foot run-up. Now, it'll be a while until your wings develop enough for this, but what you want to do is crouch."

He bent his legs, angling his torso forward, so that his centre of gravity was at the edge of his balancing zone.

"Then lean forward," he said. "When you start to fall, jump and flap as hard as you can. The key thing to remember is that you need as much forward momentum as possible. That's why you lean forward. Go on. Give it a shot."

Elena crouched and readied her wings. He adjusted her position, then nodded. She leapt, and beat her wings, sending dirt flying into Leon –

And she fell on her face.

He helped her up, chuckling. "Don't worry. Took me

months to learn. Maybe let's just focus on gliding. Get up into the air and keep those wing-tips stable."

Elena did her usual running take-off to get airborne. She flapped to pick up altitude. He nodded. Her action was smoother. Stronger.

"Don't move your wing-tips!" he said.

She nodded and stretched her wings, moving into a glide. Leon smiled. Her wing feathers were stable, not wobbling around like before. If anything, now they were too straight, but it was an improvement.

"Hold the glide," he said.

She gave him a thumbs up. Her glide carried her across the disc, towards the force field. Two hundred feet from the field, she curved to the left. Leon pursed his lips. She was still losing a lot of speed through the turn. He'd have to work on that.

Elena glided back towards him, lower than she'd been before. She landed three hundred feet away, throwing a cloud of dirt into the air.

Turns too sharp. That's what's making her lose altitude.

Leon and Elena reached each other.

"How'd I do?" she asked. "It definitely felt easier."

"Your action's better, but you lose height too rapidly."

She sighed. "Always happens when I glide. That's why I flap lots – to get higher."

"You don't have to flap to gain height. C'mon, let me show you something."

They walked across the disc. As they walked, he pointed to a patch of shimmering air.

"See that?" he asked.

She nodded.

"It's a riser: a column of hot air that comes from vents in the ground. Glide in a circle over that and it'll take you as high as you want."

They reached the shimmering air and Leon gestured at a jagged, fist-sized hole in the dirt.

"That's where the hot air comes from," he said.

He grabbed her hand and put it over the hole. Warm air blew up into them, as if someone was breathing on their hands.

"Where's the hole go?" she asked.

"Down to the bedsteel."

"What's that?"

"It's a layer of metal. Flat, impenetrable – it's the deepest we can dig. It's made from the same material as the disc's underside and it's usually a few hundred feet thick."

"So no one knows what's inside the bedsteel?"

"Probably solid all the way through. Now, you want a geology lesson, or do you want to fly?"

"Fly."

"Get in the air and glide in a circle over the riser."

Elena took to the skies. She circled in the column of hot air but gained no altitude.

"You're circling too tight," he said. "Try a wider path."

She adjusted her angle. The shimmering air carried her up, towards the force field. Leon's heart skipped a beat. She wasn't wearing her breather. If she went through the force field into space, she'd die.

"Come down!" he said.

She laughed, still circling higher. She said something, but she was too high for Leon to hear.

"Elena! The force field!"

Her wings faltered and she dropped. Leon cursed. He'd wanted her to avoid the field, but a fall from that height would kill her too.

"Don't panic," he said. "Extend your wings!"

She kept plummeting. She was six hundred feet above the ground. Four hundred feet. Two hundred feet. Leon's mouth went dry. There was nothing he could do.

Her wings stretched and her fall changed to a steep glide. She levelled out to land in a skid. Leon jogged over to her, pain spiking through his hips, muscles still aching from their frantic escape from Hargold.

He reached her. "You alright?"

She hunched over and panted. "Y-yeah."

"Always watch the force field, okay?"

"Yeah." She blushed. "I know."

Idiot! I almost killed her. I ain't no teacher.

Leon lit his pipe. Kemp smoke filled his lungs and his hands stopped shaking. Elena frowned at the pipe.

"That's enough flying for now," he said.

"But I've got so much to learn! Please, my flying's improved more today than in all the years I've taught myself. We can't stop."

Leon scowled. Starlight sparkled in Elena's wide eyes and she wrung her hands, shuffling on the spot.

"Fine," he said. "Get back up in the sky, but stay away from the force field and don't blame me if you get yourself killed."

Chapter 10

It was late afternoon, and the force field had begun to grow dark. The darkening field dimmed the sun, signalling that night would soon arrive. Leon called Elena down from the sky.

"We're near Anshan," he said.

They gathered omnicrop and sat near the force field, staring at the stars. Leon worried that eating raw roots would make him see Juliana again, so he made a fire and cooked the omnicrop. Although *cooking* was too positive a term, considering that it made little improvement to the stringy roots.

"How can you tell we're near Anshan?" Elena asked.

Leon pointed at a bright purple dot, nestled amongst the stars. "It's right there."

Elena squinted at the dot. "How do you know?"

"Look around. The stars, constellations, marks on Neebia … they all align uniquely, depending where you are. There's no place where the stars look the same, so it's just a matter of learning how everything fits together. If you learn that, then you'll always know where you are."

Elena shook her head. "Sounds complicated."

"Oh, it was a nightmare to learn. I was lucky, though. Had

a great astronomy teacher at the Academy. Professor Nane. She was brilliant. Could've taught anything."

"You're a good teacher, too."

Leon blinked. "Uh ... thanks?"

"No, I mean it. Really. I learned so much today."

Warmth spread through Leon and he smiled.

"What?" asked Elena.

"Nothing."

"No, come on. Tell me."

"Well ... it's funny, because I always wanted to teach. Had this idea that after I'd explored the discs, rubbed shoulders with royals, and done my twelve years' service, I'd teach astronomy at the Academy. Help young angels learn celestial navigation, show 'em how the discs orbit ... course, then there was the War."

She put her hand on his back. "Well, no matter where I go after today, you'll always be a teacher to me."

A lump formed in his throat. He'd forgotten he'd soon be leaving Elena. No, not leaving her.

Abandoning her.

What do I care? I've only known her for three days.

"Get ready," he said. "We're nearing Anshan."

The distant purple dot grew larger, then broke into pieces. Anshan's seven discs and the bridges between them came into view. Leon smiled. He'd forgotten how big it was. Scopus Disc – the smallest – was twice the size of Hargold. And Scopus was a speck beside Olivet Disc: a mass of yellow patchwork-quilt farmland with Lake Malilee in the middle. Then there was Ophel – disc of the Silver Towers; Old Kion – home of the All-Temple; New Kion – host of the Great Market; Murruption – domain of the Whistling Mountain;

and in the middle, dominating the six discs that circled it, was Antonia, covered by a black, impenetrable force field.

"It's huge," said Elena. "How many people live there?"

"Over a hundred thousand."

"Wow ..."

She gazed at Anshan. Her wide eyes seemed to glow, though whether that was from some youthful yearning or the reflecting starlight, he couldn't be sure.

I was like her, once. Standing on a hill, gazing at the stars, longing for adventure. All bright-eyed and innocent. And damn foolish.

"You stargazing all day?" he said. "Or you going to help me get rocks?"

"Why do we need rocks?"

"To get to New Kion Disc. We'll pass two and a half clicks under it, at a relative speed of twenty-one feet per second. We'll need to get outside our force field and jump to New Kion. Rocks will help correct course – we can throw 'em to push ourselves in the other direction. Just make sure to throw from your centre of mass to reduce spinning."

Elena frowned. "Can't I fly? Oh, no, I see."

"Damn right. Anshan's a Vahrian stronghold. Anyone sees your wings and we're both dead."

Leon tried to sound gruff but couldn't stop his voice from breaking. He gulped. Elena tucked her wings under her cloak. She and Leon gathered rocks. Once they'd got enough, they waddled to the force field's edge, pockets bulging.

Leon slapped his breathfung onto his face. "Breathers on,"

Elena rolled her eyes. "As if I'd go into space without it."

"You almost did before."

"Hey!"

They crawled out of the force field. Large clumps of soil couldn't pass through the field, so they kept their hands inside, holding onto the ground, while the rest of their bodies dangled in space. Leon frowned as they approached Anshan. They had to leap before they came under New Kion, because their momentum would carry them forwards.

Elena glanced at him. Leon shook his head. They had to wait for the right moment.

Now!

He signalled to Elena. They leapt, pushing off the disc. Their hands left the force field and they soared through space. Pomeroy glided away. Leon tried to relax. Nothing to do but wait, because it'd take twenty minutes to reach New Kion.

Judging their velocity was hard, but after a few minutes Leon thought they were rising too fast. He hurled a rock in the direction of his motion, and the force pushed him back, reducing his speed. Elena copied him.

New Kion grew larger. The blobs of colour atop the disc resolved into a mess of jumbled buildings. They were three clicks away from New Kion … Leon threw another rock to adjust his angle … two clicks away … he could see the latticework of jetties protruding from the disc … one click away … he threw two rocks to slow down … five hundred feet … the rocks bounced off the force field with a spark of light … three hundred feet …

Leon smiled. He'd land on the disc's side, beside a ladder attached to a jetty. He glanced at Elena and frowned. Her speed matched his, but she'd land twenty feet left of him: too far from any convenient handholds.

Leon slammed feet-first into the disc's side. He bent his knees, cushioning his landing, and rebounded, grabbing the

65

ladder before he floated away.

Elena bounced off the disc. Rocks tumbled out of her cloak, scattering everywhere. She stretched, trying to grab the disc, but she'd landed too hard.

Eyes wide with terror, Elena drifted away into the void of space.

Chapter 11

Leon cursed. He pulled himself up the ladder and onto the jetty. Off to his left, Elena drifted further away, towards the abyss of space. All her rocks had fallen out. She couldn't correct her course without using her wings.

Leon looked around. A Vahrian airship moored at the jetty. Two Vahrians stood outside it, holding the handrail and gaping at Leon. One held a coil of rope.

Leon used the handrail to float to the Vahrians. He grabbed the one with the rope and dragged him to the jetty's end. The Vahrian struggled out of Leon's grip, but then Leon pointed at Elena, flailing as she floated further away.

The Vahrian nodded. He uncoiled the rope and hurled it towards Elena. She grabbed it. The rope tautened, yanking the Vahrian forwards. Leon seized him around the waist and grabbed the rail with his other hand. The rope slackened. Elena drifted to the jetty and grabbed the railing with trembling hands.

Leon and Elena bowed to the Vahrian. The man stuck out his hand and Leon shook it.

Guess not all Vahrians are total assholes.

Leon and Elena floated along the jetty, gripping the handrail. They reached the end, rotated so they stood upright, and stepped through the force field into New Kion's harbour.

Gravity embraced them and noise smacked into Leon. Sailors heaved a wooden crate past him, cursing when they dropped it. A woman shooed a ragged cat away from a cage of clucking chickens. Six Payans in colourful silk gowns pranced through the harbour, while their bodyguard shoved away a dirty-fingered beggar. Dogs barked. A bell rung. In the distance, someone strummed a lute.

Leon and Elena walked around a pegasus' flapping wings, ducked under a swooping pigeon, and dodged a shifty-eyed woman trying to sell bracelets. They reached the harbour's edge and ripped off their breathers.

"That was horrible," said Elena. "I'm never traveling through space without using my wings again."

"Shh!" Leon glanced around. "Someone might hear."

"What, through this?"

The cat pounced onto the cage of chickens, knocking it over. Chickens scattered, clucking, their feathers dropping everywhere as the cat chased after them. The woman swiped at the cat with a broom. Elena arched her eyebrows.

Leon sighed. "Even so, there's spies everywhere."

"Okay. I won't say it again."

Leon swung his hands by his side. So this was it. He and Elena would part and he'd never see her again. He could get on with his life – maybe work at the harbour – and she'd leave to chase her pointless quest. No more helping a fugitive. No more visits from the Inquisition. Leon's life would return to being safe and peaceful.

He frowned. Why did he feel so hollow at the thought of the impending farewell?

"Want to grab lunch at the markets?" Elena asked.

"I ain't that hungry, but sure."

They ambled through winding streets, dodging pegasi-drawn carts and staring at the cobblestones when they passed soldiers. The lute's distant strumming grew louder.

What the hell am I doing? The longer I spend with her, the harder it'll be to say goodbye. I ain't got business walking with a fugitive. What if she's recognised? Cut your losses. Leave before she gets you killed.

They emerged into a large square filled with market stalls. The scent of spices, baked bread, and spit-roasted meat hung in the air, making Leon salivate. Payans and Vahrians bustled past stalls, while hawkers screamed themselves hoarse, trying to compete with the lutist's strumming. An immense stone castle with something hanging from the walls loomed over the markets.

"So," said Elena as they ambled. "Thought about helping me find Waverrym?"

He stared at the lute player. "Ain't changed my mind."

"Okay. Just thought I'd ask, that's all. I know that if you were helping, I'd have a much better chance of finding it."

Leon sighed. He didn't want an argument to spoil his last moments with Elena, so he stayed silent. They bought spit-roasted vegetable skewers and ambled through the markets in comfortable silence, looking for somewhere to sit.

"There's benches there," she said, pointing to a small park at the base of the castle's walls.

Leon walked towards the benches, but Elena grabbed his arm.

"Marym's tongue!" she said. "The wall."

Leon peered up. When they'd entered the square, he'd glimpsed something dangling from the castle's walls. Now that he was closer, he saw what it was.

An angel's skeleton.

Elena gasped. Leon coughed and his mouthful of vegetables splattered onto the cobblestones. His legs carried him forward to the wall with the skeleton dangling above him. Rope bound the bones together. The skull grinned at Leon and his guts twisted.

Elena stumbled to his side. "There's a plaque."

It took a few seconds for her words to penetrate the ringing in Leon's ears. He looked at the plaque, which read:

Above you hangs Beatris Clymene: the terrorist responsible for the Makrov Bombings which claimed nineteen innocent lives. May this skeleton hang forever as a reminder of her atrocities.

"She founded the Resistance," Elena said. "And that bombing killed Vahrian war criminals, not *innocents*."

"I knew her." Leon's hands trembled. "She taught History, at the Academy. Never taught me, but I knew who she was."

He clenched his hands into fists. How dare the Vahrians display Clymene like a trophy? She deserved a proper Payan funeral.

"Scum," Leon said. "Vahrians ... they're all scum!"

"Shh!" Elena glanced around. "There's soldiers over there."

"Let 'em hear me!"

Market-goers drew back from him. Two Vahrian soldiers eating chestnuts glanced at Leon. Elena tried to pull Leon away.

He stood firm. "They'll pay for this."

The two soldiers frowned and their hands strayed towards their swords.

"Leon," Elena kept tugging him. "The soldiers! If they –"

"Let 'em come," growled Leon.

The soldiers rose, finishing their roasted chestnuts, and sauntered towards Leon and Elena, pushing through the crowd. Elena cursed. She muttered something, but the ringing in Leon's ears muffled her voice. He stared at Clymene's skeleton. Elena grabbed him around the waist and tried to drag him away, but he pushed her aside. He barged past an elderly Payan and grabbed a tomato from a nearby stall.

"Hey!" said the shopkeeper. "You've got to –"

Leon hurled the tomato at the soldiers. It splattered onto the redhead soldier's armour.

"– pay for that …" the shopkeeper said, his voice trailing away.

Elena gaped. Leon glared at the redhead soldier, who watched tomato juice trickle down his armour. Everyone went silent and backed away. The lute's twang faded. The soldier looked up and he glared at Leon.

Both soldiers drew their swords with a rasp of metal.

Chapter 12

The tall soldier raised his blade. "You're under arrest, Payan."

Leon gulped. The anger drained out of him and fear filled the void. What the hell had he been thinking? He stepped back and bumped into the tomato crates. He cursed. The soldiers had trapped them against the box of vegetables. Elena's hand strayed towards her dagger. Sweat ran down Leon's spine.

The soldier raised his sword. "Now, Payan –"

Leon turned and scrambled over the tomato crate. "Run, Elena!"

She leapt over the box. The soldiers cursed and chased them as Leon and Elena burst out of the stall and sprinted through the markets. Leon pushed through the crowd and charged through stalls, scattering fruit. Beside him, Elena dodged startled market-goers and vaulted over boxes. The soldiers followed, yelling at them to stop.

"I can take them!" said Elena.

Leon tore through a hanging carpet. "Don't be stupid."

They kept running.

Hindered by their armour, the soldiers' cries grew fainter. Leon glanced back. The soldiers were gone. Together, Leon and Elena pulled out of the square, walking into a twisting laneway.

Elena punched the air and clapped Leon on the back. He grinned. His heartbeat thumped in his ears and energy coursed through him.

"That was awesome!" she said. "Did you see the look on his face? Ha!"

His grin broadened. Watching the tomato splat onto the soldier's polished armour had sent joy rushing through him. It felt great. No. Better than great. He'd experienced something he hadn't felt in years.

Power.

But when the soldier drew his sword, all that righteous anger vanished. Leon's smile faded. He pictured Clymene's skeleton hanging on the castle walls, her skull locked in an eternal grimace. Inquisitor Drayton's leering face flashed before him. Leon remembered the cadets beating Alvaro and a dozen more memories ran through his mind: cowering as Vahrian soldiers pushed past him; running from Mangold Pass; raising his knife with a trembling hand …

Leon sighed. Vahrians always won and always would.

"Well," said Elena. "I'm heading to Ophel Disc. It's got the largest library in Paya, so I'm sure it'll help me solve that riddle in the Sarahk. Want to come?"

Say no. This is my chance to get away from her.

"What riddle?" he asked.

"'Find the heart of nobility, and find the soul of the realm. Find the lungs of Severym, and find the path to safety.'"

She said it all without hesitation.

"Got it memorised?" he asked.

Elena nodded.

"You want to find Waverrym real badly, don't you?" asked Leon.

"Of course!"

He stroked his bushy beard. "That inquisitor doesn't want you to find it, does he?"

"Drayton? He's a godless Vahrian. Bet he can't name a single Archangel, but it doesn't matter if he knows about Waverrym. He'll hunt me anyway."

"Yeah." Leon frowned, turning the riddle over in his mind. "Yeah, he will."

Elena studied her fingernails. "Er ... I've got to go. Guess this is goodbye."

A pregnant pause stretched between them. Elena shuffled on the spot. Leon thought of all his years of hiding and all his years of living in fear. He thought of the battle he'd fled. He thought of all the times he'd trekked into Hargold's wilderness to climb a hill and feel the wind blow over him – the wind he could never soar upon again.

"Actually," said Leon. "I ..."

Elena looked at him with hopeful eyes. He swallowed.

Don't say it. Don't do it!

"I want to help you find Waverrym," he said.

"You do?"

Say no. You can still back out.

"Yeah," he said.

"But you said it's not real!"

"Well, we'll find out, won't we?"

"But ..."

"Want my help, or not?"

"Of course. You're a trained angel, there's so much you can teach me, but why change your mind? Why help me?"

Leon thought of Blas. He touched the half-circle pendant under his cloak, which pressed against his skin, and he remembered Juliana. Remembered her grin. Remembered the rhythmic scraping of her whittling knife.

Remembered her lips.

"Why help me find Waverrym?" Elena asked.

The taste of Juliana's lips faded, and Leon scowled. "Karym's horns. Keep asking stupid questions and I'll change my mind."

"Sorry. I just can't believe you're helping – we'll definitely find Waverrym now."

She leapt forward and hugged him.

"Oi!" he said. "Get off."

She stepped back, looking sheepish. "Sorry. I'm just so happy."

"Yeah, I get the idea. C'mon. Let's go."

He strode away. When she couldn't see his face, he smiled.

Chapter 13

"Ophel Disc's over there," said Elena as they walked through crowded streets. "We're going the wrong way."

"We ain't going to Ophel."

"But the Royal Library –"

"We don't need it."

Her eyes widened. "You've already solved it?"

"Maybe."

"But it's only been ten minutes since I told you."

"No. You told me yesterday, on Pomeroy. Haven't thought about it since, but in the last few minutes, some things made more sense."

"Come on, don't be a tease." She dodged a pegasus-drawn carriage. "What's the answer?"

Leon glanced around the bustling street. "Not here. Let's find someplace quiet."

They found an inn beside a square with a shrine in the middle. The shrine featured Mahroque-style statues of the Nine Archangels, with their hearts carved outside their chests. The statues stood around a plinth, which was missing its crystal obelisk.

Leon ducked under the low doorway as they entered the

inn. Two Payans sat around a table, talking. Another three sat at the bar, nursing drinks in silence. No Vahrians.

Leon bought his normal ale. Elena got a Molonean beer, which he'd only ever seen Vahrians drink, but it was cheap and he couldn't argue with that. They sat in the corner, away from the other patrons. Leon sipped his ale. Warmth spread through him and he leaned back against the fungcrete wall. It'd been too long since his last drink.

"So what's the answer to the riddle?" Elena asked.

"Got the text?"

Elena pulled out the Sarahk, flipped to the right page, and put it on the table:

Find the heart of nobility, and
*   find the soul of the realm.*
*   Find the lungs of Severym, and*
*   find the path to safety.*

"Let's start here," Leon pointed to the third line. "'Find the lungs of Severym.' She's one of the Nine Major Archangels – there's a statue of her in that square outside. What's she represent?"

Elena frowned. "Something to do with flying? Ascent, take-off … is that it? Wait, she represents risers too, right?"

"She does more than that. Remember, risers are patches of hot air that come from the ground. Scripture describes this air as the breath of Severym. Now, if risers are Severym's breath, what are her lungs?"

"Uh … no idea."

"Remember, risers come from the ground."

Elena's eyes widened. "Oh! The holes in the ground –

where risers come from – are those her lungs?"

"You've got it, lass."

"So we're looking for a hole that a riser comes from? That could be anywhere."

"Let me finish. There's more clues in the riddle." Leon pointed at the second line. "'Find the soul of the realm.' What realm?"

"Paya?"

"Yes. Now, where's Paya's soul?"

Elena chewed her lip. "Don't know."

"The Sarahk is translated from Old Payese, right?"

"Yes."

"The translation of soul is unclear. It could mean: self, identity, or heart."

"Hold up. How do you know so much about this?"

"About the Sarahk?"

"Yes."

"Karym's horns! You go through nine years at the Academy and it's impossible to not know everything about that damn book. We read it more than we practiced swordplay."

"But you said it was rubbish."

"It is. No way the Archangels did half the stuff it claims."

Elena frowned. Truth be told, Leon doubted Waverrym existed, but he still longed to seek it. He wanted the truth and to find it he had to follow the riddle. If there was nothing at the end, no harm done.

But if there was a secret path hidden in the Sarahk that led to Waverrym, he'd find a place where angels still lived …

Leon squashed the foolish thought and said, "Anyway, let's say instead of 'find the soul of the realm,' we say: 'find the heart of the realm.' Where's Paya's heart?"

"The capital city?"

"Which is?"

"Anshan." Her eyes widened. "Here!"

"Right."

"So we're just need to find a riser somewhere in Anshan and we'll find Waverrym? Thank the Archangels – I never thought it would be this easy!"

Leon grimaced. "It ain't. There's another part to the riddle. The first line: 'Find the heart of nobility.' That means Antonia Disc. It's home to the Queen's Palace and the main highborn families."

"The disc in the middle of Anshan?"

Leon nodded. "It's also got the biggest riser I know about, with a hole a three hundred feet across."

"Well, okay then. Let's go find it!"

"Not that easy. A fortress field covers Antonia. Anyone inside can get out, but it's impossible to enter from the outside. The only way in is through a small section where the field's permeable like normal."

"So we go through that gate."

"You don't understand. Antonia Disc has the Queen's Palace, and the Vahrian Council, who control the Queen. It's the most protected disc in Paya. They ain't letting two fugitives inside."

"So? You giving up?"

Yes. Give up. I'll get killed trying to break into that place.

"No." Leon drained his ale. "Just telling you what we're facing. Got to be realistic, is all. Now, let's work out how we're breaking in."

Chapter 14

"I count twenty-eight guards," said Elena.

"No," said Leon. "Thirty-two."

They lay hidden in tall stalks of omnicrop on the edge of Olivet Disc. The searing sun baked their necks and Leon remembered learning how Olivet's force field amplified the sun's rays to enhance crop growth. Antonia Disc floated nine hundred feet away. A black force field shrouded it in darkness, and the field sparked as it deflected debris. Rickety wooden bridges joined the surrounding six discs to a walkway that circled Antonia's circumference. The walkway widened to form a platform near Antonia's gate, where soldiers protected a transparent section of the force field.

"I only see twenty-eight," said Elena. "Where's the other four guards?"

Leon gave her the telescope. "See those four trapdoors in the platform? They lead to watch towers hanging on the bottom, which lets soldiers see people sneaking up underneath."

She peered through the telescope. Leon stood and stretched, wincing as pain jolted through his back. His body wasn't made for lying in dirt. He stood on a rock and peeked above the high omnicrop stalks surrounding them.

The crop stretched to the horizon: an ocean of brown and yellow that rippled in the breeze.

He lay back next to Elena. "See 'em?"

"Yep. How many in each?"

"Last time I was here, they had one soldier per watch tower."

"When were you last here?"

"Twenty-one years ago, a few months before the War. I'd earned my Iron Wings and they bought my class here for the Queen to give us our badges."

"Was it good?"

Leon remembered meeting his father for the first time. When he'd seen the man's name on their welcome feast guest list, he hadn't believed his eyes. Not until he'd entered the ballroom, where Leon's father stood with a crowd of laughing highborns dressed in jackets that gleamed in the chandelier's light. His enormous wings cast shadows over his companions. Shaking with nervousness, Leon checked with a servant to make sure it was the right man. Then he left Blas and Juliana and shuffled over to his father. His mother told so many stories about the angel she'd loved and Leon had spun tales about his father's bravery to his disbelieving classmates. By the time Leon reached the group, sweat coated his palms.

He sidestepped around the highborns for a few bars of music. Then he edged inside and they stared. He bowed to the man with the enormous wings, and croaked, "Father."

Leon's father frowned. "Sorry?"

Leon wanted to tell the man he was his son, but the saliva in his throat stopped his speech. As he tried to choke it down, he noticed two young men beside the man, both with wings of their own. They had Leon's hazel eyes, and his nose, and even the same half-stubble that was fashionable in highborn circles. But their jaws were sharper. Stronger. And they were taller than him, with hair slicked into neat comb-overs, and tilted smiles that made them look roguish, charming, and clever all at the same time.

A slim woman rested her manicured hand on the shoulder of Leon's father. "What did you say, young angel?"

Leon swallowed. "I ..."

Salvador and his smirking cronies lurked behind the two young men. Heat flushed Leon's face. Of course the pricks were watching him embarrass himself. As if they needed more things to bully him about.

The highborns fidgeted and one woman left the group. Leon clenched his hands into fists. If he didn't do this now, he might never get another chance.

He looked at his father. "I'm your son, sir."

"I see."

Leon's heart skipped a beat. Everyone gaped at his father. Was he claiming him in front of all these highborns?

"Is your name Gaspar?" his father asked.

"Uh, no, sir –"

"Llorence?"

"Leon, sir."

"Well, then." He clamped a hand on the shoulders of the two men who looked like Leon. "You're not one of my sons."

The highborns laughed, the two men slapped Leon's father on his back, and the group closed ranks, shutting Leon out.

Salvador bumped into him. "I knew you were lying. As if you had a *highborn* father ..."

Leon rushed to the bathroom. Blas and Juliana raced after him, but he slammed the door before they entered. He hunched over and sobbed. Blas and Juliana stood outside, stopping anyone from entering. They kept asking if Leon wanted to talk, but he yelled at them to go away. He'd stayed inside until Blas, claiming boredom, threatened to use Leon's jonshular set to play with the notoriously greasy-fingered Mateo Castellon.

"Hey." Elena tapped Leon's shoulder, bringing him back to the present. "You with me?"

"Mmm."

"So was it a good week?"

"Uh-huh."

A pegasus-drawn carriage landed on the platform. The driver helped four silk-gowned Payans float out of the carriage. A Vahrian soldier glided to the Payans, who handed him a roll of parchment. After reading the letter, the Vahrian shook the Payans' hands and allowed them to glide through the transparent part of the force field, flanked by two soldiers.

Elena put down the telescope. "If we got silk clothes and stole a carriage, could we bluff our way through?"

"No chance. Look at the emblem on the carriage."

She squinted through the telescope. "It's a coat of arms ... a bat and a shield?"

"House Faustel. The first highborn family to declare support for the Vahrians, before the War ended."

She spat into the dirt. "Traitors."

Leon winced.

They sold out. I ran. I'm as guilty as them.

"So you're saying we can't bluff our way in because we're not highborns?" Elena asked.

"Yeah."

"We could fake it, though. You'd know enough about highborns, being an angel and that."

Leon stared at Antonia.

"All angels come from highborn families, right?" she said. "My parents did. I mean, they died in the War when I was young, and my uncle never spoke about them, so I don't know for sure ..."

"Most are highborn. Not all."

"Either way, you know how highborns behave."

"Been decades since I was in a palace. Hand me that telescope."

She gave it to him. "What highborn family did you come from, by the way? Have I heard of them?"

"We talking about royals, or we working out how to get into Antonia Disc?"

"You hate personal questions, don't you?"

"No. Just want to focus."

"So tell me who your family was and I'll stop bothering you."

A Vahrian airship landed on the platform and more highborns floated out.

"What's it to you?" asked Leon.

"I like to know where people come from."

"Why don't you use that annoying curiosity to figure out how we're getting into Antonia, eh?"

"I will. Right after you tell me what highborn family you came from."

"Will you shut up if I answer?"

She nodded.

"House Comodus," said Leon. "Father was a Navy Admiral."

"But your last name's de Velasco? Oh, I get it. You changed your name after the War, to disguise yourself?"

Say yes. Save yourself the pain.

"Sort of," he said. "de Velasco was my Mother's surname."

"De Velasco … Where's that royal family from?"

"Nowhere. She was a baker."

"Wait. A commoner and a royal … but how did they marry?"

"They didn't."

"Oh."

Leon scowled.

The hell's wrong with me? That story ain't got anything to do with breaking into Antonia.

He rubbed the half-circle pendant under his cloak. On Antonia, airships and carriages arrived and departed. Well-dressed highborns bustled through the force field. Porters carried food, fabrics, and ornaments from Anshan's other discs along the bridges to the platform, where soldiers inspected them before letting the porters float through Antonia's force field.

Leon and Elena tried to form plans to infiltrate Antonia. She suggested disguising themselves as servants. Leon shook his head. Each porter carried a signed letter to prove their identity. Elena considered stowing away on board a Vahrian airship. Leon stopped her before she finished speaking. No airships entered the force field, so they'd still have to fool the soldiers outside the gate.

Scowling, Elena suggested hiding inside an ornamental vase, and making porters carry them inside. Leon didn't bother to respond.

"Would it kill you to come up with ideas?" she asked.

"If I have an idea that doesn't get us killed, you'll be the first to know."

"Least I'm trying."

He sighed. She was earnest, at least, and determined, like

he'd once been. She deserved credit for that.

"Look, it's getting dark," he said. "Let's find some place to sleep. We ain't cracking this egg today."

~ ~ ~

Leon woke from a nightmare, gasping. He ripped off the blankets and shoved his trembling hands under his sweaty shirt. No blood. The sword, the snarling Vahrian, the wound in his stomach ... it had been a dream. That's all.

In the other bed, Elena stirred. "Whatsamatter?"

"Nothing." He wiped sweat off his brow. "Go back to sleep."

They'd rented a two-bed room in the inn beside the square with the Archangel statues. For three days they'd surveyed Antonia, but the disc still looked as impenetrable as stone.

She sat up. "I'm awake now. We might as well go out, do more scouting."

"Can't it wait? The disc ain't going anywhere."

Elena buckled her dagger onto her belt and pulled on her boots. "We've never seen Antonia at this time."

"For good reason. It's past midnight."

"Which means we might see something we missed during the day, and there's bound to be less sentries."

Leon forced a yawn. "I'm too tired."

"Think about how fatigued the soldiers will be, then."

"Won't help us get past them."

"How do you know? We've never looked at night." She stood. "Come on, it can't hurt."

"Yes it will. I've had four hours' sleep."

"Oh, don't be such an old man."

"Ain't an old man. I'm forty-three."

86

"You're sure acting like one."

"If you think I'm so old, then give me some respect and let me sleep."

"You're not getting out of it that easy. You can sleep in the morning. Let's go."

He tugged the bedsheets up around him. "Not coming."

"Don't be lazy."

"You go. I'll stay. If you see something new, let me know and I'll come tomorrow night."

Elena sighed. "Why are you like this?"

"What, sensible?"

"No. Half-hearted."

Leon kept silent.

"Don't you want to find Waverrym?" she asked.

"Course."

"Argh! Find Waverrym, don't find Waverrym: you don't care. We've spent three days looking at Antonia and how many ideas have you suggested? None. I've done all the thinking and all you talk about is how none of my ideas will work!"

Leon raised an eyebrow. "Finished?"

"Finding Waverrym isn't about us, you know. It's much bigger than that. I don't know why you agreed to help me, but I know why I seek Waverrym. I want to show the Vahrians they haven't won. I want to show we can fight back. I want to show Payans that angels aren't dead and there's still hope in the world."

"Good for you."

Her face reddened, her hands shook, and Leon thought she would try to hit him. Instead she stomped to the door, the floorboards shaking beneath her.

She yanked open the door. "I'm going to look at Antonia. Stay on your fat ass and enjoy your sleep, and if you're lucky I won't come back."

She stormed out of the room.

~ ~ ~

"She don't care 'bout you," Leon slurred to himself, clutching his half-empty beer. "She's jus' usin' you to find – *hick* – Waverrym."

He drained the beer, slopping most of it down his bushy beard.

"Another, barkeep," he said, raising his voice above the chatter of the crowded inn.

Too many bloody people here. The Lowfern's never this damn busy.

He'd spent last night scowling at his bedroom's rafters. Sleep hadn't come for him until after the sun broke through the threadbare curtains. He'd woken after noon to find an empty bed beside him. After stumbling out of bed, he'd moped around in the inn, which filled with Payans as the day progressed.

"Should leave," Leon said as the barkeep handed him his fifth beer. "Run b'fore she comes back."

But I'm too weak to leave, ain't I? Too weak to help her, too weak to run. Coward.

"Shut up," he said. "Not you, barkeep."

Finish this drink, then go to another inn. Tomorrow, get a job at the port. Anshan's big enough. Elena won't find me. After a few weeks, I can pay for a flight to another disk and then I'll be free of her.

He gulped the beer. He hated when the voice in his head was smarter than him. If only Alvaro was here for a game of jonshular. He sighed.

Leon paid the barkeep, then stood.

A hand clapped on his shoulder. "Evening! What's your name?"

He glanced up at two smiling, middle-aged Payans. The man had a gold tooth and the woman looked homely, with flour on her hands. A lump formed in Leon's throat. Mother had been a baker, and her hands were always dusted in flour, too.

"Sorry." He wobbled on unsteady feet. "Got to go."

"Please," said the man. "Let us buy you a drink – you're new here, right? What's your name?"

"Leon."

"We don't mean to intrude," said the woman. "Only we heard your accent and we like to introduce ourselves to newcomers. What disc are you from?"

"Got to go." He nudged past them. "Sorry."

Leon stumbled through the crowded inn. He pushed through the doors and staggered into the cold. Rain poured from the force field overhead, pounding against the cobblestones and sending a bitter chill through Leon's cloak. The inn's door swung shut, dampening the chatter from inside. He paused. If he left, this would be it. He'd never see Elena again and he'd never know if Waverrym was real.

Leon set off across the square.

As he thought of the woman with flour on her hands, memories of his mother swarmed into his mind. He'd visited her after the War. Probably. Hard to know if he'd gone to the right mass grave.

As he walked, the inn's noise faded, punctuated by a burst of chatter as the door swung open. Leon wrapped his cloak tighter around him as he passed the shrine to the Archangels. He stumbled down an alley, grateful for the shelter of the overhanging roofs.

He stopped.

Juliana wouldn't give up, if she was still alive. Neither would Blas. What would they say if Leon abandoned this quest after less than three days?

What do they matter? They've no idea what I've been through. I don't owe 'em anything.

Leon reached inside his cloak. He pulled out the pendant Juliana gave him all those years ago and stared at the small carving of wood.

No. He didn't owe Juliana and Blas anything: he owed them everything, and if they were here, he knew what they'd do. He kissed the pendant. Put it away.

And turned around.

The middle-aged Payan couple from the inn walked around the corner, blocking his way out of the alley.

The man smiled. "Leon! Changed your mind about that drink?"

"Still no, sorry. Jus' 'membered I've got to meet someone."

The woman shrugged. "Just as well. We weren't buying you a beer out of the goodness of our hearts."

The man and woman drew knives, and the man leered. "Leon de Velasco, you're going to make us rich!"

Chapter 15

L eon drew his dagger with fumbling hands. His head pounded, his mouth dryer than a salt mine. The street wobbled before him.

"What're you talking 'bout?" he asked.

The two Payans strode towards him, knives outstretched.

"You're a wanted man," said the woman. "Outside the Inquisition's castle, there's a notice with your name on it. Leon de Velasco: one hundred dorics alive, fifty dorics dead."

Leon swallowed. "You've got the wrong Leon. My last name's de Muron."

The man laughed. "Don't try to fool us. The Inquisition described you: bushy beard, look like a tramp, rampant alcoholic –"

"Ain't an alcoholic."

"Well, you knocked back those five beers darn fast," said the woman.

"Point being," said the man, "Your capture will give us enough money to never work a day again."

"Not that we've worked an honest day in our lives." The woman rubbed the man's arm. "Have we, honey?"

Leon stepped back. His foot landed in a stream of filth that ran down the alley.

The woman threw a pair of handcuffs at Leon, which Leon fumbled. The handcuffs splattered into the filthy stream.

The man smirked. "Put them on."

Leon's heart hammered. The man and the woman were six feet away: one lunge and their knives would pierce his chest. Hands trembling, Leon crouched and grabbed the handcuffs.

The woman whispered something to the man. It sounded like, "Good thing he's a coward."

Leon scooped a handful of the mucky water running down the alley, then stood, flinging it at the two Payans. Muck splattered into the man's eyes. He recoiled, screwed up his face, and cursed.

Leon sprinted away. Howling, the woman chased Leon and tackled him. They crashed into the cobblestones and knocked a bucket of water that tipped over them and Leon spluttered as they grappled in the filth and the woman's knife swung past his face and he cursed and the knife came back and he grabbed her wrist and locked the handcuffs around it.

He dove aside as her knife cut down, striking the cobblestones, and he yanked the handcuff towards him. She yelped and her shoulder popped out of her socket with a sickening crack. Leon stumbled up, panting. He held the handcuffs' other end as the woman whimpered on the cobblestones.

Footsteps clattered towards Leon. He threw himself aside and the Payan man lunged past, his knife slicing across Leon's cloak. Pain flared through his side and he growled. The man whirled around.

Filth coated his snarling face. "Let go of my wife, you bastard."

Leon glanced down. He still held the handcuffs, with the woman's dislocated arm locked in the other end. He tugged the handcuffs and the woman groaned.

The man bellowed and lunged. Leon stepped aside but slipped in the filth and crashed onto the woman. She screamed. The man stabbed down with his knife. Leon rolled over, tugging the woman on top of him as a shield. The man's knife struck the cobblestones and he fell onto the woman, pinning Leon to the ground beneath her. Leon cursed.

The knife hilt struck him in the temple. Light exploded behind his eyes. The man drew back the knife and Leon fumbled behind him, feeling for a weapon. He couldn't die in this stinking alley. Not when he finally had something to live for.

He grabbed a metal bucket and swung it, knocking the knife away. With his other hand, Leon locked the handcuffs around the man's wrist and swung the bucket into the man's skull. He cursed. Leon smacked the bucket into the man again and the man slumped onto the woman.

Panting, Leon shoved the pair off him. He got to his knees and searched the man's pockets. He found the handcuffs' key and pocketed it, then clipped the mercenaries' knives onto his belt.

Legs shaking, Leon stood. His head pounded, his heart hammered, and filth coated his cloak, but he was alive and that was all that mattered. He stumbled back to the inn.

When he staggered inside, the chatter died and everyone gaped. Elena burst out of the crowd.

"Where've you been?" She wrinkled her nose. "I got here and I couldn't find you – what happened?"

"I'll explain later," Leon said. "Let's find another inn."

He glanced around. Half the patrons held their noses and the other half looked ready to puke. The innkeeper wouldn't miss him.

~ ~ ~

"I've been an idiot," Leon said to Elena. "I'm sorry."

They'd found another inn and he'd paid the innkeeper to use the bath. Leon had recounted what happened. Now, they sat in their room and a headache drove spikes of pain into Leon's temples.

"It's fine," she said. "I guess I've been pushing too hard."

"No. You're right. Finding Waverrym is important. We owe it to all the angels who …"

His voice faded.

Leon cleared his throat. "Any new ideas?"

"Antonia looks just as tough at midnight, but I know how to get inside."

"Yeah?"

"The Resistance. They'll know how to sneak in."

Leon frowned. Soldiers patrolled every street and you couldn't walk ten paces without tripping over a Vahrian statue. Would there even be a resistance here? He was about to say this, then stopped, because maybe Elena knew something he didn't.

"How are we going to contact them?" he asked. "Know anyone?"

"No. They use a cell system. We only know who's in our own cell. It's smart, because it stops spies uncovering all the Resistance fighters. Downside is, if all your cell members die, like mine did …" She swallowed. "You're left in the cold."

"There must be a way to get back in. How were you recruited?"

"I stole food from the Vahrian Overseer's house. Picked the lock, snuck past the guards, caught by the maid. But she didn't alert the guards. She worked for the Resistance and after helping me escape she gave me a contact. Didn't know much about the Resistance, but I signed up when they promised I'd never sleep on the streets again. Back then, I didn't care about anyone other than myself. Once I joined the Resistance, though, they showed me the world was bigger than I'd imagined."

"So they recruited you after stole from Vahrians ... what if we do that? What if we show the Resistance we're here to fight?"

"What do you have in mind?"

Leon thought of Clymene's skeleton, dangling on the walls of the Vahrian Castle. "I say we give an angel a proper cremation."

Chapter 16

"Got the gunpowder?" Elena asked Leon.

He glanced around the crowded marketplace to check no one could hear, then raised his bag. "This is it."

His heart thumped with excitement. They stood near a store of sweet-smelling spices: on the other side, above a small park, Clymene's skeleton hung from the castle's wall. They'd taken two days to gather the ingredients. After several failed trials, Leon had remembered enough chemistry lessons to concoct the proper recipe.

We'll put you to rest, Clymene. Leon stared at the angel's skeleton. *You'll be at peace at last.*

Two soldiers trooped past.

"Ready?" asked Leon once the soldiers marched around the corner.

Elena nodded and hoisted her bag of wood onto her shoulder. Leon was about to walk towards the castle when a shadow passed overhead. He glanced up. High above the force field, a Vahrian airship glided over them. Its long, streamline balloon was a dark burgundy colour and bore the mark of the Vahrian Inquisition.

Leon swallowed. "That's Drayton's ship."

Elena's eyes widened. "How can you tell?"

"It's got the Inquisition's mark on the balloon and it's bigger than a normal airship. Besides, I spent half a day unloading it. Trust me, it's definitely his."

Drayton's airship kept gliding towards Antonia Disc. After a few seconds, it disappeared behind the rooftops.

Leon cursed. "How's he know we're here?"

"The Inquisition's got spies everywhere. The couple who attacked you knew who you were. Guess it was a matter of time until Drayton found we were here."

Leon swallowed. Drayton had limitless resources, countless spies, and the full power of the Queen and the Vahrian Council. How long could Elena and Leon stay hidden against all that might?

Not long if you make a bonfire in a market. But if you leave Anshan, you'll be safe.

He shook his head. This was their best chance to attract the Resistance, and besides, laying Clymene to rest was the right thing to do.

If only Alvaro could see me now.

Alvaro had been more than just a regular jonshular opponent. Leon hoped his friend wasn't too annoyed at how their last meeting ended, but what did it matter? They'd never see each other again.

He sighed. "Let's go."

Leon and Elena strode towards the castle. They stood under Clymene's skeleton, which hung on the stone wall high above. He glanced around. No soldiers. Elena dumped the bag of wood under the skeleton and Leon poured gunpowder on top. A few people walking past frowned at them.

Leon and Elena stepped back and he took a match from

his pocket. He struck the match, then threw it onto the gunpowder.

Fire exploded into the air with the sound of a thunderclap and a pillar of flame roared up to swallow Clymene's skeleton. Heat smacked Leon's face and he fell. All around the market, Payans shrieked and a shop owner cursed as sparks set fire to his rugs.

Elena pulled Leon up. They staggered closer to the fire, shielding their faces. Above, one of the ropes supporting Clymene's skeleton snapped.

Leon stood on a bench. "People of Paya!"

Two dozen Payans stopped and watched him. The rest ran from the towering fire, pushing through the market stalls.

"For too long, Vahrians have oppressed us," said Leon. "Look at this skeleton. They've taken one of us and turned 'em into a trophy!"

Another rope snapped. Clymene's shinbone dropped into the fire with a flurry of embers.

"This skeleton's no trophy," said Elena. "This was Beatris Clymene: an angel, a Payan, a hero who fought the Vahrians. Today, we lay her to rest."

The last ropes snapped. The silent crowd watched, wide-eyed, as Clymene's skeleton fell into the fire.

"Beatris Clymene," said Elena. "May your soul find its way into the Star Spectre's heart and may you rest within Her loving embrace. Blessed be to the Archangels."

A few people in the crowd echoed Elena. "Blessed be to the Archangels!"

Armour clanked and someone shouted. Leon turned. The crowd of Payans fled as six Vahrian soldiers stomped into the marketplace.

"And now we run," said Leon.

He and Elena fled. Leon glanced at the fire as he took off. Nestled in a wreath of flames, Clymene's skull grinned at him. She was at peace at last.

~ ~ ~

Leon and Elena stopped running once they reached a deserted laneway. He grinned. Attacking Vahrians felt so damn good.

Elena smiled. "Think we got the Resistance's attention?"

"Reckon we got all of *Anshan's* attention. Just hope the Resistance find us before the Vahrians do, 'cause inquisitors will be hunting –"

A handsome Vahrian walked into the lane. Leon went silent. The young Vahrian looked about Elena's age, with a well-worn sword in his belt. Leon and Elena stepped aside to let him through.

The Vahrian sat on a barrel. "A most impressive display, friends."

Leon tensed. *He saw us cremate Clymene.*

Elena drew her dagger. "Leave us and I'll leave you with your life."

The young Vahrian grinned. "Aye, you're as fierce as you're beautiful."

Elena blushed. "I'm warning you. Run. Now."

Leon pulled out his dagger with a shaking hand. "Do as she says."

"I'm not here to harm you," said the man. "My name's Pierce McKillney and I'm part of the Resistance."

"You're Vahrian," said Leon.

"Ach! I'm not from Vahria. I'm from Murmidia."

Elena frowned. "Murmidia?"

"Country to the north of Vahria," said Leon. "Still part of the planet Neebia, and still in the Vahrian Republic."

"Aye," said Pierce. "Though I wish it otherwise."

"I've never met a Murmidian who didn't support Vahria," said Leon. "How can we trust you?"

"The real question," said Pierce. "Is how can I trust you?"

"What?" said Elena.

"Well, with that display you put on –" Pierce shifted position and Leon and Elena's daggers twitched. "– you're wanting to get our attention, yes? Or you're insane, which I'd believe of the old man, but not of a woman as beautiful as you."

Pierce bowed towards Elena. Leon scowled. He didn't trust this cocky youngster.

"My point, other than complimenting you, my lady," said Pierce, "is that a blind man could tell you want to join the Resistance. Now, you may be true heroes who believe in our cause. I hope you are. However, you could also be Inquisition spies."

Pierce drew his sword with the speed of a striking cobra, then stood and knocked Leon and Elena's daggers out of their hands. Leon cursed. Pierce's sword flicked through the air and its point stopped an inch from Leon's throat. Leon's skin turned cold.

"So," said Pierce. "Hero or spy: let's find out which one you are."

Chapter 17

Pierce marched them through winding alleys, his sword prodding into Leon's back, and Leon and Elena's daggers clipped to his belt. They rounded a corner. Five boys blocked the street, whacking each other with toy swords and yelling in high-pitched voices.

Pierce pressed the flat of his blade against Leon's back. Coldness radiated along Leon's spine. He swallowed.

The sweaty children stepped aside to let Pierce, Leon, and Elena through. The kids waved swords and jeered with mock anger. Then one boy paled. He scrambled back, nudged his friend, and pointed at Pierce's sword pressed against Leon's spine. The children's jeers faded into silence.

They left the alley. When they encountered more people, Pierce sheathed his sword, but kept close to Leon and Elena. Leon tensed. Pierce had moved that sword like lightning. One false twitch and Leon would have a blade in his chest.

"Where are you taking us?" Elena asked as they squeezed through a narrow street crammed with growling dogs.

"To the Resistance, my lady," said Pierce.

Leon swallowed. He'd never known a big difference between Vahrians and Murmidians, and he doubted Pierce was anything but a full-blooded Vahrian, about to deliver them to the Inquisition.

"Could be worse," whispered Elena.

"What?" Leon said, trying not to move his lips.

Elena glanced at Pierce, then whispered to Leon. "He's kind of cute, isn't he?"

Leon gaped, speechless.

"No private chatter, please." Pierce prodded Leon with his sword. "Anything you want to say, say so I can hear. Especially you, my lady. Your voice is as soothing as a river. What's your name?"

She fluttered her eyelashes. "Elena."

Leon scowled. He doubted her tactic would lower Pierce's guard.

"Aye. A name that matches your beauty." Pierce prodded Leon. "And you, old man?"

"Leon. And I ain't an old man."

Pierce steered them around a corner. "Is he your father, Elena?"

Leon scowled. "If I was, I'd go crazy."

"I didn't think you were related," said Pierce. "He has none of your grace, my lady."

"Give me my dagger and I'll show you how much grace I got, kid."

"Aye, you share a fiery manner. It would be a tragedy if you were spies. Especially you, Elena."

They reached a narrow alley. Pierce made Leon and Elena put on blindfolds, then led them through. Leon tripped and fell.

"Careful, my lady." Pierce brushed Leon as he stepped over him. "It's uneven, this ground."

Leon stood, glowering.

Pierce led them down the alley, squeezing them between narrow fungcrete walls until the city's sounds faded. Leon gulped. Is this how it ended, with a slit throat and a bed of mud-stained cobblestones?

Pierce's hand clamped onto his shoulder. Leon flinched. His back tingled and he waited for a knife to slide between his ribs.

Instead, someone knocked on a door.

"Who is it?" said a rough voice.

"Pierce McKillney."

"How does the pegasus fly?"

"With style, speed, and a slight lean to the left."

A door creaked open. "Good 'ter see you, Pierce."

"Aye, it's been too long. I've got two protesters wanting to join. Might be true heroes, might be spies."

"Bring 'em in."

Pierce nudged Leon inside and guided his hands onto a ladder.

"Climb until you reach the bottom," said Pierce. "We'll decide your fate down there."

~ ~ ~

After a few minutes of climbing, Leon's boots hit sand. He stepped off the ladder, wiping his sweaty hands on his cloak, then fumbled ahead, feeling for a wall. A musty smell hung in the cold air and water trickled in the distance. Boots hit the ground behind him. He wanted to whisper to see if it was Elena, but he kept quiet.

Someone grabbed him. Leon flinched and tried to stumble away, but the person tightened their grip and laughed.

"No need to struggle. I'm just here to stop your noggin colliding with a rock."

Leon's heart pounded as the stranger guided him through what sounded like a vast chamber. Voices echoed around him and the air chilled his hands. Were they underground?

They stopped.

"Remove their blindfolds," said a woman's voice.

Leon blinked as Pierce tore off his blindfold. They stood in a vast cave. Stalactites hung from the ceiling far above, their spear-like tips just visible in the darkness. Tents spread across the sand-covered floor. Glowfung lit the camp, but the feeble illumination only carved a small island of light from the sea of shadows that filled the cave. A ring of Payans circled Leon, Elena, and Pierce.

A woman with wispy grey hair sat in a wicker chair. Her wrinkled skin hung from her cheekbones with the limpness of old wallpaper. A hulking man stood behind her. His large hands rested on his sword's hilt.

"We owe you thanks for laying Beatris Clymene to rest," said the wrinkled woman. "Beatris was a good angel. A brave angel. She didn't deserve to be killed." The woman bowed her head, took a deep breath, then looked back up. "My name is Simona de Monroy and I'm the leader of the Resistance. Pierce says you wish to join us. Is this true, my dears?"

"Yes," said Leon.

Leon tried to hide his frown. This old lady led the Resistance? He doubted she could fight a stiff breeze, let alone the Vahrian Republic.

"We can prove our loyalty," said Elena. "You see, we're both angels."

Elena unfastened her cloak. Her wings unfolded and the

Resistance fighters gasped.

Simona smiled. "I never thought I'd live to see another angel. My dear, I am sorry for any mistreatment Pierce gave you. Welcome to the Resistance."

Leon exhaled a pent-up breath. *That was easy.*

Elena grinned at Pierce. "You don't have to apologise. Pierce was wonderful."

Pierce bowed. "Let me show you to your tent, my lady."

He offered her his hand. She took it. Leon rolled his eyes and moved to follow them as they walked away, but a signal from Simona made her bodyguard lunge.

The man's huge sword appeared next to Leon's neck. The massive blade hovered an inch from his skin, held one-handed despite its weight. Leon's guts clenched. One twitch and the blade would sever his jugular.

"Elena's shown her wings," said Simona. "You, my dear, have not."

Sweat streaked down Leon's back. "I'm an angel. You heard Elena say so."

Elena and Pierce stopped. She tilted her head to one side and Leon realised she'd never seen his wings despite all the time they'd been together.

"Show me your wings," said Simona.

Leon took that as an excuse to step away from the sword. He fumbled with his cloak. It fell to the sandy floor, and then he pulled off his shirt. Everyone gasped. Leon turned and showed Simona the two stubs of hacked-off flesh on his back – the stubs that were the only remains of his once glorious wings.

Chapter 18

"Leon, I'm so sorry," said Elena. "I didn't realise –"

Leon scowled. "It's fine."

Everyone stared at his back with horrified eyes. Heat rose onto his cheeks. He'd never shown anyone his sawn-off wings and now dozens of strangers were gaping at him.

"Give the man privacy," said Simona. "Teo – back to me."

The hulking swordsman stood behind Simona. He sheathed his sword with a shrill hiss and glowered at anyone who'd yet to disperse. Leon gulped. There were lots of people he didn't want to fight, but Teo now sat atop that list.

The crowd of Resistance members walked away, muttering. Now, only Elena, Leon, Pierce, Simona, and Teo remained.

"You lost your wings in the War, dear?" Simona asked.

Leon grunted. Everyone looked at him with soft faces and sympathetic eyes. Leon scowled harder. He didn't deserve sympathy. He hadn't lost his wings because he was a hero.

He'd lost them because he was a coward.

"The Vahrians cut them?" asked Simona.

Leon glanced at Elena. She already thought he was spineless, but it could get worse.

"Yeah," he lied.

106

Simona made the Archangel's Sign by steepling her fingers and touching her pressed-together thumbs above her heart. "We're all here because the Vahrians have wronged us, or someone we loved. But, Leon … they hurt you more than we could imagine. Welcome to the Resistance."

Leon tugged his shirt and cloak back on. Elena stared at him with a look of sadness mingled with disappointment. He grimaced. Why did she have to look at him like that?

"Pierce will show you to a free tent," said Simona. "He'll look after you for your first few weeks. Now, you've got the rest of today to settle in, tool up at the armoury, and learn the ropes. We meet tomorrow, after breakfast. You'll get your first mission there."

"Mission?" said Leon.

"You'll be assigned to a team, given supplies, and briefed. Our missions are varied. Sabotage airships, tail inquisitors, steal Vahrian artworks to sell on the black market, that sort of thing."

Leon swallowed. This wasn't what he'd wanted. He and Elena couldn't stay in Anshan forever. They had to get into Antonia Disc if they wanted to find Waverrym.

"Do we choose our missions?" he asked.

"Partly. We select teams based on suitability, so if you have any particular skills, let me know."

Elena frowned at Leon. He wished he could tell her what he was trying to do.

"Well, I know lots about Antonia," he said. "I've been there before, on an official angel visit, so if there's any missions there …"

Elena's eyes widened. Leon wondered if he'd overplayed his hand.

Simona stroked her chin. "There is a potential mission that requires insider knowledge of Antonia. As it stands, we weren't going to execute it, since Pierce is the only one who works there. He helps in the stables, with the pegasi. Now you're here, however, this might be the chance we need. Pierce, brief them."

~ ~ ~

"The Queen's hosting the annual royal banquet in three days," said Pierce as he walked Leon and Elena to the armoury. "Dozens of highborns and important Vahrians will be there, including several senior inquisitors. Now, I say that the Queen is hosting this little banquet. Reality is, the Vahrian Council are pulling her strings, as usual. Twenty years since the War, and the bastards are still rewarding Payans who betrayed us. This means, however, that the Palace will be full of Paya's slimiest turncoats."

Leon nodded. That explained why he'd seen so many wealthy-looking Payans over the last few days. They were arriving for the banquet.

Pierce, Elena, and Leon reached the armoury. Leon frowned. Back at the Academy, the armoury was an immense chamber with racks of swords, bows, spears, harpoons, knives, clubs, steel lashes, and dozens more weapons.

Here, a single table of weapons sat on the ground. A small rack of bows and arrows leaned against the cave's rocky wall and a stocky, bearded man stood behind the table.

"This all you got?" Leon asked.

The stocky man scowled. "Who's this ungrateful bugger, Pierce?"

"Leon," said Pierce. "And Elena. A little politeness wouldn't go astray, Rufus. They're new recruits."

"I'll be polite ta them if they be polite ta me," said Rufus. "What do you want, Pierce?"

"Simona's approved our mission," said Pierce. "The one with the royal banquet. Got the gunpowder?"

Rufus reached under the table and pulled out a bulging sack that smelled of charcoal.

"Now, our mission is to sneak into the castle during the banquet," said Pierce. "We'll disguise ourselves as cooking staff. They've already recruited me as a chef's assistant and they've brought extra workers in for the banquet, so it'll be a cinch to steal uniforms for you two. We'll each sneak several pounds of gunpowder into the Palace. Once we're inside, we'll combine our bags into one pile."

"Then?" asked Leon, fearing where this was going.

"Remember how the feast will be full of Vahrians and traitorous Payans?" Pierce grinned. "We'll blow the whole lot of them to hell!"

~ ~ ~

"This is wrong," Leon said to Elena. "We can't do this."

A clump of glowfung cast a dim light over his tent's canvas walls and shadows strolled across the fabric as Resistance fighters walked past. Pierce had taken them to their tents before Simona's messenger summoned him. Before leaving, Pierce had kissed Elena's hand.

"What are you talking about?" asked Elena. "This is what you want, isn't it?"

"I want to get inside Antonia and find that riser. Hell, so do you. That's how we'll find Waverrym, not by blowing up the castle."

"We won't blow up the castle. Just the banquet hall. Besides, we can find the riser and do the mission."

"Yeah? How?"

"After we blow the gunpowder, everyone will be distracted and we can go to the riser."

Leon scoffed. "Great idea. Ain't like there'll be soldiers crawling everywhere."

"Hmm, good point … what if we tell Pierce we need to find the riser first?"

"The boy's a fanatic. You saw his eyes light up when he talked about exploding the banquet hall. He won't jeopardize the mission."

She pouted. "Why do you hate him?"

"Because I've got more sense than you. You just like his looks."

"Take that back."

"Before, I thought you were flirting to distract him so we could escape, but you really like him, don't you?"

"Yeah." She reddened. "I do. He bought us to the Resistance and could've been an asshole about it, but he wasn't. I don't like him just because he's handsome. I like him because he's kind, and brave, and cares about something bigger than himself."

"I don't care if he's holier than the Star Spectre, because I'd never kill a Payan, and I ain't destroying a castle full of them."

She opened her mouth to retort, but before she could speak the tent's flap opened. Pierce stood outside, grinning.

"Just got away from Simona," he said. "Ready to plan our mission?"

Elena glanced at Leon, her face pale. "Leon –"

"Let's do it: I want to kill those Vahrian bastards," he lied.

They followed Pierce as he walked through the cluster of tents.

"What were you talking to Simona about?" Leon asked.

"Leon!" said Elena. "It's probably classified."

"It's alright. Simona freed from other duties so I can watch you two." Pierce winked at Elena. "Not that I need encouragement."

She smiled.

Leon cleared his throat. "You said we're planning, Pierce?"

"Ah, yes. How are your map-making skills?"

"Rusty."

"Do you remember enough of the Queen's Palace to draw us a plan?"

~ ~ ~

"… and the banquet hall's here." Leon marked it on the parchment map. "That's everything in the Queen's Palace."

"Looks right," said Pierce. "Though I only know my way around half the grounds, so you're the expert here."

Leon pulled out another roll of parchment. He used a quill to draw a circle representing the bounds of Antonia disc, then marked the Palace. Next to the Palace, he drew another circle.

"That's a gigantic riser." Leon stared hard at Elena. "Two hundred feet from the Palace's doorstep."

She looked away.

"Aye, I've seen that," said Pierce. "We sometimes use it to launch pegasi."

"Might be a good escape route," said Elena. "We could steal

111

pegasi and fly through the force field."

Leon nodded. "If that's the case, we should scout it beforehand to check it's got enough lift for a pegasus."

Pierce shook his head. "No need. I've got our escape all planned out."

Leon sighed. It had been worth a try.

After they finished planning, he pulled Elena away. They tried to work out how they'd reach the riser, but they couldn't think of a way to do it without telling Pierce.

Dinner was an hour away, so Elena practiced flying in the enormous cavern. Her standing take-offs improved. Without wind, however, she struggled to glide. Leon told her to sharpen her wings' angle and showed how to use the still air – which was heavier than normal – to aid her flight.

When she landed, scattering sand into a cloud, Resistance fighters clapped. She strutted over to Leon and Pierce, grinning.

Pierce bowed. "Your grace, my lady, is matched only by your beauty."

"I bet you say that to all the pretty angels."

"Only you."

A half dozen Payans came to Elena to congratulate her.

While she was distracted, Leon lent towards Pierce and said, "It ain't going to work out between you two."

"You don't know that."

Elena grabbed Pierce's hand. They strolled to the main clearing, where a fire shot embers into the air. Leon glowered.

What if she does fall for him? Will she still want to find Waverrym, or will she stay with the Resistance to be with him instead?

For dinner, all the Resistance fighters gathered in a circle around the fire, with Simona sitting in her chair and watching the group with the twinkling eyes of a proud grandmother. Leon gorged on meat, and when he wasn't sculling beer, he was tipping it into his hip flask.

Elena and Pierce sat beside him, gazing into each other's eyes. Every few minutes, they burst into laughter, and the remarks Leon caught from their whispers made him roll his eyes and want to puke. Him and Juliana never acted like that.

Leon rapped Pierce on the shoulder, interrupting Pierce's joke about a street rat and a chef's apprentice. "What's with Simona? She doesn't like standing, or what?"

Pierce kept speaking to Elena, so Leon repeated the question.

Pierce's shoulders sagged and he turned to glare at Leon. "A Vahrian wagon crushed her legs. The driver didn't even stop to help her."

"So that's why she leads the Resistance?"

Elena glared at Leon behind Pierce's back.

"No," said Pierce. "She was in the Resistance when the wagon broke her legs."

"Why'd you join?" Leon asked.

"Dad fought for Vahria in the War. After, he bought Mam, me, and my older sister up to Paya. Worst thing ever. See, the War was the best time of Dad's life. Afterwards, all that aggression … hurting us was his only way to vent it. Until I stopped him." Pierce glowered at the fire. "The day I stood up to my father was the best day of my life. And the worst, because I realised there were more people out there suffering because of bastards like him."

Elena leaned closer to him and her eyes widened.

In the red firelight, there was an animalistic edge to Pierce's scowling face. "When I saw soldiers beating an old Payan lady, I realised Vahrians were the biggest bastards of them all. My mam, though – she wanted me to live a peaceful life. I could've, too, since Dad was gone and the Vahrians weren't hurting us. We were Murmidian, after all. But the problem with peace is that it never changes anything. A lot of Payans don't like the Resistance. They say we're a bunch of angry fighters, too dumb to accept the way things are. Well, maybe we are stupid. Maybe we are angry. But anger's a better weapon than peace when you're fighting bastards who don't think twice about slitting an old woman's throat and leaving her in the gutter."

Elena reached out to hold Pierce's hand and her eyes shone with reflected firelight. She opened her mouth to speak but struggled to form words.

Eventually, she said, "Thank you."

There was a softness to her voice that Leon had never heard.

Pierce bowed his head. "You're welcome."

They fell back into conversation, as if Leon had never interrupted them.

~ ~ ~

The next two days passed in a blur under the cave's dark roof, from which stalactites hung like spears. No one forbade Leon and Elena from leaving, but when Leon dawdled near the exit, the guards eased swords from their scabbards. The only other exit was a hole in the rock that trickled water into a pool, but that was too small to climb through.

If Leon wasn't planning with Pierce and Elena, he was teaching Elena flying, sign language, history, and all the other

114

things he'd learned at the Academy. Her flight improved well enough, but other lessons made her stare into the distance and fidget with her cloak.

Halfway through his astronomy lesson, she yawned. "Can't we get back to flying?"

Leon sighed. He was already irritated by his itchy face – Pierce said Leon was too scruffy to impersonate a Palace worker, so a barber had cut his beard and hacked off his hair. Elena's bored tone only made him more annoyed.

"If you only care about flying, you'll be no better than a sparrow. Angels don't just fly. Angels carry messages and keep the peace. Angels talk with kings, and change kings' minds if they must. Yet they must pray with priests, haggle with merchants, and walk with commoners. If you can't navigate, you'll fly through pirate-infested space routes. If you can't use sign language, how will you communicate in space?"

Why am I saying this? She ain't ever going to live like an angel again, not with Paya how it is, so why bother teaching her?

At the Academy, he'd come to Professor Nane with similar question and asked why they learnt about dead civilisations. It wasn't like he'd ever use that knowledge.

"Do you value truth?" Professor Nane had asked.

"Of course," he had said.

"Then there's nothing more valuable than history."

Leon brought himself back to the present. "An angel must know everything – history, astronomy, maths, farming, art, song – or they'll be the village laughingstock when a peasant offers 'em a *Rube le Hart,* and the dumb angel who was too bored to learn says yes."

"What's *Rube le Hart?*" asked Elena.

115

"Goat testicle."

"Ergh."

"True story, you know. My friend, Blas, got invited to a farmer's home on the first night of his placement, and the wife gave him *Rube le Hart* as a joke. Blas never missed another farming lecture after that. Never missed a chance to tell that story, either. Heh. Funny guy, Blas. Funny guy ..."

A dead guy, now.

A lump formed in Leon's throat. He coughed, scowling.

"Placement?" asked Elena.

"Yes!" Leon winced at his eager tone, but talking was easier than remembering, so he kept speaking. "While training at the Academy, angels spend a month each year on an outer regions disc. Assist the ruler, work with the garrison, help farmers, that sort of thing."

"Right."

She nodded with more vigour than the fact deserved, but Leon appreciated the effort.

"Now, get my point?" he said. "Or do I need to tell the story about the angel who carried a message to the wrong king because he couldn't tell a map from a painting?"

"Alright, I'm sorry I yawned. Keep going."

~ ~ ~

There was no sun to light the shadowy cave, yet Leon swore it was the crack of dawn when Pierce shook him from his sleep.

"Time for swordplay, old man!"

Leon blinked sleep from his eyes. "Eh?"

"We may need to fight our way out of the castle, but with

sword skills as rusty as yours –"

"Not rusty."

"Well, I disarmed you easily enough. I'd say you need training."

Minutes later, Leon crouched in the central clearing, rubbing his bleary eyes. Pierce stood several paces away. They held wooden practice swords and Resistance fighters formed a circle around them.

Pierce twirled his sword and bowed. "Ready, old man?"

Leon bowed back and scratched his neck. He missed his long hair. This new haircut felt too damn exposing.

"Anytime, kid," he said.

Pierce strolled forward and Leon raised his sword. Pierce slashed low and Leon jumped back, but Pierce leapt forward and disarmed Leon with a flick of his blade. Then he twirled and kicked Leon's chest, making him topple onto the sand.

Resistance fighters clapped. Leon stumbled up and glared at Elena, who also clapped. He'd suffered many embarrassments in his forty-three years, but losing a fight after three seconds was a new low.

The embarrassments only grew worse, because the next three bouts ended with Leon sprawled in the sand without landing a blow on his opponent.

Leon staggered up, wincing. Tomorrow, he'd wake with a body full of bruises.

"Another duel?" asked Pierce.

The crowd grinned.

I'm done being a practice dummy, thanks.

He opened his mouth, ready to decline. Then he remembered the Academy. All those hours sparing with Juliana and Blas: practicing with blade and bow, and shield and spear, and sometimes with nothing but his body and the moves of the Harsinth warrior-monks.

The crowd of Resistance fighters jeered at him. Leon remembered another set of hostile faces and another unbeatable opponent. Salvador de Sese. Leon had defeated that highborn prick in the tourney, and if he could beat him, he could beat Pierce.

Leon raised his sword. "C'mon."

The crowd whooped. Leon narrowed his eyes and focused on Pierce, who circled around him, narrowing the distance one half-step at a time. Leon dropped into a fighter's crouch. He was taller than the boy. That gave him better reach, but wouldn't help if Pierce closed in.

Pierce stepped nearer. Leon shuffled back, shaking his sword just enough to look nervous, and Pierce raised his foot to take another stride.

Leon lunged forward, catching Pierce mid-step, and drove his blade at the boy's chest.

Pierce twisted.

Leon's sword slid past the boy's torso and Leon's momentum carried him forward. Pierce stuck out a leg, tripping him. As Leon fell, the boy's sword thwacked into Leon's arse. The crowd laughed.

"Alright." Leon picked himself up and spat out sand. "You win."

Bruised, scowling, and grumbling, he hobbled out of the ring. If only he had a wooden crate to throw at the boy.

See him dodge that.

Leon wanted nothing more than to shamble to his tent, but leaving so early would lose what little respect he had left. He stayed to watch Pierce spar with another Payan, and reflected on how pathetic he'd become.

Pierce won all but two of his fights against the other Payan. After they'd finished, he looked around for his next opponent. Elena stepped into the circle and the crowd cheered. Leon scowled. No one had applauded for him.

Elena and Pierce bowed. Then, they began.

Their wooden swords flashed through the air, clacking into each other's again and again with a frenetic beat. Pierce twisted Elena's sword from her grip. Before he could follow up, she tackled him and they crashed into the sandy ground. They grappled. When they stopped rolling, Elena lay on top of Pierce, pushing his wooden sword against his throat.

"Hope you weren't going easy on me," she said.

"Wish I could say I was."

She threw the sword away, but kept lying on Pierce.

They kissed.

The crowd whooped. Leon grimaced. Would they miss him if he walked away?

Elena's wings burst out of her cloak. The crowd laughed. Leon smirked despite himself. The first time he'd kissed Juliana, he'd done that too. Then they'd sprinted through the Academy's halls to escape the cranky caretaker, because Leon's wings had knocked over a vase.

He felt Juliana's hand-carved pendant. A lump formed in his throat. Elena and Pierce's lips were locked firm and their eyes were shut. Leon's nostalgia evaporated and he stormed away, scowling.

After dinner that night, Leon pulled Elena aside.

"Don't get too attached to Pierce," he said.

"I can take care of myself, Leon. You're not my father."

He blinked. If he and Juliana had survived the War and had

children like they'd planned, their daughter would've been Elena's age. What would this talk look like, if it was just a worried father trying to protect his daughter? When he'd seen parents do that, Leon had always thought they were stupid. But this was different. He wasn't a paranoid father afraid of his daughter's heart being broken. He was afraid something much worse would happen.

Leon glanced around to make sure they were away from the others. "Still want to find Waverrym?"

"Yes."

"Told Pierce about it?"

She looked away. "I need time to explain properly, or he'll think it's a fairy tale."

For all we know, it could be.

"When will you tell him?" he asked.

She kept staring at the sand. "He's nice, you know. And he gets it."

"Gets what?"

"What it's like to be … oh never mind." Elena chewed her lip. "If you stopped criticising him for a second, I think you'd like him."

"Elena," said Pierce, who stood by the fire. "I've got your food!"

"Be there in a minute," said Elena.

"I know you can take care of yourself," said Leon. "But there'll come a time when you have to choose."

"Between?"

"Pierce, or Waverrym."

~ ~ ~

Leon woke with a dry mouth and aching bladder. Groaning, he grabbed a clump of glowfung, crawled from his tent, stumbled up, blinked as he swayed, and staggered to the camp's edge. He undid his breaches. His piss splashed against the sand, loud in the cavern's midnight darkness. He glanced back at the camp, expecting the noise to cause groans and curses, but everything stayed quiet.

Leon buttoned his breaches. He sighed. Why the hell did his bladder have to wake him when he slept? Couldn't the bloody thing wait until morning? He never had this problem when he was young.

He tiptoed back into camp, stepping over tent ropes and praying he wouldn't knock anything over. Water dripped from a stalactite and fell onto a tent with a steady plinking.

Glad that ain't my tent. Poor sod.

He emerged in a clearing and frowned. Where was he?

Great. Of course I'm lost.

Scowling, he walked towards the central fire. The flames had died hours ago, but there was enough of a reddish glow on the stalactites above to know the way. Once he got there, he knew the path to his tent.

Someone moaned. Leon froze. The sound came from a tent a few paces away. The tent was dark, but he'd heard –

Another groan and someone rustled inside the tent. Leon frowned. The voice sounded familiar.

"Mmm," whispered Elena. "Pierce …"

Leon's guts twisted. *What the hell's she doing?*

Pierce moaned and the rustling grew louder.

Leon thought about yanking open their tent and waking the camp. He smirked. See the idiot boy stay calm during *that*. He shook his head. They'd joined the Resistance to infiltrate

Antonia, for Karym's sake, not to get laid. The stupid girl should've known better.

Leon stomped past their tent, not caring if they heard, and walked into the central clearing. He slumped onto a log and stared at the fire. Feeble embers glowed between clumps of ash and the fire coughed and spluttered with the feebleness of a dying man.

He thought of another place and another fire. Musreen Disc had been barren and cold despite the flames. An old sailor had dropped Leon on the deserted disc, because he was too poor to fly to the Academy. The pegasus-drawn ship that collected him was filled with a half-dozen other new angels – sons and daughters of highborns. They'd smirked at Leon's cloak, which bulged with stitches and was covered with dust blown onto him by the carriage's landing.

"Sure you didn't buy those wings for a Glory Day pageant?" one angel asked.

Leon's face burned with heat. These angels wore tailored suits, without an ounce of dirt. Their uniforms were a far cry from Leon's second-hand cloak. In the last few months, he'd been greeted with bows whenever he walked through the village square, courtesy of his growing wings. He'd even got donations from the ruling highborn, although Mother took it to spend on the bakery. At the time, he hadn't minded. After so long pounding bread in the bakery's back room, the attention made him strut with his head held high. Now, he wished he'd bought nicer clothing. He was already short for an angel. With a lowborn mother and clothes that looked like scraps, how would he fit in?

A girl stepped out of the crowd of angels and bowed. "I'm Juliana. What's your name?"

He bowed back. "Leon."

"Look at how short he is," said another angel. "What is he, ten?"

The angels chuckled.

Juliana glared at them. "You like jonshular, Leon?"

He'd seen men play the game on the rare occasions when Mother took him to the inn, but Leon didn't know the rules.

"I love it!" he said.

"Want a game?"

He nodded so fast that one angel muttered something about a spider flying out of his hair. They boarded the carriage, and by the time they left the force field, Juliana realised Leon had no idea how to play. He worried she'd call him a liar, but she just chuckled and taught him the rules.

A lump formed in Leon's throat. They'd met at fifteen. They could've been lovers for eight years, not four, but he'd let his new-found prestige overwhelm him. He'd got a tailored suit and used his wings, his status, and his connection to an absent father to follow the easy path, not the worthwhile one. Still, at least he'd had some time with Juliana.

The best time.

Leon watched the fire. Watched it smoulder into darkness. Watched the last embers choke to death under the weight of all that ash.

Chapter 19

The Vahrian soldier, face masked by a clump of breathfung, held out his hand. Leon gave the soldier his forged letter of employment, trying to keep his hands from trembling.

The soldier inspected the letter. Sacks of gunpowder filled the inside of Leon's stolen uniform as he floated outside Antonia Disc's entrance, clutching the handrail. Elena and Pierce were already inside. It was banquet day and servants were bustling into Antonia, crowding the platform which Leon floated above.

The soldier nodded.

Relief flooded through Leon. He took back the letter and pulled himself along the handrail, towards the small semi-circle that was the only transparent part of Antonia's otherwise black force field. He passed through and gravity tugged him down. Stifling a grin, he pulled off his breathfung.

He was inside Antonia.

Tall stone walls loomed over the cobblestoned courtyard and Vahrian soldiers prowled atop the wall. Behind him, the force field – which was semi-transparent from the inside – curved up into the sky.

Leon swallowed. Somehow, the walls towering around the

courtyard felt taller than when he'd been here with Juliana and Blas. He rubbed his pendant. Things had been rough enough last time he'd been here, even with his two best friends. Now ...

Well, it ain't going to be easier. Still, I'd rather blow up a palace than meet Father again.

He joined Payan servants marching through the Whistling Gate, which was a gigantic maw of an opening that punctured the thick walls.

It was dark inside the gate, yet light enough to glimpse the spiked metal underside of the door dangling in the shadows above the slow-moving line of servants. Leon gulped. A single pin held all that metal. If the pin loosened ...

He emerged from the gate's hulking dimness and breathed out. Squinting, he glanced around. Lush gardens sprawled in all directions, bordered by clipped hedges, and in the distance the Queen's Palace glinted gold.

In front of the Palace, a ragged-edged hole defied the sculptured gardens around it. The hole was large enough to swallow an airship and shimmering air rose from its depths.

Leon shuffled through the gardens along with the other servants, heading to the Palace. By now, Elena and Pierce would be inside. He passed a group of silk-clad highborns frolicking across the lawns, engrossed in a game of croquet. Their high-pitched laughter carried through the air. Leon clenched his hand into a fist. Before meeting his father, he'd dreamed of being like these air-headed highborns. Now, he wanted to bash their brains out with their stupid croquet sticks. These laughing men and women – and their families – had sold themselves to Vahria, because they'd worried about losing their tea parties, banquets, and dances.

They ain't the only ones who betrayed Paya. You're as guilty as them.

They skirted around the ragged-edged hole. Leon glanced inside and warm air blew onto his face. Far below, water bubbled at the bottom of the hole. Leon kept staring into the riser as he walked around it with the other servants. There had to be a hidden symbol, or a sign that appeared out of place. He thought about the Sarahk's description:

Find the heart of nobility, and
  find the soul of the realm.
  Find the lungs of Severym, and
  find the path to safety.

He understood the riddle's first three lines, but the path to safety ... was there a secret gate down the bottom of the hole? A tunnel? He'd only know if he climbed down into the riser, but he couldn't do that without arousing suspicion. He kept walking with the other servants and climbed the stone steps of the Queen's Palace.

They entered the colossal Hall of Chandeliers. The other servants gaped at the crystal chandeliers, the marble sculptures, the wall-to-ceiling mirrors, and the golden decorations. Leon scowled. The Palace had awed him when he'd visited all those years ago. When he'd discovered that the Palace's construction had almost bankrupted Paya, he'd laughed. Juliana and Blas had chuckled with him.

Now, he realised how much bread could've been bought with the money King Lerbert IV wasted on this building. Now, all that wealth, ornament, and gold made him clench his hands into fists.

The servants split up, heading to their respective jobs. Leon followed two Payan men to the kitchen, bowing to a half-dozen highborns as they bustled past. The highborns ignored them. Before he reached the kitchens, Leon ducked through a servant's door, strode through a maze of narrow corridors, and knocked on a closet.

"It's me," he said.

The door opened. He scrambled inside and shut the door. Pierce and Elena stood too close to be merely waiting, reminding Leon of another pair of young lovers hidden in this closet, and how they'd giggled, kissed, and thought nothing could tear them apart. Not the boy's lowborn blood. Not the girl's power-hungry mother. Not even rumours of impending war …

"Made it alright?" asked Pierce. "With the gunpowder?"

Leon patted his buttoned jacket. "It's under here."

The banquet was to begin after sunset, so Leon, Pierce, and Elena had nothing to do but wait. Whenever footsteps sounded in the corridor outside, Leon tensed and gripped the dagger hidden in his boot, but no one tried to enter their cupboard. The ceiling thumped above them as people walked overhead.

After four hours of waiting, the footsteps from above grew rapid and frantic, then fell away to silence.

Pierce stood. "Everyone will be in the banquet hall by now. It's time."

They left the cupboard and strolled through twisting corridors. To reach the cellar beneath the banquet hall, they'd have to pass through the kitchens, but with their waiter uniforms that'd be easy. Leon let Pierce and Elena enter the kitchens ahead of him. It might look suspicious if three people walked through at once. Leon counted to ten, then pushed through the door and walked into the kitchen.

Heat smacked Leon in the face. Pans crashed, chefs yelled, and waiters dashed around, carrying trays of sizzling meat that made Leon salivate. He threaded between the chefs, heading to the cellar door.

A monobrowed chef clamped his sweaty hand around Leon's bicep. "Oi! Second course is going up."

"What?"

"You're a waiter, aren't you? Do your bloody job."

The monobrowed chef gestured to a bench filled with plates of food that waiters stacked onto their arms. Leon nodded, muttered an apology, and strode to the bench. The chef's beady eyes followed him.

Leon cursed. How would he get to the cellars now?

"Here," said someone.

Leon glanced to his side and put out his hands in time to grab a plate that held a huge pie. The plate wobbled, but Leon held it steady. When someone rested another plate on the crook of his arm, however, Leon couldn't balance it and the plate shattered on the floorboards. He cursed. The monobrowed chef glared at him.

"I'll take this," said Leon, picking up a huge silver tray that held a whole deer before anyone could hand him more plates.

He shuffled out of the kitchen with the other waiters and before the door swung shut, he glanced back. The monobrowed chef's angry stare was fixed on him.

Leon's heart pounded as he followed the waiters up the marble stairs. How would he get past the chef? He needed to reach Elena and Pierce in the cellar before someone found them.

The waiters and Leon strode through a door and emerged into the Golden Hall. Shimmering tapestries hung from marbled walls, golden statues glinted, and raucous laughter and mouth-watering smells sprung from the long table in the hall's centre. Above it all, painted on the domed ceiling, was a panting of King Lerbert IV flying with the Archangels. Payan highborns and Vahrian councillors sat around the table, tearing into piles of food.

Inquisitor Walter Drayton sat midway along the table.

Leon's heart skipped a beat. He stopped. The waiter behind him cursed and skirted around him. Leon's heart pounded. The inquisitor sat with his back to Leon and his cane lent against his chair. If Drayton turned and saw Leon –

Leon dashed back out the door, still holding the tray of deer. "It's undercooked. Got to take it back."

The other waiters muttered. Leon bumped into a waiter as he pushed open the door and a few highborns sitting at the table turned to see what made the noise. Leon stumbled into the corridor. He looked back into the Golden Hall and as the door swung shut, Drayton turned to smile at Leon.

Chapter 20

Leon staggered into the cellar.

"What took you so long?" asked Elena.

"I got held up."

His hands shook. He'd walked through the kitchens without the monobrowed chef stopping him, but now he had bigger problems.

Did Drayton recognise me?

Leon had shaved since they'd last met and he wore a waiter's uniform, but would it fool an inquisitor?

Pierce scrambled around a stack of wine barrels and unbuttoned Leon's shirt.

Leon swiped away Pierce's hand. "I'll do it."

Pierce clenched his sword. "Hurry. If they find us here –"

"I'm getting it, alright?"

Leon unbuttoned the rest of his shirt with shaking hands and pulled out the sack of gunpowder pressed against his skin. Pierce wrenched it out of Leon's hands. Half tripping over a wine barrel, he ripped open the bag. Gunpowder poured onto the floor. Pierce tore two other bags and added to the pile. Then he unwound the fuse line.

Leon lent towards Elena. "Drayton's in the banquet hall."

"Shit. He got here fast."

Pierce wove the fuse line between shelves to give them enough time to escape, too focused on his task to hear Leon and Elena.

"At least this'll stop him hunting us," she said.

She grinned, but it looked forced. Did she feel guilty about blowing up the Payan servants along with the Vahrians? Or was she just nervous?

Leon swallowed. "I think he saw me."

"What?" said Elena.

Pierce frowned at them from behind the shelf. He'd unravelled most of the line, but still needed more distance to give them enough of a delay.

"You saw a boar stuffed inside another boar, Leon?" she said.

Pierce turned back to the fuse. Elena lent towards Leon's ear. Her warm breath washed over his chin and she whispered, "If Drayton saw you, soldiers will be down here any minute."

"They're probably searching the Palace now," said Leon. "We don't have time to set up this gunpowder and reach the riser."

"Just a few seconds," Pierce said, more to himself than to anyone else.

Leon grabbed Elena. "If we want to find Waverrym, we've got to reach the riser."

She chewed her lip. Her eyes darted between Leon and Pierce, who crouched between them and the exit, laying the end of the fuse line on the ground.

The door burst open. The monobrowed chef strode inside and goggled at Leon and the gunpowder on the floor.

"Guards –"

131

Pierce whirled and slashed his sword across the chef's throat. Blood splattered Pierce's coat, showered Leon's face, and sprayed onto the floor. The gurgling chef tottered back into the kitchens. Chefs and waiters gaped. The cellar door swung shut and screams filled the air.

Pierce grabbed a wine barrel and rammed it behind the door.

Leon cursed. "That's our only way out!"

Pierce shoved another barrel behind the door. The tendons in his neck stood out like cords of rope.

"No," he said. "It's the only way in."

He whipped around, snarling and blood-splattered. Pierce pulled a match from his cloak and held it above the pile of gunpowder.

"Death to the Vahrians!" he said.

He lit the match.

Leon tackled Pierce. They crashed into a stack of barrels, winding Leon, and the match flew from Pierce's hand, falling towards the gunpowder.

Leon lashed out with his boot and kicked the match. The match knocked into a barrel and landed beside the gunpowder and Elena stomped on it to extinguish the flame. Leon stumbled up, heart racing. Pierce sprawled amongst the barrels with unfocused eyes and blood trickled from his temple.

"You killed him!" said Elena.

"No, he's still breathing."

She pushed past Leon and crouched beside Pierce, feeling his neck for a pulse. People shouted outside the cellar door. Leon cursed. Guards would be here any moment.

"We've got to go," he said.

Leon pushed aside the barrels blocking the door. Elena hoisted Pierce up. Pierce's eyes rolled and he moaned as she pulled his arm over her shoulder, taking up his weight.

"Leave him, or we'll never escape," said Leon.

"We can't leave him!"

Armoured footsteps clanked in the distance.

Elena's eyes watered. "I can't carry him alone."

He deserves death. He would've killed me!

Leon grabbed the door handle. He was sick of the voice in his head, sick of filling his mind with fear, and sick of remembering his cowardice. Most of all, he hated how the voice was always right.

But that doesn't mean I have to listen.

He released the handle, strode to Elena, and grabbed Pierce's other side, hauling him up. Together, they staggered through the door.

The monobrowed chef lay in a pool of spreading blood, gurgling. Leon's stomach heaved, but he gritted his teeth and forced the nausea back down into his stomach. Apart from the twitching chef, the room was empty. Leon glanced out the window. The riser was so close, but now it might as well have been on another disc.

Soldiers burst through the kitchen door. Leon cursed. They were trapped.

He looked back at the window. "Elena! The window!"

Somehow, she understood. They dragged Pierce to the window. Soldiers leapt over benches, scattering knives and smashing plates as they raced towards them. Leon looked out the window. He gulped. The grass loomed far below. A fall from this height could kill them, but what choice did they have? Leon nodded at Elena, who nodded back and clenched her jaw.

Then they hurled themselves into the window.

Glass shattered and pain sliced across Leon's hands and Elena grunted and Pierce moaned and everything spun around them and –

They crashed into the lawn. Pain spiked through Leon's ankles and his knees cracked into the ground. He and Elena stumbled up, cursing, and they dragged Pierce towards the riser while shouts echoed from the kitchen above them. Pierce pulled down on them with what must've been a hundred and sixty pounds of shambling dead weight. Leon grunted, and cursed, and panted. Fire burnt through his arms and blood dripped from his cut hands.

The Palace's doors slammed open. Soldiers poured out, armour rattling, and clanked towards them. Leon and Elena quickened their slow shuffle to the riser.

Leon panted. Pierce was too damn heavy.

"How are we getting down?" he asked.

"Have to jump," said Elena.

"Are you crazy? It's three hundred feet deep!"

The soldiers were a bow shot away and closing.

"There's water at the bottom," said Elena.

"You can't swim!"

She gulped. "I know. You'll have to help me."

"It ain't deep enough."

"It has to be."

They reached the riser's edge. Hot air blasted them, rippling the crinkled skin of Leon's face and making Elena's hair stand on end.

"We can't jump," he roared over the gushing air. "We'll die!"

"It'll be fine! The riser will slow us."

The soldiers were seconds away. In the darkness of night, their helmets made them look like a herd of stampeding animals.

"We don't have a choice!" said Elena.

Leon swallowed. "No. We can surrender."

Elena cursed. She grabbed him around the back, and pushed, and Leon yelled as they fell into the riser.

Hot air ripped the scream from his mouth. His foot clipped the wall and he bounced out of Elena's grip, pain lancing through his foot. Rocky walls flashed past him. He hurled towards the bubbling water, heart hammering. All he could think was that a fall was a pitiful way for an angel to die.

Chapter 21

A hand grasped the back of Leon's jacket. The jacket yanked him back and his limbs whipped forward as he slowed. He glanced up. Elena held him with one hand and Pierce with the other, her wings half-unfolded above her.

Water hit Leon. The impact slapped the breath out of his lungs and drove water up his nose. He slammed into the metal ground. Bubbles flumed around him. He rose but the surface was too far away, and his sodden uniform dragged him down until his boots hit the ground once more. Lungs straining, darkness frayed the edges of his vision.

He clenched his teeth. *I ain't dying here.*

Leon kicked. He pushed off the ground and floated up. Bile crawled up his throat as he tore at the water with his bleeding hands –

His head broke the surface.

He coughed. Snot streamed from his nose and he gasped sweet-tasting air while the hot water bubbled around him. Elena's head burst through the surface. Pierce's body floated beside her and she flailed at the water, struggling to keep them both afloat. Her eyes were wide and she panted so loud the sound echoed off the rock. Leon grabbed her and Pierce and dragged them over to the wall. Elena scrambled up onto a rocky shelf that protruded over the water. With shaking hands, she helped Leon shove Pierce onto the rock.

"See?" Her voice trembled. "That wasn't so bad."

"They're still alive!" said a soldier.

Leon glanced up, blinking water out of his eyes. Far above, standing on the riser's edge, a clump of Vahrian soldiers peered down at them.

The soldiers started climbing.

Leon's heart sunk. They were trapped and this time they didn't even have a window to leap through.

"We've got to find that Path to Waverrym!" said Elena.

"What good will it do?" His limbs ached as he treaded water. "The soldiers will be down here in minutes."

"Remember the verse? It says, 'find the path to safety.' If we find whatever that is, we'll be alright."

Elena's voice shook as she said this. Leon doubted she believed her own words. But whatever slim hope she offered was better than resigning himself to death. He wanted nothing more than to clamber onto the rock and pass out, but he forced himself to swim around the pool.

"Look for the Archangel's Mark," Elena said. "The one with the circles inside the circles –"

"I know what the Mark looks like!"

Leon glanced up. The soldiers were a third of the way down the rocky walls. High above them, silhouetted against the force field, a cloaked figure stood on the riser's edge, bent crooked over a cane.

Drayton.

Leon swallowed and swam faster, diving underwater to investigate the ground. His tired muscles shrieked as he scoured the pool, searching for something that looked unusual.

When his lungs felt ready to burst, he resurfaced. "Nothing!"

The soldiers were halfway down.

The Sarahk said we'd find something here. There must be a gate, a hidden door, some way to escape!

But no symbols gleamed underwater. No hidden doors stuck out from the rock face.

Leon's heart sunk. The Sarahk's riddle was just a stupid verse. A dumb snippet of useless wisdom that meant nothing and led nowhere. The path to safety ... Waverrym ... *Why'd I fall for that shit?*

"There's nothing here." Leon's voice was flat. "We've got to get away."

Elena paced on the rocky ledge. "How?"

"Fly."

"But I can't take off! I don't have a run up."

"Do a standing take off."

She gulped. "With you on my back? I can barely do it by myself!"

"We don't have a choice!"

He clambered up onto the ledge. Above, the soldiers were two-thirds of the way down. Leon climbed onto Elena's back and she grunted, dropping a little. Then she stiffened and held his weight.

"Hold on," she said. "What about Pierce?"

Leon scowled at the boy sprawled on the rocks beside them. "Leave him."

"But –"

"You're struggling to carry me. Ain't room for him as well."

Elena's hands clenched into fists. Her body shook and Leon

almost slid off. For a second he thought she was about to throw him in the water. Then she re-adjusted position.

"You're right." Her voice wavered. "Just us two, then."

Mounted on her back, Leon couldn't see her eyes, but he could tell she was crying. He glanced up. The soldiers were seconds away from reaching them.

"I can't do this," she said. "You're too heavy, I don't have a run up –"

"C'mon, like we practiced," he said, trying to sound calm. "Extend your wings. Feel the riser."

Her wings stretched out and her feathers ruffled in the hot air rising from the bubbling water.

Leon's heart pounded. "Lean forward, and *fly*."

She toppled forward. His stomach lurched and he braced himself for the fall, but her wings beat down and they lifted into the air. She dropped and Leon's feet splashed into the water, but once more her wings bit into the air and they rose and hot air gusted up from below, pushing them up, and then they were rising, rising, rising.

"Turn!" he said.

She banked and they skimmed past the rocky wall, clipping a startled soldier.

"Sharper," he said.

She dipped lower and they shot away from the wall and corkscrewed up through the air. Soldiers cursed as Leon and Elena shot past them. Leon's head swirled with dizziness and blackness crept into his vision.

"Don't pass out," he said.

He wasn't sure if he meant that for Elena, or himself.

His head pounded from the strain of their upwards corkscrew. She yelled. The rocky walls blurred around them and with a scream of triumph from Elena, or Leon, or both, they shot out of the riser.

Below, the Queen's Palace, the gardens, and all of Antonia shrunk to the size of a child's play set. Leon and Elena put on their breathfung and glided through the force field.

Silence.

From here, floating in space, Antonia's force field was black as tar. Elena turned and looked at Leon. He pointed at New Kion, the nearest disc, and Elena glided towards it. Leon clung to her back.

The silence of space felt odd after the clamour of the Palace, but the abyss around Leon was nothing against what he felt within.

He glowered. Minutes ago, his heart had pounded, but now, all that adrenaline had faded. Funny. One moment, he'd been high on anticipation. Next second, he'd realised he'd been a deluded fool. He was stupid to believe in Waverrym, and that stupidity had almost killed him.

~ ~ ~

Leon and Elena glided through New Kion's force field. Noise swarmed up to them from the bustling, labyrinthine streets below, and Leon traced the patterns of the alleys, trying to distract himself from the numbness spreading through his body.

They glided down. Highborn mansions stood proud amongst the smaller fungcrete dwellings, defined by stone walls and flat roofs: perfect for angels to land on. Leon pointed to an alley. Before the War, they could've landed on a mansion and the servants would have a pegasus-drawn cart ready by the time they descended the marble staircase. Now, any highborns who'd kept their mansions served Vahria. They'd greet Leon and Elena with spears instead of champagne.

They glided into an alley. Elena's wings snagged a clothesline strung between two buildings and wet trousers flopped onto Leon's head as they landed. He stumbled off Elena's back.

"Shit," she said. "We left Pierce behind!"

He scowled and brushed the trousers away. "Good. He almost killed us."

She kicked a twig and it skittered along the cobblestones. "How can you say that? We abandoned him. He'll be on an inquisitor's rack by now and it's our fault."

"I'd feel sorry if he hadn't tried to blow us up."

He'd already abandoned too many people. What did it matter if he added another corpse to the pile?

Elena stamped her foot. "The verse said we'd find the Path to Waverrym. Why didn't we?"

Leon sighed. "Waverrym ain't real, girl."

"But you're the one who solved the riddle."

His bruised knees ached, his back twanged, and the cuts on his hands stung. Karym's horns, he was tired.

"Riddle means nothing," he said. "Just words. Ain't no secret Path hidden in the Sarahk, ain't no Waverrym, and I ain't indulging your fool's quest any longer."

He stormed away. Elena ran after him, grabbed his collar, and yanked him back.

Leon growled. "Going to stop me leaving?"

"We must've misread the clue. Is there another riser in Antonia?"

141

"No."

She drummed her fingers against her forehead, frowning. "'Find the heart of nobility' ... is there another disc more royal than Antonia?"

"No."

"'Find the soul of the realm' ... what if Antonia isn't the centre?"

Leon yanked his collar out of her hand. He strode away, longing for the warmth of an inn, the comfort of ale, and the softness of a bed.

"'Find the lungs of Severym' ..."

He stopped. "What?"

"'Find the lungs of Severym.' Third line of the verse. Don't see how we misread that, though."

Leon stroked his chin and fresh energy coursed through him. Why hadn't he thought of this before?

Don't get your hopes up. This idea's even more foolish than the last.

He swallowed. If he told her what he was thinking, he'd be opening up to fresh pain. Besides, his idea was stupid.

Stay silent. Walk away. Forget the damn quest.

"That line can only mean a riser, right?" Elena asked.

"No. It could mean something else."

Chapter 22

"What do you know about the Mahroque era?" Leon asked as he and Elena hurried through New Kion's busy streets.

"Er ..."

"We talked about it in the cave."

"Hold your pegasi, I'm remembering ... something to do with King Mahroque?"

Leon rolled his eyes. "You'd hope so, given that's how we name eras."

"I'm not done! King Mahroque ruled during the Neebian Exodus?"

"Question, or statement?"

Elena and Leon split to avoid a pegasus-drawn carriage. When they joined up again, she said, "Statement."

"Good. What was the Neebian Exodus?"

"Bunch of silly wingless commoners got angry with angels ruling everything and not caring for them. They revolted. Dumb idea. Without wings, you're useless in space."

Leon stared at the cobblestones and thought of his mother. *Silly commoners, eh?*

Her eyes widened. "Oh. Sorry, I forgot you –"

"What happened to the commoners?" he asked.

"Leaders got hung. The other revolutionaries got exiled to Neebia."

They looked up. Neebia was visible above the rooftops. The planet – around which Paya's Discs orbited – was a tiny blue dot. It was hard to imagine those exiled commoners populating that dot, forming Vahria, and returning to conquer Paya. Leon wished those revolutionaries had died along with their leaders. Then he'd still have his wings, and Blas, and Juliana.

"What did King Mahroque do after the revolution?" he asked.

"Um …"

"If you don't know, just say it. No use pretending you've got the answer when you don't."

He realised he'd stolen that from Professor Nane, his astronomy teacher from the Academy. He smiled. She'd like that. If only she was here to see him.

"Alright, I don't know," said Elena.

"He realised it wasn't just the revolutionaries who hated him. Lots of commoners thought the highborns and the angels were too powerful, too greedy, and too dismissive of common folk. So Mahroque built universities, homes, temples, and statues to appease them."

Leon led Elena down a narrow laneway.

"These statues were of a particular style," he said. "They showed Archangels with their heart outside their body, to show how angels cared for common folk. Stupid, eh? If they cared, they would've spent money on bread and homes instead of statues. Commoners can't eat stone. Anyway, this type of sculpture became known as the Mahroque style."

"And?"

"Well, you'll see in a moment."

They emerged into a small square, overlooked by the inn they'd stayed in for their first few nights in Anshan. A shrine in the middle of the square held stone-carved Archangel statues with their hearts outside their chests. On the shrine's plinth was the Archangel's Mark: a large circle containing nine smaller circles, which each held nine dots. The Mark represented the Star Spectre, her nine Major Archangels, and the eighty-one Minor Archangels beneath them.

"Alright," said Elena. "So these are Maroque sculptures. What's your point besides the history lesson?"

"Don't dismiss the past." Leon prowled around the sculptures, looking for Severym. "It's the key to the future. Ah ha!"

He pointed at the sculpture of Severym. Like the others, the statue showed the Archangel of the Risers with his heart exposed, but Severym's heart wasn't the only protruding organ.

Below the heart, Severym's lungs stood out on his chest.

Elena's eyes widened. "Marym's tongue! It was in front of us all this time."

"Severym's lungs ain't the only organs on display." Leon pointed to Harym, Archangel of home, hearth, and food. Her torso bulged in a poor attempt to emphasize her stomach. "Maroque sculptures don't just express the kindness of angels by showing their hearts. They also show each Archangel's gifts. Look damn stupid, if you ask me."

Elena and Leon ran their hands over Severym's lungs. They pushed, pulled, twisted, tapped, whispered prayers, kicked, punched, and elbowed, but the lungs lacked any hidden mechanism.

They were stone. Nothing else.

Elena nursed her bruised elbow. "Leon, wait. King Maroque ruled a thousand years ago –"

"Started in 542 AGD. That's more like three thousand years ago."

"Well, that's the thing. He ruled 542 years *after* the Great Departure of the Archangels. The Archangels made the Path to Waverrym so the worthy could find them –"

"So you say."

"– but wouldn't that mean anything made after the Archangels left couldn't lead to Waverrym? They would've made the Path before the Departure, right?"

"Oh. Yeah."

"I still think you're on to something."

He glowered. "No. This was stupid."

Elena gulped. "I didn't mean –"

"Wait!"

"Er, yes?"

"The Maroque style wasn't original. Karym's horns, it was too weird to be original. No, it was based on sculpture from the Age of Archangels, before the Departure. Yes, they made this shrine in the Maroque era, but if we can find sculptures from the Age of Archangels –"

"It'll lead to Waverrym!"

"Maybe."

No it won't, you fool. It'll only lead to more disappointment.

"But where can we find sculptures like that?" asked Elena. "They'd have to be over three thousand years old."

Forget this. This idea's even more stupid than the last.

Leon scowled. Once, that voice in his head had been so strong. Once, that voice kept him working at the port: kept him numb, yet throbbing with phantom pains. Kept him trapped in the past, yet desperate to forget. The voice kept him safe, yes, but also doomed him.

He chewed his lip, avoiding Elena's eyes. He could say he didn't know where to find such ancient sculptures and her hope would evaporate. Or, he could tell her. Fan that fragile flame burning in her eyes and fan the spark within him, too. But what if he was wrong?

"I know where we'll find them." He set his shoulders and looked at Elena. "The All-Temple."

~ ~ ~

"Find the soul of the realm ..." Elena gaped at the All-Temple. "This is it, Leon. I know it."

The Temple's great dome pierced the air above them. Yet Leon wasn't awed by the dome, or the soaring spire upon it, or the towering walls, or the huge carved friezes. No. Awe was reserved for Elena and for his past self.

What awed him now was how empty the All-Temple was. When he'd visited before the War, a constant stream of offerings flowed inside, carried atop droves of worshipers. Now, that stream was a trickle.

Leon and Elena took their weapons out of their cloaks – they'd exchanged their waiter uniforms for more nondescript clothing soon after landing. Before entering the temple, they left their weapons with a priest and shuffled inside. The air had the musty, stagnant smell of a room that needed airing. Leon swallowed. Last time he'd visited, he'd hadn't worried about surrendering his weapon, but now the lack of his dagger's weight made his skin prickle.

They passed through a hulking doorway, where the Archangel's Mark was engraved into the open door, then emerged into the temple's heart. Elena gaped at the huge domed ceiling. Despite himself, Leon glanced up and the corners of his lips twitched. Built by the Archangels, no one knew exactly what the dome was made from, though when Leon climbed to the Whispering Gallery as a young angel, he'd tapped the dome and it pinged like metal.

A painting of the Archangels covered the dome and sunlight fell through the hole in the dome's centre, illuminating a circular altar. That beam of light represented the Star Spectre. Nine alcoves pierced the temple's circular wall and each held a statue of one of the nine Major Archangels. Above them, the eighty-one Minor Archangels stood in smaller niches.

Leon looked away from the statues. Spiderwebs filled the corners, cracks lined the tiled floor, and everything was coated in a carpet of dust and dirt.

Elena pointed to the alcove that contained Severym. Leon nodded. They shuffled towards the alcove, walking around Payans lying prostrate on the ground. The dusty floor muffled their footsteps.

A red cloak rippled in the shadows. Leon froze. He almost cursed, but remembered where he was at the last moment.

"Inquisitor," Leon said to Elena, jerking his head towards the cloaked figure standing in the gloom.

Vahrians didn't worship Archangels, but they allowed Payans to do so. Having heard tales of Vahrians bombing temples in the War, Leon supposed this was a kind gesture, but the price of this freedom was that inquisitors monitored every temple.

Elena swallowed. "Let's just get to Severym."

They reached the statue. A wispy-haired female priest crouched before the kind-faced Archangel. As Leon and Elena also knelt, the priest stood and touched Severym's exposed lungs.

"Send down a saviour, gracious Severym," said the priest. "And restore Paya to her rightful glory."

The priest shuffled away.

"She touched the lungs, but nothing happened," said Leon.

Elena stood. "She's not an angel. Something different might happen if we try."

Leon glanced at the inquisitor. The man's shadowy hood made it impossible to see if he was watching them. Elena touched the stone-carved lungs of Severym. She yelped.

Worshipers scowled at her and the inquisitor's hood shifted.

Elena drew back her hand and showed Leon the spot of blood swelling from her fingertip. "It pricked me."

He frowned and tapped the lungs. A sharp pain jolted his finger and when he pulled his hand back a dot of his blood stained the marble lungs, beneath the dot left by Elena.

A tile slid back on the floor in front of Severym. Leon and Elena gaped. Beneath the pulled-back tile, a ladder led down a vertical tunnel, fading into darkness.

"Elena –"

"I see it!"

This is it. The Path is real!

He stepped towards the tunnel, ready to climb down the ladder.

"Halt," said someone.

Leon glanced around and cursed. The red-cloaked inquisitor was striding towards them.

The inquisitor stepped over a kneeling Payan. "You two!

Come here."

The priest trotted over to the striding inquisitor. "Sir, please whisper, for this is a place of worship –"

The inquisitor pushed the priest away. Angry mutters echoed from the kneeling Payans. A stocky man rose behind the inquisitor, and before the inquisitor could turn, the man punched his head. The inquisitor cracked into the floor.

The priest's eyes widened. "My child, you shouldn't have."

"He pushed you, Mother," said the man.

The man glanced at Leon. It was Rufus, the scowling armorer who worked for the Resistance.

Rufus frowned. "Where's Pierce?"

Leon gulped, glanced at Elena, then looked at the tunnel that had opened in the floor. He'd been so distracted that he'd almost forgotten it existed.

"He got captured," said Elena.

"Captured?" said Rufus.

"Don't have time to explain," said Leon. "We've got to go."

"No." Rufus stalked towards them, eyes narrowed. "Explain, now."

Leon burned with frustration. They didn't have time for this. He locked eyes with Elena and she nodded.

"We'll explain later." Leon edged towards the hole. "Promise."

Elena scrambled into the hole. Leon scurried in after her, clambered down the ladder, and slammed the tile above him back into place.

They climbed down through the darkness. Rufus bellowed for them to come back and he hammered on the tile, but it held firm and his pounding faded as Leon and Elena descended. Leon pulled a glowfung out of his new cloak

– they'd replaced their waiter uniforms before entering the temple – and a dim, purple light filled the tunnel. His heart pounded. He'd been on the verge of abandoning this quest, but now the Sarahk's verse had led to a secret passage hidden in Anshan's biggest temple. The Path was real.

The ladder ended. They dropped out of the tunnel and landed in a small room. Leon raised his glowfung to light the chamber. His heart sunk. No exit.

The floor jolted. His balance faltered, but Elena kept him from falling. He gaped. They were moving, yet the walls stayed fixed in place. Their room was ferrying them down through the rock.

Leon swallowed. The back of his neck tingled. Was it his imagination, or were the walls tightening around him? As they descended, he thought of all the dirt and rock they were passing through and a horrible thought crossed his mind.

"How are we going to get out?" he asked.

Elena's eyes darted away. "I don't know."

He gulped. What if their box descended forever? No, it couldn't do that. They'd stop when they hit bedsteel, right? He tried to think of something else to say to take his mind off their descent, but couldn't come up with anything. He gulped again. How long had they been in here?

The box stopped. Elena frowned and Leon smacked the wall. A clang of metal rang around their small box.

"We're trapped!" he said.

"Calm down." Elena's head jerked from side to side. "We're going to be fine."

"Karym's horns. Why did I get into this?"

Please. In his head, he listed all the Archangels he could remember. *If you help us escape, I swear I'll –*

One wall of the box-like room slid open with a scrape of metal. Leon breathed out. He held up his glowfung to light the way and they stepped into a room with a steel door at the end. The curved walls flowed into the floor and ceiling with no trace of an edge: it was as if they'd entered a steel cavern. Large tiles decorated half the floor, with each tile featuring a mosaic of an Archangel. The part where Leon and Elena stood wasn't tiled. Instead, they stood on a floor made from the same smooth steel as the walls and ceiling.

Elena walked forward, gaping. "So much metal."

"We're inside the bedsteel."

"That's impossible."

"The Archangels made the discs. If they made this ... who knows what's possible?"

Elena's boot landed on a tile. Leon's neck tingled. He yanked her back as a hatch opened in the ceiling and a beam of blinding light shot onto the tile. Heat slapped his face. They fell and shuffled away from the terrible heat.

The beam vanished. The hatch in the ceiling closed and darkness swelled to fill the room. After the beam of light, the purple radiance of Leon's glowfung was pitiful.

His heart hammered. "You alright?"

"Fine."

She staggered up. The beam had sliced off the tip of her right boot and the air stunk of burnt leather.

Leon gulped. "This place is trapped – like the tombs of those crazy Mahricans!"

He turned to get back in the box that had taken them here, but the door had shut.

He cursed. "Karym's horns! We're dead!"

Elena chewed her lip. "No. We can get through this. Just

calm down."

No. I don't want to be calm! I want to scream and pound the walls and curse for being dumb enough to meet you.

He took a deep breath. A thought came to him and he tilted his head to the side.

"What is it?" Elena asked.

"Thinking." He scratched his chin. "Even Mahrican tombs had a safe path through the trap-rooms, because they had to let the priests in. So there must be a safe way to cross these tiles."

"Okay. I stepped on a tile with Karym's face. I'm guessing we avoid those?"

"No crap."

Leon surveyed the tiles. They covered an area of the floor that measured fifteen feet wide and ten feet long. Each square tile was a foot-and-a-half wide. Two hundred tiles in total. Elena might be able to fly over them, but the ceiling was too low for her to flap, and then how would he cross?

The faces of the nine Major Archangels – one Archangel per tile – formed most of the tiles. Waverrym's, Karym's, and Marym's faces dominated. The remaining tiles showed the eighty-one Minor Archangels, with one tile per Minor Archangel.

Elena took out the Sarahk and leafed through the pages.

"What are you doing?" Leon asked.

"We're trying to find the Path to Waverrym, right?"

"Yeah."

"So won't we be safe on the Waverrym tiles?"

His eyes narrowed. They could reach the other side by stepping only on those tiles, although they'd need to jump at the end.

"Maybe," he said. "But that doesn't feel right. Give me the Sarahk."

She handed it to him. Leon's skin tingled. It'd been decades since he'd held the Sarahk, but the leather bound-book slotted into his hands like it had never left his grip.

Don't be stupid. It's just a book.

Leon flipped through. He took a deep breath of stale air and panic jolted through him. This place was unventilated. They'd suffocate if they stayed here too long.

Then solve the damn puzzle and get out of here.

He found *Karym's Treachery*, and read, "'Karym's wife, Marym, found the corpse of Waverrym, the Archangel Karym had killed in a jealous rage. Karym soothed her with his silver tongue. Despite their bond of love, Marym chose the righteous path and told the other Archangels of Karym's treachery. 'Murder!' The Archangel Marym cried. 'The vilest deed!' Marym led the Archangels into the wormhole where Karym had hidden Waverrym's body.

"'The Archangels wept and the Star Spectre morphed Waverrym's corpse into a disc to honour the dead Archangel. This disc was named in his honour and filled with angels who dedicated their lives and their descendant's lives to honouring Waverrym.

"'The Archangels cast Karym down to Neebia. They imprisoned him and his followers in the planet's fiery bowels, where he reigns over Hell.'"

"I know the story," said Elena. "But how does it help?"

"Don't you see?" He pointed to a tile bearing Marym's face. "Marym led the Archangels to Waverrym. She'll lead us there too."

Leon removed his boot and dropped it onto a tile of Marym.

He drew back his hand, but no light shot from the ceiling.

"See?" he said.

Elena grabbed the boot and put it on the tile she'd stood on before. Again, no beam of light incinerated it.

Leon's smile faded. "Must be weight-activated."

Elena let out a frustrated breath.

"Got any better ideas?" he asked.

"Sadly, no."

"Fine. Ladies first?"

"It's your theory, old man."

"Yes, it is." Leon waited. "Oh. That means you want me to go first?"

"If you're too scared –"

"No. I'll do it."

He raised a trembling foot above a tile of Marym. Sweat streaked down his spine and the bumps and seams of his cloak pressed against his body. He licked his lips. The tile was one row in from where he stood, so he'd need to hop to reach it. If his theory was wrong, he couldn't jump away like Elena had.

His leg wobbled. If he didn't jump soon, his leg was liable to give away. He grit his teeth. Muttered a prayer to the Archangels.

And jumped.

Chapter 23

Leon's foot landed on the tile of Marym. He tensed, waiting for the beam of burning light.

Nothing happened.

Elena punched the air and hooted. "You did it!"

"Course I did," he grumbled. "Make sure you follow my footsteps."

He turned away so Elena couldn't see his huge grin.

Tension flowed out of his muscles and warmth spread through him as he walked across the tiles, stepping only on mosaics of Marym. Elena followed. They crossed without incident and pushed through the metal door. Ahead, a corridor stretched away into darkness.

"Safe?" she asked.

"Karym's horns! I doubt it, but there ain't no other way."

They tiptoed down the corridor. Leon's glowfung cast a shallow pool of purple light, but beyond that, darkness pressed upon them, as heavy and dense as the steel above their heads.

Leon's shoulder muscles bunched up. As they followed the corridor's curve, Elena gripped his hand. He swallowed. Without her beside him, he would've curled into a quivering ball on the floor long ago. He squeezed her hand and she squeezed back.

The corridor ended in another steel door.

"Want to go first this time?" he asked.

"Together."

They pushed open the door. Teeth clenched, Leon stepped into another room and Elena walked in beside him.

Nine corridors punched shadowy holes in the opposite wall. A painting of Waverrym adorned the ceiling and a small plaque was fixed to the wall, inscribed with Old Payese. It took Leon a few moments to translate.

"'Let the Archangel be your guide,'" he read. "Hmm. I'm guessing eight of those corridors lead to death."

"Oh, really? I thought whoever made this wanted to give us nine identical ways to reach our destination."

"Sarcasm doesn't suit you."

Leon narrowed his eyes. Each corridor was taller than an average person and the widths varied between fifteen to twenty-one feet.

Let the Archangel be your guide. What did that mean?

"Can we throw things down them to find the safe one?" she asked.

"If it's anything like the tiles, it'll only activate if it senses a person."

He glanced up at the Waverrym painting. He'd seen paintings of the Archangel before, but this one seemed so real, like Waverrym was hovering right above them.

"Hmm," he said. "Waverrym, the Archangel ..."

Elena's eyes widened. "Nine corridors. One for each Major Archangel."

"Not bad, lass. Okay, nine corridors ... nine Major Archangels ... but which is safe?"

157

He looked again at Waverrym. *Let the Archangel be your guide.*

"Pass me the Sarahk," he said.

She gave him the book. He flicked through until he found the right page.

"*Guide to the Children of the Archangels*," he said. "'Let the Archangel be your guide' – maybe this is what that means. Hmm ... Most of this is about the Archangels' first descendants, but if I remember right, there's a verse that describes – aha!"

He showed Elena.

"Wingspans of the Archangels?" She frowned. "What's that got to do with this?"

Leon's hands shook with excitement. "It says, 'Waverrym's wingspan was fifteen feet and five inches.'"

"So?"

"We find the tunnel matching Waverrym's wingspan. That's why he's painted on the ceiling!"

Leon smiled. It all made sense! He couldn't measure the painting of Waverrym, because it was too far away, but it seemed like an accurate one-to-one reproduction of the Archangel, with a wingspan matching the number given in the Sarahk. That was why the painting looked so lifelike – because it was the exact size of its nine-foot-tall subject.

"How do we measure the corridors?" asked Elena

"My feet are about an inch shorter than a foot."

"About?"

"Well, that's what they measured at the Academy."

"Twenty years ago."

"Feet don't change."

She raised an eyebrow.

"Once you're an adult, they stop growing," he said.

"If you say so."

Leon removed his boots and paced out the corridors' widths. After several minutes of measuring and a few more to double-check, he put his boots back on.

He pointed. "This one."

"Sure?"

"Yeah."

"Sure you're sure?"

"Shit, no."

She sighed. "Great."

"Don't worry. I'll go first."

"No. I trust you."

She stepped up beside him and together they walked into the corridor.

No blinding light. No incineration.

Leon exhaled.

Elena smirked. "For someone so confident, you look relieved."

"This is my normal face."

They shuffled along the corridor. Leon smiled. Despite the death traps surrounding them, he hadn't been this happy since the Academy. After all those years of drudgery, locked in a prison of ale and regret, he finally felt alive.

He felt like an angel.

They entered another room. Leon gaped. He and Elena stood on a small platform overlooking a pitch-black abyss.

His smile vanished. *Dead end.*

Behind him, the door shut. He hammered on it, but the steel was far stronger than his fist.

Leon's eyes bulged. "We're trapped!"

A sea of darkness surrounded their platform and his glowfung's light failed to penetrate the inky blackness. He leaned over the side. If the abyss had a bottom, it was further than his light could reach.

Tremors shook his hands and he dropped the glowfung. It landed on the platform's edge. Elena grabbed it before it fell into the darkness.

"Careful," she said. "We're ruined without that."

Leon pressed his back against the locked door. Vertigo shot through him. If he leaned forward, gravity would pull him off the tiny platform and claw him down into the abyss.

Elena peered over the edge. She tore off a small clump of glowfung and dropped it into the darkness. Terrified that he'd fall, but too curious to resist, Leon edged forward and watched the light shrink as it fell … fell … fell … and landed on the floor far below.

"So there is a bottom," said Elena.

Light flashed. Leon stumbled back, shielding his eyes. When his vision returned to normal, he squinted down at the floor, but couldn't see the glowfung.

"Vaporised," he said.

"We're not going down there, then." Elena stroked the steel walls. "And there's no way to climb this. Even an ice-pick couldn't carve handholds."

"There's got to be a way through."

He tore off a small patch of glowfung and hurled it into the darkness. It fell in a curved arc, moving away from their platform as it plummeted. Leon waited for the glowfung to hit the floor.

Instead, the glowfung stuck to a wall.

Elena gasped. Leon chewed his lip. The glowfung's

light was too dim to illuminate more than a few feet of its surroundings, but there was no mistaking that it had attached to a wall perhaps one hundred and fifty feet away.

Light flashed. The glowfung disappeared.

"Of course," said Leon. "We need to fly."

"What?"

"This place exists to test us. To make sure only angels can get through. We needed knowledge most commoners lack to solve the first two puzzles, but now, only angels can overcome this obstacle. You'll need your wings, Elena."

She unfurled her wings. In the dim purple light, her feathers looked like they'd been carved from obsidian.

She frowned. "What about you?"

Pain raced through the stubs on Leon's shoulder-blades.

"You go," he said. "I'll wait."

"I won't do that. I won't abandon you."

"Karym's horns, I didn't ask that. Fly out there, scout, then come back." He tore the glowfung and gave half to Elena. "Go."

She stared down at the glowfung.

"Any time before we starve to death, please," he said.

"I'll come back, alright?"

"Bloody hell, I trust you, okay? Just get going."

Elena nodded. She walked to the platform's edge, glanced back, then dove into the darkness.

Fear shot through Leon.

What if the light vaporises her?

She soared away from his platform and the glowfung's light bobbled as she flew. A wall loomed ahead of her and she banked away. Her altitude dropped and Leon's heart rate spiked.

She circled. As she regained height, her light illuminated a small platform attached to the wall on the chasm's other side. An empty steel altar sat on the platform.

"Should I land?" she asked.

"Yes!"

She landed on the platform. Her boots skidded on the steel and she gripped the altar to stop herself falling off.

"There's no door," she said.

"I can see that. Is there anything on the altar?"

"Altar?"

"The big hunk of steel in front of you! What did you think it was? A lounge?"

Elena muttered under her breath. She inspected the altar.

"Nothing," she said.

Leon remembered the statue in the All-Temple and how its lungs drew blood from their fingertips to open the trapdoor.

"Touch it," he said.

Elena tapped the altar. "It pricked me."

Leon grinned. His guess was right.

A great rumbling filled the chamber and Leon stumbled back. The steel walls glowed with golden light. Shielding his eyes from the sudden brightness, he gaped as the chasm's floor rose. The room shook, making his legs wobble.

He fell to his knees and warmth spread through him. Warmth like a blanket. Warmth like a campfire. It was almost like he could feel Juliana's embrace.

Tears streaked through the grime that coated his face. Why had he doubted Elena? Why hadn't he believed in the Path left by the Archangels? He covered his face, so Elena couldn't see his tears, and trembled.

Chapter 24

A hand touched his shoulder.

"Leon?" said Elena. "You alright?"

He sniffed, wiped his tears with his cloak, and stood. "Fine."

Elena crouched in front of him. Golden light suffused the walls and the chasm's floor had risen to fill the gap between the platforms, without trace of a seam. Elena had strolled over to him.

They walked to the altar. Leon gaped at the ground. Moments ago, the metal beneath him was nothing but an abyss. He was walking over a void. Flying, almost . . .

Leon walked behind the altar. "There's an inscription."

"Where?"

Leon pointed.

This steel garden is a lonely place,
  watered by legacies of pain.
  May ye not suffer its embrace
  for it is truly the angel's bane.
  Yet in this field of speeding death,
  safety the noble-hearted will find
  in the flowing path of the great Archangel's breath.

Leon's straightened up, frowning at the text, and his heart thumped. The Path to Waverrym was real.

Don't get excited. I ain't finding any angels unless I can solve the riddle. And even if I find angels, I can't bring back Blas, or Juliana.

He scowled.

Stop it. I've had a win, so be happy, damn it.

"That's a verse from the Sarahk," said Elena. "Or close enough, anyway. From *Wisdom of the Star Spectre*: 'Safety the noble-hearted will find in the path of the Archangel's breath.'"

"But the rest ain't from the Sarahk."

A breeze blew on his neck. He glanced over the altar. The door they'd entered through had slid open.

"Got these words remembered?"

"Give me a moment."

They spent a few more minutes re-reading the inscription. Then they walked to the door. Leon spun to view the room one last time and took a huge breath, as if breathing deep enough would draw the room's golden glow into his soul. For a moment, he smelled amethyst poppies – the wildflowers that dotted the fields on Amwedd, where he'd spent weeks camping with Juliana and Blas.

Juliana loved those poppies.

Leon took another breath, but the smell had vanished. He shook his head.

Stop imagining things.

Their path back through the rooms was easier than before. Leon assumed the traps were deactivated, but didn't want to risk it, so they retraced their steps over the tiles and entered the box that had taken them down.

The door slid shut and the box rose.

"Nice work," said Elena.

"You too, lass."

They grinned at each other.

"So what does the riddle mean?" she asked.

"Must lead someplace like this. A secret chamber only angels can find."

"What do the words mean, though? Any ideas?"

"'Angel's bane' could be anything. Nets … trees … space debris … plenty of things can ruin an angel's day."

"It says 'speeding death,' though. Trees and nets don't speed, right?"

"Mmm. True."

"So what goes fast that's bad for angels?"

"Arrows. Asteroids. Airships. And like I said, space debris."

"What's that?"

"Pray you never encounter it. In space, there's no gravity or air friction, so junk flies at insane speeds. Imagine a splinter hitting you at three hundred clicks per hour. Not good."

Elena winced. "Is debris common?"

"Oh yeah. People drop things through the force fields all the time and they keep flying through space until they hit something. Angels are fairly safe, though. Wings create a current that pushes away debris, but some angels still carry shields while flying."

Leon frowned. He'd talked about angels in present tense, like they were still alive.

But was it a mistake? He sure as hell wasn't an angel, but Elena grew more like one with every lesson. And if Waverrym existed, which was looking more likely, and angels lived there like the stories promised …

Elena furrowed her brow. "Do asteroids count as debris?"

165

"I guess, but asteroids are mapped and easy to see. Can't stop 'em with a shield, though."

"What about, 'the flowing path of the Archangel's breath'?"

"Jetstreams."

"Huh?"

"Like wind currents, but they flow through space. Most are well-mapped and angels use 'em like boats use rivers. They're dangerous, though, because they accelerate you without stopping. Safer to fly beside one, not inside it."

"So 'the Archangel's breath' is a jetstream?"

"Probably."

"Alright ... so is there a place with lots of space debris and jetstreams?"

"Well, there's plenty of debris in the decay zone."

"Where?"

Leon blinked. "You don't know?"

"I've never been to this decay zone, so no."

"Plenty of places I ain't been, but it don't mean I'm ignorant of them. Karym's horns! A ten-year old angel could tell me where the decay zone is."

"I didn't train at the Academy, alright? Just tell me where it is."

"You know where Neebia is, yes?"

"I'm no fool."

"Sure act like one, sometimes."

She rolled her eyes.

"Most discs are in the inner regions," he said. "That's the stable orbital zone around Neebia. The rest of the discs are in the outer regions, which is further away, but that ain't important right now. Between the inner regions and Neebia is the decay zone. Discs can't orbit there, because it's too close

166

to the planet and gravity will pull 'em down. This means the decay zone's full of debris spiralling towards Neebia, where it'll crash onto the planet, or burn in the atmosphere."

"So the riddle points to the decay zone?"

"Maybe. Still not sure."

Their box stopped rising. A hatch opened in the ceiling and a ladder glinted in the light of their glowfung. They climbed.

An hour before, Leon's limbs ached from the exertion of running across Antonia and swimming in the riser. Now, fresh energy flooded his muscles. Newfound vigour had replaced his fatigue, just as hope had replaced his doubt.

"What about those other lines?" Elena asked. "'Steel garden' … 'legacies of pain' … something about an 'embrace' … "

"Plenty of iron floating in the decay zone. Plenty of pain, too, for those traveling through it. As for an embrace … might mean Neebia's gravity?" He frowned. "One part don't fit, though. No jetstreams pass through the decay zone, because of the stronger gravity."

"Oh. So that's not it, then?"

"Doubt it."

Elena sighed. Her feet crashed onto the ladder's rungs a little louder.

"Oi," said Leon. "Don't be so damn glum. We found this place and we'll find the next. We can do this. We're angels."

Elena gaped down at Leon as they climbed. She was so busy staring at him that her head bumped into the trapdoor's underside.

Leon smirked. "Watch where you're going."

Elena smiled and rubbed her head. "Thanks for the tip, professor. Now, how do we open this?"

She fiddled with the trapdoor. A crack of light appeared,

and the tile slid open, flooding the tunnel with brightness. Elena scrambled out.

Payans gasped as Leon emerged back into the All-Temple.

"Just checking the foundations," he said.

The trapdoor slid shut. Leon and Elena strode towards the exit.

"Where'd that inquisitor go?" He said as they strolled through the door. "And what about Rufus?"

A meaty hand clasped Leon's arm. "The Vahrian bastard went where you're about to go."

Leon turned. Rufus stood beside him. Six more Resistance fighters stood behind Leon and Elena.

Leon gulped. "We can explain –"

"Oh, don't worry," said Rufus. "You will. Now, let's go outside. Don't want to make a scene in a temple, eh?"

Chapter 25

Rufus marched Leon out of the All-Temple, while another Resistance fighter dragged Elena along beside them.

The bright sunlight made Leon squint. "Can you let us get our weapons?"

Rufus released his arm. Leon gave him a weak half-smile.

A blow cracked Leon's jaw and light exploded behind his eyes. Pain spiked through his head as his back smacked into the cobblestones. He groaned.

Rufus loomed above him and the sun flickered around his head. "Pierce McKillney was a good man and you betrayed him."

No, he was a crazed fanatic.

He yearned to say it, but Leon knew it was best to stay silent. Rufus spat. Saliva struck Leon's face and dribbled down his cheeks. He winced.

"Hey!" Elena tried to hit Rufus, but two Resistance fighters grabbed her. "Let go!"

In the square around them, Payans gaped. No one interfered. Most just glanced away and hurried onward, although a cloaked figure in the square's corner kept staring.

"Get up," said Rufus.

Leon stumbled up. Rufus seized his arm and tugged him through the streets. The other Resistance fighters dragged Elena along.

"Where are you taking us?" she asked.

"Quiet, girl," said Rufus.

Leon scowled. "You can at least tell us –"

Rufus drove his elbow into Leon's stomach. Pain shot through his abdomen and he doubled over, wheezing.

Rufus kept pulling him along. "I said, quiet!"

They walked through the streets. When they passed through a marketplace, a crowd blocked Rufus and Leon from Elena and the other Resistance fighters. Leon's arm twitched in Rufus' iron grip.

"Don't think about running," said Rufus. "You won't get far with a knife in your side."

He flashed a gleaming dagger in front of Leon's nose.

Leon swallowed. "Put it away. I ain't running."

"I think I'll keep it out." Rufus pressed the flat of the knife against Leon's aching back. "How's that feel, *spy*?"

"Karym's horns! We ain't spies. Won't you just –"

Rufus cracked his elbow into Leon's skull. Elena and the other Resistance fighters reached them and they kept walking. Leon glanced back as Rufus tugged him into a laneway.

In the distance, a cloaked woman strode through the bustling marketplace. Leon frowned. Was she the same woman who'd stared at him in the square outside the All-Temple?

Rufus kept marching Leon onward. The cloaked woman ducked behind a cart. Leon swallowed. She was following them.

Should I tell Rufus?

The woman's cloak was brown, but she had to be an inquisitor. If she followed the Resistance to their hideout …

Leon's heart beat fast. The Resistance already thought he and Elena were spies, and having abandoned Pierce in Antonia, Leon doubted he could change their minds. Leading a spy into the hideout could be the distraction they needed to escape.

Do what you have to do to survive.

Rufus led them down a familiar alley and sweat made Leon's hands clammy. Last chance to warn Rufus about the cloaked woman. He glanced at Elena, praying she'd somehow understand his thoughts and give him guidance, but she couldn't read his mind.

This decision was his alone.

Leon looked down at the cobblestones and stayed silent. Rufus led him, Elena, and the other Resistance fighters into a crammed hut and forced them down the ladder into the Resistance's cave.

Shame flooded through Leon as he climbed. *I did the right thing, didn't I? The Resistance can take care of itself, but we've got to find Waverrym.*

Rufus marched Leon and Elena across the sandy floor, towards the tents. Leon looked away from the Resistance fighters as he and Elena stumbled into the central clearing. He'd eaten with these people. Laughed with them.

And now he'd betrayed them.

The inquisitor from the All-Temple knelt in front of Simona, who lounged in her wicker chair. Teo stood behind her, clutching his sword with meaty hands. Blood trickled from the inquisitor's skull, staining the sand, and his hands were chained behind his naked body.

A boot crunched into the back of Leon's leg. He sprawled onto the sand and Rufus made Elena kneel beside him. Leon rose to a crouch, wincing.

Simona rubbed her wrinkled face. "Just when I thought Paya could decay no further, I am betrayed by two *angels*. Angels!"

"We didn't –"

Teo lunged and kicked Leon in the chest. He crumpled, gasping.

"Is that how you survived the War, Leon?" asked Simona. "By cutting a deal with the Vahrians? Dear me. I should have realised your treachery sooner."

Leon's hands clenched into fists and he flushed. "Ain't how I survived the War. Wasn't a traitor then and I ain't a traitor now."

"We're not spies," said Elena. "Just listen! We can explain."

Simona pointed one gnarled finger at the bleeding inquisitor. "That's what he said, my dear. Pray that you do a better job."

Elena swallowed. She glanced at Leon. He was about to explain the story of Waverrym and why they sought it, when a metallic crash echoed in the distance.

"What was that?" Simona asked.

Someone screamed. Everyone turned towards the tunnel with the ladder. A Resistance fighter plummeted out of the tunnel, shrieking, and smacked into the ground with a crack of breaking bone.

Blood bubbled out of his mouth. "Inquisition."

His head slumped into the sand. Leon's chest grew hot. If he'd told Rufus about the woman following them, the man sprawled in the sand would still be alive.

"Oh dear," said Simona.

Before anyone could move, an armoured Vahrian soldier clanked down the ladder and landed with a crash. More soldiers streamed after him. Leon's guts twisted.

What have I done?

A Resistance fighter brandished her sword. "Charge –"

An arrow whistled through the air. It punctured her neck. Her voice cut off in a strangled yelp and she staggered into a tent, which collapsed under her weight. More soldiers flooded into the cavern. Leon gulped. The soldiers outnumbered the Resistance three to one and the Vahrians wore better armour.

Everyone looked to Simona.

She clenched her jaw. "Fight. Fight for Paya!"

Resistance fighters unsheathed their swords, bellowed Archangel's names, and charged at the Vahrians. An arrow toppled one charging Payan, who tripped the woman behind him, but then the Resistance slammed into the soldiers with a clash of steel. Roars and curses and shrieks deafened Leon. A figure loomed over him and he covered his head, even though his bare arms would do nothing to stop a blade.

"Come on," said Elena.

Leon glanced up. Elena stood above him, her hand outstretched. He took her hand and she hoisted him up, and he gaped at the frenzied bodies hacking each other around the cave's entrance. The fight had drawn away the Resistance fighters, leaving Leon and Elena alone.

"There must be a secret escape route," said Elena.

She pointed at Teo, who carried Simona in her chair as he sprinted away from the cave's entrance.

"Let's go," said Leon.

He and Elena sprinted towards Teo and Simona. Leon's heart hammered. They couldn't get too close, or Teo would see them, but they couldn't stray too far back either. Crashing blades and cries of pain echoed through the cavern. Leon's neck prickled. He didn't like having his back to the battle. Too damn easy for an arrow to slice into his spine –

A bow thrummed.

Leon dove onto the sandy ground. An arrow hissed through the air five paces to his right and stabbed into Teo's bicep. The hulking Payan grunted. He fumbled the chair and Simona's frail body toppled onto the sand.

Elena hauled Leon up. He cursed. Teo stopped running, unsheathed his blade, and swung the weapon one-handed towards three soldiers who'd leapt out from behind a tent. Even with one hand, Teo kept the soldiers back, but that didn't help Leon. He needed Teo running. Needed Teo to find an escape route, so they could leave this mess.

A wooden barrel hurled through the air and crashed into Leon. The impact jolted through his elbow and knocked him into Elena, making them sprawl onto the ground. Leon tasted sand. He pushed himself up, groaning, and a blade touched his back. He froze.

"Look up," said a voice.

Leon glanced up, trembling. Rufus towered over him and his sword touched Leon's spine. Blood stained Rufus' shoulder and his left arm dangled at his side. Two other Payans held blades to Elena's neck.

Rufus drew back his sword. "This is for Pierce."

Leon closed his eyes and covered his head with his shaking hands. A sword punctured flesh and someone shrieked. Leon winced. Then he realised he was fine. Leon opened his eyes.

Rufus collapsed, a jagged wound gaping in his chest. A ring of Vahrian soldiers encircled the other two Payans. The Resistance fighters dropped their swords, which hit the sandy ground with muffled thumps. Soldiers slapped handcuffs around the Payans' wrists.

Rufus rolled over and glared at Leon.

"You …" Rufus' gurgling voice was soft. "You … won."

Leon's stomach twisted. "No. We ain't traitors, I swear."

But Rufus' eyes glassed over and his head slumped into a pool of his own blood. Leon gaped. This was his fault.

He glanced at Elena, who sprawled beside him. Her pale face contrasted with the blood soaking into the sand.

A Vahrian soldier shoved Leon's head into the ground and locked handcuffs around his wrists.

Chapter 26

The Vahrian guards shoved Leon into a cell and slammed the door shut. Quivering, naked, and covered in dozens of tiny cuts, Leon sat against the rough stone wall in the darkness. He sobbed. He was trapped in the Inquisition's castle. A castle from which no Payan escaped alive.

Huddled on the cold stone floor in a puddle of freezing water, Leon thought of Elena.

Where've they taken her? What are they doing to her?

Slipping on the wet floor, he stumbled up and hammered the door. He smashed the wood with all his feeble strength, but the door held firm. Pain throbbed through his fist. He slid to the floor and curled into a shaking ball.

He sobbed. The worst part was that they'd taken the pendant Juliana carved for him. He'd worn that for two decades. And now it was gone. Gone, like Juliana herself.

Time passed in a blur of damp, stinking darkness. His stomach throbbed with hunger, but no food came. His lips cracked with dryness, but no water arrived. He crapped in the drain in the corner, filling the cell with a foul stench, but no bucket came for him to wash himself with.

After an age, the door scraped open. Blinding torchlight

flooded his dark cell. He squinted at the bulky silhouettes of two Vahrian soldiers.

In his mind's eye, Leon pictured himself leaping and slamming their helmets together, making them collapse onto the foul-smelling floor.

In reality, the soldiers yanked him up and pulled a bag over his head. Leon slipped and stumbled as they dragged him through corridors and up stairs, and every clink of their swords made him swallow and lament his nudity even more.

They ripped the bag off his head and pulled Leon into a room with a single chair, a torch in a bracket on the wall, and a tiny window covered by iron bars overlooked jagged rooftops. The soldiers shoved him into the chair and bound him with rope. They retreated to the corner of the room.

In the distance, a boot dragged along the floor with a scrape. A cane tapped on stone. Another boot clumped onto the ground.

Scrape.

Tap.

Clump.

Leon swallowed. Whoever was making the sound was approaching. *Is that ... him?*

Scrape.

Tap.

Clump.

Leon gulped.

Please let me be wrong. Don't let it be him.

The door behind Leon creaked open. He tried to twist to see who'd entered, but his bonds kept him from moving as the stench of yhona paste filled the room.

Scrape.

177

Tap.

Clump.

Inquisitor Drayton limped into Leon's vision. His twisted leg dragged along the floor and he leant on the cane, gasping. Splotches of blue paint covered his crimson cloak.

Drayton twisted his haggard face into a smile. "It's most unfortunate to keep meeting like this, dear fellow."

Leon swallowed. He wanted to swear, wanted to shout at Drayton, wanted to say something brave, but any confidence he'd possessed had been torn away when they'd ripped off his clothes and shoved him into the stinking cell.

"When we met in your humble cottage, all those days ago, I made an offer," said Drayton. "An offer to preserve your life. Nay, an offer that would improve it. All I wanted was one tiny piece of information, but you refused, and now we're here."

Leon stared at the ground and his hands trembled. His naked legs shivered. What would Drayton do to him?

The inquisitor's smile grew. "You've heard stories of me, perhaps? From Elena? And the other terrorists?"

"Y-yes," said Leon in a high-pitched voice.

"What do they call me? A filthy Vahrian? An Angel-Killer? A monster?"

Leon gulped.

Drayton chuckled. "I'm all those things, in a fashion. All Vahrians that live in Paya are filthy. Contaminated by your world. You know, after the War, I just wanted to return to Vahria, hold my wife in one hand, my child in the other, and watch the sun rise over the countryside. But your cursed lower gravity weakened me, and the gift your angels gave me –" he tapped his twisted leg "– meant my return to Vahria was

178

filled with agony. I suppose that's why I'm a good inquisitor. Pain follows me from when I wake to when I sleep. Pain's my friend. My teacher. My aide. And I know better than anyone how it can twist you.

"This brings me to that second term. The Angel-Killer. It's true, dear chap. My motive, I'm sorry to admit, is rather primitive: revenge. If not for your kind, I'd be with my wife, my child, and the sunrise. As for that last term? A monster? There are no monsters. Only those twisted by the past. I believe you also suffer the burden of a heavy past. How does it feel to be a wingless angel?"

Leon scowled. He struggled, wanting to clasp his hands around Drayton's murderous throat, but the ropes held him tight and his fear held him tighter.

"In a way, my dear fellow, I suppose your lack of wings helped you survive the War's aftermath," said Drayton.

Leon stared at the floor. *That's what I thought, too.*

"Far easier to pass as a commoner without feathers tucked under your cloak," said Drayton. "Still, I imagine the pain of a soldier's blade slicing through those wings would've –"

The inquisitor paused. Leon scowled harder.

Drayton cocked his head to one side. "Those wings weren't cut by someone else, were they? You cut them!"

Leon's hands trembled. He swore and spat a mouthful of saliva onto Drayton's cloak.

The inquisitor laughed. "Oh, this is too good, dear chap. In all my years, I've never found an angel who's done what you have. I suppose this will make the next part easier." Still grinning, Drayton wiped a tear from his eye. "Leon, in your cottage, I made you an offer. Today, I want to make another one."

Leon frowned. This had to be a trick. He glared at Drayton's smiling face, resolving that whatever the inquisitor said, Leon wouldn't give him anything that could help with the inquisitor's quest.

"Earlier today, you and Elena entered a secret chamber beneath the All-Temple. What was inside?"

"Nothing."

"You climbed down a ladder, stayed underground for forty-three minutes, and emerged looking like you'd won the royal jonshular tournament. You need to do better to fool me. Of course, I doubt you'd betray the chamber's secrets at a whim, which is where my offer comes in. Tell me what's inside, and I'll free you, remove your charges, and give you enough gold to buy a castle."

"What about Elena?"

"The girl? Do you wish her freed, too?"

Leon nodded.

"Then your freedom will be hers."

Leon swallowed. He sensed Drayton really would grant freedom and fortune if he told him about the chamber. But some instinct warned him to not tell the inquisitor about the inscription, because if Drayton discovered the Path to a place where so many angels lived ...

"You'll free us right away?" Leon asked.

"Yes. I give you my word as an inquisitor that if you tell me what's in the chamber, I'll free you and Elena."

The room's chill sent goose bumps rippling along Leon's skin. He shivered.

Glancing down at the floor, he cleared his throat. "There were two puzzles. Death traps, for those who don't know Payan lore."

He described the room with the tiles of Archangels, and the hall with the different-sized corridors. When he talked about the last room, he recounted how the floor lifted to fill the abyss, but didn't mention the inscription on the altar.

Drayton's eyes narrowed. "And how did you get out?"

"After Elena touched the altar and the floor rose, all the doors behind us opened. We walked back the way we came and took the rising room to the surface."

"Fascinating. A hidden chamber, crafted by the Archangels. Hidden in the bedsteel, no less." Drayton frowned. "Tell me, is that all? Or was there anything you neglected to mention?"

Leon tried hard to not blink. "That's all, sir."

Drayton kept staring. Leon's eyes watered and after holding the stare for several moments, he swallowed.

"No." Drayton gripped his cane tighter. "You haven't told everything, dear chap."

"I swear that's all there was!"

"Don't lie. I'm an inquisitor. Lies are my business."

The door creaked behind Leon. He again twisted, trying to see who'd entered, and coughed as the stench of burning lead filled the room. A soldier wheeled a metal bucket containing hot coals into the room. The bucket hissed, and steam rose through the damp air. Leon gulped as Drayton removed an iron rod from the bucket with a gloved hand. The stench of yhona grew stronger. Drayton held the red-hot iron an inch from Leon's nose and the heat made sweat run down Leon's face.

"You've expended my goodwill for today," said Drayton. "Once again, I made a good offer and you tried to take advantage of me. Bravery doesn't suit you, Leon."

Leon closed his eyes. He lent back as far as his restraints

181

allowed, but the rod's heat stayed plastered to his sweat-stained face.

"You and Elena seek Waverrym. Is this correct?"

Leon opened his eyes. "Yes."

He cursed. Drayton's knowledge of Waverrym had shocked him so much he'd responded without thinking.

"How do you know about Waverrym?" Leon asked, trying to ignore the red-hot iron hovering in front of his mouth.

Did Elena tell him? No, that ain't possible. She never would've given into torture.

"I'm an inquisitor. It's my business to know motives and rumours, although until today, I thought the Path to Waverrym was just that. A rumour. An old legend to make Payans think their precious angels still exist. Today, however, you proved this legend has a factual basis. My spy tells me you touched the Severym statue, opening an entrance to a secret chamber. Now, in the Sarahk, the verse that inspired the legend of the Path says: 'find the lungs of Severym, and find the path to safety.' Yes?"

Leon gulped. Sighing, Drayton lowered the red-hot iron and tapped it against Leon's stomach. Heat seared his skin. He bellowed as pain flooded through him and he doubled over, tears streaking down his face.

"Y-Yes," Leon said.

"You touched the statue because you seek Waverrym. Understandable, as it offers a chance to reunite with other angels. This brings me to the part of your description you neglected. There must be something in the chamber, a map, or engraving, or something else that shows Waverrym's location. A riddle perhaps, for it is said the Path contains many puzzles, only solvable by true angels. Tell me, what was it?"

Drayton twirled the iron through the air. Leon swallowed. If Drayton found Waverrym, he'd destroy the last remnants of Paya's angels. If they existed.

"Ain't telling you," said Leon.

Drayton pressed the iron rod into Leon's thigh. Pain burnt through Leon and he screamed and his skin bubbled under the iron's pressure and he bellowed but Drayton kept pressing the metal against his blistering skin and his nerves burst into flame and his blood boiled –

The inquisitor lifted the rod. Leon's leg spasmed and he grit his teeth.

Block it out. It's all in my head.

"Perhaps you think you're a hero, dear chap," said Drayton. "Very well. I'll show you what happens to heroes."

Drayton clicked his fingers. The door opened and two soldiers dragged Pierce into the room. Cuts and bruises covered his naked body, and he dripped blood onto the stone floor. Leon swallowed. Pierce was alive, but he looked on the verge of death.

Blood bubbled down Pierce's cracked lips. "Sorry ah called you a spy, Leon."

"It's okay. I'm sorry I got you into this mess."

Drayton raised his hand and a soldier held a sword to Pierce's throat. Pierce glared up at the inquisitor. Despite the wounds across his back, his countless bruises, and the cuts lacerating his flesh, Pierce's handsome face burned with defiance. Something about that stoic glare lessened Leon's pain.

"Leon," said Drayton. "Please tell this fine young gentleman about Waverrym."

Leon gulped. "It's a disc. A secret disc, where angels still live."

"Sounds m'ghty fine," said Pierce through swollen lips.

"Leon's just visited a chamber," said Drayton. "Inside, a clue leads to Waverrym. Leon, you'll tell me what it said, or young Pierce here will have his throat slit."

Pierce spat blood onto Drayton's robes.

The inquisitor smiled. "There's a reason my robes are red, young chap."

"Leon, don' tell 'im," said Pierce. "'e can't find Waverrym. 'e can't kill the angels."

"I can't let you die!"

"'e'll kill me anyway. Listen, angels are our last hope. 'e's already killed so many. 'e can't kill any more."

Leon's heart hammered. "Pierce –"

"This is more important than me." Pierce clenched his jaw. "Aye. My death means nothing if it stops him killing 'undreds o' angels."

Drayton leered. "Give the hero his wish."

The soldier pressed his sword against Pierce's throat.

Pierce nodded to Leon. "Glory to the Archangels."

The soldier sliced Pierce's throat, tearing the flesh, ripping sinew and muscle and spurting blood onto the floor. Pierce hit the ground with a wet crunch. His handsome head lolled back, and his dead eyes glared at the ceiling.

Chapter 27

A scream echoed from a nearby room. Drayton muttered something to a soldier, who raced out the door. Moments later, the scream stopped.

Drayton dipped the iron rod in the bucket of smouldering coals. "Last chance, Leon. Tell me what was in the chamber or share Pierce's fate."

Pierce's blood spread across the floor, tickling the tips of Leon's bare toes. Leon remembered the boy's defiant glare, and he tried to capture the same anger, righteousness, and bravery as he scowled at the inquisitor.

An angel cares for the greater good. An angel cares naught for himself.

"Go to hell," Leon said.

Drayton chuckled. He took the rod out of the coals and pressed it into Leon's thigh. Leon screamed until his throat turned raw –

Drayton removed the iron, but the agony continued. "Tell me what was in the chamber."

Leon's eyes watered. A pink blister throbbed on his thigh and blood filled his aching mouth. He'd bit his tongue.

"Five seconds." Drayton held the smouldering iron an inch from Leon's thigh. "Then you get it again."

Pain pulsed through Leon's leg and he whimpered. He thought of Juliana and Blas.

He thought of the battle he'd fled.

He thought of the friends he'd betrayed.

"Four seconds..." said Drayton.

He thought of slicing off his wings, and his guilty joy at surviving all those years after the War, while angels' heads appeared on stakes around Paya.

"Three..."

Didn't take much to conjure those memories.

They haunted him always.

Reminded him what he was.

A horrible friend.

A false angel.

A traitor.

"Two..."

Tears streaked down Leon's face. If he told Drayton what was in the chamber, what did it matter? He'd always been spineless. No one could say he'd gone against form.

He'd always been a coward.

And always would be.

"One–"

"P-p-please!" said Leon. "I'll tell you! There was an inscription: 'This steel garden is a lonely place, watered by legacies of pain. May ye not suffer its embrace for it is truly the angel's bane. Yet in this field of speeding death, safety ye will find, in the flowing path of the Archangel's breath.'"

Drayton grabbed Leon's hair and yanked up his head to peer into Leon's eyes. "Where does this riddle lead to?"

"D-d-don't know."

Drayton stabbed the iron onto Leon's thigh, making Leon

shriek. His leg twitched and he sobbed –

"The asteroid b-b-belt!" Leon said.

Drayton raised the rod so that it hovered above Leon's thigh. "More precision."

"In the Mallean asteroids – in the mining c-c-colonies, there's a ring-shaped asteroid. Paracelsus-7. A jetstream passes through it."

Leon gaped. Until then, he hadn't known the answer, but somehow the searing pain had dragged the truth from him.

"Convicts mine zinc from Paracelsus-7." Drayton frowned. "How do you know it's part of the Path?"

"It's in the r-r-riddle. 'Steel garden' – zinc's a steel. 'Legacies of pain' – slaves and convicts have mined the asteroids for centuries. That's why you don't want to 'suffer its embrace.' Asteroids are 'the angel's bane,' because they can kill us in collisions. The asteroids orbit faster than the discs, making them a 'field of speeding death,' and the 'Archangel's breath' refers to jetstreams."

A strange numbness spread through Leon. He'd betrayed his fellow angels.

Again.

The door scraped behind him. A soldier dragged Elena into the room, a gag across her mouth. Bruises marred her naked body, and her right arm dangled limply at her side. Anger surged through Leon. He wanted to ask if she was alright, but then her face twisted into a glare and Leon realised she wasn't the one who needed help. Gulping, he looked down.

She'd heard Leon tell Drayton everything.

Tears dripped down her cheeks as she stared at Pierce's body sprawled in a pool of his own blood, and she struggled and cursed, but the gag muffled her cries and the soldier held her firm.

"You're lucky, girl," said Drayton. "Your friend told me everything I wanted, so there's no need to torture you."

Elena struggled harder. Leon gulped. He had to say something. Anything. He had to make her realise he'd done the only thing he could. Had to make her know he'd done the right thing. Had to make her understand he wasn't brave like Pierce, that he wasn't a hero, that he'd never been a hero, and never would. His treachery today was just another act of fear in his pathetic life. He tried to catch her eyes. Tried to form the words to explain all that.

But no words came.

Drayton gestured and the soldier dragged Elena out of the room. Pain throbbed in Leon's leg, but the pain was dull compared to the anguish of seeing Elena's devastated face. She'd trusted him. Maybe even admired him. Now he'd shattered that trust, like he'd shattered the trust of everyone who'd ever believed in him.

At a gesture from Drayton, a soldier smeared ointment on Leon's burned thigh. Blessed coolness numbed the agony, although it still stung like hell.

Drayton flicked blood off his cloak. "Thank you for your service, Leon. Tomorrow, we'll set off on our journey to the asteroid belts. You, dear fellow, will be my hunting dog, and with you on my leash, you'll lead me to Waverrym."

~ ~ ~

Guards threw Leon back into his cell. He scrambled to the puddle on the floor and pressed his thigh against the water, gasping as the chill lessened the pain. He should've cried but he couldn't muster the energy. All his strength had leaked away, just like how Pierce's blood leaked from his slashed neck ...

Cut off from the stars, Leon couldn't tell how long passed before the blade of grass sprouted from the floor.

He frowned. More grass pushed through the stone, covering the floor in a layer of soft, green lawn. The cell's walls faded. Grass stretched out into the distance, dotted with patches of sweet-smelling amethyst poppies. Leon stood and gaped at the meadow around him. Cicadas rustled and wind caressed his face. Stars blinked through the force field above and he recognised the constellations with a smile.

This was Amwedd, the disc full of rolling plains and boundless meadows, but famed for its uselessness. It belonged to the de Bernal highborns, had no natural resources, and its location in the Outer Regions rendered it useless for trade. This left the de Bernals in constant poverty.

Despite that, it was Leon's favourite disc, and the two reasons for that stood in front of him when he lowered his gaze back to the ground.

Juliana smiled. She fiddled with a whittling knife and a lump of wood and Blas de Bernal stood beside her, grinning.

Leon hugged Juliana and kissed her. Warmth spread through his body. He held her tighter and she patted his back, chuckling.

"Juliana," he said. "It's been so long."

Leon's eyes grew wet, but he didn't wipe them. He trusted Juliana and Blas more than anyone, and he wasn't afraid to show them his tears.

"Damn right," said Juliana. "It's been twenty years."

A jolt ran through Leon. The warmth inside him faded

and he remembered Juliana and Blas had died in the Battle of Mangold Pass. Leon released Juliana. His face softened as he gazed into her shining eyes and the voice insisting this wasn't real vanished.

Leon strode towards Blas, arms outstretched.

Blas held up his hands. "Just a hug, buddy. No kisses for me, thanks."

Leon laughed. He hugged his best friend. When they let go, a campfire crackled on the ground and three one-person tents crouched around the cheerful flames. They sat. Juliana whittled a jonshular piece and Blas roasted a hare over the dancing fire. Leon grinned. War had yet to rear its bloody mane and he was camping with his lover and his best friend. All was right in the world.

Juliana set her hand-carved piece on the ground. "I'm carving a whole set. I'll give it to you when I'm finished."

Leon kissed her. "A master gift from a master artist."

Juliana screwed up her face. "You stink. Go easy on the omnicrop root."

She looked back down at her whittling and touched the spot where Leon kissed her. A faint smile played with her mouth. Leon grinned.

"One day, you'll flee from home," said Blas.

Leon frowned. "Eh?"

"You won't have time to take the jonshular set and you'll regret leaving it, even though you had to," said Juliana.

"What?"

Blas turned over the hare. "That regret will be nothing compared to the anguish of abandoning us."

"I-I didn't abandon you. I mean, I won't –"

"You will and you have." Juliana's face turned hard and

190

flinty. "In the Battle of Mangold Pass, a Vahrian arrow will cut me down and you'll flee, terrified."

Coldness clutched Leon's heart.

Blas tore the hare in half, splattering greasy fat onto Leon. "You'll fly to the nearest disc and in a dirty alley you'll cut your wings."

"You'll spend the next twenty years hiding from the past," said Juliana. "You'll smoke and drink and try to forget, but no matter what you do, we'll haunt you."

"And then," said Blas, "When all hope's lost, a young angel will come to you."

"You'll have a chance to find Waverrym."

"A chance for redemption."

"But you'll throw it away, because you're a coward."

Juliana and Blas stood and unfurled their wings. Leon stood, but almost fell. His feet sunk into the ground, which was rocky and littered with bones.

Juliana and Blas flapped, and took to the skies. High above them, the other dead angels from the Academy glided in the air, glaring down at Leon. Above them flew the eighty-one Minor Archangels, and the nine Major Archangels. And over them all, a great shadow blotted out the feeble sun, casting the barren ground into darkness. Leon gaped at the disc-sized underbelly of the Star Spectre.

She was as the paintings foretold – a being with an enormous triangular body, flapping and rippling as She glided through space. A gigantic tail swayed behind her, long enough to encircle Hargold. Starlight warped around Her and She glowed with an ethereal radiance.

His knees weakened. Awed by Her immensity, he dropped to the ground and tears flowed down his face. She was like nothing he'd ever seen, nothing he'd ever imagined …

Juliana and Blas soared up to join the flock of angels.

"Don't leave me," said Leon. "Please!"

"We'd never leave you," said Juliana as she and Blas rose into the air. "You abandoned us."

The fleet of angels passed through the force field. They soared away from the disc. The ground sucked at Leon and dragged him down, swallowing him into the field of bones. Darkness pressed against him and he screamed.

"Leon, shut up! The guards will hear."

A dirty hand clamped over his mouth, muffling his shrieks. He rolled over, gasping. Elena stood above him, dressed in inquisitor's robes, a ring of keys chained to her belt and Leon's cloak in her hands. His cell door was open behind her and a bag lay slung over her shoulder.

"Elena? How –"

She threw him his cloak. "I'm breaking us out. Get dressed!"

Chapter 28

Leon scrambled into his cloak. After being naked so long, the coarse fabric weighed down against his skin. "How did you –"

"I grew up on the streets." She pulled him into the corridor. "I could pick locks before I could add two and two."

"Wait."

Leon felt in his pockets. Breathfung. Matches. Smoking pipe. Where the hell was Juliana's pendant?

"C'mon, let's go," Elena said.

"I said wait."

He reached deeper into his pockets. Omnicrop root. Glowfung. Knife. He gulped. That pendant was his only keepsake of Juliana. If the filthy Vahrians had taken it –

His fingers brushed something small and wooden. Exhaling with relief, he hung the pendant around his neck and tucked it down his cloak.

"Alright," he said. "Ready."

They crept along the dark corridor, Leon limping behind Elena. He swallowed. The guards had treated him like an animal. What would they do if they caught him escaping?

"How come you're wearing an inquisitor's cloak?" he asked.

Elena's lips curled as she looked at her red robes. "I've got my normal cloak in my bag, but I figured it'd be easier to sneak around wearing this. Would've got one for you, but I only found one. It's … strange to wear."

Leon kept patting his cloak pockets. Something was missing.

He cursed. "The bastards stole my hip flask! And my kemp!"

"Probably for your own good. And keep your voice down."

Leon scowled. *Bloody Vahrians. Left me with a pipe, but nothing to smoke.*

Elena pushed through a sturdy wooden door. They emerged at the bottom of a crumbling stone staircase, with torchlight flickering from the room at the top of the steps. Leon turned to tell Elena the room looked like a guard room, but she was already climbing the steps. Leon cursed. He tried to pull her back, but she brushed away his hands.

"It's safe," she said.

She climbed the steps. Legs shaking, he stumbled after her and entered the guard room.

Three armoured Vahrians sprawled on the floor amongst a mess of broken chairs and smashed tables.

Leon gaped at Elena. "You did this?"

"No. A magic fairy did it." She rolled her eyes. "Keep moving. Think I know the way out."

She opened the door, but Leon glanced back down the stairs.

"What about the others?" he said.

"What others?"

"The Resistance. It's our fault they got captured."

Elena scowled. "They wouldn't be here if they'd believed us. Forget them."

"No. I'm sick of abandoning people."

194

He walked to the stairs and Elena grabbed him.

"Leon …" Her face grew haggard and she looked older than her twenty years. "I wanted to make this easier for you, but the Resistance … we can't help them."

She led him to a narrow slot window. The window overlooked the castle's battlements, where Resistance fighters' heads sat atop blood-stained spears. Leon gulped. The nearest head's wispy grey hair blew in the breeze. Further along the row of spears, a cord of bloodied flesh dangled from an eye socket and crows picked at the head.

Leon's mother had fed crows in the laneway behind their bakery. She'd made him scrape breadcrumbs off the floor and out of the crevices behind the display shelves. Then she'd grab a handful with her thick fingers, roll them around her palm like a gambler weighing dice, and toss them to the birds.

"One day you'll fly like them," she told Leon when he was seven. "Be sure you remember how to fly back here, eh? Mumma will always have bread for you."

He hadn't known what she meant. Then he'd grown his wings, flown away, and never returned. Had she kept feeding the crows after he'd left? He hoped so.

His mother's face disappeared and all that remained were the crows, picking at flesh instead of bread. Bile crawled into Leon's mouth. He'd done this. He'd led the Inquisition to the Resistance, hoping to save himself.

"It's not your fault," said Elena.

She touched his shoulder and he shoved away her hand.

"Leon –"

"What's your escape plan?" He wrenched himself away from the window but couldn't wipe the sickening image from his mind. "Come on, girl. Tell me you've got a plan."

Her lip trembled. "Yeah."

Despite Leon's better judgment, he took one last glance through the window. A hulking figure strode onto the battlements, his cloak flapping in the breeze, and knelt before the head with wispy grey hair. Leon frowned. The man looked familiar. Leon lent closer to the window and the man turned and locked eyes with him from across the courtyard.

Leon jumped back. "Shit. I saw Teo."

"Simona's bodyguard?"

"He must've escaped. Crap. He thinks we're Vahrian spies. If he finds us –"

"We'll be fine. He doesn't know we've escaped."

Leon winced.

"Ah, great," she said. "He saw you?"

"Yeah." He stumbled to the door. "C'mon, tell me you've got an escape plan."

"We can't escape the castle. It's too well-protected."

"Well that's bloody useful to know, ain't it?"

His voice was a few octaves higher than normal and his heart pounded. Teo moved his sword like lightning. The thought of his blade tearing through Leon's flesh made him gulp.

"Let me finish," said Elena. "A Vahrian slave ship's about to leave from the main courtyard. We can sneak on board."

"How will –" his voice cracked, and he swallowed. "How's being on a slave ship better than being in a dungeon?"

"The ship's got a load of convicts. Before, after I broke out, I saw them marching on board. I also overheard the captain, and the ship's heading to the mining colonies in the asteroid field."

Leon nodded. "Where Paracelsus-7 is. Alright, then."

They left the room and strode through the castle, cloaks flapping behind them. Shadows filled the narrow, stone-carved corridors, broken by dim pools of harsh red candle-light. Fingernail scratchings etched the walls and a thick layer of dust and dirt carpeted the floor. A scream echoed in the distance. Then, from much closer, a guttural sobbing leaked through a gap in the stone walls. Leon swallowed. How many Payans were trapped here? How many would die and water the floor with their blood, like Pierce? He wanted to break every door and rip the chains from the walls. But the weaker part of him wanted to hunch in a dark corner and curl into a ball. If it wasn't for Elena, he might've done just that.

Footsteps clunked around the corner. Leon froze. His neck prickled and he pressed against the cold wall.

Elena tiptoed to the corner. Leon's hands clenched into fists and his nails bit into his palms. What the hell was she doing? He wanted to scream at her to stay back, but he had to keep quiet. Sweat streaked down Leon's nose and he wiped it in case it hit the floor and the person heard.

The footsteps grew nearer.

Elena peeked around the corner.

No!

He tensed, waiting for the person to shout. Waiting for soldiers to storm the corridor, knock him to the ground and stab his back so hard the sword burst from his chest –

The footsteps receded. The person must've walked down another junction. They hadn't seen Elena!

She nodded and they kept walking. Leon strained to hear approaching guards, but the only noise bouncing through the corridors were distant shrieks. The lack of people should've relaxed Leon's clenched hands and bunched-up muscles. But the quietness made his heart beat faster.

They rounded a corner and emerged in a wide corridor. When he saw that light spilled from an opening at the end, Leon released a pent-up breath.

Leon and Elena stopped by the opening. Beyond, a hulking Vahrian airship floated in a dusty courtyard. The airship's gherkin-shaped balloon hovered above its wooden cabin, and the vessel strained at its anchor ropes. The captain stood outside, overseeing a worker loading one last crate of cargo on board. Six soldiers stood around her.

"Okay. There's the airship." Elena fingered the hem of her inquisitor's cloak. "Now, how to get on board?"

Grunting, the worker pushed the crate into the hold. The captain said something to him and the worker untied the anchor ropes.

Leon cursed. The airship would leave any minute.

"If we race out underneath it while it takes off," said Elena, "we can grab the underside and climb into the hold."

"No," said Leon. "Got a better plan. Well, ain't much better. You're wearing an inquisitor's robes, so act like one and I'll be your prisoner. Tell the captain you're transferring me."

"How's that a better plan?"

"It's our only chance. Come on. You've got the robes. No one refuses an inquisitor."

The worker unfastened another anchor strap and the six soldiers climbed onto the ship.

Elena sighed. "If this goes sour, it's your fault."

"Act well and it won't go sour."

She put her hand on Leon's shoulder. As they strode across the courtyard, Leon tried to look meek and defeated. It wasn't hard.

"Captain," said Elena. "I have another prisoner."

She spoke with a distinct Vahrian accent. Leon hid his grin. She had a slight Payan lilt, and was taller, darker, and skinnier than a Vahrian, but her accent was strong enough for her to pass as the mixed-raced daughter of a Vahrian and a Payan.

The captain raised her eyebrows. "Inquisitor, they said to transport only these convicts."

Leon's hands grew clammy. He stared at the ground, hoping his nervousness wouldn't betray them.

Elena pulled a metal badge out of her pocket. Leon blinked. That was a real inquisitor's badge. Whoever she'd stolen it from would be pissed.

"Change of plans," she said. "Or are you refusing an inquisitor's direct order?"

The captain bobbed her head. "Certainly not, ma'am. Come aboard."

Leon exhaled a pent-up breath. Elena pushed him into the cabin and he tried to wipe the relieved smile off his face. Inside, six soldiers watched a dozen Payan convicts. The prisoners sat on low benches, their iron slave-collars chained to the wall. One convict gaped at Leon and Leon's heart missed a beat.

It was Alvaro.

Chapter 29

"Leon," said Alvaro. "What are you doing here, old buddy?"

A soldier punched Alvaro's stomach. "Quiet."

Alvaro doubled over, coughing. Leon swallowed.

This is my fault. If I'd never fled Hargold, the Inquisition wouldn't have arrested him. Karym's horns! Why does everything I do turn to shit?

The floor wobbled under Leon's feet as their airship ascended.

"Here's a spot for your prisoner, ma'am." The captain gestured to the bench, then frowned. "Where's his slave-collar?"

"He's an informer, not a convict," said Elena.

Alvaro's shocked expression transformed into a glare.

He mouthed, "Traitor."

Leon shook his head, and his cheeks burned with heat, but there was nothing he could say. The airship kept rising, and the wood creaked. Leon frowned at the tar patched over holes in the wall. This ship had seen better days.

Alvaro kept glaring, so Leon looked away and peered out a porthole. A cloaked figure stood in the courtyard below, watching the rising airship.

Teo.

Leon swallowed. They'd escaped the Resistance fighter for now, but all Teo had to do was steal a pegasus and follow them.

Leon attached his breathfung to his face. It was too early to need it, but it calmed his nerves. He kept avoiding Alvaro's eyes.

The captain smirked. "Your informer doesn't look too smart, inquisitor."

Leon frowned and looked at Elena. What was the captain saying?

"We've got a Mainwright Generator, which makes its own air," said the captain. "You don't need your breather."

Leon didn't understand how that worked, but no one else wore a breathfung, so Leon removed his breather. The captain's smirk grew. Leon bowed his head, trying to look meek. His acting came too damn easy.

"I need to talk with my prisoner," said Elena. "In private. Do you have a room for me?"

The captain opened a door and gestured to a room filled with bunk beds. "I'll be in the wheelhouse if you need me."

Elena dragged Leon into the room. Leon glanced at Alvaro. His old friend's glower was sharp and Leon broke eye contact straight away.

A soldier tried to follow them into the room, but Elena raised her finger.

"No need to join me. I can handle this myself."

The soldier nodded. He backed out and closed the door behind him. Elena collapsed onto the nearest bed, folded her arms around herself, and stared at the porthole.

"Pierce is dead," she said.

Serves him right.

She pulled a metal pendant out of her robes and cradled it. The half-circle pendant was a metal version of the one Juliana had carved for Leon.

Lightness swept through him and the pendant floated above Elena's hand. Leon glanced out the porthole. The airship had passed through the force field into space, yet air still filled the cabin. He grabbed a rail to stop himself floating into the ceiling.

Elena's pendant spun in the air. "He gave me this before the mission. Said it was a traditional Payan gift."

Leon thought of Juliana. "I know."

She stared at her pendant. "See how it's a half-circle? He has … no, he *had* the other half. Represents how we're only complete together. But now … he doesn't deserve to be dead."

"No. He doesn't."

Leon thought of Pierce screaming death to Paya's enemies as he held a match above the gunpowder.

"He was brave," she said.

She sat so still Leon wondered if she'd stopped breathing. He remembered Pierce's sword tearing through the chef's throat, sending blood spraying everywhere.

"Yeah," said Leon.

"You're not brave."

Heat tingled his face and he stared at the floor.

"He gave his life for Paya," said Elena. "But you couldn't last a minute of torture. Now Drayton knows how to find Waverrym, and if he gets there first …"

Leon scowled. He floated to the porthole. Anshan, city of the seven discs, shrunk beneath them as their airship glided away.

"You're a coward," she said, her voice shaking.

He hunched his shoulders. Elena crossed her arms and an ugly twist distorted the corners of her mouth.

"Aren't you going to say something?" she asked.

"No. You're right. I am a coward." Sighing, he sat beside Elena. "And a traitor to Paya. Name it and it fits me."

The fire faded from Elena's eyes. Had she expected a fight? Wanted one, even? Too bad. He was in no mood to argue and after the things he'd done he had no right to defend himself.

Elena cleared her throat. "Look, maybe I've been too harsh –"

"No. I deserve it."

"Hey, under that torture, anyone would've given in."

"Pierce wouldn't. Or you."

"Leon, just because you gave in to Drayton doesn't make you a coward."

Leon pulled out his own half-circle pendant. Unlike Elena's, his was carved from wood and attached to a frayed cord.

"See this?" he said. "The only woman I ever loved made it for me. Juliana was … a great whittler. And you know what I did in return?"

Elena's face softened. "What?"

"Juliana and I were at the Battle of Mangold Pass. In the shield wall. We were joking. Laughing. My best friend, Blas, teased us, asking when we were going to get married. In the distance, Vahrians marched around the corner of the Pass. But what the hell did we care? This was the War's first major battle and we thought we were invincible. We were angels."

Leon gritted his teeth. "Juliana was mid-sentence when the arrow impaled her throat. Hadn't held her shield high enough. Hadn't expected the Vahrians to shoot so early. I

203

thought it couldn't be real. Couldn't have happened, not to an angel. She reached for me with her hand, and it was bloody from touching the wound in her neck. I tried to grab her, but her strength faded and … you know, the sound a body makes when it falls sounds just like a sack of grain hitting the dirt. Don't sound like nothing special.

"I looked up. When I saw the Vahrian army marching towards us, I ran from the front lines, screaming for a medic. Except after a while, I wasn't screaming for anyone. I was just running. By the time our armies clashed, I'd fled the Pass. Know what the worst thing was? I didn't even think about my best friend Blas until I'd flown to another disc and hacked off my wings."

Elena's eyes widened. "You cut your wings?"

"Yeah. Didn't want to fight and I wasn't worthy of being an angel."

"But your wings!"

"Do what you have to do to survive." Heat radiated through Leon's cheeks. "Told you. I'm a coward."

He stared at the porthole. The glass muted the stars and made them look faint. Distant. A dull headache throbbed through his skull and he cursed the Vahrian who'd stolen his hip flask and his kemp. He'd give almost anything for either of them. Preferably both.

"No," said Elena.

"Eh?"

"You're not a coward. You were, but now you don't have to be. Forget the past. You're who you choose to become."

Leon scowled. "Old pegasi can't fly new routes."

"Aren't you the one who said stories like that are full of lies?"

He chewed his lip. Didn't have anything to respond with, so he went back to staring at the porthole. Silence stretched between them. He thought of Alvaro, sitting in chains on the door's other side. Leon ran his fingers over Juliana's pendant.

Maybe Elena's right. Or am I just saying that because I want her to be right?

"There's a convict out there called Alvaro," he said. "He's my friend. I want to rescue him."

Elena gaped. "Er ... is that a good idea?"

Someone knocked.

"Busy," said Elena.

The door opened a crack. "Sorry to bother you, Inquisitor –"

"Close the door. I said I'm busy."

The captain's head poked through the opening. "Afraid it's urgent, ma'am. A vessel's approaching at speed. It's ... it's –"

"Spit it out," said Elena.

The captain swallowed. "It's a pirate ship."

Chapter 30

"How many hostiles, Captain?" Elena asked.

She floated into the main cabin, pulling herself along the handrails. Leon glided after her. Alvaro glared and Leon avoided his friend's angry eyes.

The captain mopped her sweaty brow. "It's a pegasus-pulled corsair. Room for a dozen pirates."

Leon swallowed. With only six soldiers on their airship, the pirates outnumbered them two to one. He peered out the nearest porthole. The corsair was a speck in the distance but grew larger at a frightening rate.

"Can't you outrun them, Captain?" Elena asked.

"Afraid not, Inquisitor. Our vessel doesn't have their acceleration. They'll catch us in minutes."

"Do you have an escape pod?"

"No, ma'am."

Leon frowned. He and Elena might be able to flee if she flew and carried him ... no. Silly idea. A corsair pulled by six pegasi had more endurance than a young angel's wings. Besides, once Elena revealed her wings, the captain would try to kill her and so would the pirates. A dead angel would fetch a bounty far more valuable than anything stolen from an airship.

206

"How far are we from the nearest disc?" asked Elena.

The captain frowned. "I'd have to check my star charts –"

"Six hours." Leon squinted at the stars. "At our current velocity, at least."

The captain scowled. "Does your prisoner always interrupt Vahrians?"

"When he knows more than them, yes," said Elena.

The captain swallowed. "May I suggest providing breath-fung to the soldiers and prisoners, Inquisitor?"

Elena nodded. Soldiers glided around the cabin, slapping breathfung onto their faces. Leon attached his. It wriggled into place and newfound energy mingled with his nervousness. Viewed through the porthole, the pirate's corsair was close enough for Leon to count six pegasi lashed to the front. The vessel was a sleek wedge of wood, with a sharp steel prow, designed for stealth and speed. Unlike Vahrian airships, it had no floatation balloon to reflect the sun, which was why it had only been spotted this late.

Elena frowned at the soldiers. "Don't you have any external defences? Crossbows? Spears? Harpoons?"

The breathfung over her mouth muffled her voice.

"We've a few swords in the armoury," said the captain. "But save that, nothing else. We used to have more weapons, but this route's been safe so long there didn't seem the need."

Elena sighed. "Handy."

She acted the picture of inquisitor apathy, but her hands, bunched in her robes, shook. The captain's face turned ashen as she watched the approaching corsair. Chained to their seats, the prisoners hugged themselves and stared at the floor. A few moaned. Most had resigned themselves to a life of enslavement in the brutal mines, and so the prospect of slaughter by pirates gave them no cause to yell.

"Inquisitor," said Leon, his heart thumping. "May I suggest something?"

The captain fingered her knife and glared at Leon.

"Proceed," said Elena.

"Give the prisoners swords and free them to fight the pirates."

"In Menon's name!" said the captain. "Inquisitor, let me beat your insolent Payan for you."

"You'll do no such thing, Captain. Free the prisoners."

"You can't be serious –"

"Now."

Grumbling, the captain ordered the soldiers to unlock the convicts. The prisoners floated up, gaping. Alvaro glared at Leon. Leon nudged the wall and floated backwards, putting a soldier between him and Alvaro.

"We'll give you knives," said Elena to the prisoners. "And if we survive, you'll have your freedom, too."

Convicts gasped, soldiers gaped, and the captain cursed.

"Surely you jest," said the captain.

"It's the only way to motivate them," said Elena. "You can't ask them to risk their lives only to return to chains." She turned to the prisoners. "And as a warning: if you want to survive, don't turn against us. Pirates take no prisoners."

She nodded to the captain, who gave knives to the convicts, shaking her head. Leon wiped his sweaty palms on his cloak. He didn't like how Alvaro's white-knuckled hand clutched his new knife.

"Take defensive positions on the outer deck," said the captain.

A soldier opened the main door. Air hissed out into space

and everything faded into silence. Vahrians and Payans floated onto the deck, which was more of a walkway that circled around the cabin. They floated shoulder to shoulder, clutching the rail.

The pirates were less than three clicks away. Leon's hand trembled so much he almost dropped his knife. Beside him, Elena's jaw throbbed as she grinded her teeth.

The pirates' corsair glided closer. Six pegasi pulled the ship, and on the deck swords bristled in the starlight.

All was silent in the darkness of space.

Movement rustled across the corsair's deck and a cloud of thin objects sprung from the enemy ship.

Leon tried to shout, "Down!"

But in the vacuum, no one heard.

He seized Elena and pulled her down as a wave of arrows impaled the men and women around them. Leon grabbed a handhold. He wrenched himself and Elena towards the cabin's door, his heart hammering in his eardrums.

A harpoon loomed, massive and silent, and punched through the airship's side. The harpoon's trailing rope snapped tight.

The airship jerked.

Leon slammed into the wall and Elena crunched into his back. Soldiers flung off the walkway into space. The corsair crashed into the airship and pirates swarmed on board as Leon yanked himself and Elena inside the airship's cabin. Swords slashed in eerie silence outside on the deck.

Elena pointed at the far wall. A cracked porthole offered escape onto the side of the ship with no fighting. Leon's hands tingled. If they went through the porthole, they could glide away from the battle unnoticed and Elena could fly them to the asteroid belt.

Then Leon remembered Alvaro.

He glanced back at the battle and gaped as Alvaro's sword skittered out of his hand. His pirate opponent drew back his knife.

Leon pushed off the wall. He shot back through the door, stretching out his arm to point his knife ahead of him. Leon's blade punched through the pirate's ribcage. The impact jarred Leon's arm. The pirate tried to stab him, but the man's strength faded and his elbow tapped Leon's head.

Leon yanked on his knife. His heart pounded and vomit crawled into his mouth. He cursed silently. He couldn't pull out the damn knife and now he floated off the deck and into space, stuck with the dead pirate.

Someone grabbed his leg and stopped him. He glanced down. Alvaro, one hand clasping Leon's boot, the other gripping the rail, nodded at him.

Leon smiled. The weapons brandishing around them vanished and they were back in the Lowfern Inn, congratulating each other for a well-played jonshular game.

Then a sword punctured Alvaro's chest.

Chapter 31

Alvaro's eyes bulged. Globules of blood floated out of his body. The sword yanked out of his chest and coldness pierced Leon's heart as he stared at his friend's gaping wound. Alvaro released the rail. He ripped off his breathfung, pointed up at Leon with a trembling finger, and spoke three words. Even without sound, Leon understood:

Not coward. Hero.

Alvaro squeezed Leon's boot. Then his grip faded and Leon drifted away. Alvaro's body floated in place for only a second before a pirate knocked it away.

A soundless growl rumbled through Leon. He released the knife stuck in the dead pirate and pushed off the body to hurl himself at the man who'd killed his friend. He reached for the pirate's throat.

Elena dove out of the cabin and tackled Leon. They glided away from the airship. Leon struggled, trying to throw her away, trying to reach the pirate who'd murdered Alvaro, but Elena's wings snapped out, smacking him in the face. They zoomed away from the battle. Leon thrashed as the airship shrunk to the size of a dot. Ant-sized bodies floated around it and light flickered off the swords slashing through space.

In the distance, someone rode a pegasus. Leon wasn't sure if its rider was fleeing or approaching, but what did it matter?

Alvaro was dead.

He struggled, trying to escape Elena's grip. Didn't she understand? He had to go back to slaughter the pirates and the filthy Vahrians who'd put his friend in danger. He had to make them pay. For killing Alvaro. For killing Blas. For killing Juliana.

Elena pushed him away. He floated through space and fear surged through him. Had they shot her? He looked for a wound, but then she used sign language to spell one word:

Waverrym.

Leon sagged and the heat inside him died. She was right. Killing wouldn't bring Alvaro back. Or the others. They had to stick to their quest and find Waverrym before Drayton did. Leon nodded. Elena grabbed him and they flew away from the desperate carnage.

Leon swallowed. He turned away from the battle to glare at the stars ahead.

He's dead because of me.

Leon growled. The growl built into a yell and then he was screaming for his friend, cursing the Vahrians, cursing the pirates, cursing himself.

But his cries were soundless.

In space, there was only silence.

~ ~ ~

Leon coughed.

There was no noise, because they were still flying through space, but the cough racked his body and made him shake in

Elena's grip. He frowned. Another cough exploded through his chest. Spots flickered before his eyes. He twisted around to face Elena and signed, *Is my breathfung brown?*

She frowned. He pulled out a clump of glowfung to illuminate himself and repeated the sentence, signing slower this time.

Elena nodded.

Leon cursed. He swallowed and his heartbeat quickened when he tasted stale air.

His breathfung was dying.

More spots danced before his eyes. He took a deep breath and tried to calm down. That was hard, though, because within hours his breathfung would shrivel into nothing and he'd choke to death.

Get some of Elena's breathfung.

No. That wouldn't work. Her breathfung was too thin. If he ripped off a clump, she might not have enough left to cover her mouth and nose. Besides, his breathfung had turned brown in under two hours of flying, so a simple replenishment wouldn't be enough. He'd need a new breather.

He signed, *Land on nearest disc.*

She nodded. He turned around to face ahead and nausea washed through him. He gulped.

Stay calm. Don't breathe so hard.

He scanned the stars, trying to use the constellations to figure out their location, but his head pounded and he couldn't distinguish between the stars and the spots flickering in his eyes. He squinted. Were wings flapping in the distance?

Bile crept into his mouth. He choked it down, knowing that vomit would get stuck in his mouth. He cursed. Why couldn't he triangulate their location?

A faint purple-red dot glowed in the distance. Leon squinted. Hard to tell, but it looked brighter than any other light around them. He pointed to the dot. Elena shifted course and they glided towards it. He didn't know where they were or what disc they were shooting towards, but he didn't care. Air was all that mattered.

Time passed. The disc didn't grow bigger. He took another shuddering breath of thin air that strained his lungs and chilled his insides. He cursed.

Why didn't I grab another breathfung on the ship?

He stared hard at the disc, as if focusing would make it bigger. It didn't. He closed his eyes and tried to relax, but his muscles were stiffer than steel. Elena squeezed his hand. After a moment, he squeezed back. Her warm hand fit well against his calloused, thick-fingered hands.

He opened his eyes. Darkness frayed the corners of his oxygen-deprived vision, but there was no mistaking that the purple-red dot had grown. He smiled. They were going to make it.

Excitement quickened his breath. He forced his breathing to slow and tried to relax his muscles. There wasn't any need to do that, though, because within minutes the purple-red dot expanded into a disc. A huge mountain sat in the disc's middle and patches of fire glowed on the dark ground. Leon would've seen more if it wasn't for the force field's dimness.

They shot through the force field and everything went dark. The only light came from patches of glowing redness scattered below.

Leon ripped off his breathfung. He gasped. The air tasted hot and metallic, but it was the sweetest thing he'd ever inhaled.

"Land away from the fires, Elena." He gulped another beautiful breath. "Don't want anyone seeing us."

"Those aren't fires," she said as they glided.

Leon was too busy sucking in lungfuls of air to pay attention to her words. "Eh?"

"They're not fires. It's lava."

They glided closer to the ground. Pools of seething lava dotted the rocky terrain, sending waves of heat shimmering through the air.

"Don't land in those!" he said.

"You think?"

Her sweat dripped onto his neck, and she panted. They dropped like a stone. Rock and fire flashed underneath them, and Leon covered his face with his arms. Elena swept her wings down, trying to slow their flight, but he was slipping out of her grip –

They crashed into the dirt.

Elena thudded onto Leon's back and pain smashed through his knees and elbows. He wriggled out from under her. Stood up. Helped a sweaty-faced Elena stand. Then he looked around the disc they'd landed on.

"Shit," he said.

Pools of lava dotted the jagged landscape and sulphur and ash clogged the sweltering air. A distant mountain dominated the wasteland of fire and rock.

"Where are we?" asked Elena.

Leon looked up. The tar-black force field obscured the stars. The only transparent part of the field was a tiny circular section above the towering mountain, but that gave too small a window for him to identify constellations.

"Don't know," he said.

Elena frowned at the force field. "Why can't we see through?"

"No idea. Hang on, give me your breather."

She gave it to him. He trudged towards where the force field hit the disc's edge a half-click away. Elena followed.

"Don't slip," he said. "These rocks look sharp."

She rolled her eyes. "I can take care of myself, old man."

He coughed as he stumbled across the rocky ground, circling around pools of lava. The air didn't taste so sweet anymore. Now it tasted like a blacksmith's workshop.

They reached the disc's edge and Leon slapped the breath-fung onto his face. He waited a few seconds. Then he held Elena's hand and lent out of the force field to check the stars.

His head cracked against the field, making him recoil.

"What happened?" she said.

He tapped the field. It was solid.

"Shit," he said. "It's like Antonia's force field, but reversed. We can get in, but can't get out."

Her eyes widened. "We're trapped?"

"Bloody hope not. These lava pools will roast us if we stay too long." He pointed above the distant mountain. "There's a transparent part of the field up there, right above the peak. Might be able to escape through that."

"What if we can't?"

Then we're dead.

"It'll be fine," he said. "Besides, I need to find a new breather before we leave, anyway. C'mon."

They staggered across the desolate landscape, heading towards the mountain.

"Ever been on a disc like this?" Elena asked.

"Nah."

"Did you learn about them, though?"

"A little. Hold up, lemme see if I can remember … lava pools … they're fed from underground or caused by – oh. Crap."

"What?"

He pointed at the mountain. "That ain't a mountain. It's a volcano."

He stopped. His legs muscles tightened and he fought the urge to run.

"Why are we stopping?" she asked.

"Because I ain't walking up a damn volcano!"

"But the force field above it's the only way to escape."

"I ain't climbing a volcano."

"Look, there's no other way to get off this disc. Besides, it probably won't erupt."

Leon winced. "Don't jinx us."

A speck of whiteness flashed in the corner of his vision. He turned and watched a pegasus soar through the force field on the disc's other side, several clicks away. Leon cursed. He grabbed Elena and crouched behind a boulder.

She grabbed her sword's hilt. "What?"

He pointed at the pegasus. She frowned as the animal glided towards the ground, wings beating a laboured rhythm. A rider sat atop it. Leon gulped. Just as well the creature was landing so far away.

"Looks like a tired pegasus," she said.

"That ain't surprising, considering the rider. It's Teo."

Elena's eyes widened. "From the Resistance? Crap. How'd he follow us here?"

"Must've trailed us from a distance. Saw my glowfung, maybe. Shit."

The pegasus disappeared behind the volcano. Leon swallowed. The animal looked too exhausted to fly any time soon, but once it recovered, Teo would be able to scour the disc with ease.

Leon stood. "Keep going. We've got to get to the volcano before he finds us."

"We won't reach it before night falls."

"Damn, you're right. Fine. Walk as far as we can, then find someplace safe to sleep. Someplace Teo won't find us."

They stumbled across the jagged landscape. Leon clenched his teeth. This disc was bad enough by itself, but with Teo here to hunt them it had become even worse.

~ ~ ~

Leon and Elena staggered down into a ragged crater with walls tall enough to hide them from view.

Also tall enough to hide anyone who approaches.

Leon looked around the crater. He considered finding another place to sleep, but the thought of more walking made his knees ache. He sighed. This would have to do. He and Elena collapsed onto the ground and Leon pulled omnicrop roots out of his cloak.

Elena screwed up her face. "Yum."

"Unless you're hiding a chicken under your cloak, it's all we got. Besides, it's –"

"Great for my wings and it'll cure poisons and blah blah blah, whatever. Doesn't make it taste any better."

They sat in the darkness, munching the roots. Leon shifted position, trying to find a comfortable part of the rocky ground to sit on. He didn't find it. The rocks were hard and sharp, like the sword that pierced Alvaro's chest –

Leon growled. He shook his head, trying to dispel the image, but the sword and blood and Alvaro's wide-eyed face had been burned into his mind's eye.

The image of Alvaro's face thinned. The hair lengthened, and the cheekbones sharpened, and a sparkling blueness gleamed in the eyes, and now the gaping mouth and the ragged wound and the scent of blood belonged to Juliana –

Leon stood. "Elena, get up."

"What's wrong?" she asked.

His hands shook. "You want me to train you, right?"

"Yeah, but can't it wait? I'm tired."

No, it can't wait. If I sit and stare into the darkness, I'll see Juliana's death a thousand times. Your tiredness is nothing. Get up, you lazy girl.

He took a deep breath. "It won't be hard. I promise."

She yawned and stood with a slowness that made Leon want to yank her up.

"What's the lesson?" she asked.

Leon bent and grabbed an armful of pebbles. He paused. They'd been lucky to avoid Teo, but what if the bodyguard heard them training? Leon thought about stopping, but as he considered the choice, he realised the air was noisy with bubbling lava. Added to the darkness – and them hiding in a crater – meant Teo wouldn't find them unless he stumbled right past their spot. That was unlikely. Besides, Leon couldn't return to his thoughts.

He threw a pebble at Elena. "Catch."

She caught it.

"You're right." She raised an eyebrow. "That isn't hard."

"It will be. Catch this next one without your hands."

He chucked the pebble. She caught it in the fold of her cloak.

"Still easy, old man."

He scowled. "No cloak this time, or anything that's not your body."

"What? But how –"

He hurled another pebble and she dodged. Leon's next pebble hit her stomach.

"Hey," she said.

Leon winced, but Elena had enough sense to keep the noise quiet, and the crater's walls would dampen the sound.

She sidestepped his next throw.

"Catch," he said.

"But I can't use my hands."

"That's what I said. Is there an echo in here?"

She scowled and his next pebble bounced off her elbow. He grinned. He'd been on the receiving end at the Academy and it felt better to be the one throwing.

"C'mon," he said. "You're an angel. You can do this."

Leon chucked a pebble and it bounced off her scrunched-up forehead. She glared. Then her eyes widened.

"My wings …" she said.

Good girl.

Leon kept his face expressionless. Didn't want to give away the answer, after all.

She shrugged her wings out of her cloak. "But how do I catch with them?"

"That's for me to know and you to learn."

He threw another pebble. Softer, this time. She twisted and the pebble bounced off her outstretched wing.

Leon shrugged. "You hit it, at least."

220

"Shut up, old man."

She tried to catch his next pebble, but it skittered onto the ground. Leon threw again and again. A dozen throws later, she still hadn't caught a pebble.

"Want to call it a night?" he asked. "You've made a quick start, you know. Took me ages to try using my wings."

"Keep going. I can do this."

So they continued. After the thirtieth throw, scratches covered Elena's arms. After the fiftieth, Leon's wrists ached. Then, well after he'd lost count, Elena slapped her wings together and caught the pebble. Her eyes widened. She beamed at Leon and opened her mouth, about to cheer.

"Shh," he said. "Good work, but keep quiet. Don't want anyone hearing us."

"Oh. You're right."

He patted her on the back. "I mean it, though. Good work."

She squeezed his shoulder. "Good teaching."

Leon smiled. "Thanks, lass."

They ate more omnicrop roots, passing a water skin between them. After they'd finished, Leon tucked the leftovers into his pocket and they lay under a shelf of rock. Wasn't much cover, but it was better than nothing. Leon spent half the night awake on watch duty and the other half sprawled on sharp, pointy ground, while seething lava hissed and a man who hated them prowled in the darkness.

It was one of the most peaceful nights he'd ever had.

Chapter 32

"Craters," said Leon. "How are they formed?"

It was morning. Or at least whatever passed for morning on this disc of darkness and fire. Leon and Elena walked towards the volcano, which was lit by a thin column of sunlight from the transparent part of the force field far above.

Elena frowned at a pool of bubbling lava. "Is this a test?"

"Ain't everything?"

"Okay. Asteroids make craters."

"How?"

"They fall from space and smash into the ground."

"What about the force field?"

"What about it?"

"Doesn't the force field deflect asteroids?"

"Oh." She frowned. "Yeah. But then how do asteroids make craters?"

Leon grinned. "That's for me to know –"

"– and me to learn. Alright. Let me think."

He chuckled as they strolled. Leon supposed he should've worried. They were stranded on an unknown disc with a ruthless swordsman hunting them and they couldn't leave until Leon found a new breathfung. Despite that, a smile creased his weathered face. He kept his smile hidden from Elena, though. Didn't want her thinking he was soft, even though warmth rushed through him whenever she solved one of his puzzles. He wondered how long it would take her to solve this one.

"Asteroids definitely make craters, right?" she said.

"No. Craters are the footprints of giant lizards."

She glared. "Just checking."

"Don't check. Give me the answer."

"Do force fields have cracks in them?"

"If they did, what would happen to the atmosphere?"

"Oh yeah. It would leak into space ..."

They clambered over a clump of scattered boulders. Sweat dripped down Leon's face.

Why's the volcano so bloody far away?

"People can pass through the force field," said Elena. "So the field doesn't block everything."

Leon nodded.

"Are some asteroids made of a special material that lets them through the field?" Elena asked.

"No."

"Airships and pegasus-drawn carriages get through too, so it's not just natural objects ..."

"And what do pegasus riders do before entering the force field?"

"They slow down."

Leon nodded. "C'mon. You're so close."

He fought the urge to blurt the answer. It was so obvious, wasn't it? Then again, he supposed he'd once been as ignorant as Elena. No, he couldn't give the answer, or she'd never learn.

"Is it something to do with speed?" she asked.

"Maybe," he said.

Her eyes widened. "You've got to go slow to get through the force field!"

"Yes. Although the smaller and lighter something is, the faster it can pass through. An airship must slow to enter a field, while a single angel can travel faster, but you still haven't explained how craters are made."

They trudged up a slope of slippery, tar-black rock.

"Wait," said Elena. "I think I've got it. The force field deflects most asteroids, but some go slow enough to pass through. Having an asteroid big enough to make a crater but slow enough to get into a force field would be rare, though. Am I right?"

Leon pressed his mouth into a tight line.

"Aw, come on, tell me!" she said.

"Yeah, you're right."

She thrust her fist into the air, grinning, and Leon smiled. They crested the slope. Ahead, the tattered remains of a cloak lay between two boulders and a clump of glowfung cast light onto the rocks.

Elena drew her sword. "Reckon it's Teo's?"

"Bloody hope not."

Fumbling, he unsheathed his blade, wincing at the loud rasp.

A bare chested Payan ambled out from behind a boulder. He yelped.

"Er–hello!" His voice was high-pitched, yet sounded like he was choking on gravel. "C-can I help you?"

The skinny man chewed his lips and stared wide-eyed at their swords. His ribs strained at a thin coating of mottled skin and his three-fingered left hand locked around his other wrist to stop himself trembling. Blackened holes pockmarked his ragged trousers.

Not a threat.

Leona and Elena sheathed their swords.

"Just passing through," said Leon.

"Oh, that's a relief," said the skinny man. "You get some real crazies on this disc. Are you a Penitent?"

Elena frowned. "What's a Penitent?"

"People like me. We came to this disc after the War, to repent."

"For what?" asked Elena.

"Losing."

The man's lip trembled. He shrieked, ran to the nearest boulder, and head-butted it. Elena reached towards him.

Leon held her back. "Don't touch him."

"But he's hurting himself!"

The skinny man collapsed onto the floor. A line of blood trickled down his forehead and he stared cross-eyed at Elena.

"My sins are great," he said. "But the Star Spectre's mercy is infinite."

What the hell is this man doing?

"We'd best be going," said Leon.

He bowed – more a bob of the head than a proper farewell – and shuffled around the skinny man.

"Oh. Goodbye." The skinny Payan rubbed his head. "Where are you heading?"

As if I'd tell a lunatic like you.

"The volcano," said Elena.

Leon groaned. Why was she so damn trusting?

"I'm going there, too," said the man.

"We'd rather travel alone," said Leon.

"But I can help! I know the best paths, the safest routes – you're not from around here, right?"

"We could use help," Elena said.

"No," said Leon. "He's crazy."

"I can hear you," said the man. "And I'm not crazy. I'm Don Paquito, at your service."

He bowed so low that he almost toppled over.

"Leon," said Elena. "We need to reach the volcano as fast as possible. He'll help us do that."

Don displayed a crooked grin. "That I sure will do, brother!"

Leon sighed. Don looked harmless enough.

"Fine," said Leon.

"Woo-hoo!" Don clapped. "You're in for a fast and safe journey. People say I'm the best navigator on this disc. Or are they talking about the other Don? Anyways, let's go!"

He rolled up his bedding-mat, slung it over his shoulder along with a rucksack, and walked away in a wobbling line. Elena strode after him. Sighing, Leon followed.

"So what brings you to this fine disc?" Don asked.

"The weather," said Leon.

"Aha! Me too, brother. Provides a good air for repenting, does it not?"

Leon scowled at a pit of bubbling lava, then scanned the landscape, looking for Teo. No sign of him. Then again, the countless ridges and canyons and craters and spiked rocks could hide an army a stone's throw away and Leon would never know. His hand rested on his sword's hilt.

"How long have you been here, Don?" Elena asked.

Leon glowered. Why was she speaking? Silence was better than talking to a lunatic.

"Eighteen years," said Don. "Came here after the War, with

a few other Penitents. I suppose you'll become Penitents, too?"

"No," said Leon.

Don laughed. "But everyone here becomes a Penitent. Or goes crazy. Or dies. Plenty of ways to do the latter. You've got the lava, the lack of food, and the toxic gasses."

Leon swallowed. The stench of sulphur grew stronger.

"Toxic gasses?" he said.

"Oh, yes. I normally wear a breather, to stop the fumes from the lava, see, but it's hard to talk through a breather and I want to talk." He blinked. "Talk with you two, that is."

"Put on your breather," said Leon to Elena.

"We'll share." She put on her breather. "I'll give it to you in an hour, okay?"

"Good plan."

Don frowned. "Don't you have a breather, brother?"

"No." Then against his better judgment, Leon said, "Know where to find one?"

"Of course." Don pulled a quivering breather out of his pack. "Have it, brother."

"I can't take your breather."

"You won't." Don pulled out another breathfung. "I've got two, see."

Leon stared at the breather. His instinct was to refuse, but the breathfung looked healthy enough.

"Thanks," he grumbled.

Don handed it to Leon, grinning. "Always happy to help a future fellow Penitent! He he. Future fellow is a funny phrase."

Leon slapped the breathfung onto his face. The breather plugged his mouth and nose and pumped fresh air into his lungs. He wished it would block his ears, too. Then he wouldn't have to hear Don's prattling.

The ground steepened as they neared the volcano. Don scrambled up the rocks, pausing to reach into a crevice and extract several glistening worms. He offered one to Elena.

"I'm … full, thanks."

"Leon?"

"Hell no."

Don shrugged. "More for me, then."

He popped the worms onto his tongue and chewed with a look of blissful ecstasy. Wet squelches sounded from his half-open mouth. Leon shuddered.

Elena wrenched her gaze away from Don and pointed at several Payans descending from the volcano's peak. "Who are they?"

"Fellow Penitents." Don swallowed the worm, his throat bulging. "Probably said prayers, or made a sacrifice. Sure you don't want a worm?"

"Yes," said Leon. "What sacrifice?"

"To honour the Archangels, see," said Don. "And pray for our forgiveness. Nothing big. Not too many animals left here. We just sacrifice little things. Stones carved into Vahrians. Rare plants. Fingers."

Don held up his three-fingered hand. Leon's skin crawled.

"Haven't done a finger in a few years," Don said. "Might do one today … then maybe I'd be as penitent as ol' Lommy Two-Fingers. He would have been Lommy One-finger if he hadn't fallen in the volcano last year."

Leon gulped. Don was insane. Leon would've run away if Don hadn't picked a path that had taken them further in half an hour than they'd walked all of yesterday.

As they climbed the volcano, Leon peered around. Still no sign of Teo. That should have reassured him, but instead it made his skin tingle.

With much grunting and a lot of cursing, Leon scrambled over the volcano's ridge. Heat slapped his face. He stood on a ring of jagged rock which sloped down towards the centre, ending in a sharp drop which led to a pool of bubbling magma. The magma cast flickering light onto the rock. The transparent part of the force field was only a three hundred feet above. Stars gleamed beyond the field. Beckoning him.

So close ...

Leon wiped sweat off his brow and helped Elena clamber onto the ridge.

Don sprung up onto the rock, grinning. "Beautiful, isn't it?"

Leon raised an eyebrow. Sulphur, soot, and ash choked the air and heat pressed against his skin. Walking across the ground had been sweltering, but this place had the heat of a furnace. On the plus side, the hot air would aid Elena's flight.

"Well," said Leon. "We've got to go."

"Thank you so much for your help, Don," said Elena.

Don cocked his head to the side. "Where are you going?"

Anywhere away from you.

"Got a friend up in space," said Leon. "We'll light a fire and she'll come down on her pegasus."

Don gaped. "You're leaving. Wow. Didn't think you could leave this place."

Elena stared at the ground. "We would ask if you want to come with us –"

"But there's no room," said Leon. "Alright, then. We'd best go light our fire."

"I can help you," said Don.

229

"No. Our friend's twitchy. If she sees three of us instead of the two she was told about, we'll get shot."

"Oh."

"Thanks for your help, Don," said Elena. "We're both really grateful. Aren't we, Leon?"

She glared at him.

"Yeah," Leon said. "C'mon, let's go."

Don held out a water skin. "Will you at least have a drink with me before you go?"

"No," said Leon.

Elena scowled at Leon. "Thanks for the offer, but you need it more than us."

"No, have some," Don said. "It's a rain-day tomorrow. I'll refill then."

"Well, in that case, thank you," said Elena.

She took the water skin, popped out the stopper, and drank. She handed it to Leon.

"Not thirsty," he said.

Don's smile fell and his hands twitched. "Please, brother. It's all the hospitality I have to offer."

Elena nudged Leon. "Be nice."

He sighed and drank. "Thanks."

After the disc's heat and smog, the water soothed his parched mouth and sent a pleasing chill down his throat. Tension flowed out of his muscles.

He yawned. "Ready, Elena?"

She stared at Don. Leon groaned.

I swear, if she goes soft-hearted on this fool –

She yawned and looked away from Don. "Yeah. I'm ready."

Leon handed the water skin back to Don. "Bye."

Don grinned. Ash stained his tongue and gummy holes

230

filled the spaces where several teeth should've been. Leon looked away.

He stumbled along the ridge, Elena beside him. He wobbled. Spots danced before his eyes. Why'd he feel so sleepy? The climb must've taken more out of him than he'd thought. He yawned.

"You tired?" Leon asked.

Her eyes drooped. "What?"

"Tired. You feeling …"

His voice trailed away. Weakness flooded his knees and he collapsed. Elena fell beside him. Leon tried to stand, but he couldn't. He swallowed and it felt like he'd lodged a rock in his throat.

What the hell's happening?

Don loomed over him, grinning. Leon gulped. Those ashen teeth looked worse from down here.

"Don," Leon mumbled. "Help me up."

"'fraid I can't do that."

Leon blinked. "What?"

Don's lopsided grin widened. "Sorry 'bout this, but like I said, it's been too long since I gave the Archangels a good sacrifice. Throwing you and Elena in the volcano will make up for that, don't you think?"

Chapter 33

Don grabbed Leon's numb legs and dragged him towards the volcano's mouth. The rocky ground tore at Leon's skin and ripped lines of bleeding pain into the back of his hands. Leon tried to move, but his floppy limbs refused to obey him.

"Been years since I sacrificed someone," said Don.

Leon's head cracked into a rock as Don dragged him, sending pain pounding through his skull. His heartbeat raced.

The water must've had a sedative. Fast-acting, but not poisonous. Crosshade? Or Winterspell?

He'd made antidotes for both at the Academy, but his memory of those classes was hazy. Besides, he had no time to brew a potion.

Don hummed as he dragged Leon. "Last person I sacrificed was old Lommy Two-Fingers. Easy to push him into the volcano, with him missing eight fingers and all. No way for him to climb out. Ha!"

Leon strained to grab a passing rock. His hand twitched, but didn't grab the stone. He cursed. The words came out as a mumble.

"Sorry 'bout this," said Don. "But you shouldn't have come here if you didn't want to be a Penitent."

As Leon's head bumped along the ground, he glimpsed Elena behind him. Her limp body sprawled on the rocks. Panic raced through him. Don had dragged him halfway to the ridge's edge and Leon was seconds away from being pushed into the volcano. He pictured the lava engulfing him and smothering his cries.

Focus.

He needed an antidote for the sedative. His eyes widened. He had one: the omnicrop root in his pocket. Leon groaned. Why hadn't he thought of this sooner? It had only been on Pomeroy Disc that he'd told Elena how the root cured most poisons and she'd mentioned it again last night.

Don dragged Leon over ash that marked his back with faded heat. Leon swallowed. The volcano's mouth loomed a dozen feet away.

He strained, trying to reach into his pocket. His numb arm flopped onto his chest.

Okay. Now, into the pocket.

He pictured his hand's intended path and willed it to move. His hand missed the pocket and slapped onto the ground. A rock sliced his palm. Pain streaked through him. He growled and focused on the pain, forcing his hand to flop back onto his chest. He shoved his numb fingers into his pocket.

He felt his pipe. Then the matches. Then something dry and hairy. His fumbling fingers clenched the omnicrop root and he pulled it out and pushed it into his mouth. He chewed.

Don dropped Leon's legs. They thudded into the rocky ground. As Leon mashed down on the omnicrop root, fear jolted through him. He was running out of time. To his right, the ridge cleaved away and lava seethed and bubbled below, sending heat roaring onto Leon's ash-stained face.

Don took a rope out of his pack and tied it around his waist, then around a rock. "Don't want to fall when I push you, brother, do I?"

Leon's teeth ground against each other. He'd finished the omnicrop root, but how long would it take to counteract the sedative?

Don raised his arms and stared into the volcano's maw. "I dedicate this sacrifice to the Star Spectre. May you receive this gift in your name –"

Leon's finger twitched.

"– and the names of the nine major Archangels –"

Leon raised his hand.

"– and the names of the eighty-one minor Archangels –"

Feeling flooded back into Leon's legs, making him wince.

"– and the names of the Payans that serve you –"

Leon tried to move his foot and his boots twitched. The volcano's stench grew stronger.

"– may you look humbly on my sacrifice and may it be worthy of your glory."

Don put his foot under Leon's side, ready to push him into the volcano.

Leon grabbed Don's ankle.

Don's eyes widened. Leon bared his teeth, and yanked Don's leg, and Don slipped, tripped on Leon, and fell off the ridge. The rope snapped tight and bones broke with a dry crunch. Leon peered over the edge.

Don dangled below, spinning as the rope twisted. A groan bubbled from his mouth, his arms hung at his sides, and blood dribbled from a cut on his forehead.

Leon stumbled to the boulder Don had tied his rope to. The boulder teetered. One push, and the rock would roll down the slope and plummet into the volcano, taking Don with it.

He tried to kill us. A tooth for a tooth's only fair.

Leon crouched, picked up a smaller rock, and wedged it against the boulder to fix it in place. In the scheme of things, it didn't help much. Don still had to climb out of the volcano, but at least this way he wouldn't die and he'd stay away until Leon and Elena left.

A shadow shot overhead and Leon ducked, cursing. A pegasus landed with a clatter of hooves and a roar of wind. Ash blew into Leon's face, stinging his eyes. He squinted.

Teo leapt off the pegasus. "Hello, traitor."

Leon's stomach twisted. His mouth went dry and weakness shot through his legs, making him clutch the boulder for support.

Run!

But Elena lay sprawled behind Teo and Leon knew that he'd kill her if Leon fled.

Leon gulped. "I'm no traitor."

Teo dashed forward. He leapt onto the boulder and his sword materialised an inch from Leon's nose. Leon's heartbeat spiked.

"Don't run," said Teo.

Leon held up his open hands. "Please. I ain't a traitor."

"Don't lie. Girl talked in corridor outside my cell."

"She was being dragged to Drayton's torture room!"

"No. After I broke door, you boarded airship. She dressed liked inquisitor."

Leon swallowed. His heart pounded and sweat made his palms clammy, but he couldn't think of anything to say. Teo was right. It sounded suspicious. Hell, it was impossible to argue against, but Leon had to try.

235

"We're looking for –"

Teo pressed his sword against Leon's mouth. "No more lies."

The blade pierced Leon's lips. Blood dribbled onto his chin and the ash and the fear and the pain stung his eyes. Tears dripped down his face.

Teo scowled. "Kneel."

His sword twirled, sending the flat of his blade crashing onto Leon's head. Leon dropped to his knees. Down here, he was level with the rock he'd wedged against the boulder Teo stood on. Fitting, Leon supposed. He belonged down in the dirt.

Teo drew back his sword and in a flash of dry-mouthed panic, Leon scooped a handful of ash. He threw it up. Teo leant to the side, the boulder wobbling under him, and the ash missed his face. Didn't bother Leon, though, because that was a distraction.

Leon kicked the rock wedged against the boulder.

The rock skittered away. The taunt rope jerked on the boulder Teo stood on, and the boulder tilted, rearing up to smack the Payan. Teo fell off, landing on the rope. The boulder slid down the slope, crunching into Teo, and the rock and the hulking Payan fell into the volcano with a grunt and snap of broken bone. A thick, gloppy splash echoed from below.

Leon crawled to the drop-off. The volcano's maw snarled back at him, showing only rock and bubbling lava.

He stood. Leon's legs shook and for a heart-pounding moment he wobbled and almost stumbled off the edge. He staggered away from the drop-off.

I killed him.

Leon ignored Teo's pegasus and knelt beside Elena's limp body.

And I killed Don, too. So much for sparing his life.

Growling, Leon tore off Elena's breathfung and shoved omnicrop root into her gaping mouth.

"Chew." He hoped she could hear. "It'll cure you."

I killed them. Ain't I got anything to say about that?

Elena's jaw stayed slack. Leon waved his hand in front of her eyes, but she kept gazing at the stars.

Wasn't me that killed them, though. Was it? Didn't mean to kill Don, even though I could've. And Teo – well, the rock snuffed him, didn't it? Not me?

Leon tapped Elena's cheeks with his thick fingers. "C'mon. Chew."

No, I don't kill. Do I?

A tremor shook Leon's knees. He closed Elena's mouth, turned her onto her stomach, and moved her jaws up and down. Omnicrop root squelched inside her mouth.

Except I killed those Resistance fighters, didn't I? Could've warned them about the inquisitor, but I kept silent. Coward.

Another tremor rattled Leon's knees. The ground shook. He worked Elena's jaw harder and tried to ignore the voice in his head.

And I killed that cadet in the forest on Hargold, or will I pretend that wasn't my fault, either?

A splash of gloppy liquid echoed from the volcano's mouth. A rumble made Leon's neck tingle.

Sweat dripped from his nose onto Elena's neck. "C'mon, girl."

Shit. I'm pathetic.

Leon shook his head, but it didn't drown out the voice.

237

And killing the cadet, the Resistance, Don, Teo ... they ain't even the worst things I've done.

Heat flared behind him and lava splashed onto the ground near the pegasus' hooves.

No. They ain't the worst. Not by a long way.

The pegasus neighed and flew away. Leon worked Elena's jaw faster.

No. The worst thing happened in Mangold Pass. Remember?

"Shut up," said Leon.

Remember Juliana and Blas?

"Shut up!"

Elena twitched.   Leon turned her over with trembling hands.

She blinked. "Who are you talking to?"

"No one. You alright?"

"Mmm." She yawned. "What happened? I remember falling …"

Another tremor shook the ground. Leon slung Elena's arm over his shoulder, and hauled her up, grunting.

"Don poisoned us," he said. "Tried to sacrifice us into the volcano."

A huge clump of lava sprayed from the volcano's mouth and splattered onto the ridge.

"And now it's erupting," Leon said. "We've got to leave."

Elena yawned. "Think we climbed up from over there."

She tried to stumble away.

Leon held her back. "No. We need to fly."

"But I feel like the plague."

"We've got to! The eruption could destroy the whole disc. Look." He pointed up at the force field's transparent part. "We can't fly up there from anywhere else. Too far away. This

238

is the closest we can get. C'mon, the air's hot here. Ride it up to the force field."

"It's hot because the volcano's erupting!"

She swayed and yawned, blinking through heavy-lidded eyes.

"You can do this," Leon said.

He sure hoped she could, or they were both dead. Another tremor wobbled his legs.

"I believe in you," he said.

More lava splattered onto the ridge. Heat choked the air. Leon gulped. Only a matter of time before lava showered onto them.

"Shit, Leon. Why can't we do things the easy way?"

She slapped herself and yelled so loud he jumped.

"What the hell you doing, girl?"

"Waking up. Get on my back."

Leon gave Elena her breathfung and she fixed it to her face. He checked his own breather. Hadn't fallen off. Just as well, because every bloody other thing had gone wrong in the last few minutes.

She unfurled her wings. Leon climbed onto her back, making her knees buckle and her wings sag. She yawned and Leon prayed for the pegasus to return so he could fly on it instead, but Elena was already staggering towards the ridge's edge. Leon didn't even have time to curse before she leapt off the volcano.

They plummeted.

Rock thrust up towards them and wind ripped through Leon's hair. He screamed. Then Elena's wings snapped taunt and Leon's face thudded into her shoulder. The breeze caught them.

They circled the volcano and Elena's wings beat at the air. They rose until they glided above the volcano's mouth. Leon looked down, gulping. Lava hissed and spat below. Hot air smacked into them. Leon tightened his grip and they spiralled up on a column of heat towards the force field, and as they shot into space the volcano's angry bellowing cut off.

They flew onwards, back into silence.

Chapter 34

They landed on a deserted micro disc and slumped to the ground. The asteroid belt and Paracelsus-7 were only three hours away, but Leon and Elena needed rest, even if it let Drayton increase his lead.

Leon shivered. Damn micro discs were always freezing. This place was no exception. Groaning, he stood and gathered timber. There were no trees or plants, but plenty of driftwood had crashed onto the disc. His fatigue-numbed hands snapped three matches before lighting the fire. Flames flickered into existence, bathing them with feeble warmth. They roasted omnicrop root and ate.

"Don't taste so bad now, eh?" said Leon.

A tiny smile creased Elena's face. "Got any stories?"

"Eh?"

"Well, we're around a campfire and I could use the distraction."

"I ain't got stories."

Blas had been the storyteller. Whenever they camped, he entertained Leon and Juliana with tales of angels, romance, and mill workers who looked under the bridge for the ghostly screeching noise no matter how much Leon shouted at the idiots to stay away. He'd kept them enthralled until the fire burnt to embers and they realised they had to wake before dawn. He could've made a damn good bard. Leon sighed. If only he remembered Blas' stories.

"That's okay," said Elena. "Because I've got one."

Leon yawned and munched his omnicrop root. "Too tired."

"You're still eating."

"Fine. One story."

Elena grinned. "Alright. I heard this one when I was a child, from an old lady who sat on a street corner and told fairy tales for food. Me and the other children used to –"

"I've almost finished eating ..."

"Okay, okay!" She cleared her throat. "Before the Great Departure, there lived two Minor Archangels, who were twins. Ines: the Archangel of flowers, and Murio: the Archangel of dirt and sand. Ines lived in a floating palace weaved from masinth vines and toras petals. Murio's citadel was carved under the earth. Her domain was damp, and cold, and earthworms wriggled through the walls.

"Ines' palace was adorned by fine trophies and artworks: gifts from angels seeking her approval. These pilgrims hoped to become blessed like Ines' chief entertainer, Ramonet. Highborns from distant discs would travel to attend Ines' lavish balls, where Ramonet sang ballads so beautiful that distant mountains wept.

"Murio's citadel had no trophies, artworks, or balls. Her home was a realm of squalor and darkness. Ines often invited her sister to balls in her floating palace. Murio refused, for she feared heights, but not as much as she feared scorn. And so in her cave that dripped with water and smelled of rotting moss, Murio lived with only her sand-servants for company.

"One morning, Hieronyma – the captain of Ines' soldiers

– received a letter. She snuck into a storeroom to read it, hoping it would be from her lover. Alas, it was from Ines. The Archangel's writing was loopy and full, with the neatness of a row of flowers. The letter contained dire news. Murio had sent her sand-servants to abduct Ramonet, and the bard was trapped in Murio's underground citadel. Ines could not confront her sister, for the Star Spectre forbade Archangels from challenging each other, so Ines tasked Hieronyma with rescuing Ramonet.

"Hieronyma hated being underground. But she equipped herself with spear, torch, and rope, and journeyed to Murio's cave. She wished to prove her loyalty to Ines. More importantly, she wished to rescue Ramonet, who was her secret lover.

"Murio's citadel was a labyrinthine construction of narrow tunnels and low-ceilinged halls, all carved from dirt. As Ramonet snuck through the passageways, she worried less about being caught and more about the structure collapsing and burying her. Murio's dungeons were empty, save for the sound of soft singing from behind a stone door. Hieronyma smiled, for she recognised her lover's voice. She rolled aside the door and the singing stopped as she peered into the shadowy room. A figure stood inside.

"Hieronyma recognised Ramonet's outline and raised her torch to see his delicate face, but Ramonet cried out. He warned she must not look at him. Murio's curse would ensnare them both if she cast her gaze upon him before they escaped her citadel. Hieronyma longed to see her lover's countenance, but she cared for his safety more. She led Ramonet out of the underground citadel. The corridors were carved through dirt, full of loops, strange angles, dead ends. After hours, Hieronyma discovered a hole that led to the outside. She crawled into the hole. Then she held out her hand for Ramonet. Seconds passed, but Ramonet's thin, clever fingers did not intertwine with hers. She called for him to climb after her. Ramonet did not respond. Footsteps echoed in the distance, growing closer. Hieronyma called for Ramonet again. His silence hung over her with the weight of a shroud. The footsteps grew closer. Hieronyma longed to look back at Ramonet, but she kept her eyes averted. Instead, she begged Ramonet to join her.

"'Lover!' she said. 'We must escape!'

"A cackle sounded from behind Hieronyma. Her heart sunk. Murio had caught them. Hieronyma had failed Ines and she'd doomed Ramonet.

"'You can look, child,' said Murio.

"Hieronyma refused to turn, terrified of seeing Ramonet, but a force compelled her head to twist. Ramonet stood in the corridor. Alone. Hieronyma's heart blossomed with love and she opened her mouth to call his name, but then he sneered. His face bubbled. His skin twisted. He morphed, growing taller, and his hair lengthened, his cheekbones sharpened, and he transformed into the Archangel Ines. Hieronyma gasped.

"'So,' said Ines in a voice that matched her twin's. 'You sought to steal Ramonet's heart?'

"Hieronyma tried to respond, but flesh closed over her mouth and her hands melted into stubs.

"'I've known about your secret meetings for weeks,' said Ines. 'Ramonet is mine. How dare you try to steal him from me?'

"Ines clicked her fingers. The scent of blossoming flowers exploded through the corridor. Hieronyma's legs and arms melted. She shrunk. A new mouth ripped open on her face, and her transformation into an earthworm was complete. Ines stalked away. Weeping, Hieronyma burrowed into the soil and never emerged again."

Elena stared into the fire and her face glowed red. Leon yawned. He lay down and rolled his cloak around himself. Wasn't much warmth, but it would do.

"What are you doing?" asked Elena.

"I've finished eating."

"But what about my story?"

"I listened, didn't I?"

She scowled. Leon remembered his literature professor at the Academy. She'd had the same frown when Leon didn't applaud after she argued that a poet's description of blue curtains endorsed the Tovarn War.

Leon wriggled, trying to position himself to avoid the sharp pebbles. Problem was, every pebble was sharp. Elena pulled off her half-circle pendant and rested it on her hand. She stared at the crackling fire. Her hand drifted towards the flames and her pendant's chain dragged in the dirt.

"Why do you keep your pendant, Leon? The one Juliana carved for you."

Leon groaned. "Can't it wait 'til morning?"

"I need to know. Why keep something that reminds you of loss?"

Leon struggled into a sitting position, wincing as stones pressed into his arse. He grabbed his own pendant. The flames cast light over the scratches from when he'd once thrown it off a cliff.

"I already abandoned them. I can't forget 'em as well. It's the least they deserve."

"You mean, even after twenty years ..."

He glared at her. "They'd do the same for me."

Elena swung her pendant by the chain. The tiny metal half-circle swung over the fire, then back towards her. Over the flames ... then back ...

"Does it get easier?" she asked.

A lump formed in Leon's throat. He dreamed of Juliana and Blas most nights. The worse part of his day was when he woke and realised those dreams were just that: dreams. When he saw dewy-eyed young couples holding hands, something cold and hard sank into his guts. He never ate spit-roasted hare, because every bite was a mouthful that should've been cooked by Blas. Whenever he moved, Juliana's pendant pressed against his skin.

"Yeah," Leon lied. "It gets easier."

Elena nodded. Her pendant swung over the fire and then she hung it back around her neck and tucked it under her cloak.

"Alright." She exhaled a huge breath. "Alright."

Why had Leon lied? Did he want to spare her the pain of knowing she'd carry Pierce's death forever? Or did he think he could fool himself into believing things could improve for himself?

Elena wrapped her arms around herself and stared at Leon with bloodshot eyes. "I've done bad things, Leon."

He sighed and thought of Mangold Pass. "Me too, girl. Me too."

"You don't understand. It's ..." She swallowed and tucked her knees under her chin. "I shouldn't have mentioned it."

"Hey. Look at me."

She raised her head.

"Whatever you did, it's history. Ain't nothing you can do to change it, so move on."

You're telling her to move on? Hypocrite, much?

She wiped her glistening eyes. "You don't understand. I ..." She sniffed. "No. Never mind. It's fine."

Whatever she'd done, it wouldn't be half as bad as she thought it was. Besides, Leon could help. It was too late for him to change, but she still had a future.

She plastered a shaky smile onto her face. "Good night."

Leon sighed. "Night."

They wrapped themselves in their cloaks and lay on opposite sides of the lukewarm fire. Leon stared up at the night sky. If only people were as straightforward as his star charts.

Chapter 35

There it is, thought Leon as he and Elena crested over an asteroid. *Paracelsus-7.*

The colossal, ring-shaped rock floated in the Mallean asteroid belt, encased in a spherical force field. A faint blue jetstream ran through the ring's centre like a shimmering thread.

Leon gestured for Elena to circle Paracelsus-7 before landing. She nodded and they glided around the asteroid. Below, iron-collared convicts tore at the surface with pickaxes, while armoured Vahrian soldiers watched them. Three airships floated above a mess of stone shacks huddled in a large crater: the main barracks, Leon assumed.

They circled the asteroid. A cluster of tents and another three airships anchored around a steel mound. His heart leapt. One of those airships bore the distinctive mark of the Vahrian Inquisition, printed onto its balloon. That was Drayton's ship. Judging by Elena's shudder, she also recognised it.

They landed in a crater, trusting the darkness would hide their descent. A puff of dust rose into the air as they landed. Leon stumbled off Elena's back and they removed their breathers. The chink of pickaxes and the faint grunting of convict miners sounded in the distance.

"Nice flying," he said.

She nodded, swaying on the spot.

He pulled an omnicrop root from his cloak. "Here."

She yawned. "Not hungry."

"You're tired. You need energy and this'll give it to you."

She scowled, but ate the root. They trudged towards where Drayton's airships hovered over the mound of steel. Elena tucked her wings under her crimson inquisitor's cloak.

They crested a hill. In the valley below, a hasty camp sprawled around the steel mound. Three airships hovered above, tethered to the ground by anchor ropes. The steel mound looked like a mineral deposit, but with four Vahrian soldiers guarding a hole in the steel, Leon guessed it was the entrance to another secret chamber.

"Leon?"

"Mmm?"

He turned to look at her. She stared at Drayton's airship and creases formed around her eyes.

She gulped. "I need you to promise something."

"Sure."

"If he catches me, you have to escape. Don't try to rescue me, don't try to kill him, just get away. Fast."

Like I did with Juliana and Blas?

She glanced at him. "Promise me."

"You know I can't do that."

"We've only survived because we've been running from Drayton. But if you run *at* him …" Elena sighed. "I know this guy, Leon. I read his files when I broke into the Inquisition's office. After the War, he was assigned to hunt forty-three angels. Know how many he caught?"

"Do I have to find out?"

"All of them."

Silence stretched between them. In the camp below, soldiers laughed and flames rose as cooks roasted meat. The smell made Leon's mouth water.

"You don't know what you're dealing with," Elena said. "If I'm captured, escape without me. Promise?"

"Alright," he lied. "But he ain't gonna catch us. Now, how are we getting into that camp?"

She frowned. Leon doubted she was convinced, but he didn't care. He wouldn't leave her. He'd already abandoned too many people.

"We can't sneak through without being seen," she said. "Too many people."

"Don't sneak, then."

"And get skewered by a sword?"

"Karym's horns, girl. You're wearing inquisitor's robes."

"Oh. So, same plan we used to get on the slave ship?"

Leon grimaced. Playing prisoner had grown old.

"Not exactly," he said.

~ ~ ~

Elena strode through the camp and up to the steel mound with the careless assurance of an inquisitor. Leon strode beside her, holding his head high. They passed meek-looking Vahrian scientists, linguists, and historians, who nodded when Elena and Leon swept past them.

Leon kept his trembling hands stuffed in his cloak. Every time they rounded a corner, he expected to see Drayton, smiling at them while he lent on his cane, but he and Elena faced no opposition.

Until they reached the steel mound.

"With respect, Inquisitor Drayton told me he's the only inquisitor on this site," said a sentry outside the tunnel into the steel.

Elena looked down her nose at the soldier. "He was, until I arrived. I've brought Professor Melasco." She gestured at Leon, who bowed. "He's a Payan archaeologist and will help with our mission."

"Sorry, ma'am, but Inquisitor Drayton said –"

Elena brandished her inquisitor's badge. "Let me in, or you'll be in a slave collar by nightfall."

The soldier gulped. "As you wish, my lady."

Elena strode into the tunnel. Leon scurried along in the wake of her flapping cloak.

"Nice going," he said.

She grinned. They strode through the tunnel, which felt more like a corridor than a natural formation. They twisted around the corner and stopped. The tunnel ended in a flat wall of smooth steel, bearing a circle holding nine other circles, each containing nine more dots. It was the Archangels' Mark.

Looks like a door.

Leon and Elena tapped it. Something pricked Leon and he pulled his hand back to see blood welling into a dot on his fingertip. The foot-thick steel door slid to one side, revealing a huge chamber.

They grinned at each other and walked inside.

The door slammed shut behind them.

Leon jumped. Footsteps echoed in the distance and someone hammered on the door. Leon and Elena drew their swords. More fists clanged on the door and someone cursed.

251

"Can't open it," said a muffled voice. "Damn it. What will we tell Drayton?"

Leon clenched his hands into fists. The voice sounded like the soldier they'd spoken to at the entrance.

"Follow my lead," Elena whispered.

Leon frowned. "Eh?"

"Help!" She knocked on the door. "We're trapped."

"How'd you get in?" said the soldier on the other side.

"My archaeologist did something!"

Leon gulped. Elena glared at him.

"Say something," she whispered.

"Blood!" he said. "Angel's blood! I had it in a vial and when I smeared it on the door, it opened."

"Why'd it shut?" asked the soldier.

"Something clicked when we walked inside. Pressure plate in the floor, maybe?"

The soldier cursed. "Why didn't you wait?"

"Pretend I hit you," Elena whispered.

Leon yelped. He slapped the metal door for extra effect.

"Because he's a right idiot, he is," said Elena. "He walked in and I went to grab him, and then it closed behind us."

A rhythmic clicking sounded from behind the door and the soldier cursed. "Damn it."

"How do we open it?" asked the soldier. "Battering ram?"

"It's a foot thick," said Elena. "And Archangel-made. No ram could break it."

"I've studied similar tombs," said Leon. "The tombs of the Mahrican ancients."

"For Menon's sake, get on with it, man."

"Sorry. See, Mahrican tombs had several puzzle rooms between the entrance and the sarcophagus. Once you solved all the puzzles and reached the end, the main entrance would open and you could exit. This should be the same."

"And if you don't reach the end, the door stays shut?"

"I presume so, sir," said Leon.

The soldier cursed.

"Alright," said Elena. "Me and this idiot professor will fix this. Soldier, you stand guard outside."

A pause. Leon frowned. Was someone whispering on the door's other side? He shrugged. Probably just his ears ringing in the aftermath of the door slamming shut.

"Alright," said the soldier. "We'll wait outside the tunnel entrance."

Footsteps receded.

Leon grinned. "We fooled 'em."

"If we get through this, we should be actors."

"Yeah, right. As if any playhouse could afford us. C'mon, let's figure this out."

He surveyed the huge, circular room. He hadn't noticed it before, but thick moss covered every surface, and when he rubbed it the moss was hard, like fungcrete. Out of curiosity, he pulled a match from his pocket, lit it, then held the flame against the moss. As he watched the flame, he wished he still had his pipe and kemp to go along with the matches. Stupid Vahrians.

After a minute, the match extinguished before it could leave a scorch mark. This wasn't ordinary moss, then. Leon stroked his chin. The first chamber on Anshan had been like a steel cave, but this one was like a cavern sculpted inside a lump of fungus.

Above them, the domed ceiling was smooth enough to be Archangel-made, and light beamed down from the dome's centre, even though there was no hole. Dozens of empty niches circled around the walls beneath the dome. On the ground, nine openings led into short corridors.

Elena strode around. "These corridors are all dead ends. Not even any doors."

"Don't go into them until we find the right one."

She rolled her eyes. "Thanks for the safety tip."

"You count eighty-one niches?" he asked.

She counted. "Yep."

He pulled out the Sarahk and flipped to the *Tellings of Ellarmun*, the ninth book of the Sarahk. Then he found the eighty-first chapter within the *Tellings*.

Elena peered over his shoulder. "What are you looking for?"

"I don't know, but there's nine corridors, and eighty-one niches. It might be a code."

Together, they read the chapter:

In the outer reaches of the realm was a disc called Grunai, populated by settlers who had struck out for the disc many years ago. They were faithful to the Star Spectre, but the disc was far from civilisation and harsh for living. Snowy mountains covered most of the land, and what little arable land remained was barren and poorly suited for grain. So, as the years marched on, the settlers struggled to provide.

In Anshan, the prophet Ellarmun had a visitation from Harym, Archangel of Home, Hearth, and Food. She told him to travel to Grunai and fast for nine days on the tallest mountain. When Ellarmun arrived at Grunai, their village leader, Garbulan, greeted Ellarmun with grace.

"My lord," said Garbulan. "We wish our finest welcome to thee,

but our feast shall be meagre indeed. We are struggling to grow crops, and do not know if we will survive the coming months."

Ellarmun longed to climb the mountains and begin his fast, but he knew the Archangels would not begrudge his charity. He instructed Garbulan to show him their fields.

They walked amongst the crops, which were sickly and dying. The farmers greeted Ellarmun with good cheer, for they recognised a man of strong faith, but it was clear they had fallen upon harsh times.

Ellarmun gathered the farmers and the other villagers. "I have communed with the Star Spectre, and she has given instructions for solving your plight. You are to burn your fields, destroy the grain, and throw any stored food you have into space. Then, you will climb the mountains with me and fast for nine days hence."

Anger erupted through the crowd. The villagers yelled at Ellarmun, saying that this was a foolish idea that would only starve them. Ellarmun held firm. Seeing his conviction, and knowing he was a holy man, the leader Garbulan calmed the crowd and convinced them to accept Ellarmun's plan.

So the villagers razed their fields and destroyed all food they possessed. Then they climbed to the highest peak. With Ellarmun leading them in prayer, they fasted for nine days. Even the frailest among them were given strength to persevere.

When the nine days were done, they descended back to the village. To their amazement, fresh crops stretched across the field. Unlike their previous grain, this crop towered above them and was imbued with such healthy sheen that the farmers set to weeping. Their village was saved.

Ellarmun gathered the villagers again. "Let all remember, a full bucket cannot hold more water. Those who seek to know must first forget, and those who seek to be filled must first be emptied."

"That's how omnicrop was made," said Leon. "Although it wasn't named until later."

He looked around the circular room. Nothing seemed different and he wondered if he was missing something obvious.

"Do we have to empty ourselves, somehow?" asked Elena. "Like fasting for nine days?"

"Maybe. But we don't have that much time. What if those soldiers work out how to open the door?"

"Then what do you think the story means?"

Leon stared at the Sarahk, mind racing. At the Academy, they'd been taught codes for hiding information within a letter. He applied some of those now – the ones he remembered, at least – but no meaning arose from the pages.

Leon sighed. "Maybe this was a false lead. Let's step back and start from the beginning. We're in a circular room with a domed ceiling. Nine corridors, eighty-one smaller niches above them –"

He gasped. It was so obvious – why hadn't he realised this before?

"Nine Major Archangels and eighty-one Minor Archangels!" Leon pointed at the light beaming from the domed ceiling's highest point. "And above, the Star Spectre."

Elena's eyes widened. "So it's a temple?"

It was, although with moss covering the walls instead of marble and stone, it had taken Leon a while to make the connection.

"Help me measure," he said.

They paced across the floor.

"Diameter of one hundred and forty-seven feet," she said.

"I got one forty-four, but it's close enough to match my

256

theory. This ain't any temple. It's a replica of the All-Temple, in New Kion."

"The one with the first secret chamber!"

Leon rolled his eyes. "No. A different All-Temple on a different New Kion."

"Hey, I'm just checking. Anyway, how does that help us?"

Leon paced around the chamber. "In the All-Temple, touching the Severym statue opened a secret entrance. Here, all the corridors lead to dead ends. But if we go into the corridor that matches where Severym was, a secret entrance might open."

"Might?"

"Well, it could incinerate us instead."

"Great."

"Got to be realistic, is all."

And besides, joking eases the fear. Not by much, though.

She sighed. "Which corridor matches Severym's position?"

Leon counted three corridors clockwise from the entrance door. "That one."

He didn't tell Elena his memory of the All-Temple was hazy at best. They stared at the corridor, which looked like the others: ten paces long, terminating in a dead end.

Hope that ain't a literal term.

Leon removed his shoe and threw it down the corridor. No hidden blades chopped it into pieces. No beams of light incinerated the shoe. Wasn't much consolation, because the shoe was probably too small to set off traps.

"Want to go first?" he asked.

Elena gestured at the corridor. "Your guess, your privilege."

"Alright. If it incinerates me, throw half my ashes into space. Throw the rest into a Vahrian's soup. If I'm going to die, at least give the bastards indigestion."

"Don't say that! You'll be fine. Like you said, this theory's logical, it explains why this room's a copy, it –"

"Relax. It'll be fine. And if it ain't, don't put my ashes in soup. Put 'em all in space."

"You're going to be fine."

Leon smiled. Felt more like a grimace, but it bolstered his bravery and he needed all the help he could get. He turned away from Elena to face the corridor. He stopped smiling. If he was wrong …

No. Like she said, it makes sense.

Still didn't make it easier to take that first step. He muttered a prayer to the Archangels. Then, tensing his muscles and holding his breath, Leon shuffled into the corridor.

Chapter 36

Nothing happened.

Leon breathed out and put his boot back on. "It's safe."

"I can see –"

The floor jolted beneath him. Then the patch of moss he stood on descended. Elena raced towards him and slid across the floor, dropping onto the descending platform. She yelped.

"Marym's tongue!" She tried to put weight on her injured leg, grimacing. "Twisted my ankle."

"Here, hold my shoulder."

The platform lowered them through the ground with a squelching sound that made Leon think of food being swallowed. He winced.

Not a good image.

He pulled glowfung from his cloak and purple light illuminated the shadows under Elena's eyes.

The mossy walls opened around them. With a shuddering halt their platform stopped in the corner of another massive chamber.

A door stood on the room's other side, blocked by a snarling bull statue. Unlike the mossy platform they'd descended on, dirt covered the rest of the floor. A deep pond ran along one side of the room.

"What do you reckon?" he said.

Elena pointed at the bull statue. "Odd place to put a sculpture."

Leon frowned. She was right. The statue stood in front of the door, so they'd need to climb over it to leave the room. He gulped. He didn't like this. Not one bit.

"See any other doors?" he asked.

"No. Unless they're in the water."

Leon couldn't see the bottom of the pond. He imagined a tentacle emerging from the dark water, and he shuddered.

"Let's not go in there," he said.

She rubbed her twisted ankle, scowling. "Let's not."

"Yeah. Let's not."

Elena arched an eyebrow. "Did you just copy –"

"Shut up."

Quit delaying and get on with it.

He stepped off the platform and onto the dirt. A rumbling growl echoed through the chamber and Leon cursed and leapt back onto the platform.

His heart hammered. "The hell was that?"

"I don't know. You waved the glowfung around too much for me to see."

"You hold it, then."

He thrust the glowfung into her hand and she held it above her head. The feeble light gleamed off the bull statue. Leon frowned. Had it moved?

"Swords out," he said.

He tried to sound gruff, not scared, but he doubted that he'd fooled either of them. They unsheathed their swords. Elena stood on one leg and jiggled her twisted ankle, wincing.

"You holding that glowfung?" he asked.

"What's it look like, old man?"

"Just asking."

Dryness made his voice croak. He licked his lips. Tensing, he stepped onto the dirt. A rumbling growl shook the room as he squinted at the bull statue. Then, it moved.

"Shit," said Leon.

The bull charged. Terror locked up Leon's knees, froze his muscles, and as the bull lowered its horns, Elena yanked Leon back onto the platform.

The bull skidded to a halt at the platform's edge, snarling.

Leon's heart pounded. He and Elena backed up against the wall, holding their swords. Leon swallowed. His blade was a twig against the bull's hulking mass. A puny, useless twig.

"Don't move," Leon said.

The bull paced along the platform's edge. Leon's sword trembled in his sweat-stained hand.

Elena frowned. "I think –"

The bull's angry bellow cut her off.

She gulped. "We're safe on the platform."

"W-what?"

"It can't step onto the platform."

The bull roared. Leon shied back, but he realised she was right. The bull's stomping hooves hadn't touched the platform. Elena limped forward. The bull's nostrils flared and it bellowed, making Leon flinch, but the beast stayed off the platform.

They were safe.

He walked up to Elena's side. The bull's eyes narrowed as it paced beside the platform, snorting.

"How –" Leon's voice cracked. "How are we getting past?"

"Fly?"

Her voice was higher than usual. That made Leon's frantic heartbeat slow a little. He wasn't the only one who was scared.

"Ceiling's too low," he said.

"Can we outrun it?"

The bull tossed its horns and snarled.

She gulped. "Scratch that."

"We're safe on the platform. Stab it without stepping off?"

"Yeah. Good idea."

"Thanks."

They shifted from side to side.

"Are we, like, both doing this?" Elena asked.

He nodded.

"Okay," she said.

"Ready?"

"Yeah. You ready?"

"Karym's horns, girl! I just said that."

"So you're ready?"

"Shit, no."

The bull narrowed its eyes. Leon took a deep breath and tried to ignore the horns glinting in the light.

No! Don't ignore them. Watch the hell out for them, or they'll end up in my chest.

Elena tightened her grip on her sword and her knuckles whitened.

"Alright," he said. "I've got the neck. You take the head. Let's do this."

They stepped forward and Leon swung a two-handed blow at the neck as Elena stabbed the eyes. The creature roared and slashed his horns left and right, catching and slicing Leon's wrist. He cursed. His sword twisted out of his grip and he stumbled back, blood dripping from his throbbing wrist.

Elena stepped back from the thrashing bull. "I got him!"

"Where?"

"Right in the eye, but he didn't even blink."

"This ain't a normal bull." Fresh pain lanced through his left wrist. "Karym's horns!"

Elena looked at Leon's arm and her eyes widened. "It cut you?"

"No. My wrist's always like this. Quit the dumb questions and help me bind it."

Elena muttered under her breath. She tore a strip off her cloak, wrapped it around the bleeding cut on Leon's left wrist, and bound it. The makeshift bandage soaked with blood straight away. Leon inspected the bandage, not because he thought she'd tied it wrong, but because he didn't want to look at the bull.

"Crap," Elena said. "It got your sword, too?"

Leon glared at her.

"Sorry!" she said. "Dumb question, I know!"

He clenched his hands into fists and looked past the bull. His sword lay beside the pond a dozen paces away from the platform. Too far to reach.

Leon frowned. *The pond ...*

"Reckon it can swim?" he asked.

"Looks too heavy."

She was right. The bull looked carved from stone, despite it pacing along the platform's edge. Leon swallowed. Elena's sword hadn't hurt the creature. Would Leon's ploy do any better?

He pulled out his breathfung with a trembling hand and told Elena his plan.

263

She gaped. "Marym's tongue. That's insane."

"Forget it. It's a dumb idea –"

"No. It might work, but it's still crazy and if it goes wrong … hell, look what it did to your hand."

Leon didn't need reminding. Pain thudded through his arm and every heartbeat stabbed needles into his wrist.

"You can't risk yourself," Elena said. "I'll do it."

"What? No!"

"It's the only way to defeat it. That's why the pond's there, isn't it?"

"Well, yeah. But if I ain't doing it, you ain't either, girl."

"What the hell's that mean, old man? You reckon you're better than me?"

"Course not, but can you swim?"

Elena stared at the ground. "Screw you."

The bull bared its teeth. Leon prayed the creature couldn't understand them.

"Hold my cloak, will you?" he said.

She sighed. "Of course."

He slapped the breathfung onto his face, pulled off his boots, stripped down to his undergarments, then gave his cloak to Elena. He stared at his sword, which rested next to the pond, and clenched his hands into fists.

"Leon?"

He glanced at Elena. Her eyes were wide and for a moment he remembered how young she was.

"Good luck," she said.

A lump formed in his throat. "Thanks."

He took a deep breath and the bull snorted.

Leon ran.

He sprinted off the platform too fast for the bull to react.

264

Dirt churned under his toes and he shot towards where his sword lay next to the pond. Hooves thundered behind him. Leon skidded to a halt at the pond's edge, grabbed his sword, whirled to face the mass of stone-carved muscle thundering towards him –

But as the beast charged, Leon dove to the side.

The bull's hoof crunched into his flailing leg, knocking him into the pond. He splashed into the water. Coldness pierced his sides and he gasped for a second before the bull fell on him, plunging them both under the water.

Leon tried to squirm out from under the beast. The bull thrashed. Its horn stabbed into Leon's breathfung and dragged him down as the bull sunk. He punched the creature's snout. His blows bounced off the bull's head, dampened by the water.

The beast yanked back, tearing the breathfung off Leon's face. Leon yelped. Bubbles billowed from his mouth and he swallowed water. He shut his mouth, choked on water, and tried to swim away, but the bull pinned him with its legs and Leon kept sinking. Lungs straining, he reached for something to grab, but his hands slid down the mossy walls.

He was going to drown.

Chapter 37

Bile crawled up Leon's throat as he hammered the bull's ribs, his hands bouncing uselessly off the creature's torso. He glanced up. The surface was far away and darkness frayed the edges of his vision. A dull splash sounded somewhere above. His lungs screamed for air and he stretched up a trembling hand –

Elena grabbed it.

As Leon gaped, she slapped her breathfung onto his mouth. Fresh air swelled into his lungs.

She twisted, put her feet on the bull's side, and pushed, holding his arm. His legs wrenched free of the bull's grip. Leon kicked. They floated upwards. Elena's flailing arms didn't help much, but he had enough strength for them both. Light shimmered above them. Leon clawed at the water and they broke through the surface.

They crawled from the pond and Leon tore off the breathfung and spewed water onto the dirt. He coughed. Fresh pain throbbed through his wrist. Elena winced as she put weight onto her rolled ankle. Water dripped from her cloak.

She panted. "Cold."

"Water's like that." He clapped her on the back, making her cloak squelch. "Thanks."

"Is the bull gone?"

"Looked too dense to float, but let's not stick around to find out."

He scrambled into his trousers and shirt and stepped into his boots. He was halfway through pulling on his cloak when he saw Elena shivering. Water dripped from her sodden clothes.

He offered her his cloak.

Her teeth chattered. "Thanks, but I'm fine."

"Don't be stupid. You'll get a cold."

"I don't need it."

He didn't move his outstretched hand.

"I can't take your cloak," she said.

"I've got my shirt and my trousers. I'll be fine. Besides, I'll have it back once yours has dried."

She stared at the cloak.

"Hurry up and take it," he said.

"You sure?"

"Karym's horns! I wouldn't have offered if I wasn't."

"Well, alright then. Thanks."

Leon transferred his belongings into his trouser pockets, gave her the cloak, and turned his back while she changed. He buckled his belt, sheathed his sword, and tucked his breathfung in his shirt. No way was he losing that.

Elena wrung out her sodden cloak and laid it on the floor. They crossed the room and entered a narrow corridor with a glowing door at the end. Carvings covered the ceiling, walls, and floor. Leon recognised a few Psalms from the Sarahk. Halfway along the corridor, a dark opening punched a hole in the wall, blocked by prison bars. Leon frowned.

Elena hobbled forward, but Leon stopped her.

"Might be traps," he whispered. "Let's go slowly, and watch that opening."

They crept down the corridor. Elena held his shoulder as she limped beside him. They stopped before the opening. Leon swallowed. Bars obstructed the shadowy hole in the mossy wall and he worried an animal would leap out when they walked across the opening.

"No other way to get around," Elena said.

Leon glanced at the phrases etched on the walls. Nothing warned against the opening.

"Blades out," he said.

He drew his dagger and Elena pulled out her sword. He clenched his knife's stained leather grip with a white-knuckled hand as he walked past the opening.

"Hello?" said a voice.

Leon jumped. Someone had spoken from inside the opening. Leon held up his glowfung, but the purple light couldn't penetrate the inky blackness behind the bars.

"Is someone there?" said the voice.

The speaker sounded deep, dry, and desperate, as if he hadn't used his voice in a while.

"Keep going," whispered Elena. "He can't see us."

Leon glanced along the corridor. The golden door at the end was edged open a crack. He should keep moving. Push through the door, continue through the chamber, and reach the end.

Instead, he said, "Who's that?"

"Oh, thank the Archangels! I'm but a poor convict, good sir. Wandered into this place and been stuck ever since."

Elena tried to pull Leon away.

"This is a trap," she whispered. "He couldn't have gotten in here unless he's an angel. He's lying."

"Thank you so much, good sir, for rescuing me," the voice said. "I haven't seen the stars in months."

"We didn't say anything about rescue," said Elena.

"Oh, and a kind lady too!" The voice paused. "Forgive my hearing, but did you say you're not rescuing me?"

"We're here to find the Path to Waverrym," she said.

"Oh. Alright, then. Go find your fancy Path and I'll just sit here and rot."

Elena scowled. "Leon, this is a trap. He couldn't have survived here for months."

"What do you think I am?" said the voice. "A ghost? Water drips through the ceiling and fungus grows on the walls. Tastes like dung, but it feeds me."

Elena tugged Leon's arm. "Come on."

He hesitated. Something about the voice kept him rooted in place.

"Back in my day, Payans used to help each other," said the voice.

"If we were to free you," said Leon. "How would we do so? There's no lock on these bars."

Elena groaned.

"A thousand praises for you, good sir. See the hole next to the bars? On your left."

The hole was ragged, dark, and made Leon think of scorpion nests.

"There's a button at the back," said the voice. "When I was wandering along here, I pressed it and the bars opened. I peeked inside and chains sprung out and pulled me in. Maybe if you press the button, the bars will open again?"

Leon blinked. "I have to put my hand inside that hole?"

269

"Please and thank you, good sir!"

Leon gulped. Anything could lurk in that crevice. Spiders. Serpents. Rats. Maybe the hole would constrict and crush his hand, or slice off his fingers with a hidden blade.

"Is there a stick I can use?" he asked.

"I'm afraid the button can only be depressed by a Payan finger, good sir."

"Forget it," said Elena. "It's a trap."

Every instinct yelled at Leon to scurry away. Then he remembered his cell in the Inquisition's castle. Cold, damp, and crowded with fear. What would it feel like to lay trapped in a cell for months and then have your hope of rescue dashed?

"Elena, you told me something a while ago," said Leon. "An angel always helps those in need. Remember?"

"This is different. You can't even see who's in there."

"I'm chained to the wall, kind lady."

"Argh!" said Elena. "This is stupid. Come on, let's go."

Leon stared into the dark cell. "No. I'm sick of abandoning people."

He plunged his uninjured hand into the ragged hole. Elena cursed. She tried to pull his arm out, but Leon pushed her away and reached deeper into the hole. He pressed something that clicked.

The bars across the opening retracted into the walls. Light flared, scattering the darkness to reveal an empty room.

Leon stepped inside and Elena hobbled in behind him. He frowned.

Where is he?

"That was close," said the voice.

Goosebumps rose on Leon's arms. The speaker sounded like he was right next to him, but there was no one there.

Karym's horns! Leon's heart beat faster. *He's a ghost.*

"If it wasn't for you, good sir, you two would have come to an unfortunate end," said the voice. "That golden door at the corridor's end leads only to death. Now, don't forget this."

A new carving, etched in gold, appeared on the wall:

21/32/851.31

Elena pulled off her boot and scratched the numbers onto the sole with her knife. "Is that a date?"

"No." Excitement raced through Leon. "Coordinates. For a disc. First two digits means the distance from Neebia, in astronomical units. Second two digits give the orbital angle, relative to Neebia's equator. Third set is the orbital period, in days."

"So where's it lead to?"

Leon stroked his stubbled chin and ran the calculations. With an orbital distance of twenty-one units, the location was somewhere in the Outer Regions. An angle of thirty-two meant the disc was removed from other discs: most orbital angles were under ten degrees. He smiled. With a period of almost three years, the location could only be one place.

"Nustune," he said.

"Quick calculations, good sir," said the voice. "When you wish to exit, take the route that got you here, except in reverse."

Leon looked around for the voice's source. He stopped.

Pretend he's behind you. Don't think about him being a ghost, alright?

Leon winced. "Er … thanks. Wait, it's Nustune for sure?"

"Erm. I'm not supposed to tell you that. Technically, I'm not allowed to even talk with you like this. Sorry. Nothing personal, just how they made me."

"Where's Nustune?" asked Elena. "I've never heard of it."

"Not many have," said Leon. "It's the most isolated disc in Paya. It's a small two-disc system, inhabited by monks. No Vahrian presence. Too damn far away from anything for the Vahrians to bother."

Leon strode back along the corridor to the door they'd entered through. Newfound energy shot through him. He knew where to go and Drayton didn't. He and Elena were going to find Waverrym!

Elena limped after him. "Any plans for escaping without getting caught by the soldiers?"

Leon's smiled faded. He'd forgotten they were surrounded by a Vahrian camp. He stalked across the room, glaring at the pond, then stepped onto the platform. Elena retrieved her cloak and hobbled onto it. The platform ascended.

"Same as how we entered," he said. "Stick with the story. Tell them we solved the puzzle rooms and say we need to go to our tents to write a report before we forget anything. Then, soon as we're near the edge of camp, we fly away."

"And if that doesn't work?"

"Fighting's an option, I guess. Anything to get us through the tunnel and into the open. But pray like hell we can bluff our way outside, because there were four soldiers guarding the tunnel before, and there's only going to be more now."

Their platform stopped at the level of the main chamber. Leon licked his lips. If they could escape, Drayton wouldn't be able to solve this chamber, and he wouldn't know to fly to Nustune. Leon and Elena would have a head start. Drayton might be eliminated from the race for good!

Leon supported Elena as she staggered across the chamber towards the open entrance door. The corridor beyond the door was empty. No guards.

Perfect. Now we just have to get outside.

Elena hobbled behind him. He hoped she could take off from the ground, or they were both screwed.

"Ankle still bad?" he asked.

She winced. "It's fine."

Leon stepped over a steel pole jammed in the doorway. He helped Elena over the pole. Then he gazed back at the cavernous chamber and a smile creased his weathered face. As he waited for the door to slide shut, he muttered thanks to the Archangels.

But the door didn't shut.

Metal scraped and grinded, but the pole stuck in the door kept it open. Leon's eyes narrowed.

"My thanks, once again," said a familiar voice.

Leon whipped around. A dozen soldiers swarmed into the corridor and Inquisitor Drayton limped around the corner.

Chapter 38

Leon's throat tightened and the memory of Drayton's red-hot iron made his leg flare with pain.

"Take them," said Drayton.

The soldiers rushed forward. Leon snarled, dropped into a crouch, and drew his sword, ready to go down brawling. He couldn't return to the inquisitor's torture room.

Elena grabbed a fistful of his cloak and hurled him back into the chamber. Leon slid across the metal floor. A soldier tackled Elena to stop her running after Leon, but as she fell, she kicked the pole blocking the chamber's door.

The pole skittered across the floor.

"No!" said Drayton.

The door slammed shut, cutting Leon off from Elena, Drayton, and the soldiers.

He staggered up and hammered on the door. "Elena!"

"Leon! Go –"

Her voice cut off. He pictured a soldier's hand clamping over her mouth and Leon screamed, pounding the door, yelling at it to open. The door stayed shut.

"I'll rescue you, Elena!" he said. "I'll save you, I swear! And then we'll find Waverrym!"

No response came from behind the door.

His hands trembled. "Elena?"

No reply.

He pictured a soldier dragging her towards Drayton. Leon cursed. Elena had scratched the co-ordinates for Nustune on her boot. Drayton would read them, follow them, and find Waverrym.

Leon bellowed.

His scream echoed through the chamber. He stumbled to the centre and stood in the beam of light streaming from above. He pulled the Sarahk from his pocket. Still yelling, he tore apart the book with shaking hands, ripping the pages into tiny scraps that fluttered onto the floor around him. Tearing the pages hurt his wrist, but he didn't care. He glared up at the light. Leon pictured the Star Spectre gliding overhead and heat surged through him.

"If this is how you treat us, it'd explain why you've got no friends!"

He pictured Drayton's red-hot iron scorching Elena's side. Leon collapsed onto his knees. He sobbed.

"Good sir?"

Leon looked up. "Who's that?"

"It's me again, good sir."

He recognised the voice. It was the same one that spoke from the walls in the corridor below.

"Just checking," said the voice. "That bit about not having friends: you weren't talking about me, were you?"

"No."

"Oh, good. Have a nice day, then."

A nice day?

Leon bunched his hands into fists. An inquisitor had captured Elena and this stupid voice wanted him to have a *nice day?*

He stood. "Oi! Come out and face me, asshole!"

"Sorry, good sir, but I'm just a voice. Afraid I'm not blessed with a body like you."

"Blessed?" Leon stamped his foot. "I ain't blessed. An inquisitor captured my friend. He'll torture her. He might kill her."

A lump formed in his throat. He swallowed it. He needed anger. Rage. Needed it hot and sharp, so he could picture slicing through Drayton's smiling face and not think about Elena screaming ... Elena hurting ... Elena dying ... leaving Leon more alone than he'd ever been before.

"Human thoughts are not my specialty," said the voice. "But I assume you wish to rescue your friend?"

Leon wiped a bead of moisture from his eyes. "Yeah."

"You wish to escape this chamber, then?"

Elena had so quickly become everything to him ...

"Yes." A vision of soldiers swarming through the open door sent fear flashing through him. "Wait! I can't go through the main door."

"But that is the only door."

Leon swallowed. "There has to be another way out. Please."

Silence.

"I've got to get out. I need to save my friend."

The floor vibrated under his boots. He gaped as a steel cylinder lifted him up through the shaft of light, towards the apex of the domed ceiling. The ceiling winked with light. Then, a patch of the dome opened like a flower and the steel cylinder carried Leon through the opening.

"Thank you," he said.

Leon ascended through the ceiling. The walls fell away

276

around him and with a click, the rising cylinder stopped, depositing him on top of the steel mound.

He crouched, muscles bunching at the thought of arrows. But while the Vahrian camp spread out around the steel mound, no heads tilted to look up at him.

A snapping sound echoed from the camp. Drayton's airship and two other vessels broke free from their anchors. The ships rose. They glinted as they ascended through the force field and glided into space. Dull pain throbbed through Leon.

They're heading towards Nustune.

He watched the three airships until they disappeared. Elena was on board. He could sense it. Drayton needed an angel to solve whatever riddles lay at Nustune.

Leon wrenched his gaze away from the stars. He glared at the convicts hacking at the asteroid with pickaxes. Soldiers watched the prisoners and a settlement loomed in the distance. The settlement held a cluster of soldiers' barracks and convicts' sleeping quarters. Three airships hovered above it, anchored by long ropes.

If Leon wanted to pursue Drayton and rescue Elena, those airships were his only way off this asteroid. But how to reach them? With an army he could hold the Vahrian soldiers hostage on the ground and force the airships to land, but he was just a lone man.

His gaze flicked back to the toiling convicts. Leon frowned. *Maybe I do have an army.*

~ ~ ~

The padlock broke with a twist of Leon's knife. Muscles tensed, he waited for soldiers to burst from the barracks behind him.

All was quiet, save for distant laughter.

Leon winced at his knife. The blade wasn't made to lever open chains and he'd worried his weapon would snap.

He glanced back at the barracks. Why hadn't the Vahrians posted a guard outside the convicts' sleeping quarters? He supposed it wasn't like the convicts could escape the asteroid. The airships floated too high to climb up their anchor ropes and were always manned by Vahrians.

Or maybe there's guards inside the sleeping quarters.

Rubbing his aching wrist, he looked at the door, as if he could see through by staring hard enough. He couldn't. Leon thought of Elena, gritted his teeth, and opened the door.

The room stank of sweat. A mound of cloaks lay heaped in the middle of the stone-walled room and as the pile shifted, Leon realised the cloaks held convicts.

Bodies of bone and skin twisted to face him. Sunken yellow eyes stared at Leon.

"I'm here to rescue you," he said.

A shaggy-bearded convict with a scrawny chest sat up. "Piss off."

A few convicts laughed, sounding like wheezing crows. A bald woman glared at the bearded man. A couple of the other convicts looked at her, like they were expecting her to do something.

Leon blinked. "Didn't you hear me?"

"Don't think you heard me," said the shaggy-bearded man. "See if you hear this: guards! Come here!"

Chapter 39

Leon gaped. "Karym's horns! What the hell are you doing?"

The bearded man shrugged and a door slammed in the distance.

"I'm here to free you!" said Leon.

"Nah," said the bearded man. "Unless by freedom, you mean death. Best not risk it."

Outside, ambling footsteps crunched across rock, growing louder. Leon's heart hammered. If he bolted through the door, he could escape before the guards arrived, but if he wanted to leave this asteroid, he needed the prisoners' help. Leon stared at the withered bodies sprawled around him. A few watched with mild interest. Most slumped back onto the ground and stared at the ceiling.

"The price of freedom may be death," said Leon. "But life with an iron collar around your neck … is that really a *life*?"

The bearded man smirked. "Best start running, mate, unless you want to try it for yourself."

Outside the building, the footsteps drew closer.

"I used to be like you, you know." Leon pointed at the bearded man. "But I've changed."

"Too bad for you."

The bald woman and a few other convicts sat up and watched.

"Didn't use to care about anyone," said Leon. "I thought cutting myself off would help me forget the past, but all it did was enslave me to it. And now, I've met a woman who's changed everything."

"Well bloody done for you," said the bearded man. "Looks like old pegasi can fly new routes after all."

"She ain't just any woman," said Leon. "She's brave. Honourable. And she's the last angel."

The bald woman's eyes widened and convicts gasped. An elderly woman made the Sign of the Archangels and muttered a prayer.

"Angels don't exist," said the bearded man. "Not anymore."

"They do." Leon swallowed. "I'm one, too."

"Yeah, right. You said she's the last –"

The bearded man choked on the rest of his words as Leon pulled down his cloak and showed the two stubs on his back where he'd hacked off his wings.

"She is the last angel," said Leon. "The last decent one, anyway. But an inquisitor's taken her and she'll die unless I get off this asteroid and save her."

This time, the bearded man kept silent. The bald woman exchanged a glance with the elderly woman who'd uttered a prayer when she saw Leon's sawn-off wings. Something passed between them.

The approaching guards were near enough to hear snatches of them talking.

Leon's gaze swept across the convicts. "Our past has as much power as we give it, but even if we've been cast into hell for what we've done, we're still alive. And if we're still alive? Then it ain't over. Whatever we did, whatever got us here, what we do now will define us."

A few convicts glanced at the bald woman, as if they were waiting for orders.

"This is your chance to escape," said Leon. "To choose freedom over slavery. This ain't just freedom from chains, but freedom from whatever you've done before. This is your chance to rise from the ashes and cast aside the shackles of your past!"

The door opened. Two Vahrian soldiers gaped at Leon.

"For freedom!" said Leon.

He charged at the nearest soldier, drawing his sword. Metal crashed on metal as the man's blade slashed into Leon's sword. Pain flared through Leon's wrist. The second soldier drew his sword, ready to plunge it into Leon's exposed side.

And then the bald woman tackled the soldier.

Leon gaped. *Someone listened. Someone's helping!*

Distracted, he turned back to the first soldier and fell, cursing, as the soldier's blade whistled above him. The soldier's sword plunged towards Leon. Before it pierced his chest, two convicts crashed into the Vahrian, knocking him to the ground.

Leon stumbled up. He couldn't believe it – the convicts had knocked out the two soldiers! Noise rustled behind him. He turned and the mound of prisoners rose, cheering. From holes in the wall and from under their beds and from dozens of other hiding places, they pulled out shivs and clubs and sticks. They charged forward, and the swell of roaring bodies pushed Leon out the door and into the courtyard.

More soldiers burst from the barracks. They charged towards the convicts. Leon raised his sword in his right hand

281

and his knife in his left and screamed Elena's name as he ran. Brandishing their makeshift weapons, the convicts followed.

Leon crashed into a soldier and they both lost their swords as they slammed into the dirt. They grappled. Boots and bare feet stampeded over them. Shrieks and blood and flashing steel crowded the air above as Leon strained and growled as he edged his knife towards the Vahrian, the man's sweaty hand pushing at Leon's forearm. The soldier's eyes were wide and pale. A pang of guilt streaked through Leon. The man thrashing beneath him was more boy than man and his eyes bulged with fear.

Then he gripped Leon's throat and squeezed.

With a guttural shout, Leon plunged his knife into the soldier's neck. Blood spurted onto Leon, blinding him. He growled and held down the knife until the Vahrian stopped thrashing and his hand fell from Leon's throat.

Leon grabbed the soldier's sword. He stumbled up, slipping on the blood-slicked ground, and gaped at the battle raging around him. Screams and shouts and moans pierced his ears and the air was clogged with sweat and struggling bodies and biting steel.

A Vahrian lunged at him. Leon swung his sword but the leather grip twisted in his sweaty hand and the blade bounced off the soldier's armour. The man's knife sliced a line of red-hot pain across Leon's arm as he tried to dodge.

Fear surged through Leon. He stumbled back, holding his sword between him and the knife-wielding Vahrian. A hand tripped him. Leon crashed onto a snarling soldier, whose arm pressed down on Leon's throat. Leon thrashed, his eyes bulging. Above, the other Vahrian stalked away and the mass of stampeding bodies swallowed him.

Spots danced behind Leon's eyes. He hit the Vahrian beneath him with his elbows, but his attacks bounced off the soldier's helmet and the man laughed. Spittle gurgled down Leon's chin. He growled. Death wouldn't take him here, not on this blasted asteroid. He had to escape.

Must save Elena.

A guttural snarl filled his throat. He dug his fingers under the soldier's arm and pushed, his heart hammering and lungs straining. The iron-clad arm left his neck. Leon gasped. He twisted, rolled off the soldier, and kicked the Vahrian's head, knocking him out.

Blood thumped through Leon's skull. He stood and rubbed his bruised neck with shaking hands.

"Well fought, mate," said a voice.

Leon whipped around. He stood outside the battle and the bearded convict leant against a wall, holding his hands behind his back.

Leon scowled. "Thanks for the help."

"I'd rather watch. Besides –"

An arrow sliced through the air from above and punctured the man's chest. Bone cracked and blood burst. The man pulled his hands out from behind him, revealing five stolen swords.

"Give 'em hell," he gurgled.

He threw the swords into the dirt at Leon's feet. Then he fell.

An arrow hissed from the sky and thudded into the ground next to Leon and he remembered he was in a battle. He grabbed a sword, gave the rest to nearby convicts, and looked up. Three Vahrian airships floated above the battle, lit by torchlight from below. Arrows shot from one airship and rained upon the struggling convicts and soldiers. Fear surged through Leon.

More arrows plunged down, cutting into the raging fighters. Screams tore the air. A group of convicts abandoned battle, running for the nearest building.

"Hold," said Leon. "Hold!"

They rushed into the soldier's barracks, ignoring him. Leon cursed. The convicts were skinny and malnourished from toiling in the mines, but mining had also made them strong. Combined with their greater numbers and the element of surprise, they'd dispatched most of the soldiers, but if arrows kept pelting down, their chances of victory were slim.

"Grab the anchors." He pointed at the long ropes tethering the huge ships to the ground. "And pull down the airships!"

Chapter 40

L eon sprinted through the battle, pushing through soldiers, leaping over slashing steel, and ducking piercing knives. He grabbed the biggest airship's anchor rope and tugged. Pain burned through his injured wrist. High above, the vessel bobbled, but even when Leon hauled himself up to put all his weight onto the rope, the airship stayed afloat. It seemed the three-hundred-foot long vessel was too heavy for one man to drop.

The bald woman burst through the battle that raged around the anchor. She heaved on the rope. Above, the airship dipped. An arrow lashed through the air, carving a bright red gash into the bald woman's arm. She grimaced and pulled harder. Sweat glistened on the beard-like stubble on top of her head and she nodded to Leon, baring her teeth.

Another convict added his weight to the rope. And another. And another, until a clump of convicts seethed around Leon, cursing and pulling. Their bodies were lean and scrawny from months of hard labour and poor eating, and the airship was so huge it cast them all into shadow. But despite the airship's size, it was a vessel designed for lightness and it was already loaded with a cabin full of soldiers. Together, the mass of convicts dragged it to the ground.

Up on the vessel, a soldier tried desperately to sever the anchor rope. But before he could break the cord, the airship crashed onto the barracks. Wooden splinters flew through the air as the stone walls crumbled, falling onto the ground with a thump that shook Leon's boots. Savage joy swept through Leon. He and the other convicts swarmed over the barrack's ruins and clambered into the airship. Everything disintegrated into a blur of clashing steel.

Leon's sword took a Vahrian in the armpit, more by accident than design. He ripped out the blade, gasping. Leon's knees ached, his chest heaved, and wooziness made his head spin. Why had he started this?

Then he thought of Elena, screaming in Drayton's torture room. He gritted his teeth. Couldn't stop, not until he rescued her. He growled and cut and stabbed and clawed and yelled and bit and kicked and sliced until the last Vahrian collapsed onto the bloody floor.

Fatigue washed through Leon and he stumbled shaky-legged to the railing. He puked. A hand crashed onto his back. Leon turned to see a grizzled-looking man, grinning a bloody smile.

"Where's your fighter's stomach, angel?"

Leon's hands shook. "Death's nothing to cheer."

"No, but freedom is."

He thought of what Professor Nane had told him at the Academy, all those decades ago. *An angel cares for the greater good. An angel cares naught for himself.*

Convicts pulled the other two airships down and swarmed into them. Corpses littered the ground and the air reeked of spilled organs. Leon swallowed. He'd done this. With words of foolish bravery, he'd killed scores of convicts and soldiers,

286

as swift as if he'd slashed a blade across their throats.

Leon stumbled off the airship and onto the crimson soil. Thundering applause greeted him. Up close, the stench of dead meat watered his eyes. Convicts raised their swords and chanted.

"Angel! Angel! Angel!"

Lumps of bloodied flesh sprawled on the ground. Leon stared at the gaping, sightless faces, frozen forever in death's embrace.

"Angel! Angel! Angel!"

There was no glory here. Only death. He fought the urge to vomit again.

"Angel! Angel! Angel!"

Leon's legs shook. He longed to run from the chanting crowd, slump onto a patch of grass, roll his cloak around his body, and sleep forever.

But Elena needed him.

And so did Waverrym.

An angel cares for the greater good. An angel cares naught for himself.

He clenched his jaw. Setting his shoulders, he raised his hands and the chanting faded.

"Thank you for your bravery," said Leon.

Thank you for slaughtering these men and women: for killing sons, daughters, fathers, mothers, husbands, wives.

"I still mean to rescue my friend, so I'll need one of these airships, but you're welcome to the other two."

The bald woman frowned. "Don't you want us along, Angel?"

Leon glanced at the carnage strewn around him. "You've already helped me enough."

Angry mutters drifted through the crowd.

"We want to help," said someone.

"Yeah!"

"We want to save the other angel."

Sickness dribbled into the back of Leon's throat. The thought of leading more of these Payans to the slaughter made him shudder.

Then he thought of Elena.

Drayton already had dozens of soldiers. He might recruit more if he passed through a garrisoned disc. Leon couldn't free Elena by himself. He'd need an army. And it wasn't just Elena he had to save, because Drayton meant to destroy Waverrym: home to a civilisation of angels, if the stories were true.

An angel cares for the greater good.

Leon swallowed. "You're free to go your own way, but if you wish to join me, you can."

The crowd cheered. Half the ex-convicts surged forward and bowed to him. Leon counted. Eighteen men and women, with grim determination etched onto their faces. He didn't know how many soldiers Drayton had, but this would even the odds.

Leon stared at the Vahrian soldiers' rotting carcases. He tried to imagine them as animals. Tried to forget they'd been humans until a blade snuffed their lives. He couldn't.

That would make this next part tougher, but still necessary.

An angel cares for the greater good.

"Strip their armour." Leon pointed at the soldiers. "And ransack the barracks. We'll need four days of supplies."

Chapter 41

Leon brought the airship in to land on an empty micro disc. He'd wanted to push further towards Nustune, but he was exhausted after a day of navigation, especially since he'd plotted a complex route that avoided all inhabited discs. Pushing himself had worked, though. They'd covered half the distance to Nustune in a single day's travel. Not bad considering he'd wasted two hours learning how to fly the three-hundred-foot-long Vahrian airship.

Gravity pressed upon him as he glided through the force-field. His legs were weak after hours in space. Behind him, the ex-convicts grumbled as gravity gripped their own bodies.

He landed the ship. The bald woman – Mencia was her name – was the first to rip off her breathfung and leap out to survey the land.

Leon shuffled outside, wincing at the pressure gravity put on his knees. He always found these places strange. Far away from anywhere important, too small to hold a decent population, and without so much as a rat scurrying across the barren surface. What had the Archangels been thinking? Or maybe they hadn't been thinking at all, and this was less about design and more about randomness.

No. That was the old Leon talking – the old Leon who was

always certain in his disbelief. After what he'd seen in recent weeks, he'd realised certainty was only a few steps removed from stupidity. The universe was vaster than he could have imagined, and he'd learned there was truth to the Sarahk.

Yes, this disc must've existed for a reason. It just wasn't one he could see.

"There's springs!" said Mencia, who'd already dashed up a hill.

The other ex-convicts climbed out of the airship, and with Leon following them they circled the hill. Sure enough, shallow pools of water bubbled in the hill's shadow. Leon dipped a hand into the warm water.

The ex-convicts stripped off and clambered into the hot springs, sighing as the warmth relaxed their aching muscles. Some of them closed their eyes, and a few even smiled. A faint trace of blood leaked into the water – trailing from beneath bandages that hadn't been wrapped quite tight enough.

Standing on the bank, Leon watched. He wasn't a prudish Vahrian who thought nudity was somehow shameful, but there was a reason he'd avoided the public baths after the war. Entering the water meant showing his hacked-off wings. Even though the ex-convicts had already seen the stubs on his shoulder blades, he didn't want to repeat the experience.

He turned away and strode up the hill. They had plenty of food, but he might as well search for more omnicrop.

"Angel!"

He turned.

Mencia waved at him from the pool. "Coming in?"

The other Payans opened their eyes and watched.

"I've got to check things in the ship," he said.

"That can wait," said Mencia. "It's so nice in here."

Leon paused. He was asking these men and women to fight for him, maybe even die for him. If he wasn't willing to bathe together, what message did that send? Besides, they'd already seen his shame. Showing them again wouldn't hurt him anymore.

"You're right," he said to Mencia.

He removed his clothes and slipped into the water, trying to ignore the ex-convicts gaping at the hacked-off wings on his back. Staring was frowned upon in bathhouses, but most people didn't have anything as eye-catching as a pair of severed angel wings.

Warmth loosened his muscles. The water soothed the scarred burn mark on his thigh and relaxed his injured wrist. Both injuries still hurt like hell, but over the last day they'd faded a little. Thank the Star Spectre for the bandages and the burn ointment he'd found when they ransacked the Paracelsus-7 barracks.

Leon closed his eyes and groaned in appreciation. The ache in his knees lessened and the stiffness faded from his joints.

"Angel?"

Leon opened his eyes. An eldery woman with kind eyes stood beside him, a look of reverence on her face. He thought her name was Salome, but so many ex-convicts had introduced themselves on Paracelsus-7 that all their names had blended together.

Leon blinked. She was talking to him. Karym's horns, it felt odd for a stranger to call him an angel.

"Yes?"

"You don't have to tell us, if you'd rather keep it private." Salome's eyes flicked to Leon's back. "But if you're comfortable … we all want to know your story, sir."

The other ex-convicts watched with poorly disguised curiosity. Leon glowered. After an exhausting day of travel, the last thing he wanted to do was talk. Hell, even if he hadn't travelled, these people were strangers and he hated telling strangers about himself. Especially considering what he'd done over the last few weeks. Yes, there'd been moments of pride, but when he thought about it fully, those moments were outweighed by his cowardice.

The woman raised her hands. "It's fine, I know you're tired –"

"No." Leon steeled himself. "I've asked you to help me. It's only fair that you know who you're helping."

He took a deep breath, and then he spoke. He spoke about his wings growing when he was a boy, about entering the Academy, about bonding with Blas and Juliana. He talked about the War, how he'd lost everyone he cared about, and his wings. He paused. They didn't know he'd cut them and it was well within his rights to let them think a Vahrian had done it. But lying felt wrong.

Gritting his teeth and looking down into the water, he told them what he'd done. A few of them gasped, and Salome made the Sign of the Archangels.

"I ain't proud of it," Leon said.

He paused. With shaking fingers, he pulled Juliana's necklace up so he could see the carvings in the wood. It was his only possession he hadn't left with his clothes on the bank of the springs.

Leon swallowed. "Every day I think about what I'd do if I had that choice again. And … I don't know if I'd be strong enough to change it. It was horrible, but it let me survive, even while all the other angels …"

His voice faded. Clenching his hands into fists, he cleared his throat and told them about Elena. Thinking about her made his voice quiver. He hoped she was still alive. What would he do if she wasn't?

Leon recounted their escape from Hargold, how they'd joined the Resistance, how they'd found a hidden chamber under the All-Temple. As he described how golden light illuminated the final room, it was as if that same light shone from him onto his audience. Their hard faces grew softer, more youthful. Hope filled their eyes. In that All-Temple, his faith had been restored, and with it came the knowledge that there was something more powerful than the Vahrians. Leon remembered the peacefulness he'd felt, bathing in that golden light. He took courage from that and his voice grew strong.

"… and then, after Drayton's airship left Paracelsus-7, I realised the only way to escape was with an airship of my own. So I went to you."

Salome bowed. Her reverent expression had become one of awe.

She made the Sign of the Archangels. "And we thank you, angel."

The others nodded and clapped. Leon scowled. He didn't deserve their praise. If it wasn't for Elena, he couldn't have done any of it. And now that she'd been taken …

Eager to draw attention away from himself, he asked: "What about all of you? How'd you end up in chains?"

The ex-convicts looked at each other. Leon wondered if asking how you'd been arrested was a faux pas, but then Mencia raised her chin and looked at him.

"I used to be a mercenary, sir," she said. "And I'm ashamed to admit it, but I worked for Vahrians as often as Payans. Coin was the only thing that mattered, so I guess it wasn't that surprising when my partner sold me out and they sent me to the mines. Truth be told, I deserved to be there, for all the bad I'd done."

Mencia looked off into the distance, and Leon realised that all these men and women had endured horrible things, things that were probably far worse than what he'd experienced. Yet instead of choosing freedom, they'd followed him. What had he done to deserve their trust?

"I was planning to throw myself through the force field, until Salome arrived," said Mencia. "But she wouldn't let me give up on life. And thank the Star Spectre she didn't, because it was only a few months later that you arrived."

The ex-convicts watched Mencia with admiration. Leon smiled. Maybe it was less about them trusting him, and more about them trusting her. She seemed the closest thing the convicts had to a leader and she'd been one of Leon's first supporters.

"You give me too much credit," said Salome. "I didn't give you your strength to survive."

"Maybe," said Mencia. "But I won't let you escape without swelling your ego, Mother."

"Mother?" Leon frowned at Salome. "You're a priest?"

"Until I was excommunicated." Salome sighed. "We had a half-dozen young men stumble into my temple. They were ragged and bloody, and bore a strong resemblance to wanted posters the Vahrians had nailed around the disc. But I chose to believe my eyes saw differently, and I offered them shelter. It is our holy duty to give hospitality to all who ask. My Brothers and Sisters thought otherwise. However, they did not wish to turn a priest over to the Vahrians, so first they stripped me of my office. Then they called the Inquisition."

Leon gaped. He'd never been overly fond of priests, but he'd always thought they were too passive to betray one of their own.

"Do not think ill of them, sir," said Salome. "It is an age of pressure, and we're not all built to withstand it. Besides – I don't need my robes to do the Star Spectre's work."

More people told their stories. There was Raul, the hulking man who was a secretary for a Vahrian governor, until the Governor's rival framed Raul for sedition. Garcia – a woman who looked about Elena's age – had stolen food for her family, and so the Inquisition had stolen her in turn. Eloy had been secretly courting a Vahrian noblewoman, until the woman's father discovered them and threw Eloy into jail.

As they talked they drew closer together, moving from their spread-out positions until they were all sitting in a tight circle, half-submerged in the bubbling water. Leon tried to listen as close as he could, but the convicts' stories began to blend together. They were all the same, at their core: a Vahrian had disliked them, and so they'd been ripped from their life and sent to break rocks on a desolate asteroid, away from their homes, families, and loved ones. The tales should've angered Leon, but he already knew that Vahrians were self-serving, ruthless bastards.

"They arrested you for a *song?*"

Leon snapped out of his reverie. Fernan had just spoken. He was a grizzled man a decade older than Leon, who'd given a two-word answer to how he'd ended up in chains: the War. Fernan was scowling at Oscar, a young boy with nervous eyes.

Oscar gulped. "Yes."

"Surely your voice isn't that bad," said Fernan.

"It isn't," said Mencia. "I heard him sing when he thought he was alone in a crater. You have a wonderful voice, kid."

Oscar blushed and sank deeper into the water. He was scrawny and knobbly-limbed, and didn't look like he got much praise.

"What was the song about?" asked Leon.

Everyone looked at him. His every word seemed to carry so much weight with the ex-convicts. Leon wished they wouldn't pay him so much attention.

Oscar gaped at Leon. He opened his mouth, but no words emerged. Leon sighed. How had Leon's younger self dealt with people who'd never seen an angel? Back then, awed strangers were easier to deal with. Probably because his ego had been the size of Neebia.

Oscar looked down at the water. "It was about the Governor – the one on my disc. There were rumours and I thought it'd be funny to match them to a tune."

"Can we hear it?" Leon asked.

Oscar's eyes widened. "My song?"

Leon nodded. "Could do with some fun."

The other convicts chorused in agreement, except for Fernan, who rolled his eyes. Oscar looked at Mencia, who nodded.

"Okay," said Oscar. "My voice is rusty, and it's better with an instrument, but here it goes."

Oscar cleared his throat, then sang:

"There was a husband stiff and fair
his wife beside him in her chair
with belt of chasteness that she wear

for dinner was a formal affair."

Oscar's voice wobbled, but as he continued, his words grew clear and powerful. The ex-convicts leaned forward.

"Now these folks were Vahrians
they were proud and pink and prude,
so to tumble with each other
was considered rather rude."

Leon smirked and the convicts chuckled. That was an understatement – Vahrians seemed to consider it scandalous to so much as hold hands in public.

Drawing heart from their reaction, Oscar's voice strengthened as he continued:

"The man watched the woman
suck deeply on her spoon,
eating with such fervour that
the food caused her to swoon.

The man scowled with anger up at their clock,
wishing that those lips
were wrapped instead around his cock."

The group roared with glee. Leon smiled. This was the kind of bawdy song he'd spent many an evening singing in taverns with Blas. It felt nice to remember the good times they'd shared, especially when the memory wasn't followed by the agony and wistfulness that was normally attached. Leon had barely a second to reflect on how precious this was before

Oscar leapt into the next verse.

"So late that night
  the man snuck quick into the dining hall
  he grabbed the spoon
  but knocked the plates all across the floor
  and his shrieking darling wife
  came bursting through the door

She watched with a face aghast
  but the husband was too fast
  and before she could stop him
  he tightened his grip
  and shoved the spoon up his ass."

The group erupted into laughter. Leon threw his head back, gasping for air in between bouts of cackling. He hadn't laughed this hard in ages. Mencia clapped Oscar's shoulder, and then everyone was crowding around him, cheering and slapping the boy's back. When they cleared away, a wide grin stretched across Oscar's young face.

Leon surveyed the group, still smiling. Vahria had enslaved their people, destroyed the angels, and stolen everything that mattered to Paya. But this laughter, this bonding, this heart – Vahria could never take this, and for that Leon was grateful.

Chapter 42

"Angel, can we speak privately?"

Leon turned. Mencia stood behind him. They were in the midst of rolling cloaks out on the airship's floor, preparing for sleep.

Leon stood, wincing at the pain in his knees. "Sure."

She strode outside. Leon limped after her. Above, the force field dimmed the sun, showing only the light of the stars and Neebia far away. Even after all these years, Leon didn't know how that worked. If the field blocked the sun, shouldn't it also stop the starlight? He didn't begrudge it, though. The stars were always so beautiful at night.

"I know who you are, sir," said Mencia.

Leon frowned. "Eh?"

"I know you're an Archangel."

Leon gaped. It took a few seconds for her words to sink in, and then he bellowed with laughter. A few people stuck their heads out of the airship to watch. Leon waved to let them know everything was fine and laughed so hard that tears streamed down his face. Mencia kept staring firmly at him.

"Oh, Karym's horns!" Leon wiped his tears. "That's funnier than Oscar's song."

"It's okay, your grace. I won't tell anyone else. I know you're here for a purpose and it's not my place to disturb that."

"Wait, you're serious?"

"In the mines, I had a vision we'd be saved by an Archangel. Then you came." Mencia leaned closer. "I don't deserve this, but thank you. I used to be a non-believer. Then Salome showed me the way, and I had the vision. If it wasn't for the hope it gave me ... I would've died in the mines."

"I ain't an Archangel, Mencia."

She dropped to one knee. "I promise you, your grace. I will die before telling another soul. Your secret is safe with me."

"Mencia, stand up. I'm not a bloody Archangel, alright? Why the hell would an Archangel look like me?"

She stood. "Salome told me a story from the Sarahk, about the Minor Archangel Taryn. He was prideful and arrogant, and boasted that he was greater than the Star Spectre. So the Star Spectre stripped his wings and sent him to live in squalor, on the streets of Anshan. No one knew his identity. He was beaten, arrested, almost killed. But through it all he came to understand the poorest of the poor, and eventually grew to love them. He set up a soup kitchen, and forgot he'd once been an Archangel, dismissing it as a fever dream of his time spent drunk and sprawling on the streets. Then, on his deathbed, he was visited by nine tall strangers. The Major Archangels, themselves. They blessed him. In that moment he remembered he'd been an Archangel, too, and wings sprouted from his back and the Star Spectre's voice boomed in his mind, telling him that he'd lived a worthy life, and he'd been forgiven. From that day on he became the Archangel of the Poor, and he continued to walk the streets and help the helpless until the Great Departure."

Mencia leaned closer. "It isn't the first time an Archangel has taken the shape of man, and I hope it won't be the last. Your secret is safe with me, your grace. If there is anything I can do to help your mission, I am yours to command."

Leon gaped. This was the most ridiculous thing he'd heard, but nothing he said would change Mencia's mind.

"Er, right," he said. "I'll ... get back to you."

Mencia made the Sign of the Archangels. As they walked back to the airship, Leon kept waiting for her to smirk and reveal that it was all a jest. But as they walked into the airship, her serious expression remained unchanged.

The other ex-convicts watched him as he strolled through the cabin and laid down on his cloak. Did they all share Mencia's thoughts? Did they think Leon was a saviour, sent by the Archangels? A revolutionary leader who'd free Paya from Vahria's yoke?

Leon was none of those things. He was a scared, ordinary man, who'd been too afraid to stick by his friends, too hurt to believe in the Path to Waverrym, too weak to protect Elena ...

He didn't have what it took to lead. But Mencia thought he did and so did the others. Maybe that was enough. Maybe that was all that mattered.

Chapter 43

"Karym's horns, there's a lot of the bastards," said Leon.

Leon and his crew stood on the edge of Nustune's forest disc, overlooking the monastery on the disc below. An hour ago, he'd landed their airship on the far side of the forest, approaching from an angle that used the disc to hide them from the monastery's view. Then they'd hacked through vines and bracken, emerging sweaty and dirt-stained in this clearing at the edge of the force field. Leon pried his sweaty shirt off his chest. The forest was thick with the stench of rotting vegetation, and the air was sticky and humid.

Nustune's second disc was a click away, and several hundred metres below. In the centre, a nine-sided stone wall enclosed a dusty courtyard seething with Vahrians, with a tower in the middle. Intricate carvings were etched into the stone. Huge crimson blocks formed the monastery, slotted together without mortar. Life-sized Archangel statues stood atop the broad walls, and more Vahrian soldiers prowled between them, their swords shining in the sun. Compared to the nine-foot-tall Archangels, the soldiers looked like children.

Six airships floated in the courtyard. One bore the distinctive markings of Drayton's ship.

Leon clenched his hands. At least he'd guessed what Drayton would do. He prayed his theory about Elena was correct as well. What would he do if she wasn't here?

"You said this was a monastery," said Fernan. "Not a castle."

Mencia scowled at him and looked at Leon, like she was waiting for his permission to throw Fernan through the force field. Nervous murmurs sounded from the ex-convicts. Were they having second thoughts about helping Leon? He'd said they'd have to fight to free Elena, but even Leon hadn't expected Drayton to have so many soldiers. There were at least thirty – and the Vahrians had the benefit of a fortress.

"It is a monastery," said Leon. "Just a damn big one."

At least he had the element of surprise. Outnumbered as they were, it might be their only advantage.

Garcia pointed. "Leon, what's that?"

"Eh?"

Garcia gestured above the monastery disc's force field. Leon frowned. Along with the others, he scanned the stars, trying to follow her finger.

A distortion bulged in space. It looked like ripples in a pond, except these ripples stayed static, warping the stars behind them. Leon's gaze swept across space and he saw eight other distortions. The hairs on the back of his neck stood up and warmth radiated through his chest.

"They're wormholes!" he said.

"They ain't in no dirt," said Fernan.

"Not that kind of wormhole. Karym's horns, these are rare. Never seen 'em, only heard stories –"

"Mind saying what the hell's a wormhole?"

"It's a porthole through space. Like a door. When we go

through one of 'em, we'll come out another one, somewhere else in the universe. If we're lucky."

The ex-convicts gaped at each other. Leon wondered if they believed him. Then he remembered how Mencia thought he was an Archangel, and he realised these Payans would probably swear by anything he said.

"And if the dice don't fall our way?" asked Fernan, still squinting at the wormholes.

Leon shrugged. "Don't know. Ripped apart. Squished to a pulp. Like I said, wormholes are rare. A few hundred years back, an adventurer mapped a few and made a bloody fast trade route. Then she went into a new wormhole and never returned. Within a decade, her wormholes vanished. Fickle things."

Mencia stabbed her finger at the wormholes. "Have these always been here?"

"No record of 'em," said Leon.

"Why've they appeared, then? And how recent d'you suppose they are?"

"If I may suggest something, sir?" asked Salome.

Leon nodded at the priest. "Of course, Mother."

"In the Sarahk, it's said that when Karym murdered Waverrym, he hid Waverrym's corpse in a wormhole. When the Archangels found Waverrym and turned him into a disc, there's no mention of them removing him from that wormhole. Sir, if you seek Waverrym –"

"We have to go through a wormhole." Leon's eyes widened. "Do one of these lead to Waverrym?"

The ex-convicts gazed at the wormholes with awe. Certainty filled Leon's bones. The quest. The Path. It all led here. All finished here. He and Elena were a fingertip from finding

Waverrym and reaching safety.

He just had to rescue her first.

"A disc of angels ..." Salome stared with wonder at the warped and twisted stars. "It could be right there."

"For all we know those wormholes could send us into a sun," said Fernan.

The other convicts glowered at him. They wanted to believe, but Leon knew why Fernan was so cynical. Leon's old self would've snorted at the idea of going through an uncharted wormhole. Now, though ... he couldn't explain it, but it felt right. There was no record of these wormholes before, yet here they were, right where the Path had led him. Still, he wasn't about to charge into them. He remembered the secret chambers, where only one path led to survival. He guessed these wormholes were the same. No sense rushing in, then. Besides, he needed to rescue Elena first, because the wormholes might be a one-way trip.

An airship appeared in the distance – a tiny blot against the darkness of space. The ship landed outside the monastery. A cloud of rust-red soil billowed into the air and ant-sized soldiers leapt out to fasten the anchor. More soldiers unloaded barrels of gunpowder.

The monastery's bronze gate opened. Leon stiffened as a cripple with a cane limped through the gates to greet the airship. Soldiers followed him.

Drayton.

"Mencia?" Leon said.

"Yeah?"

"Give me your bow."

She frowned and gave him her bow, which she'd taken from a corpse on Paracelsus-7.

"And an arrow," he said.

She handed him an arrow. The other convicts watched, frowning. Leon slotted the arrow on to the bowstring, drew it back to a half-draw, and sighted down the shaft at the speck that was Drayton. Leon's disc was about a click from the inquisitor's, but the arrow would fly through space without losing speed or its trajectory.

Leon pursed his lips. The rational part of him warned that this shot was impossible. Drayton was too far away. The angle of error was non-existent.

But the part of him that never stopped thinking about Elena screamed at him to shoot, to strike the inquisitor and make Drayton's blood leak into the dirt.

Mencia frowned at Leon's trembling hands. "Sir?"

He drew the bowstring. He pictured the arrow sailing through space, passing through the force field, and falling towards Drayton –

And missing.

Drayton would turn, see Leon and the ex-convicts, and send soldiers to the forest. Any hope of freeing Elena would die.

He thrust the bow into Mencia's hands. "Good weapon."

"Er … thanks. What now, sir?"

Drayton limped back into the monastery. An extra five soldiers had joined the Vahrians following behind him. Leon stared at the monastery's central tower. Elena was in there. He knew it.

"Now, we plan," said Leon.

"Plan what?"

The monastery's bronze gates shut and rust-red dirt swelled into a cloud.

"For the attack."

Chapter 44

L eon stood on the disc's edge in the pre-dawn darkness. Beyond the force field, the monastery squatted on the disc far below: solid, crimson, and unyielding.

He turned to his army. Laughable to call it that, but it made him feel like they had half a chance, and his courage needed all the bolstering it could get.

"Below us are our conquerors," he said. "They killed our angels. Enslaved us. They're stronger and better equipped. Luck ain't with us."

He took a deep breath and surveyed the scared faces around him. Leon swallowed. His back ached, but his armour's burden was nothing against the knowledge he was leading these Payans to the slaughter.

No. The plan will work. It has to.

"Below us are our conquerors, but so long as there are Payans like us, people who'll fight back?" Leon drew his sword and held it in the air. "Paya will never be conquered!"

Swords left their sheaths with rusty scrapes and his army brandished their weapons. They cheered.

"Glory to Paya!"

"Glory to the Star Spectre!"

"Glory to the angels!"

Leon forced himself to grin. The cheering sounded small and weak within the forest's expanse. Almost as weak as his speech.

Say something like that before a battle and everyone cheers. Say that in a tavern and they'll tease you senseless.

Leon scowled. However hollow they were, his words put smiles on the Payans' faces and filled his soldiers with fire.

That was worth something. Right?

"May the blessing of the Star Spectre be upon us," said Salome.

Leon nodded. The priest was too frail to join their attacks, so she'd stay here and watch. Having her blessing reminded Leon that they weren't just fighting for Elena. They were fighting for Paya's soul.

Leon's gaze swept over the convicts, the supplies they'd gathered for the fight, and the small escape pod they'd removed from the airship. Then Leon turned to face the force field. He sheathed his sword, lest his shaking hands drew blood before he'd even reached the monastery. He slapped breathfung onto his face and re-adjusted the grappling hook coiled over his shoulder. Feeble cheering sounded behind him. Leon donned his helmet and tried to forget how he'd pried it off a Vahrian corpse.

He squared his shoulders. *For Elena.*

Leon walked through the force field and silence snapped off his army's cheers. The sun's undimmed brightness made him squint. Holding the rope he'd placed earlier, he floated down and positioned himself against the disc's side. Casting a prayer to the Archangels, he pushed. He glided through space, soaring towards the monastery disc.

Alone.

Like he'd always been.

And always would be.

Unless I rescue Elena.

As he drifted through space, Leon pulled out the pendant Juliana had carved for him. He tried to imagine the wood feeling warm, as if she'd handed it to him, but in space the pendant was colder than a corpse. A lump formed in his throat and he stuffed the pendant back into his cloak.

Halfway to the disc.

If only Juliana could be with him now. And Blas, too. They'd made Leon braver, dampened the other angels' taunts, and made his years at the Academy tolerable. A weak smile tugged at his mouth. If those two were with him, Leon's pocket would hold a jonshular piece Juliana had carved last night, and his stomach would be full, courtesy of a meal cooked by Blas.

Tears welled up in his eyes. He dragged a hand across his face and the tears floated away.

He swallowed. The monastery disc was near and he needed to focus. He uncoiled the rope wound around his shoulder and checked the anchor tied to the end. His eyes narrowed as he approached the disc. He would land on the side, nine feet below the force field. That meant he'd bounce off into space unless he could dig his makeshift grappling hook into the disc's surface.

Now!

He hurled the rope. The throw cast the anchor through the force field, where it dropped into the dirt and raised a puff of rust-coloured dust. Leon pulled himself along the grappling hook as he glided towards the disc's side. The rope went taunt. Leon jerked up. He accelerated towards where the force field hit the disc. He slammed into the rock and the impact punched the air from his lungs. Growling, he crawled into the force field. Gravity slapped him onto the ground. He pulled off his breathfung and choked on a cloud of powdery red dirt.

Went as well as expected, I guess.

He stood, wincing. He'd plundered his armour from a dead soldier on Paracelsus-7, and while the bloodstains made him think twice about donning it, that crash made him glad to be wearing armour.

The monastery loomed in the distance, flanked by gleaming airships. Leon marched towards the crimson-walled building. Rust-red dirt puffed up from the ground with each heavy footstep, coating his armour in powdery dust as he trudged through the darkness. He curled his gloved fingers into a fist. Elena was in the monastery.

And so was Drayton.

One way or another, this ended today. Either Leon's army captured the monastery, freed Elena, and killed Drayton, or –

He cut the thought with an angry flick of his head. No need to entertain those ideas.

Leon stopped three hundred feet from the Monastery's bronze gate. Close enough to be heard, but far enough away to dodge a bow shot. He unslung the shield from his back, slipped it onto his left arm, and drew his sword with a rasp of steel.

"Drayton!" he yelled. "I've come to make a deal."

Metal clanged atop the monastery's wall. A sentry shuffled to the edge, gaped at Leon, and rang a bell. The noise sounded feeble against the monastery's might.

Sweat dripped down Leon's brow. Waiting was a tough

game, made harder by the heavy metal pressing against his aching shoulders. The shield pulled down on his arm. He longed to drop it, but a sore arm was better than an arrow through his chest.

A dozen soldiers joined the lone sentry and stood between the Archangel statues lining the top of the wide wall. Leon's stomach clenched.

Drayton limped to the wall's edge with a clack of his cane and stopped beside a statue of the Archangel Harrhi. Leon clenched his gauntleted fingers into a fist.

Hope the damn cripple falls off. Hell, I should've bought a bow.

"Just you, dear chap?" said the inquisitor. "No hidden friends? No archer ready to shoot me?"

Leon swallowed. He'd wanted to get close enough to kill the inquisitor, but now that he remembered Drayton's red-hot iron, Leon's spine tingled and sweat streaked down his back.

"I've come to make a deal!" Leon said, his voice cracking.

Soldiers guffawed at his high-pitched squeal and Leon's cheeks flushed with heat.

Drayton smiled. "I heard you the first time, dear fellow. Very well. Speak."

Leon glanced up at the force field. By now, his army should be in position – seventeen men and women holding on to the escape pod and floating above the force field – but they were too far away for Leon to see them. If they were even there.

He looked back at Drayton. "Free Elena, leave this disc, and I'll let you live."

The inquisitor chuckled. His soldiers' laughs echoed across the disc's dusty plains.

Drayton raised his hand and four soldiers aimed bows.

Leon hunched behind his shield. He gulped.

"Surrender," said Drayton. "I have a task that requires your skills and if you perform it, I'll even free the girl. I swear it on my honour as an inquisitor."

Drayton smirked, like he was in on a joke. Leon didn't like the man's smile, but something in the inquisitor's voice rung true.

No. He's lying. He'll never free her.

"No," said Leon. "I think I'll kill you instead."

"This shall be entertaining," said Drayton. "A single hero, fighting against the odds, defeats a score of Vahria's finest warriors!"

Movement flashed from high above and Leon smiled. "Wrong on two counts."

"Which are?"

"I ain't a hero. And I ain't alone."

"Eh?"

A soldier shrieked and Drayton's warriors looked up to see Leon's army fall from the sky. Except they weren't falling. They were flying. Large squares of airship canvas billowed above them, slowing their fall so that they floated down to the monastery.

And then their arrows fell upon Drayton's soldiers.

Chapter 45

Arrows rained from the sky. One stabbed into a Vahrian soldier, who howled, toppled off the wall, and landed with a wet crunch in the rust-coloured dirt. Drayton cursed and limped away. A soldier held a shield over the inquisitor's head.

Vahrian archers fired at the descending Payans. Leon's crew had dismembered their airship to get enough material for their makeshift parachutes, which had removed their only escape route, but it'd been worth it for the surprise.

A cluster of arrows ripped through one man's canvas and he plummeted with a shriek, smacking into the ground with a sickening crack.

Leon charged at the wall. A Vahrian shot an arrow at him. The arrow clanged into his shield and the impact thudded up his arm.

People screamed and cried and thumped onto the monastery's walls as the ex-convicts floated down, raining arrows upon the Vahrians. Leon reached the base of the walls. He sheathed his sword, uncoiled his grappling hook, and hurled it over the wall's edge. He tugged.

The rope went taut and Leon pulled himself up. His feet scrabbled on the smooth stone walls, fighting for grip, and he cursed his armour's weight as pain twanged through his arms and injured wrist. His shield cracked into his nose. Blood dripped from his nostrils, filling his mouth with a metallic taste.

He heaved himself over the wall. A boot clanged into his helmet, making his ears ring. Leon cracked his shield into the soldier's ankle, knocking him off the wall, sending the soldier crunching into the dirt below.

Leon stood, still holding his rope. Dozens of nine-foot-tall Archangel statues stood on the wide wall. His grappling hook had snagged on a Severym sculpture. People fought amongst the Archangels, stumbling over the discarded canvas squares which littered the wall. Most of Leon's army had cut themselves out of their harnesses, but some sprawled dead on the floor, tangled in ropes and blood. More fights raged in the courtyard below.

An axe-wielding soldier charged at Leon, screaming, and Leon sidestepped, pulling his anchor rope taut. The rope tripped the soldier. Leon dropped the rope and drew his sword as the Vahrian struggled to rise.

Strike!

But Leon's shaking arm locked up.

The Vahrian lashed out with his axe. The back of the weapon crunched into Leon's ankle and pain spiked up his leg. Stumbling, Leon thrust his sword into the soldier's back and his blade punched through the man's chainmail. A shock jolted Leon's arm.

The Vahrian scrabbled at Leon's boots with trembling fingers. Leon stepped back. Nausea swelled through him as blood stained the soldier's shirt. Around him, the clash of blades made his ears ring.

"Nice fighting."

He looked up. Mencia hunched beside a statue, teeth bared, sword stained red, and chest plate heaving. Leon grunted. He was terrified he'd vomit if he spoke.

"Behind!" Mencia yelled.

Leon whipped around, raising his shield. The soldier's blade crunched into his shield, knocking him into a statue, and the next strike ripped the sword from Leon's hand. He ducked and the Vahrian's sword decapitated the statue. Broken marble showered everywhere. Leon lunged, crunching his shield into the soldier's torso and pushing the man back. Mencia's blade sprouted from his chest.

It took three tries for Leon's trembling hands to pick up his sword.

"Thanks," he said.

Mencia gurgled.

Leon glanced up. An arrow protruded from Mencia's neck and her eyes bulged. She tried to speak, but coughed blood instead.

"I'll see you," Mencia spluttered. "In the next ..."

She crumpled.

An arrow bounced off a statue beside Leon, leaving a deep gouge. He swivelled. The archer drew another arrow. A snarl rumbled in Leon's chest and blood thumped in his ears and his nostrils flared and he charged, yelling so hard his throat felt like it was tearing.

The wide-eyed archer fired a half-drawn shot. Leon whacked the sluggish arrow with his shield. He slashed. His sword cleaved through the archer, splitting him in a line from shoulder to hip. Blood sprayed onto Leon. He bared his teeth, whirled around, and looked for another enemy to fight.

The courtyard below was a mess of broken bodies. Mainly Payans. But it was too far for Leon to leap to the courtyard and he couldn't see any ladders, so he turned to the Karym statue, where three Payans duelled five Vahrians. He charged.

A Vahrian sliced through Raul. Leon roared. He reached the fight and his blade whistled through the air, biting into the Vahrian's side. The soldier collapsed into a statue's arms. Leon bellowed and hacked at the man. His sword rattled and his blows dented the soldier's helmet until the man's skull caved in with a dry crunch.

Dispatching another soldier, Fernan gave Leon a bloody grin, then pointed over Leon's shoulder and shouted a warning. Leon whipped around and parried a blow. He deflected the soldier's next strike into a statue, where it lodged in the stone. The soldier cursed. He tried to pull out his sword, but Leon screamed with blood-red rage and stabbed through the man's gaping mouth. He ripped out his blade.

And as the man crumpled, it was as if Leon had cut down all the fear he'd ever faced.

He grinned. All those songs about war's glory were truer than he could have imagined. He spun, deflecting another blow. He thought of the songs they'd sing about him and a mad laugh bellowed from his snarling mouth. His opponent's eyes bulged with fear. Leon focused on the blade. His enemy's blade, and his own. For that length of razored steel had power to maim, kill, avenge his fallen angels, and rescue Elena.

For in the blade's power lay Leon's redemption.

He feinted high, then swung low, but his sword crashed into a statue's legs and bounced out of his hands. The Vahrian lunged but slipped on a corpse. Leon dove onto him.

They grappled. Leon pummelled his shield into the soldier,

clobbered him with his elbows, and bit him, all while rolling in the fetid stickiness of a dead man's blood.

Leon grabbed the soldier's neck and squeezed. The Vahrian spluttered. He slapped Leon's helmet and the helmet twisted around Leon's head, blinding him, but he just squeezed harder. Nails scratched his wrists. Spittle drooled onto his hands. The Vahrian gurgled, crying for his wife, or maybe his mother.

Leon didn't care. This soldier was stopping him from saving Elena and for that Leon could spare no mercy.

The man went limp. Leon stood. Panting, he readjusted his helmet.

A howling woman charged at him and he cursed, dodged behind a statue, and grabbed his sword from the ground. He beat away her blows. The sword pulled down on his arm and his lungs strained and his heart hammered and he wanted nothing more than for this to end, but he had to win.

Have to free Elena.

He growled and sharpened his rage into newfound vigour. She dodged his cut and her knife sliced across the back of his gloved hand. Pain swelled through him. He dropped his sword but didn't have time to curse before the woman lunged with another knife, forcing him to back away.

Leon tripped on a dead body. It was Eloy's body – one of the Payans he'd freed. Leon stumbled, barely keeping his feet. He caught the Vahrian's next blow on his shield. As she drew back for another strike, he punched the heavy shield into her face, pain wrenching through his shoulder. Her nose cracked with a spurt of blood. She stumbled back and Leon pushed her off the wall.

He grabbed his sword, then leaned on it, panting, and surveyed the battle. Bodies draped over the walls, rested at statues' feet, and lay in the courtyard below, sprawled in blood. Equal numbers of Payans and Vahrians, but the Vahrians had started with an advantage, so attrition favoured them. Leon swallowed.

We're losing.

His ragged breath caught in his throat. Down below, Garcia sprawled in the courtyard's rust-red dirt, her skull split in two, showing her brain's pinkish flesh amongst chips of bone. He tried to muster emotion, tried to use her death to bolster his rage. But his knees ached, his breath came in ragged gasps, and his heavy armour made his shoulders burn. All he wanted was for this bloodbath to end.

He growled. Thinking like that wasn't an option, not when he needed to save Elena.

Leon turned, seeking his next opponent. A blurred shape flashed through the air and an arrow sliced a line of pain across his forearm. He howled.

A bulky soldier charged at him. Leon raised his shield, arm straining at the weight. The Vahrian shouldered Leon's shield, which crunched into Leon, making him step back.

His feet hit empty air.

Leon toppled off the wall and weightlessness overcame him. He flailed. Flapped his arms in a mockery of how his wings used to beat the air. He crunched into the ground.

And his leg broke.

Pain made Leon roar until his voice went hoarse, made his eyes swell with tears, made a thousand curses leap from his mouth. The clash of swords and thrum of arrows faded. Against the red-hot agony that burned through him with every frantic heartbeat, those sounds meant nothing. He gritted his teeth. Tried to push himself up. More pain flared through him and he slumped back onto the ground, inhaling a lungful of bitter-tasting dirt.

"Leon!"

With a throb of agony, he glanced up. Oscar raced across the courtyard, a line of blood dribbling down his forehead. Leon's breathing eased. Oscar had medical supplies. The boy could help him.

An arrow punctured Oscar's chest, bursting out the other side. The boy gaped at the hole in his torso. Another arrow stabbed through his body, spilling his innards. He collapsed, jerked around, scuffled in the dirt, then stopped.

Leon wanted to scream, but his throat was red and raw and the pain in his broken leg overwhelmed him. He stared up at the force field as it lightened. The sun grew bright and painful, boring a hole into the back of Leon's eyes, but he kept staring up, because to look anywhere else meant seeing the Payans he'd led to the slaughter.

He cursed. What was worse? The agony in his leg, or knowing his arrogance had snuffed the lives of eighteen Payans? His broken leg didn't come with guilt, so he focused on that. He let the pain overwhelm him, like he deserved, while swords ripped flesh and Payans shrieked and Vahrians yelled in triumph.

A soldier loomed above him, blocking the sun. Leon raised his blade, but the soldier grabbed the sword and tore it from Leon's shaking hand. Fear throbbed through Leon. He closed his eyes, waiting for a sword to cleave through his chest.

Instead, the soldier grabbed Leon's ankles.

Fresh pain lanced through his broken leg. He cursed and tried to sit up, but the soldier marched away, dragging Leon, and his head flopped back into the dirt. The rough ground bumped Leon's armoured back, scraped his unprotected buttocks, and bruised his hip. Leon wondered if he'd already died and Karym was dragging him to hell. Then an airship blotted out the sun. The soldier stopped dragging him and ripped off Leon's armour, batting aside Leon's feeble blows. Seizing a fistful of Leon's sweat-stained cloak, the soldier hurled him into the airship's cabin.

"Ingenious plot, dear chap. Too bad it didn't work."

Leon's blood turned cold. Still sprawled on the floor, he glanced up. Inquisitor Drayton, cane in clawed hand, stood at the front of the cabin, flanked by six soldiers. And, kneeling in front of him, her hands chained, a gag across her mouth: Elena.

Chapter 46

Leon swallowed and horror washed through him. His army had lost. Now how would he free Elena? He tried to stand, but a soldier crossed the cabin and used his boot to force Leon back to the floor.

Karym's horns! Why does every bloody thing I do turn to shit?

The floor rumbled under Leon and the airship floated into the air. A bruise had bloomed on Elena's face and Leon shuddered to think what else Drayton might have done to her.

Leon forced a smile. "Didn't think you'd get rid of me that easy, eh?"

Her eyes crinkled. Was she grinning? Leon couldn't tell, not with a gag stretched over her face, cutting into the corners of her mouth. Her grin looked feeble, anyway. Best she could do given their situation, he supposed. Elena tried to speak, but the gag muffled her words.

Drayton rapped his cane onto the floor. The soldier's boot pressed harder onto Leon's back, making his spine ache and driving the breath from his lungs.

"I hate to cut your reunion short," said Drayton. "But there's a task I need you to do, Leon. Let him stand, Henry."

The soldier's boot lifted. Leon gasped and sucked in

lungfuls of air, wheezing. He pushed himself up, but as soon as his broken leg took his weight, pain seared through him and he collapsed, whimpering, turning away from Elena to hide his tears.

"Pathetic," said Drayton. "Henry, pull him up and bind him."

The soldier's hands dug under Leon's shoulders. He struggled, but he was weaker than a new-born and couldn't stop the soldier hauling him up and slamming him onto a wooden bench.

Through a veil of tears, he glanced at Elena. Her eyes were hard as steel. She nodded. The pain in Leon's leg faded and knowing she still felt brave made him hold his head higher.

Drayton limped towards Leon. His cane clicked and his twisted leg scraped on the floor. Leon jutted out his jaw, and glared at the inquisitor, but the memory of Drayton's torture room made Leon's lip tremble.

Drayton tapped his cane against his twisted leg, then against Leon's broken one. "Fitting, isn't it?"

Leon tried to spit at the inquisitor, but nothing came out.

Drayton laughed. "You know, I didn't cry when the angels mangled my leg."

"Not crying," said Leon.

Drayton's finger jabbed into Leon's eye. Leon yelped.

Drayton held up his glistening finger and smiled at Elena. "Your hero's bravery doesn't match your stories, eh?" He turned back to Leon. "No. When they mangled my leg, I crawled for an hour to reach my brother's tent. As it was … I shouldn't have bothered."

Leon scowled. He didn't give a damn about anything Drayton had to say, but he hoped the inquisitor kept talking. The longer he prattled, the more time Leon had to plan his escape. Leon glanced around the cabin.

"When we last met, dear chap," said Drayton, "I showed you what happens to terrorists."

Leon swallowed. The air turned stale and the foul-smelling memory of Pierce's death wafted into his nostrils. Elena stiffened.

"I think you could do with another lesson, don't you?" said Drayton.

A soldier mushed Leon's face against a porthole in the wall, covered with spiderweb cracks – an arrow must've hit it. Leon squinted at the monastery's courtyard below. Bodies lay piled in the middle.

Payan bodies.

Light flared and flames crackled around outstretched arms. Licked at ankles. Played with strands of hair. Sent smoke drifting up to the ascending airship.

Leon rammed his hands against the porthole, tried to twist out of the soldier's grip, tried to tackle Drayton and smash away his stupid smile. The soldier held him firm. All Leon achieved was a wet flopping noise as his hands slapped the porthole. Sounded like a dying fish. Drayton chuckled and angry mumbles sounded from Elena's direction.

Their airship floated through the force field and a sheen of shimmering purple blurred the funeral pyre below. Weightlessness swooped through Leon. He slumped against the cracked glass, half wishing Drayton had made a mistake, and that this airship had no air generator, and that the vacuum would rip away Leon's breath. At least death would cure his guilt.

But the stronger half of him wanted to weep with joy that there was still air and that he still lived.

Pathetic. He grit his teeth, but it didn't stop bitterness spreading through his mouth. *I'm pathetic.*

He stared at the funeral pyre. Drayton's soldiers might have lit the fire below, but Leon had surely pushed the Payans into the flames. Their deaths were his fault.

It's always my fault. Mangold Pass. The caves. The asteroid. Now this.

The soldier wrenched Leon away from the porthole and smacked him down onto the bench. His leg throbbed. Didn't hurt as much, not now that his insides were hollow and twisted. Elena gaped at him.

Am I going to get her killed, too? Will she join Alvaro, Blas, Juliana? Another friend I've led to their death?

"Now, the wormholes." Drayton gestured at the porthole. "If the monks told the truth – and I'm good at making people do that – the wormholes appeared when you left the hidden chamber on Paracelsus-7."

Leon glanced out a porthole. Beyond the cracked glass, the wormholes were further away than he'd thought, but close enough to see the foreign constellations inside them. Those strange stars made Leon uneasy. Ain't no place in Paya where he didn't know the stars around him. He blinked. A strange constellation shone from the smallest wormhole.

Looks like a person. Leon's heart quickened. *No. That ain't a person. It's an angel.*

An angel with wings formed of stars, a nebula cloud for a heart, and eyes twinkling blue with the light of distant suns. The hairs on Leon's neck tingled. It was as if someone struck a gong inside him, reverberating his bones, and his stomach, and his soul.

That's the Path to Waverrym!

325

He'd never felt more certain. Or afraid. Drayton would see the constellation, see the angel in the stars, and he'd know. Then he'd have no more use for Leon.

Or maybe ...

Leon licked his lips. Faint hope sparked inside him and he fought to keep himself from smiling. Drayton had been here for days, but despite the obvious signs, he'd yet to see the truth. What if the signs *weren't* obvious?

Leon thought of the time a blacksmith refused his silver coin, because he claimed it was cracked. Leon had argued with the man. Then the smithy put a magnifying glass over the coin and barked at Leon's short sightedness.

Maybe the same thing was happening here. Leon had an astronomer's eye. He saw constellations Drayton couldn't see, and that meant Waverrym's location was safe, so long as Leon kept silent.

All this passed through his mind in a half-second.

He gulped. Whatever happened, he couldn't let Drayton realise the wormhole led to Waverrym. Leon glanced away from the porthole and caught Drayton's cold eyes.

The inquisitor tilted his head. "You've seen it."

Leon's mouth went dry. "Seen what?"

"Nine wormholes. Eight lead to death, but one leads to Waverrym."

Don't blink don't blink don't blink–

"That so?" said Leon.

He tried to keep his voice level. Tried to hide the terror racing through him.

"You've seen it." Drayton's eyes bored into Leon's. "You know which one goes to Waverrym!"

"What the hell are you talking about?"

Leon blinked.

Damn it.

Pain cracked across his face and he twisted off the bench, crashing to the floor. Leon groaned. He floated back off the floor and raised his arms to ward off another blow from Drayton's cane.

"Don't lie," said the inquisitor. "I always know. Believe me, I've had practice."

The soldier hoisted Leon back onto the bench. Leon winced.

Drayton licked his lips and gazed at the wormholes. "So close … now, dear chap, which is the correct wormhole?"

Leon built up a mouthful of saliva. This time his spit splattered onto Drayton's coat.

"Go to hell," he said.

"Heh." Drayton drew a tiny knife with a finger-length blade. "Last time we did this, you lasted all of one minute. See if we can beat that record, shall we?"

He sliced Leon's forearm, making a line of blood bubble across his skin. Leon grunted. The pain made his eyes water. He glanced at Elena, trying to find courage, and she nodded back at him with wide eyes. He grit his teeth.

Drayton cut again. "Which wormhole leads to Waverrym?"

The inquisitor sliced again. And again. Leon screamed and sobbed, but kept his teeth gritted and mouth shut. Drayton didn't stop until Leon's arms were a bloody mess of screaming tendons.

Drayton nodded. "Two minutes. An improvement."

He gestured. The soldier grabbed a handrail, pushed Leon onto the floor, and stomped on his broken leg. Leon's scream tore his throat. The agony made his heart hammer, made the wounds on his arm bleed faster, made him feel as if he'd been tossed into a fire. Globules of sweat floated around him.

The soldier stamped down harder. A snap echoed through the chamber and bloodstained bone tore through Leon's skin. For a few moments, he felt nothing. He almost fooled himself into thinking the bone wasn't his.

Then the pain hit.

He screamed and thrashed and cursed and fire seared inside his mouth and blood dribbled through his bared teeth and he realised he'd bit his tongue. Warm blood oozed from his leg. It floated around him in balls of shining liquid that splattered onto the cabin's walls and Drayton's robes. Sweat drenched Leon's face and his throat ached. He glanced at Elena. She looked terrified.

"Water," Leon mumbled.

"I'll give you water," said Drayton. "Just tell me which wormhole leads to Waverrym."

Leon cursed the inquisitor. He tried to grab Drayton's ankles, but Drayton's cane stabbed onto his injured wrist and pinned his hand to the floor. The inquisitor floated up and held onto the ceiling.

"Wrong answer," said Drayton.

The soldier's boot crunched down again. Pain stabbed into Leon and he blacked out. When he came to, he puked. Globules of vomit floated through the air. His puke splattered onto the grumbling soldiers and a strange calmness washed over Leon. He grimaced.

"There's nothing you can do to me" – he coughed blood – "That'll make me tell you that."

Drayton frowned. He stared at Leon for a long moment and in the end, the inquisitor looked away first.

"Perhaps you're right, dear fellow." Drayton pushed off the handrail he'd been holding onto, floated to Elena, and held his knife to her throat. "Tell me which wormhole leads to Waverrym, or she dies."

Chapter 47

E lena's eyes bulged. Leon cursed. He tried to dive at Drayton, but the soldier's boot kept Leon pinned to the floor.

"No," said Leon. "Please!"

Drayton pulled the knife closer to Elena's throat. "Tell me, or she dies."

Elena shook her head. Muffled curses sounded from under her gag. Leon's heart pounded. If he told Drayton, the inquisitor would wipe out the angels who lived on Waverrym. But if he stayed silent …

Leon pictured the knife tearing across Elena's throat, her head lolling backwards, and blood spluttering from the slit in her neck.

Tears streamed down his face. With a wet, soft chuckle, he remembered teaching her to fly on Pomeroy … remembered her joy when they'd solved the riddles in the chamber hidden under the All-Temple …

He'd spent the last two decades with one foot in his grave, but she'd torn away the drudgery and the gloom and made him feel alive again.

He swallowed. A life without her would be worse than death.

"It's the smallest one," Leon said. "The smallest wormhole."

"Point to it," said Drayton.

Leon raised a trembling finger, and pointed.

Drayton stared at Leon. The inquisitor's chest heaved and his face twisted into a look of ecstasy. He sheathed the knife. Leon released a pent-up breath a second before the soldier hauled him up and Drayton flew across the room, smothering Leon in a hug.

"Thank you," said Drayton.

Leon struggled, but the inquisitor hugged him tighter. Leon gagged on the stench of yhona and the matches in his pocket pressed against his bruised hip. Drayton sobbed.

"Thank you!" The inquisitor's tears streaked onto Leon. "Oh, I'm going to miss you, dear chap."

Drayton trembled. He cried harder, and more tears dripped onto Leon's face. Revulsion shot through Leon. He tried to push the inquisitor, but Drayton clung to him with the desperate strength of a soldier meeting his lover after years of separation.

Drayton released Leon. The inquisitor wiped his eyes with his handkerchief and beamed. For once, the smile reached his eyes. He gave a curt order to the captain and the airship glided towards the wormhole that led to Waverrym. Seven more Vahrian airships rose from the monastery and followed. Leon swallowed. The wormhole was half an hour away, but it didn't matter if it took three days to reach it.

Leon had doomed Waverrym.

Traitor coward traitor coward traitor coward –

"Apologies for the emotion, dear fellow," said Drayton. "It's just … I've waited so long for this. You have no idea of the gift you've given me. It's only fair I give you one in return.

331

Guards, free Elena."

What?

A leer played with the corners of Drayton's smile while a soldier untied Elena's gag and removed her handcuffs. She used the rails to float into a standing position, shaking her hands, but didn't look at Leon. He couldn't blame her. She shouldn't be surprised, anyway, not when his life had been a series of betrayals, each worse than the last.

A soldier gave her a sheathed sword. She buckled it onto her belt.

Leon gaped. *What the hell's going on?*

Elena met his eyes. "Sorry, Leon. I … I've been lying to you."

She spoke with a Vahrian accent.

His stomach clenched. "Elena, I don't understand."

Drayton smirked. "She's my spy. She used you to find Waverrym."

Leon waited for her to stab the inquisitor. Instead, she stared at Leon.

"No!" he said.

She'd been his ally. His friend. She'd saved him from his miserable life and been the daughter he and Juliana never had. This couldn't be real.

"Please," said Leon. "Tell me it ain't true."

Her eyes moistened as she looked at the floor. "I'm sorry. You didn't deserve this."

Leon's guts twisted. "You bastard!"

He lunged, but a soldier held him back.

"You're the only bastard here, aren't you?" Drayton asked. "Elena told me all about your parents –"

"Shut up," said Leon.

332

Drayton chuckled and clapped his hands together. "Oh, what jolly fun! Elena, my girl, you did a superb job on him."

Leon's blood pounded in his ears, but he took a deep breath and bottled his anger. Had to stay calm to survive.

Which should be easier now that I don't have to rescue someone else –

He cut off the thought before it grew more painful, then curled his fingers into fists. Strength wouldn't help him. He needed brains. Needed to use his captors' weaknesses and distract them until he formed an escape plan.

"Surely there were easier ways to find Waverrym than by using her," he said in a strangled tone.

"Not at all, dear chap," said Drayton.

Come on. Take the bait.

If Leon knew one thing about the inquisitor, it was that the man loved his own voice.

"Why, I spent months trying every other route," said Drayton.

Got him.

"I heard about Waverrym a year ago," said the inquisitor. "The thought of angels living on a secret disc haunted me. Myself and my apprentice" – he patted Elena's back – "set about finding the Path. I thought it was a myth at first, dear chap. Most scholars thought the same, although a few believed the tale. Still, I investigated. Didn't take long, however, until I realised I'd need an angel's help. A classically trained one. Not like Elena here, who for all her merits, lacks a proper angel's education. We found an angel to help us. One who'd survived the War."

Leon spat. "Me."

"No. Fabian de Castellan."

"Who?"

"A coward who fled the War, like yourself. He'd somehow got to Neebia, where he was working in an exotic brothel in the Far West. I offered him gold if he would find me Waverrym. He accepted."

"Fabian had all the Inquisition's resources," said Elena, still looking down at the floor. "But he couldn't –"

"Shut up," said Leon. "You don't get to talk, bitch."

Drayton gestured and a soldier clubbed his elbow into Leon's head. Pain thudded through his skull.

"Please remain civil," said Drayton. "I'll not have you insult my apprentice."

Leon's hands shook. He stared at the floor and bottled his anger. Rage wouldn't help him survive.

"Fabian had unlimited resources," said Elena. "But he couldn't solve the first riddle. Took us on a trek halfway across Paya, but didn't come close to Anshan. He – he wasn't as smart as you."

"Fabian lacked desperation," said Drayton. "He had all the money and time one could wish for, but still couldn't do it. To fix this, I made him desperate."

Leon pictured Drayton prodding a red-hot iron into Fabian's sweaty back. He winced.

"Still no result," said Drayton. "Very disappointing."

"Then I came up with the idea of using you, Leon," said Elena.

"No," said Drayton. "I did."

"But I found the file –"

"Which I made you look for. When you're the master inquisitor, you may take credit, but not until then."

Elena glowered. Leon licked his lips. There was a rift

between master and apprentice. Could it be exploited?

He glanced out the window. Leon gulped. They'd reach the wormhole in under twenty minutes.

"You had the idea to use me," said Leon, looking at Drayton.

"Yes, but I tried a different tact with you. I developed the ploy that Elena was a fugitive, a young Resistance fighter for whom Waverrym was a last, desperate hope. You leapt onto my hook right away."

"Our hook," said Elena.

Drayton waved a hand at her. "Whichever. My role was to provide external pressure and give you the desperation that Fabian lacked. 'twas a fine balancing game. I stayed close enough to make you fear failure, but not so close that you abandoned your quest."

"And it was my job to motivate you in a different way," said Elena. "I had your file, see. I knew you lived a miserable life and would jump at a chance for redemption."

"There were times when I thought you'd fail," said Drayton. "Your capture on Anshan was particularly chancy. Another inquisitor led the raid, not knowing about my secret mission, but it worked in the end. Elena and I had tea. We gave her a few bruises, to make it look like she'd suffered the same treatment as you, and then she helped you escape. Easy enough, since all the guards cleared out of your path. I apologise for torturing you, Leon. Elena told me everything, but if I followed you to Paracelsus-7 without extracting information from you, it would be suspicious. Elena and I had quite a nice catch up, though, didn't we?"

"Yeah," said Elena.

Leon glared. "Enjoy Pierce's death, too?"

She swallowed and clenched her hands into fists.

"I warned you to avoid attachments," said Drayton. "Emotion is the enemy of success."

She scowled. "I'm over him."

Struck a nerve, eh?

"He loved you," said Leon. "And you loved –"

Elena shot through the air and kicked Leon's broken leg. He howled.

"Sh-shut up about Pierce," she said. "Or I'll break the other one."

She floated back to Drayton. Leon tried to form an insult, but his aching leg scrambled his thoughts.

"Apart from that, it was smooth sailing," said Drayton. "Oh, of course there was this bother here on Nustune. I must confess, it was arrogant to assume Elena and I could solve this final puzzle on our own. I was about to launch a ship back to Paracelsus-7, but thankfully you saved me the trouble."

"What about the Palace on Antonia?" Leon said. "She tried to blow you up. Did you know that?"

"Elena's no fool. She added a chemical to the gunpowder before the mission, making it inert. There was no concern of an explosion, though of course she had to pretend the gunpowder was active."

Crap. That did nothing. C'mon, I need to make Drayton mad at her.

A thought crossed Leon's mind and he jumped on it. "Elena, back on Paracelsus-7, you helped me escape Drayton. Why?"

"Yes." Drayton frowned. "That was disappointing."

"I said I'm sorry, alright?" Elena said. "I know I shouldn't have, but I thought we could find Waverrym without Leon's help."

"No," said Drayton. "You wanted him to escape. Dear me, I

336

warned you to not form attachments."

"I wasn't attached," she said in a quivering voice.

"Elena," said Leon. "Surely you don't want this. Karym's horns, he'll kill the last angels!"

She glanced at Drayton.

"Oh, I see your ploy," said the inquisitor. "You're trying to turn us against each other, eh? It won't work. You've known her a few weeks, but I've raised her since she was a child."

"Angels deserve to die," said Elena. "They're arrogant. Greedy."

"How can you say that?" said Leon. "You're an angel and so were your parents!"

"My parents left me to fight in the War! They stuck me with my uncle, who beat me every damn day. My only hope was that my parents would come back. That thought kept me alive through the War and even a few months after it ended. Then I realised the truth. My parents? They weren't coming back. They'd got themselves killed because they cared more about their pride than their daughter."

"But why help the Vahrians when your parents fought them?"

"My parents didn't care about Paya, or commoners, or even their family. They cared about themselves! They wanted favour, and stupid War badges to wear at tea parties, like every other damn angel."

"Not all."

"As if you can talk."

"I ain't talking about me."

"Oh, so Juliana and Blas were heroes, then?"

Leon clenched his shaking hands into fists. "Shut up."

"Or what?"

337

Leon uncurled his fingers, pressed his hands flat against the wall, and took a deep breath. Anger wouldn't help him. He had to keep them talking, so he could plan his escape.

He gritted his teeth. "How'd Drayton find you?"

"My uncle kicked me onto the streets when I grew my wings. He worried the Inquisition would see them. Turns out he was right. Except he never lived to see it, because the Inquisition only found me after I killed him. When the city guards found me, they were shocked by my wings, but not as shocked as they were by all the blood. Drayton interrogated me, asking who'd helped me kill my uncle. I hadn't needed help. By then I was seven, and I'd had more than enough experience fending for myself."

She glared out the porthole at the approaching wormhole. Leon scowled. Elena deserved to burn in hell for her lies, but now ... now he saw a scared young girl. A girl hurt because of her wings. A girl abandoned by her family. A girl who'd learned to hate, because what other choice did she have? Despite himself, he felt sorry for her.

"Drayton made me his apprentice," she said. "I owe him everything. I certainly owe him more than I owe any filthy angel. Besides, angels were evil. Tell him how you became crippled, Drayton."

Drayton stiffened. "I'd rather not."

"Fine, I'll do it. During the War, Drayton got captured. In the prison camp, he fell in love with a guard who was an angel."

"Wasn't love," said Drayton.

"But you thought it was, didn't you?"

Drayton stared at the floor.

"Anyway, the angel – what was her name?"

The inquisitor scowled. "Doesn't matter."

"She freed Drayton. Sent him in an airship back to a Vahrian camp and came along for the ride. The Vahrians wouldn't normally let angels near their camp, but she was delivering prisoners, so they trusted her. Bad move. The angel got Drayton and the other ex-prisoners to stand on the airship's deck, so the people in camp would see them. Then, as they passed through the force field, she pushed them off. All except Drayton."

"She did it to give me a fighting chance, I'd say," said Drayton. "Not entirely sure if it was much of a chance, because after she pushed off the others, she flew away and the airship exploded. I woke in the rubble of a tent. Somehow, I'd survived the fall with only a mangled leg. Everyone else hadn't been so lucky. There'd been rocks hidden in the ship's cargo hold, which fell onto the camp, killing dozens. Including my brother." Drayton swallowed. "I found the woman, you know, after the War. The angel."

Silence filled the cabin. The soldiers glanced at each other, fidgeting, and Drayton stared at the stars, looking haggard and broken.

"What?" said Leon. "Want me to cry? You're monsters, the both of you."

The inquisitor smiled, and the smile was creased with resignation, and age, and sadness.

"There are no monsters," said Drayton. "Only those twisted by the past."

Leon glanced out the porthole. The wormhole to Waverrym was minutes away. He swallowed. Part of him wished the Path was a lie and that there wasn't a secret angel civilisation on the wormhole's far side. But the stronger part of him craved to be right. Craved to know angels still existed, even if his treachery meant they wouldn't live much longer. Leon scowled. He was pathetic. He deserved the pain stabbing through his broken leg and all the other wounds Drayton had given him.

"Are you wondering what I'll do when we reach Waverrym?" Drayton asked.

"No."

Drayton chuckled. "I'll tell you anyway. It'll pass the time."

He clicked his fingers. Heavy objects thumped against the walls. Soldiers floated barrels into the middle of the cabin, leaving a trail of black powder hovering in the air. The smell of gunpowder filled Leon's nostrils. His heartbeat raced.

Drayton turned to Elena. "In a way, I'm glad you told that story. It'll help Leon appreciate how poetic this is. Now, Leon, as I'm sure you can deduce, these" – he gestured at the wooden barrels – "are bombs. Crude, but they'll fit the task. Especially considering that I've got another seven airships worth of them. When we reach Waverrym …"

Drayton mimed an explosion with his hands. A vague sense of horror trickled through Leon, but his mind raced too fast for him to worry. He'd formed a plan.

"I'll dispose of you after, dear chap," said Drayton. "You deserve to see Waverrym destroyed. After all, you helped me find it."

Leon gulped and watched gunpowder dust float into the air.

Running out of time.

Soon, they'd reach the wormhole. The other seven airships had glided within a stone's throw from Drayton's vessel, ready to enter the wormhole.

"And what will you do once Waverrym's gone and I'm dead?" asked Leon.

Am I trying to distract him? Or just stalling?

Drayton shrugged. "Retire. Bring my family up from Neebia and settle someplace quiet. Sleep in, paint in the afternoons. It'll be nice to see my wife again. And my daughter, too. I haven't seen them in years."

Elena frowned. "You're leaving the Inquisition?"

"After the angels are dead, what else can I achieve?"

Elena's eyes widened. She spluttered, her chest heaving and her face contorting into a snarl.

"No!" she said. "No, you can't do that to me. You promised there would be more – you said you'd give me a purpose!"

Drayton raised his hands. "And I will, Elena. When I retire, you'll take my place as a senior inquisitor. The angels will be gone, yes, but our mission continues. There are many Payans who still plot revenge against Vahria, Payans who seek chaos and turmoil. Who better to stop them than a master of deception like yourself?"

Elena's snarl melted away. She bowed her head before Drayton, then clasped his hand.

"Thank you, master."

Drayton grinned. "You're welcome, master."

Elena straightened up. A contented smile spread across her face and she looked more peaceful than Leon had ever seen her. Karym's horns, he wanted to puke.

Now's my chance.

Drayton and Elena were distracted, and the soldier behind Leon had floated a few paces away. Leon swallowed. If he did this, he'd die. But if he didn't do it, everyone on Waverrym would be slaughtered. If Waverrym even existed.

341

An angel cares for the greater good. An angel cares naught for themselves.

He grit his teeth. Easy enough to spew out that stupid platitude. Much harder to follow it.

Drayton and Elena released each other. Leon's heart hammered.

Now.

Or never.

"Remember the Angel's Oath, Elena?" asked Leon.

She frowned. "What?"

"You said it on Hargold, when you were convincing me to help."

"Yeah."

"Can you say it, please?"

She glanced at Drayton.

"Only proper to fulfil a dying man's last request," said Drayton. "It's harmless enough."

I wish.

"'I am sworn to valour,'" Elena said. "'My heart knows only virtue. My words uphold the peace. My blade defends the helpless. I care for the greater good, and I care naught for myself. My soul belongs to the realm, and, if need be, I pledge to lay down my life for the good of the realm. This I swear in the name of the Archangels.'"

Leon nodded. "Reckon it's high time I followed that oath, don't you?"

He reached into his pocket and pulled out a match.

Soldiers yelled. They drew their swords and Leon pushed off the floor and floated up. He grabbed onto a porthole and held the match against the wall, ready to strike, ready to blow up this gunpowder-filled airship –

"Hold your swords!" said Drayton.

The soldiers froze. Leon tightened his grip on the porthole's frame to stop himself floating away. The match shook as he held it against the wall.

"Swords away," said Leon. "Or I'll do it!"

"Do as he says," said Drayton.

Swords rasped as they slid into sheaths. Leon swallowed. Strike the match. Then this ship and the others packed tight around it would explode. Leon would die, but Waverrym would be safe. One stroke. That's all it would take.

So why am I still waiting?

"Stop this ship," said Leon. "Do it!"

Drayton's eyes twinkled with a calculating gleam. "Or?"

"Or I'll blow up this bloody airship, I will!"

The match was slick with sweat. Leon gulped.

If I drop it ...

"If we stop the airship, will you give me the match?" asked Drayton.

"Hell no."

"We have a stand-off, then," said Drayton.

Leon cursed. This was no stand-off. As soon as the other airships passed through the wormhole, they'd spread too far apart for this ship's explosion to hurt them. And he couldn't hold the match much longer, not with his shaking fingers.

"Ain't no stand-off," said Leon. "I'll do it, I swear!"

"You don't believe that. I see it in your eyes."

Leon's left hand gripped the porthole's rim tight enough to whiten his knuckles and his right hand gripped the match so hard he worried it would snap.

"You don't have to die," said Drayton. "There's an escape pod on this ship. I can equip it with food, water, enough gold to buy a disc. You can leave with your life."

Leon's hand trembled. "That'll never work!"

"But of course it will. I'll send my soldiers into the captain's room and lock the door. Then I'll give you a small barrel of gunpowder, so if you feel threatened you can strike it at any time to explode this airship. The captain – not a soldier – can escort you to the escape pod."

Leon glanced out the porthole. The airships would reach the wormhole in under ten minutes. Whatever he did, he needed to act before they arrived.

"You can watch the captain load the supplies, check the air tanks, and whatever else you need," said Drayton. "All this time you'll be holding the match and the gunpowder. If we do something you don't like, blow us up. Once you're happy with the pod, you can climb inside and fly away."

"You'll shoot me with your cannons!"

"My dear fellow, have you tried hitting a fly with a grain of rice? While you're both moving? I assure you, targeting the pod would be equally difficult."

"Then … then you'll send a ship after me!"

"All my ships are moving in the same direction. When we jettison the pod, it will shoot you the opposite way at a frankly ridiculous rate. By the time we decelerate enough to reverse, you'll have a huge head start, and with a tiny pod that could fly in any direction, how would we see you?"

Leon frowned. The Keronian Jetstream ran nearby. Given what he knew about Vahrian escape pods, he could reach it in fifteen minutes and use it to reach the other side of Paya. It'd be risky, of course. But he'd learnt how to fly an airship, and from what he'd heard, escape pods were even easier to manage.

Six minutes until the wormhole!

"Even if I escape, you'll hunt me," said Leon.

Drayton shrugged. "I do hate lose ends, so you'll have to accept that. Consider, though: I have ninety-one gold dorics in my strongbox. Imagine how useful those will be to someone on the run."

Leon gripped the match tighter. That was enough money to buy a castle. Hell, it was enough to buy *ten* castles. With those kinds of funds, Leon could pay for bodyguards. Spies. Protection. A new identity as a rich highborn, or merchant. He could craft a disguise so complete even he wouldn't recognise himself.

"Be rational, Leon," said Drayton. "Accept my offer and you'll live. I swear it on my honour as an inquisitor."

Leon gulped.

"Come on," said Elena. "Do what you have to do to survive. You told me that, remember? Get in the escape pod and everything will be okay."

"Sh-shut up," said Leon in a shaking voice.

"There's no need for you to die, Leon." Drayton spoke in a soft voice. "Fly away and you can live out your days in peace. Why sacrifice yourself for Waverrym? What if it doesn't exist? And if it's real, what *have* Waverrym's angels done for you? Did they help in the War? Did they offer solace when you lost your wings? No. They've hidden from society, aloof from your problems. You owe them nothing."

Leon remembered the father who'd never claimed him. He remembered the angels at the Academy who'd called him a half-breed. A bastard. A fake angel. He remembered all the years he'd wallowed in misery, nursing the pain of his missing wings and his missing friends.

Four minutes.

"Don't sacrifice yourself for Waverrym," Elena said in a trembling voice. "Whoever's hiding there doesn't deserve it. I know you're angry because of what I did, but I swear on my life: everything with you – it was real. It was real, damn it. You were the best teacher I ever had and you're not like the other angels. You're not greedy, you're not selfish, you're not corrupt. You're a good man. Please, Leon. Take Drayton's offer and you can live. Please, Leon."

As Leon floated there, he thought of Juliana and Blas.

He thought of the battle he'd fled.

Thought of the friends he'd betrayed that day.

Thought of slicing off his wings, and his guilty joy at surviving all those years after the War, while angels' heads appeared on stakes around Paya.

Didn't take much to conjure those memories.

They haunted him always.

Reminded him what he was.

A horrible friend.

A false angel.

A traitor.

Three minutes until the wormhole.

Tears streaked down Leon's face. If he gave Drayton the match, what did it matter? He'd always been spineless. No one could say he'd gone against form.

He'd always been a coward.

But he didn't have to be one now.

A strange sensation spread through him, loosening his muscles, warming his stomach. Didn't feel like bravery. Felt more like peace. He looked up at Drayton and the inquisitor's smile crumbled. Elena stiffened.

"Wait!" said Drayton. "Blow us up and you'll never know if Waverrym is real!"

Leon smiled. "It's real. And this is the only way I can reach it."

He struck the match.

Drayton howled. He dove towards Leon as a spark blossomed. Gunpowder puffed.

Flame flashed –

A thunderclap deafened Leon and a shock wave smashed into him, breaking bones, slamming the breath from his lungs, and hurling him through the porthole with a shatter of glass. He shot into space. Leon tried to grab his breathfung, but it flew from his pocket and vanished into the distance.

Everything went silent.

He cursed soundlessly. In space, you'd last fifteen seconds without a breathfung before blacking out. Death would come soon after. He supposed he was doomed, anyway, owing to all the blood spewing out of him and the pain stabbing through his veins.

A fireball engulfed Drayton's airship. Leon gulped as he floated away, the stars twirling around him.

That's it? The ship ain't even –

A huge, soundless explosion stabbed Leon's eyes, blinding him. He covered his face. Rubble bounced off his cloak. A broken sword spun through space and sliced off his hand, but he felt only a numb disbelief.

He looked over his chopped-off arm. Clouds of raging fire died into nothingness and debris bloomed out from where the Vahrian airships had been.

Something small and hard pressed against his throat. He fished the pendant out from under his shirt and held it with his remaining hand. Was it his imagination, or did it feel warm?

He didn't have any breath left in him, but he tried for a relaxed sigh anyway. Didn't know why he bothered. Couldn't hear anything in space. Darkness crept in on the edges of his vision and his lungs strained to suck air that didn't exist, but despite it all, he smiled. He'd destroyed the airships.

Waverrym was safe.

As he drifted away from the wormhole and the debris, his vision flickered …

Leon stood in a meadow …

He was floating through space, dying …

Soft grass brushed his bare feet … he ambled forward, enjoying the tickle of the grass … cicadas rustled … wind caressed his face …

Saliva boiled off his tongue and coldness crawled inside him …

"Leon!"

He looked around … the voice was familiar, and it sounded like it was close, but the meadow was empty …

Numbness spread through his fingers … his toes … his feet … his arms … the stars dimmed …

"Leon!"

He gazed up. A smile creased his youthful face. Juliana and Blas circled overhead and a great cloud of angels flew above them … there were normal people, too, riding on the backs of pegasi … Mencia, Oscar, Fernan, and all the other ex-convicts he'd freed … Alvaro, grinning from atop a pegasus … Professor Nane, floating beside him … his mother, looking proud … and above them flew winged figures who looked too big to be human … Archangels, Leon realised … and over them all, the Star Spectre hovered against a backdrop of glittering stars, an immense being of ethereal beauty

...

The blood had caked solid onto his stump of an arm ... his heartbeat slowed ...

Blas glided overhead. "Come on!"

"Where are you going?" asked Leon.

Juliana pointed up at the great blanket of shimmering stars. "Onward."

Feathers brushed Leon's back ... he glanced behind him and gaped at the pearly-white wings sprouting from his shoulder blades ... sensation flooded back into his body ... he could feel every muscle in his wings, every tendon, every feather ... he'd forgotten how glorious wings were, how joyous it was to know the freedom you carried upon your back ...

Lungs strained for air ... eyelids flickered ...

Juliana hovered above him and extended her hand, smiling. Starlight sent a blue glow washing over her face, and her dark hair rippled in the breeze.

"Come on," she said. "We're waiting!"

Warmth filled his soul ...

And as his eyes closed for the last time, he took flight, and with his friends beside him, Leon soared towards the stars.

Acknowledgements

Thank you to everyone who helped make this book a reality.

First, to my family. Your support and love means a lot to me.

For Joshua de Souza, James Heald, Rebekah Craggs, and Raine Bianchini – thank you for letting me ramble about this story to you, way before a single word was written. A double thanks to Rebekah for serving as my incredible editor. Thanks for letting me steal your ideas!

For my wonderful early readers: Marci Low and Caitlin Shaw.

For your mentorship and emotional support: David Castelanelli, Mitch Bruce, and Gabriel Bergmoser.

And lastly, thanks to you for reading this book and being part of Leon's story.

Please Consider a Review

If you enjoyed this story, I'd massively appreciate an honest review. It's hard to get discovered as an author, but reviews make it easier. They boost search results, encourage more readers to try my books, and tell me what you enjoyed so I can give you more great stories.

So if you had a good time, please consider reviewing *Across the Broken Stars* on Amazon or Goodreads. Amazon reviews, in particular, really help new readers discover my books.

Thanks!

- Jed Herne, author of *Across the Broken Stars*

About the Author

Jed Herne is a fantasy and science fiction author from Perth, Western Australia. His novels include **Fires of the Dead** and **Across the Broken Stars**. His short stories have been published in *The Arcanist, Scarlet Leaf Review, Flintlock*, and more.

In addition to writing, he hosts the *Novel Analyst* podcast. Each episode, he deconstructs a book to help his listeners become a better writer. He also hosts the *Half-Baked Stories* podcast, an improvised storytelling show where three writers are locked in a room and have thirty minutes to combine three random ideas into a single story.

Outside of writing, you can find him playing board games or falling off walls in a bouldering gym. (Although probably not at the same time).

To learn more about him and his books, go to: **jedherne.com**

FIRES
OF THE
DEAD

JED HERNE

Also by Jed Herne

Fires of the Dead

Wisp is a pyromancer: a magician who draws energy from fires to make his own flames. He's also a criminal, one job away from retirement. And it can't come bloody soon enough.

Leading his misfit crew, Wisp ventures into a charred and barren forest to find a relic that could change the realm forever. But they aren't the only ones on the hunt, and the forest isn't as barren as it seems ...

A jaded gang leader longing for retirement
  A bloodthirsty magician with a lust for power
  A brutish fighter who's smarter than he looks
  A young thief desperate to prove herself
  A cowardly navigator with secrets that won't stay buried

Together, they must survive fights, fires, and folk tales that prove disturbingly real – if they don't kill each other first.

"The perfect read for someone looking to be quickly immersed in a magic system unlike anything else."
  – Nicole Wallace, editor of *Synopses by Sarge*

"Did not put this one down til I finished."
  – Katelyn Dickinson, editor of *From Cover to Cover*.

an
ACROSS THE BROKEN STARS
story
THE
LANGUAGE
OF
LIES
JED HERNE

The Language of Lies
A free prequel to Across the Broken Stars, featuring Walter Drayton and set a year after the Invasion War.

Walter Drayton is a broken man. Crippled by the war and unable to live with his family on his home planet, he has returned to Paya, wandering between discs without purpose or passion. Pain is all he has.

When an important noble is murdered, Drayton is called in to help with the investigation. And, in doing so, he discovers a cause he can put his pain towards …

There are no monsters. Only those twisted by the past.

To read 'The Language of Lies' for free, go to:

jedherne.com/lies

This also lets you join Jed Herne's email newsletter, which gives you more insights into the world of *Across the Broken Stars*, free stories, behind-the-scenes exclusive content, and much more. You'll also get author updates and be the first to hear about new books.

Made in United States
Troutdale, OR
12/02/2023

15233001R00224